He's Either Dead or in St. Paul

He's Either Dead or in St. Paul

D.B. Moon

Three Waters Publishing, LLC
Savage, Minnesota

Interior and cover design by Three Waters Publishing, LLC.

The characters and events portrayed in this book are fictitious and are used fictitiously. Apart from well-known historical figures, any similarity to real persons, living or dead, is purely coincidental and not intended by the author.

ISBN: 978-1-942930-13-6

First Edition: March, 2015

Published by
Three Waters Publishing, LLC
Savage, Minnesota

Visit us on the web at
http://threewaterspublishing.com

Printed and bound in the United States of America

Contents

Acknowledgements

I would like to acknowledge and dedicate this book to my family. Their support is appreciated more than I can express. Also David Fingerman, Christy Perry, the Minneapolis Writers' Workshop, and the Woodbury Writers' Group, without which this book would not have happened.

Prologue

Agony

SYLVESTER HOBBS GRIPPED the dynamite in his small hands. The slicing January winds cut through his tattered clothes and punished him for what he was about to help his father do.

"Sly! Stop daydreamin' and make sure that dynamite is tied tight. Double-check your knots, boy!" his father yelled as he pointed toward the railroad bridge. Every breathy word punched out hot steam.

Sly closed his eyes, attempting to focus on the sweet white-pine scent, but his stomach twisted when a train whistle echoed across the lake.

His father stopped wiring blasting caps and held his breath. He hitched up his pants with serious purpose before hooking his thumb under a sagging right suspender and looping it back over his shoulder. His glazed eyes grew two sizes larger and his raw pink ears perked up when the train howled in the distance.

"C'mon! Train's comin'!" Sweaty curls stuck out from under his father's grey flat cap.

As the man knelt in the snow untangling blasting cap wires, Sly stared at him as though the monster under his bed had come to life. But this monster got drunk and inflicted punishments using lit cigarettes. And at nine years old, Sly still wasn't sure what his father's real name was. He thought it might be Thomas, but his mother only referred to him as "Agony." "All he says, all he does, and all he is, is

1

agony," his mother always said, usually while crying.

Sly wondered why Agony continued to bitch about the recent presidential election. He thought back to November when he and his mother and father made the rough trip to Superior, Wisconsin via horse-drawn carriage in the freezing rain to cast their votes for Charles Evans Hughes of New York, the *Unified Republican candidate for president in the year of our Lord nineteen hundred and sixteen.*

"Goddamn it, boy, move your ass! We need blasting caps in those two bundles, there and there! Go!" Two blasting caps landed in the snow at Sly's feet. When he dug them out, the snow no longer felt cold against his blackening finger tips.

Sly stood on the ice near shore and turned to check the train's progress, then looked up at the railroad bridge that spanned the frozen waters of Lake Nebagamon. Standing taller than any surrounding white pine, the bridge was held up by timbers so strong and broad that even Paul Bunyan couldn't have chopped them down.

The numbing in Sly's hands began to burn instead. He fought to shove blasting caps into the bundled dynamite tied to two load-bearing timbers. Smoke curled on the horizon above the pine tops.

The train closed in.

Snow crunched under every step as Sly ran the blasting cap wires back to shore, dragging lengths of fraying rope and twisted wires behind him. Agony knelt, unscrewing wing nuts and connecting wires to the T-box. This marked the third day without sleep for Agony, whose driving force was a dangerous mix of adrenaline, cheap whisky, and revenge.

"We're gonna blow that son of a bitch straight to Hell, aren't we, boy?" he asked through gritted teeth. "I'll teach that bastard to give our jobs to Chinese! I built this railroad and, by God, I can take it down!" The grit in Agony's voice became coarser every time the wing nuts twisted tighter. Sly knew this was very wrong, but the bitter cold kindly reminded Sly of the aches and bruises from last week's beatings.

"Goddamned Democrats. Hughes got robbed. There is no way Wilson should have won that election. It was rigged, I tell you."

A murder of crows used raspy caws to cheer from pine trees onshore—keen spectators able to spot a potential meal. Sly looked up at them and they stared right back. The crows could tell, just as Sly did, that death was in the air.

"Check those bundles and make sure they're tied tight!" Agony yelled. Sly turned his feet outward and plowed snow toward the nearest bundle hoping his dawdling would go unnoticed.

A sharp pain clamped down on Sly's right ear, sending him to his knees. He screeched and held Agony's callused hands, along with the pliers, trying to pull upward to relieve the tension. The top of Sly's ear tore open and warm blood dripped down his jaw.

One of Agony's powerful hands wiggled the loose bundle of dynamite while the other hand clenched the pliers on Sly's throbbing ear.

"I told you to double-check these knots! Look at this shit. It's about to fall right off! Now we gotta check the next one."

A violent yank ripped more of Sly's ear before he was able to pull upward and gain enough leverage to ease the tension. The cold did little to numb the pain as he stumbled, dropping to one knee every few steps while trying to keep pace.

When the train pounded onto the bridge, loose dirt, pebbles, and old cobwebs fell from between the timbers. The ice trembled and the bundles of dynamite vibrated. Agony stopped and Sly crouched at his side. The pliers opened and Sly fell in a heap, clasping his bloodied ear.

Sly tore a strip of cloth from his undershirt and wrapped it around his head. He wiped his nose on his sleeve and felt the cold start to kill the pain while the blood warmed his ear.

"Here it comes," Agony whispered. "Avery's on that train. Him and a bunch of his high-falootin' friends."

Sly remembered meeting railroad tycoon Everett Avery several times. On one occasion Mr. Avery had given Sly an all-day sucker, which Sly then left on the seat of the family's carriage on a hot sunny day. Sly spent the rest of the day rubbing the welts across his ass, cleaning melted sugar off the seat, and resenting Mr. Avery for having given him the sucker in the first place.

The train roared closer. The ice cracked under Sly's feet as he sprinted for the T-box onshore. Sly heard his own gulping breaths and pounding heart over the mocking crows and raging train. He tried to keep pace, but water spit up between the cracks and caused Agony to slip and fall and Sly to trip over him. They sprang up and continued to shore.

The crows looked on and squawked as they bounced on their branches waiting for lunch to be served.

Agony slid like a baseball player and grabbed the T-box, kicking up a cloud of powdery snow. Sly stared at the dirty white knuckles wrapped around the T-box handle, and then turned his attention to the train. The rumbling train.

Sly felt the ground quake beneath him. Guilt and fear served up one-two punches directly into his stomach. Steam rose from the sweat across his father's forehead. Coal smoke billowed into the frigid Wisconsin sky. Agony sat motionless—other than licking the sweat from his upper lip and watching the train the way a hungry cat watches an empty birdbath.

When the train hit the halfway point, Agony muttered, "Now he's going to get his come uppin's."

Snap! A loud metallic zip cut the air. Sly turned to see the plunger thrust into the T-box. He flinched as a sharp tingle shot through his body.

The blast force full of wood and ice knocked Sly and Agony off their feet. Timber chunks and splinters showered down. Sly uncovered his head to see the black engine slide sideways off the tracks, pulling the other cars with it. The whole train squirmed like a severed earthworm.

Sly struggled to his feet and watched the bridge timbers crack and moan before buckling under the pressure. The train swayed to one side and gained speed as it slammed to the ice. It landed on its side, shattering the lake ice like fine porcelain, and sending a geyser of ice, snow, and steam skyward.

Back on shore, the ground shook followed by a flood of water, ice, and splinters, soaking Sly and Agony above the ankles. The scene froze Sly in place. His mouth hung open and he ignored the feeling of a thousand needles stabbing at his feet. The open water was only a few yards away. The crows fell silent.

The train lay on its side like a dying monster, wheezing and gasping its last breaths. Sly watched water flood the passenger cars as the train began to sink below the ice. A woman held a crying baby out a shattered window. The woman's wide-brimmed hat covered her eyes but couldn't mask her screams.

People attempted to climb out broken windows, but their clothes and limbs caught on broken glass. Another woman strained only to have her shawl become a noose holding her in place. Steam hissed. People wailed. A baby cried. His eyes welled.

The doomed train took its last breaths before the final plunge. Like a chain tied to an anvil, the locomotive sank beneath the murky depths, followed by the passenger cars.

Sly stood next to Agony and watched the water eddy. The open water seemed to be a boiling cauldron of tumbling ice chunks and shattered timbers—like some horrific stew using death as its secret ingredient. Sly wondered how many souls the churning water had claimed and how long he'd been watching the rising bubbles. So many bubbles.

At first, the rippling water made the image difficult to see, but Sly saw a thin, pale man just beneath the surface of the water. Blood flowed and swirled, like red chimney smoke, in and around where eyes should have been. The man wore the satisfied grin of a glutton after a large meal. He stared at Sly and mouthed the words *Thank you.*

After Sly wiped away his tears, he could see nothing in the water except debris and more bubbles.

Agony's calloused hand slipped over Sly's. Sly stepped away from the edge of the ice and turned to search his father's face. Agony smiled down at the open water like a man who had just outsmarted the Devil.

1.

Well Done, Sly. Well Done.

12 Years Later

Cold. Goddamn, what a cold day. A small coal stove in the corner did all it could to warm the frigid warehouse. But wind whipped through the open cargo doors and chilled Sly to the marrow. After all, it was December in St. Paul.

The sweat under Sly's flat cap had frozen since the last shipment. Whenever he stopped rolling barrels for more than a minute, his dark curls froze to his head.

A train had just arrived. Another of Dapper's workers ran outside to take care of paying off the engineer leaving Sly to prepare the boxcar for unloading. The train's belly was chocked full of hooch. Looked to be a big haul and that meant a big wage. Sly smiled and rubbed his hands together. Sly loved money.

After setting the plank ramp from the cargo door to the warehouse floor, he positioned the barrels at the box car's door just right, then eased them down the ramp, being sure never to lose control along the way. A five-hundred-pound barrel could do a lot of damage, especially if you wound up under it. Splinters by the dozen bore into Sly's hands. He had become real good at using his teeth to pull them out.

Hauling moonshine off trains hijacked by his boss "Dapper" Dan Hogan kept Sly from freezing solid. And he was paid *good*. Good enough to keep him out of the breadlines. A man like Sly who couldn't read so great—truth be told, not at all—could make a solid living during Prohibition. All a guy needed was a strong back and enough balls to pull his gun if he ever needed to get out of a scrape. Sly *really* loved money.

This train had been "rerouted" from an illegal distillery somewhere up north in Stearns County and was supposed to end up in Chicago. The load caught Dapper Dan's attention because it was *big*. He didn't bother with cars or trucks—he hijacked booze by the trainload.

And that meant someone down the line was going to miss that much hooch. Many a Chicago mobster were none too happy with Sly's boss. Ruthless men like Capone and the deadly DeLuce. Outside of St. Paul Dapper would have feared for his life. But St. Paul had a system in place, established by former chief of police John J. O'Connor. The "O'Connor system," built from the top down by mayors and cops, protected guys like Dapper. Even the Mob thought twice about shedding blood in the streets of St. Paul. Mobsters and gangsters alike lived by one rule: violence was bad for business.

St. Paul allowed big dreamers with low morals the opportunity to take advantage of certain loopholes—such as doing a little rerouting—knowing no cops or competitors would come after them. Prohibition was more like a candy store with no one minding the counter. Sly would tolerate the cold and the risks as long as wads of cash kept filling his splintered hands. The last thing he wanted was to trade all that *fresh lettuce* for stale bread. Never again.

Sly rolled the final barrel over the grit and sawdust on the wood floor and into position with the others, then he got right to the task of chewing and pulling splinters from his hands using his front teeth like tweezers.

BOOM

Dust and cobwebs fell from the ceiling and the barrels even wavered a bit. Through his worn work boots, Sly felt the floor quake. And he swore he heard screaming.

That was an explosion—Sly knew the sound all too well.

He flew outside. After skidding to a stop, Sly soaked in the fiery scene. Dapper Dan's Paige Coupe was engulfed in flames and pumping out fat, angry smoke that choked out the bright blue sky. Sly slid across the ice and snow toward his boss's car. A body was splayed out on the hood. Burning.

No reason for Sly to risk his neck for a lost cause. But his empty pockets pushed him closer to the flames. He raised his hands to block the heat. Fire crackled and blistered across Sly's palms causing him to slow to a shuffle. Flames roared and meat sizzled. If he didn't act now, he would not be getting paid for all the barrels he had just unloaded.

Sly leapt into the black smoke. He yanked Dapper off the hood, back through the metal frame of the windshield, and into the driver's seat. Two hunks of flesh peeled from Dapper's hands when they hit the steering wheel, left dangling in the ten o'clock and two o'clock position.

Sly grabbed Dapper under his armpits. Smoke thick as boiling oil clogged Sly's eyes, throat, and lungs. He hacked until his chest hurt, but managed to drag Dapper about thirty feet from the burning car.

Dapper's legs continued to burn. His sock garters bubbled and melted into the skin on his calves so Sly tossed handfuls of snow over them. The flakes turned to water and then bubbled against the wounds, as did the snowdrift Sly had set Dapper in.

The man moaned and wheezed and gurgled, but couldn't talk. Sly crouched down and cradled Dapper's head like a newborn baby. The whites of his eyes glowed against charred, black flesh. They were glossy and scared and full of *agony*.

Agony. The flames. Sly couldn't stop the flames. Fireballs consumed a bridge. Timbers shattered. Screams cut through the rural Wisconsin afternoon. The train sank. Everyone died. Agony had held tight to Sly's hand and *smiled*.

Now Dapper smiled wide and bright. The flesh around his face cracked like burnt chicken skin, revealing raw, pink flesh underneath. "I'm so proud of you, son," he said.

Sly pulled back, not understanding how Dapper could be smiling. He looked completely at ease, as if resting on a lounge chair waiting for a busty waitress to deliver a cocktail. Smoke still rose from Dapper's face. The air stunk like overcooked meat and almost made Sly gag. Curiosity pulled Sly in closer, though. He blinked hard. Dapper had closed his eyes. His smile had disappeared. Dapper trembled in Sly's arms.

The shock of seeing his boss on fire must have gotten to him. Yeah, that's it. The heat and action all played with his head. Sly waved off the smile as just seeing things—After all, his boss now lay in his arms, wheezing like a flattening tire, smoldering like a log, his head tilted back and one foot in the grave. Okay, make that both feet and sinking fast. No way would he live through the day.

Any money Dapper had on him burned up along with his pockets, so there was no need to rummage. The hopes of climbing the ranks within Dapper's organization had just gone up in smoke. Time to find a new boss.

2.

Gangster Barbeque

A LOT OF SMELLS defined St. Paul: coal smoke, car exhaust, piss, gunpowder, corruption. The stink clung to your clothes, you took it home to your wife and family—the same people you'd taken an oath to protect from the stench. You couldn't scrub hard enough to wash it off.

There were two ways to make big money during Prohibition. One was as a gangster, the other as a cop. But how much money you made as a cop depended on which side of the law you enforced. And if you could tolerate the stench.

What interested St. Paul Police Chief August Murnane most on this frigid December day in 1928 was the luscious smell of burning gangsters. He negotiated the slick streets toward thick black plumes that billowed between downtown buildings. As he approached Dapper Dan's warehouse, Murnane slowed to bump over a double set of well-used railroad tracks. When he hit the brakes, the police cruiser slid on an icy patch, finally coming to rest in a snowdrift. As soon as Murnane opened the door, the stink of burnt rubber tires and smoldering human hair slithered up his nostrils and wouldn't let go. Another hit ends in a bad-guy barbeque. Nauseating, but oh, so satisfying.

The call had come in that Gangland boss Dapper Dan Hogan had had some car trouble. As Murnane tromped in for a closer examination, he could still sense the heat from the burnt car. All the windows of Dapper's Paige Coupe were blown out and the interior was no more than a charred mess of charcoal seats and wire framing. While the fire department rolled up hoses and tucked them back on their trucks, white smoke curled in the whirling winds. The driver's side door lodged askew in a snow pile more than ten feet away. Hunks of Dapper's cooked flesh still dangled from the steering wheel.

He got what was comin'. Play with fire, eventually you get burned.

Officers had cordoned off the area with rope and were milling around mumbling about whodunit and who'd most likely be next. They acted more like a sewing circle than police officers.

Murnane spotted a rookie and called out. "Hilliard."

"Yes, Chief." Hilliard came closer, writing in his notepad as he walked.

"What do we got?"

"We got one well-done bad guy. Ambulance took him away already. You just missed him."

"Ambulance?" Hilliard might be a rookie, but a school kid could tell the difference between an ambulance and a hearse. "Don't you mean a hearse?"

"No, sir. He's alive."

"Hogan lived through this?" Murnane re-examined the carnage. Dripping water began to form icicles all over the husk of what used to be a real swanky car. Dapper was one tough son of a bitch.

"He's alive, but he's not long for this world. Poor guy looked like one of my wife's pork chops. Surprised someone would bump him off though. I mean, everybody likes the guy, he's a real darb," Hilliard said.

"Any witnesses?"

"We got one guy." Hilliard used his pencil as a pointer in the general direction of a young, lanky thug leaning against the building. The guy held a lit cigarette down at his side and pondered the burnt-out car—like he might share the same fate someday.

"Well, bring him here."

Hilliard waved the young man over. Murnane watched the kid close in. He sure didn't look like much: typical lowlife gangster hopeful. Probably trying to work his way up the ranks in Dapper's organization. The kid was dressed for the Minnesota winter. Thick wool overcoat burnt badly at the cuffs, clodhopper boots, and a blackened wool flat cap. Murnane wondered why the kid's jacket was wide open and his boots were unbuckled. While still holding a cigarette, the kid ran his thumbs under grey suspenders before hitching up his sagging pants pitted with burn holes.

The buckles flopped and clanked as the kid approached. He stopped in front of Murnane, wiped a snail trail of snot across his forearm, then sucked his cigarette down to the cracked skin on his soot-covered knuckles.

"What's your name, kid?" Murnane asked.

"Sly." Smoke seeped from the kid's nose and mouth when he answered.

Hilliard checked his notepad. "Says here his name is Sylvester Hobbs."

"People call me Sly."

"Like your *mom*, maybe?" Murnane asked.

Sly shuffled in place, shifting his weight from one foot to the other.

"How about you tell me what you saw."

"I didn't see nuthin'."

Murnane savored the young gangster's darting eyes and quick twitches.

The kid's sleeves smoked a little and his face was coated in soot. "You wanna play tough? This could happen to you." Murnane pointed at the black metal skeleton. "Now tell me something useful."

"Actually, Chief, he might be telling the truth. Said he was in the building when he heard the explosion. Came out to find Mr. Hogan on fire and hanging halfway through the windshield. Mr. Hobbs here pulled him to safety and used snow to put him out."

"Well, Mr. Hobbs, looks like you're the hero of the day. I'll notify the papers."

"I said, call me Sly."

The defiant little asshole wore on Murnane's thinning patience. "Did Dapper happen to say who did this?"

"He wasn't much in the mood for talkin'."

Murnane lifted one side of his mouth. Sly had moxie, that's for sure. Murnane hated gangers with moxie. Then again, he hated any gangster with air in his lungs. But cops and gangers worked within the same system. Every time the system rubbed Murnane raw, he pictured his wife and kids out on the streets. Standing in the breadlines, feeling the cold through the holes in his shoes—he'd be goddamned if that was in his future. Someday he'd get out from under the system. Someday the dirt would wash off for good and he could look his wife and kids in the eyes without being coated in guilt. For now he went with the system because he knew damn well how his bread got buttered.

"Tell Officer Hilliard how best to get a hold of ya'. And stay in town. We may need to talk to you again. Mr. Hobbs."

Sly sneered at Murnane. The kid took a final drag, heaved his chest outward, and held in the smoke. He flicked the butt, causing a shower of orange sparks cascading like a small firework, into the smoldering car. Cigarette smoke hissed from his nostrils as he turned and walked back into the building. One more smell Murnane would take home to his family.

"Asshole," Murnane said.

"You want me to go after him, chief?"

"No. Leave him. Something tells me we'll be seeing him again soon enough."

Out of all the gore and misery that surrounded him, it was the kid that raised the hair on Murnane's arms. Sly's parting played out again amid a tornado of other thoughts and crept down Murnane's spine. Something about that kid stood out. Like the kid had the Devil in him.

A voice deep inside nagged at Murnane—the next time he crossed paths with Sylvester Hobbs, there would be blood.

3.

Dark Descent

OH GOD, please help me get into this gang. I know I'm not a praying man and I've done some bad shit, but if you do me this favor I'll think about going to church. You have my word.

Sly stood before two men he'd never met, but knew their grim reputations all too well. The Boss sat behind an oak desk. A single floor lamp cast thick shadows throughout the dark office. The Boss's eyes glistened and studied Sly. Another man sat in the corner watching in silence, a lit cigarette dangling from his mouth.

The air was dry, the kind of dry only winter brings, and it made Sly's skin itch. The faint scent of urine sullied the room. Sly bathed about as often as he went to the dentist, so he figured if the stink was coming from him, he best keep away from the desk.

"What's your name, kid?" the Boss asked. His baritone voice rumbled through the dark.

"Sylvester Hobbs, but people call me Sly."

"Sly, eh? How old are you?"

"Twenty-one, sir."

The Boss addressed the cigarette ember glowing in the dark to his left. "What do you think?" A sigh cut the silence the question left behind. The ember illuminated the man's harsh face framed by matted hair.

"Eightball, what do you think?" the Boss asked again.

14

Eightball slouched in his chair, seemingly more concerned with his dwindling cigarette than the current gang status of one Sylvester Hobbs.

"Maybe," Eightball said.

Eightball pinched the cigarette between his thumb and index finger. He sucked hard, holding in the smoke and narrowing his eyes at Sly.

The Boss turned his attention back to Sly.

"So you're here because you want to be part of our organization, is that right?"

Sly shifted his weight from his left foot to his right, then back again—a nervous tic he carried since childhood.

"Yes, sir. Very much."

Sly kneaded his checkered flat cap at waist level in front of him. A thick tuft of hair flopped into his eyes, which he quickly combed back between his bony fingers.

"You worked for Dapper Dan, is that right?"

Sly nodded.

Dapper Dan Hogan had talked a lot about the Boss. The Boss was Dapper's best customer. Sly was privy to many dealings because Dapper loved to talk big about himself and others—including the Boss. As a result, Sly had a clear picture of how deep the Boss's pockets really were.

The Boss leaned forward. "He was a good egg. Too bad his car got blown up with him in it. Occupational hazard, I guess. So now your former employer is dead and you need work." The Boss set his pudgy hands on the desk. "How long did you work for him?"

Sly attempted to count backward, and he was already plenty bad at counting forward. His face crunched and his eyes rolled up as he fought inside his head for an answer.

The Boss slapped a folded St. Paul *Pioneer Press* newspaper on the corner of the desk. "You need to take a look at today's date, genius?"

Sly looked down at the newsprint. It may as well have been chicken prints in the mud since he couldn't read.

"What is today?" Sly asked. He knew it was 1929, he knew it was

January, but didn't know the day. He shifted his feet and fought to count the months and years he worked for Dapper, not counting the month since he was blown up.

The Boss said, "It's January twenty-third, like it says right there." He pointed at the paper. "You know it's January, right?" The Boss chuckled.

"I'm reminded every time I step outside, sir."

Sly wanted this job something awful. If the Boss didn't accept him, he would be out on the street. Sly figured his best bet would be working for one of Dapper Dan's competitors, unloading, stacking, and guarding shipments of booze off the Midway train line again. He was tired of lifting oak barrels full of alcohol in a warehouse that froze in winter and sweltered in summer, combined with the constant fear of being hijacked or arrested. He felt a bigger and better future was waiting within the Boss's organization. The risks would increase, but so would the rewards.

Sly cleared his throat. "I guess, around a few years, I guess . . ."

"That's a lot of guessing." The Boss leaned back. The moaning of overworked chair joints filled the shadows. "I'll tell you what. I'll send you on a little assignment and see how you do."

Sly's heart jumped while he shifted his weight from one foot to the other. He held his emotions in check by squeezing his lips together and holding back a smile.

"Yes, sir. I won't let you down."

"To be honest, I don't like you. You remind me of a panhandler without the confidence."

Sly stopped fidgeting.

"You don't agree with my assessment?" the Boss asked.

Sly sharpened his glare enough to convey a hearty *Fuck you*.

"Eightball may look like something out of *Grimm's Fairy Tales*, but he's proven himself to be a tough son of a bitch."

Eightball stood but stayed in the corner.

"You, on the other hand, just walked in off the street looking for a job. Now understand, I'm real sorry about what happened to Dapper, but I don't know you from Adam except what Dapper told me before he died—and that wasn't very much. For all I know you could be a fed. So if you want to work for me, you have to prove yourself first. Now you can stop giving me that tommy gun stare."

Sly raised his eyebrows and tucked away his "tommy gun stare" for another day. Swallowing his pride felt worse than swallowing a broken bottle.

"So like I said, I have an errand I want you to run. You and Eightball are going to intercept a package and bring it here."

"What package?" Sly asked.

"Setup money from a Chicago Mob boss trying to expand his business. Mobsters don't take us gangsters seriously and think they can push us around and take whatever they want. They don't like or respect us, and we sure as hell don't like them. Anyway, Eightball will fill you in on the rest."

Eightball came closer to the light where Sly got a better look at him. Sly had a hard time guessing how old Eightball was under all that matted hair and scar tissue, maybe midtwenties. His face backed up his reputation for brawling. His sporadic teeth resembled a piano keyboard and his nose bent toward the southeast.

Eightball crushed out his hand-rolled cigarette in the crystal ash tray on the Boss's desk and exhaled with authority, never taking his sunken eyes off Sly.

"When do we go?" Sly asked.

Eightball walked around the Boss's desk at a slow pace, his eyes studied Sly along the way. The urine stink followed him.

"Maybe," he said.

"Tomorrow afternoon," the Boss answered. "Take him to the Outhouse, Eightball. I'll tell them you're coming."

"C'mon kid, let'sss go." The letter s whistling through Eightball's missing teeth.

Sly followed Eightball down creaking stairs. They came to the small entryway Sly had passed through on his way in. Sly reached for the door.

"Wait."

"What is it?" Sly needed some fresh air. Eightball smelled like a pissing post.

"It's colder than a well digger's ass out there." Eightball removed a stained and ragged stocking cap from his hip pocket and stretched it over his head.

"Okay, ready."

Sly pushed the door open and squinted into the blinding afternoon sun. The January air felt anything but warm. It bit Sly's skin, burned his lungs, and made walking along the streets of downtown St. Paul miserable.

"Are you sure we want to go to the Outhouse?" Sly remembered Dapper mentioning the Outhouse by saying, "Sly, if you ever find yourself in that place, sit by the door so you can get out fast when the shooting starts."

Eightball walked briskly, his hands stuffed in his tattered pockets. "It'll be fine. Yeah, it's a shithole, but there hasn't been a murder in weeks. The liquor might have killed some folks, but that's the chance you take, am I right?"

"Why do they call it that, anyway?" Sly wondered how such a bad place earned a worse name.

"You're right. They could have called it the Shit hole just the same."

Sly had darkened the doorway of more than his fair share of blind pigs. They catered to the poorer, more unsavory, drunks. The owners frequently cheated Prohibition by bringing in an animal, usually a pig, and charging patrons a fee to see it. With the fee came a free drink. Each time customers paid, they got a peek at the pig and another shot of crudely distilled alcohol. Sly didn't like the four *or* the two-legged animals at any blind pig he'd ever been in.

While Sly didn't like pigs, he *resented* speakeasies. Even if Sly could afford to drink at a speakeasy, they wouldn't let him in because of his shabby clothes—and shabbier attitude.

Speakeasies were classier establishments that beat Prohibition by selling illegal liquor to anyone who knew the correct password at the door. Sly usually couldn't find the door, and on the rare occasions he did, he never knew the password. Speakeasies catered to the type of folks who could handle their liquor in a high society way. With a belly full of good bathtub gin or high-grade Minnesota Thirteen, the speakeasy patron burst into song while the blind pig patron would likely pull out a knife.

Ice and snow crunched underfoot and cars honked and sputtered through the streets. The wind sliced through Sly's torn clothes exploiting any shortcut to exposed flesh. The cold easily poked through the holes in his shoes.

Sly followed Eightball along slippery, but bustling, sidewalks. Thick coal smoke and car exhaust filled Sly's nose and stung his eyes—the smells being one of the most charming parts of St. Paul.

Eightball ducked down an alley and stopped at a small wooden door secured by large wrought iron hinges. He knocked three times.

Then paused. Another knock.

Then paused. Finally, he knocked two more times.

The eye slit opened. *Thwack.*

"The Boss sent us," Eightball said.

A muffled voice responded, "Bullshit."

"Goddamn it, you horsse'sss assss. You know who I am."

"Don't know who *he* is though."

"He's new. Now open the goddamned door."

"What's the password? Say *Sally serves sarsaparilla on the Mississippi,* and we'll let you in."

"You asssess. It's fucking freezing out here. Open up!" Eightball pounded his fists on the door.

Sly heard breathy chuckles from the other side of the door.

"Password, please."

"I'm going to kick the shit out of every one of you! Mark my words! The Boss is going to hear about thisss."

Eightball kicked the door like it owed him money.

"Okay! Okay! Settle down."

Eightball clenched his fists and leaned in toward the door when the heavy iron locks clanked open. Before the door opened an inch, Eightball thrust his shoulder into it, barging inside.

It took three men to hold Eightball by the arms. He flailed and spit curse words at a man who was a solid wall of muscle, stood six inches taller than Eightball, and was twice as wide. Eightball showed the same tenacity as a starving lion.

"We were just having a lark. No big deal. Settle down."

When they released Eightball's arms, he pointed as if his finger were the stinger on an angry hornet. "Don't fuck with me, Walter." His breath pushed in and out of him like a fireplace bellow. He removed his hat and shoved it back into his hip pocket. "You buncha horsess' asssess."

A large rack piled high with current newspapers and stacks of magazines filled the wall in front of Sly. Walter waved him toward the shelves. Sly had to duck to avoid the single incandescent bulb dangling by a frayed wire.

Sly scratched his head. "Is this it?" *It is the size of an outhouse—but no hooch.*

"Walter, get the door. Make yourself useful for once." Eightball said.

Once Eightball calmed down, he stopped hissing.

Walter smiled and shoved the rack. It glided on rails in the floor like a miniature train car, exposing another door. Walter bent down and opened the second door, revealing a staircase. Eightball crouched and started down the dimly lit stairs squeezed between rust-stained sandstone walls. He stopped after two steps and looked over his left shoulder.

"You coming or what?"

Sly unplanted his feet and followed. He cleared the doorway and started down the dilapidated stairs, Walter slammed the door behind them. Sly heard the rack sliding back into place and felt the vibration on the stairs.

The wood planks bowed when he stepped down. He was unsure what the darkness held at the bottom of the stairs, but it sure as hell didn't look inviting. Apprehension was a feeling he had never understood very well, until now.

4.

Counting

SLY STEPPED LIGHTLY. The stairs creaked and wobbled and the dim stairwell smelled like a wet basement. Rusty water streaks bled down the sandstone walls and glinted in the weak light.

A dangling spider web stopped Sly in his tracks. He stared at it and remembered being six and crawling under the house to check on a leaky pipe for Agony. Cobwebs wove nightmares so thick they blocked what little sun shone down there. He came out of the crawlspace wrapped in a cocoon of silken horror. Agony whooped and hollered at the hatching egg sacks in Sly's hair. Since that day, he hated spiders.

"You comin' or what?" Eightball asked.

Sly didn't dare show his fear of spiders or anything else.

The dingy light and musty smell reminded Sly why he steered clear of blind pigs—the kind of place you grip your wallet as tight as your pistol. Where men with hair-trigger tempers carried the weapons to finish any argument. Dapper Dan had told him blind pig patrons usually consisted of America's most wanted felons and prison escapees. As the saying went, *If you can't find him, he's either dead or in St. Paul.*

Sly thought he'd calm himself by providing a little chatter. "What's with all the cloak and dagger stuff?"

"The Boss can't be too careful. The Purity Squad sticks their nose everywhere lately."

Sly took a moment to examine the strange beaded curtain at the bottom of the stairs. Everything from doll parts to hat pins dangled from the curtain, like fish in a gill net.

The small barroom proved more dank than the stairway leading to it. Sly had heard tales about the Outhouse being a silica sand mine, then a mushroom farm, before the Boss took it over and converted it into a ramshackle blind pig. Low ceilings helped contain the smells of fungus, cigarette smoke, and a small coal-burning, potbellied stove. Large logs supported a crisscross timber skeleton that kept the sandstone ceiling from drying out and caving in.

Humming Edison bulbs hung from wires and attempted to hold off the darkness. Sly could just make out the rickety bar. The bar was made of wood planks set on stacked soda pop crates. It bowed while supporting a few huddled men speaking in hushed voices as Sly and Eightball walked in. Sly could see that sin and death were as common here as dirty glasses and food poisoning.

"Let's grab a booth in the corner," Eightball said.

The irregular walls provided small coves and outcrops tailor-made for private conversations. Eightball chose a table: a whisky barrel turned on its end accompanied by two wobbly stools and an oil lamp set on top.

"Have a seat."

When Sly turned to sit, he noticed what looked like names carved in the walls.

"Who are those guys?" he asked.

Eightball pointed at each and read aloud, "Dapper Dan Hogan, Creepy was here, J. Dillinger. I thought you worked for Dapper Dan. You didn't recognize his name?"

"It's dark in here."

Eightball responded by taking out rolling papers and making a fresh cigarette. He glanced up every few seconds. Eightball was a slow-burning fuse.

"So what's this all about?" Sly asked.

"Whoa, Nellie. Let's get a drink first. They got hooch here that'll make your insides sit up and beg." Eightball smiled and slapped the tabletop.

What would my insides beg for? Sly thought.

"I'll just have a beer." Sly shifted on the stool.

"They don't have beer. The Boss is fighting with the Schmidt brewers. They have bootleg. It's not Minnesota Thirteen, but it'll do the trick."

Minnesota Thirteen was the high-grade alcohol Sly unloaded off the Midway trains as it came in from Stearns County. Dapper hijacked thousands of barrels of the corn liquor over the years by bribing rail yard workers who rerouted trains bound for Chicago to Dapper's private warehouse instead. Dapper then sold the barrels to the swankier speakeasies in St. Paul and Minneapolis for huge profits. Minnesota Thirteen got mixed into cosmopolitans and highballs for blue bloods who sported fur coats and bank accounts. Sly hated breaking his back so those people could drink the good stuff. With the backroom moonshine they served in the Outhouse, he figured he'd be lucky to not go blind after a few sips.

"What's in it?"

"Shit, I don't know. Could be goat piss for all I know." Eightball scanned the room. "Where's the damn waitress?"

Eightball put the unlit cigarette in his mouth before he waved over a woman who looked to be worse off than Sly's shoes. The waitress nodded at the wave, but remained at the bar, stacking dirty glasses.

"So what do you know about the Boss?" Eightball asked.

"Only what Dapper told me and what I've heard on the streets. That he can be a mean guy when he wants to be. And that he runs pretty much everything in St. Paul."

"You got that right. Minneapolis is a lot tougher without the O'Connor system and the Mob has a lot more power over there, so the majority of the Boss's business is done in St. Paul."

Sly understood the O'Connor system inside and out thanks to working for Dapper Dan. When Prohibition began in 1920, St. Paul police Chief John O'Connor established a system. In a city built to keep secrets, police and gangsters worked together to establish a set of rules to keep the dirty money flowing in. Criminals were required to do three things when they arrived in St. Paul. First, they provided a bribe to the officer who greeted them when they got off the train or boat. Second, they had to check in with Dapper Dan Hogan and let the gangsters know they were in town. Third, they were to commit no violent crimes while inside St. Paul. If gangsters and mobsters alike abided by these three simple rules, they were able to go about their business. If they didn't, there was hell to pay from both the police and fellow gangsters. Violent crimes were bad for business.

Sly shifted in his seat when he noticed Eightball staring—the kind of stare always followed by an uncomfortable question. The kind of stare meant to pull things out of a guy faster than a skilled surgeon. Sly hoped all Eightball wanted was basic information and not internal organs.

"So, where you from anyway?"

"Northern Wisconsin. A place called Lake Nebagamon."

"Lake Nebba-gamma-what? Where's that?"

"Northern Wisconsin. I just told you."

Eightball leaned forward. "Hey. Don't get a fresh mouth with me, kid."

Sly sensed the edge in Eightball's voice.

"I didn't mean nuthin' by it."

Sly caught sight of a skeletal waitress stacking glasses behind the bar. She stopped stacking and stepped out to take their order. She wore a green chemise that hung off a pair of shoulders no wider than a wire coat hanger. Uneven bobbed hair stuck out from beneath her white flapper hat. Her eyes held dark circles probably from too much mascara and moonshine and not enough rest. The woman looked like someone the Grim Reaper would take pity on. But she made Eightball smile.

"How's tricks, Doris?"

Doris turned away like a scolded dog. Sly noticed her eyes tearing up and her lip quivering.

"What would you like?" she asked Sly.

Sly paused to see if she would break down. What with her looks and working in a shithole like the Outhouse, her dance card seemed chock-full of grief.

"Um . . ."

"He'll have the Boss's special hooch. Make it two."

Doris shuffled back to the bar, flashing a backward glance over her coat-hanger shoulder every few steps to keep an eye on Eightball.

"What was that about?"

"Aw, nuthin'. She's one of the Boss's prostitutes who doubles as a waitress. Actually, most every waitress here doubles as whores."

"She sure doesn't like you very much." *Probably the smell,* Sly thought.

"That's because I roughed her up a little last time we were together. She got smart and I put her in her place. Nowadays, women think they can do what they want. That's not how I operate. Any woman I take on's gonna do what I say or there'll be hell to pay."

In the short time he'd known Eightball, Sly realized that violent fits of rage were more the norm than the exception. Eightball seemed to be a booze-fueled fighting machine. Sly wondered how many drinks it would take to start Eightball's engine. Doris was probably one of many molls trying to keep from drowning in the lousy palooka's wake.

"So how've you been making your way on the streets up till now? Word was that you were a hijacker before Dapper took you under his wing."

"I'm not about to rob liquor off the Boss's train cars then ask him for a job, if that's what you're thinkin'. I unloaded the boxcars and kept lookout on a lot of shipments to make sure hijackers didn't come around. Got paid pretty good too. Worked for Dapper Dan for a while and then the Karpis gang before that. I guess I see more of a future with the Boss than those other folks."

"And you want to try out for the big time? This ain't no stroll through the garden."

Sly's memory flashed to Agony locking him in a cellar full of spiders and then sticking a pitchfork between the floorboards just for laughs. "I can handle myself."

"I hope so, or you could get us both killed."

"What are we up against?"

"It's like this. There's a Mob boss outta Chicago named DeLuce trying to set up a bootlegging operation here in St. Paul. The word is

Capone is muscling him out of Chicago. The Boss says DeLuce wants to get up and running right under our noses before we can react. Lucky for us, the micks DeLuce cut the deal with work for the Boss. So they dropped dime on him and told the Boss all about it. DeLuce's sending a courier named Mario Pancetti with a bundle of setup money. Pancetti will be at the warehouse on Fifth and Cedar tomorrow around noon. We beat the shit out of him to send a message, take the money, and deliver it to the Boss."

"Won't he have company?"

"Since DeLuce wants to keep this real quiet, we expect one other guy. Two tops. They figure if the cops at the train station don't recognize them, they can be in and out of town before they even have to check in with us gangsters, since Dapper is no longer . . . in charge."

"So it's just us and them? No help from the cops?"

"Just us. You're not turning chicken on me, are you?"

"No, no. I'm okay." Sly thought about how many things could go wrong even if everything went according to plan. Assaults were considered violent crimes and violated the O'Connor system. And Sly wondered if the rumors were true—that one good punch from Eightball could send a man to the morgue.

Worse still, his fellow criminals called DeLuce "Devil" on the streets: a man so twisted even his shadow could kill you. When crossed, the Devil would seek revenge.

The oil lamp bathed Eightball's scarred face in an eerie amber light. "This is your one shot, kid. Don't fuck it up."

"I said I'm okay. Just tell me what I gotta do."

"There should only be two guys. You take one, I'll take the other. Like I said, we beat the shit out of them, grab the money, and run. No sweat." He glanced around the bar. "Where is Doris?"

Sly looked around the bar only because he thought Eightball expected him to. "Will they have guns?"

"We're not going to an ice cream social. Yeah, they'll have guns."

Sly took a deep breath.

"These questions are making me nervousss. If you're not ready, tell me now," Eightball said.

"I'm ready. I'm fine. Don't worry about me."

"I swear if you get me killed, I'll kill you."

If Eightball intended to question the size of Sly's balls, it was time to change the subject. "How much do you think the Boss makes off one of these shitholes?"

Eightball rapped his knuckles on the table. "Well after all the grifts to the police chief, the mayor, the district attorney, flatfoots, and some members of the Purity Squad, he still pockets some good cake. His swankier places on University and Wabasha pull in way more than this place, but the grifts are a lot stiffer over there." His unlit cigarette bobbed between his chapped lips as he spoke.

Doris showed up balancing a tray containing two stained glasses filled with a yellowish liquid. "About damn time," Eightball said, scowling. Keeping her head down, she placed the drinks on the table and backed away. Eightball stared at his drink like it held the cure for everything from leprosy to bad breath.

"What's the Boss's name?" Sly asked.

"You call him Boss. That's all you need to know."

"You don't know his name?"

"Of course I know his name."

"What is it then?"

"You'll find out if you get into the gang."

"You have no idea, *do* you?"

Eightball removed the cigarette from his mouth and held it between his index and middle finger before narrowing his eyes at Sly. "One more word and I'm comin' over this table and choking you out."

"Don't get steamed. All the time I was out on the streets, no one called him by anything but Boss. I just found that weird."

"I got a question for *you*." Eightball stiffened. "How many guys have you killed?"

Sly took a hefty slurp of his drink. "Jesus Christ! What *is* that shit?" He had never tasted varnish before, but thought it must be very similar. His tears flowed and a few violent coughs drew laughter from Eightball. Sly now understood how his insides could sit up and beg.

Eightball laughed. "Great hooch, right?"

"You could strip paint with that!"

"Settle down, kid. Finish up, it's good for you. Puts hair on your chest."

Sly winced and took another sip. "How many have *you* killed?"

"Plenty. Mostly in bare-knuckle fights the Boss sets up. If they're dumb enough to fight me, I beat them to death." Eightball raised his hands to the table lamp and clenched his fists. His scarred and misshapen knuckles looked more like clumps of cauliflower. "I've broken every bone in my hands more than once. These are more like clubs made of bone than knuckles anymore. I've killed seven men and can't wait for number eight—you know, because my name is Eightball and all. I've killed men and dames with knives and guns, even a straight razor. But I really only remember the ones I beat to death." Eightball gulped varnish and inhaled between gritted teeth. If he put that cigarette in his mouth and lit it now, his face would go up in flames. "How about you?"

The question snapped Sly from studying Eightball's hands. "Why is that important?"

"I want to know who I'm working with. Now answer the fucking question. How many?"

Beyond the cave walls, Agony kneeled in the snow. Sly saw fireballs and shattering ice. Exploding timbers and swaying trains. A woman tangled in her shawl. He heard a baby's cry. Agony smiled.

The memory sank its teeth into Sly and wouldn't let go. He felt it crawling under his skin like someone covered in shadow was showing him a moving picture.

"Sly!" Eightball's voice shook Sly from the memory. "Are you running through the daisies or what? Ansssswer the question."

Sly answered, "I was counting."

5.

Finders Creepers

TUCKED BEHIND A PILE OF CRATES in an alley on the corner of Fifth and Cedar, Sly and Eightball waited for Mario Pancetti and his cargo of money. Sly looked up between the buildings to see the noon sun shining, but couldn't feel its warmth. The winter air stank of car exhaust and the warm sewer steam rising from the grates along the sidewalks.

"Where the fuck is thiss guy?" Eightball rubbed his arms. Sly adjusted his checkered flat cap. He blew in his hands and rubbed his palms together before jamming them back in his coat pockets. Although Sly was sick and tired of Eightball bitching and whistling about the cold for the past hour, he wondered too, *Where the fuck was this guy?*

A black Ford Roadster turned the corner and slowed.

"I think we got something here," Sly said.

The car stopped next to the dirty, snow-packed sidewalk. Two men wearing identical black, soft-crowned hats got out, one of them doing his best to conceal a Thompson submachine gun under his black wool overcoat. The driver wore spectacles and fumbled a set of keys in his skinny fingers as he approached the padlock on the wooden warehouse door.

"Looks like there's only two of 'em. The one with the peeper cheaters is Pancetti. Wait till he goes inside, and if the lookout stays out here, we're taking him down," Eightball said.

"What? He's got a Tommy under his coat. And we're only supposed to rough them up."

"The Boss gave you iron same as me, right? Use it. I say when they bring the big guns we're allowed to change the rules."

Sly felt his stomach twist and kick and checked the pistol in his pocket for reassurance. He didn't remember swallowing an angry wolverine, but that's how he felt. Pancetti unlocked the door and went inside, shutting the door behind him.

"Walk up like a bum looking for change. Distract him long enough so I can move in behind him. And let's keep this quiet. Don't shoot unless you have to."

"Are you crazy? He's got a machine gun," Sly said.

"I'll take him out before he can get off a shot. Don't worry about it. Now go."

"Don't worry about it?"

Eightball gritted what teeth he had left. "Pipe down." Sly felt a pistol barrel press against his rib cage. "I swear I will plug you right here and do this myself, the hard way. Now move."

Sly palmed the pistol in his pocket and considered slinging hot lead at Eightball, but the thought of getting cut down by a Tommy gun seconds later kept his anger in check.

The same chill Sly had felt in the Outhouse the day before crawled under his skin again. He stepped from behind the crates and approached the gunman. Sly took two steps before the lookout spun and the barrel emerged from beneath his coat.

Sly's world squeezed into a tunnel of vision focused on the tip of the gun. Lightning struck from the Tommy. The movie of his life flashed like the start and end of a picture show—showing nothing in between. Sly closed his eyes and waited for the burning bullets to rip through his flesh. Nothing. Sly opened his eyes. The man was still holding the Tommy on him. But no holes. No blood. No smell of burnt skin from the entrance wounds. No sensation of falling to the sidewalk. Sly raised his hands slowly as his heart tried to kick its way out of his chest.

"Stop," the lookout ordered.

Sly stopped, hands still in the air.

"Who are you? What do you want?"

Sly fixed his gaze on the black steel glinting in the afternoon sun. "Um. I just need some change for a warm cup of joe, Mister."

The man waved him away. "You're lucky I don't cut you in half. Get the fuck out of here."

The man's head snapped back when Eightball came from behind and clamped his left hand over the man's mouth. The shiv shimmered before Eightball drove it deep into the man's neck. Thick metal smacked the concrete when the Tommy gun dropped on the sidewalk. The lookout gurgled and flailed, making a feeble attempt to shake Eightball. Eightball managed to kick the machine gun toward Sly. Blood from the man's neck spewed like an open fireplug, staining the snowdrifts.

Sly watched the man's life drain onto the icy sidewalk. Eightball's forearm was coated in steaming blood. The man finally dropped to his knees.

Sly was startled when Pancetti emerged from the warehouse. Pancetti carried a suitcase in one hand and used his free hand to shield his eyes from the sun. He frowned and shut his eyes before turning around to lock the door.

Pancetti turned back to see his partner doing the dead man's float in a pool of blood. Pancetti immediately fixed on Sly.

Eightball wiped the shiv on the dead man's pant leg and yelled, "Don't just stand there, get him!" Pancetti yanked at the latched warehouse door. Sly gripped the pistol in his pocket and stepped forward. He had forgotten about the Tommy gun on the sidewalk before he accidentally kicked it. He released the pistol and picked up the Tommy and bore down on Pancetti.

Pancetti fumbled for the warehouse keys inside his jacket pocket. Sly raised the gun but slipped on the pool of blood covering the icy sidewalk. His finger pressed the trigger. Four rapid blasts rattled against his arm. Sly steadied his feet and saw the top of Pancetti's head splatter against the warehouse door. A sludge of brain, hair, and skull slid down the door on a sheet of blood. The rest of Pancetti hit the sidewalk like a deer struck by a truck. Sly felt the thud come across the concrete and up through his feet.

Shrieks and wails were everywhere. People ran yelling, jumping into doorways and ducking down alleys.

Sly's gut screamed at him to get the hell out of there.

"Grab the case! Let's go!" Eightball yelled.

Sly lifted the case, but it seemed much too light. "I think it's empty!"

"Open it!"

Sly opened the case and found nothing. He held it up for Eightball to see. Eightball stepped over Pancetti's carcass and hammered at the door latch. The pistol butt sparked against the lock.

"What are you doing?"

"I'm getting the Boss's money." Eightball used his bare knuckles to smash open the lock. He unhooked it from the door and threw it to the sidewalk. He kicked the door and took one step over the threshold. "Stay here." Eightball disappeared into the warehouse, leaving Sly covered in blood, holding a smoking Tommy gun in broad daylight, and standing over two dead mobsters.

Church Bells gonged their guilt-ridden song, signaling the end of Sunday mass. The people leaving church were greeted by blinding sunshine and Sly's bloodbath. The church crowd bled into the already panicked street crowd. People ran, snatched up children, shuttled grandmothers, slipped on the ice and snow, called for help, and searched for cover. The scene resembled a wolf entering a sheep pen.

But Sly wasn't in the pen. Everything slowed. The feeling reminded Sly of a raging storm that takes a deep breath before it unleashes Hell.

A quiet but forceful voice spoke louder than his inner thoughts and easily overpowered his knowledge of right and wrong. The whisper told him to search the dead men's pockets—*Now.*

The lookout carried a wallet and a gold pocket watch. Pancetti's pockets coughed up a flask, another wallet, and a folded piece of paper.

There was something mesmerizing about the paper. Folded, creased, yellowed, and apparently very old. The paper warmed in his hands as he rubbed it. The soft, thick paper felt so comforting between his fingertips like it was a beautiful woman's hair. He licked his dry lips while unfolding it. Sly looked left, then right, as if someone was peeking over his shoulder.

The images on the wrinkled paper looked like a child's drawing but without the innocence. Rows of dark, scratchy stick figures faced the same direction in a single-file line along the bottom. His eyes narrowed and widened and his face strained with concentration. His head began to ache and his frustration grew. There were triangles and wavy lines and some strange writing all over it. The fact he couldn't read caused him to curse and mumble and gnash his teeth.

On the right-hand side was an area covered in gold dots. Sly turned the paper in all directions, unsure which way was up. He felt as though a spider wriggled in his throat when he studied the gold objects causing him to cough and gag. A nearby scream snapped him back into the mayhem on the streets. He quickly stuffed the paper in his right pocket along with his pistol. The flask, wallets, and pocket watch he stuffed into his left pocket.

Eightball crashed through the door and stumbled over Pancetti's body.

"Let's! Go!" Eightball blurted, gasping for air.

"Did you get the money?"

Eightball lifted a potato sack he clutched in his left hand, staggering as he ran down the block toward the car. Sly stayed on Eightball's heels. Sly arrived at the car and jumped in the passenger side and slammed the door. Both men pumped out frosty clouds of hot breath. "We. Are. Fucked."

"No. We're not." Eightball pushed in the starter pedal and clutch. The grinding gears kicked and whined in protest against the cold.

"Why not?" Sly asked.

Eightball tried to catch his breath as he maneuvered the car onto the street. "We got . . . the money. That's . . . the main thing. He won't be too . . . sore. I know it."

A world of shit whirled inside Sly's head during the bumpy ride back to the Boss's office. The Boss had instructed them that no one was to be killed. His arm still tingled where the Tommy gun had thrust and jerked when it fired accidently. Sludge ran down the warehouse door. He smelled the smoke of a freshly fired Tommy gun. The Boss would have his ass. There was no chance of getting into the gang now.

An even bigger problem loomed, though. They had just broken the cardinal rule of the O'Connor system: no killing. Sly understood it wasn't the police he needed to worry about as much as other gangsters. Killing in the streets cost gangsters big money. And costing gangsters money meant you're only worth whatever the urchins could strip off of you after you're gunned down on the sidewalk.

Not that murders didn't happen inside St. Paul's city limits, but Sly had learned the proper way to handle that situation was to take the body outside of town and dump it.

"We should just take the money and get out of town," Sly said.

"Are you cracked? There is nowhere we could run where the Boss won't find us. You know that. And if we get pinched, he'll have us killed in jail—*any* jail. Like I said, he won't be sore. We got his money."

Despite his world hanging in the balance, Sly's thoughts switched to the paper. It nagged at him worse than having corn stuck in his teeth. He hoped it led to a treasure bigger than he could imagine. If he'd blown his chance with the Boss, at least now he had an insurance policy. If he lived long enough to cash it in.

Eightball parked in front of the Boss's office. He paused to examine the blood covering his hands before pulling the hand brake. He got out while grasping the potato sack firmly. Sly didn't want to face the Boss so he sat and watched Eightball walk around to the passenger side. The three quick knocks on Sly's window sounded like Eightball had used a rock instead of his knuckles. Eightball scanned the immediate area for onlookers as Sly rolled down the window.

"Look, if you're that worried about it, I'll let you hand the Boss the money and tell him it was all my idea. Now come on. I'm out here in broad daylight covered in blood."

Sly followed Eightball inside. Warmth wrapped around Sly as the door closed. One of the Boss's assistants greeted them in the entry and took their coats. The pudgy greeter reacted to all the blood by sneering and pinching the stained coats between his fingers before dropping them on the floor.

Sly's sight had barely adjusted to the dark entryway before the Boss's booming voice shot from upstairs. "Is that Sly and Eightball? Tell them to get their asses up here. Now!"

"Gentlemen, the Boss would like a word."

6.

Costly Mistake

"GET UP HERE!"

Sly heard the Boss's anger from the upstairs office. They had fucked up, no matter how much Eightball tried to sugarcoat the situation. The Boss simply told them to send a message, not to leave a mess for God and the cops to sort out. The only part of Pancetti that survived now lined Sly's pockets—including the mysterious piece of paper. It nagged at him like a throbbing tooth.

Loud, drawn-out creaks echoed through the small entry as Eightball stepped slowly on the stairs, as if trying to sneak into his parents' house after a night of drinking. Sly noticed the closer Eightball got to the top, the slower he climbed.

"Goddamn it, I said get up here now!"

Eightball gripped the burlap sack tighter and stepped faster. He stopped at the top of the stairs and tilted his head toward the half-open door, motioning for Sly to enter first. Sly soured his puss at Eightball before entering the Boss's office.

With the shades pulled down tight, the office had the feel of a cave. The bulb in the floor lamp buzzed and cast deep shadows.

"So what was that?" the Boss asked.

Eightball shrugged. "Ssso what was what? It was the kid's fault. I told him jusst to rough them up. The kid went crazy."

Sly clenched his fists and his jaw. "You son of a bitch."

36

"Don't play with me, Eightball. You were supposed to leave them alive and now every cop in the city is pissed off. The chief of police is jumping down my throat. I just got off the phone with Murnane himself."

"But how did you know? . . ."

"I had you tailed. You think I'd send you out there without a back-up plan? They told me exactly what happened—*everything* you clowns did. I know the kid didn't start a thing. He's so green he wouldn't know if he'd been kicked, shot, fucked, or snake-bit." The Boss looked down and sighed like a boiling kettle. "Give me the money."

Eightball flopped the burlap sack onto the Boss's desk and took a step back. The Boss opened the sack and began stacking the bundles of cash neatly in front of him.

"Thanks to the circus you made out there, most of this money will go straight to the mayor's office so they can keep the feds out of town. We can't afford to have him or the cops pissed off. Chief Murnane is the last cop you want on your ass. And you had to pull this shit during an election year, goddamn it." The Boss stopped stacking money.

"What's the first thing we do when we kill someone inside the city?" The Boss stared at Eightball. Eightball's silence answered for him.

"We dump him along the roadway outside of town like we're supposed to. You don't watch him bleed in the middle of a busy sidewalk in broad daylight so everyone can get a real good look at you. Let's face it, when you're covered in blood you don't exactly blend into a crowd. The guys I had follow you couldn't clean up your mess because a swarm of flatfoots came running right after you took off."

"But Bosss, they had a Tommy . . ." Eightball sounded like a child trying to explain how the cookie jar broke.

"Where did you think you were going? To take an all-day sucker from some snot-nosed kid? Come on Eightball, I trusted you. It was the kid I was worried about. I thought you could keep your temper in check and focus on the task at hand."

"But I got the money."

"We'll be lucky to break even after all the grifts are doled out." The

Boss counted on his sausage fingers. "Murnane, the mayor, the head of the Purity Squad. You really fucked up. We won't have two nickels to rub together."

The Boss shook his head and mumbled. "It wasn't even about the money; it was about sending a message. The only message you sent is what fuck-ups we are."

Sly removed his checkered flat cap. When he bowed his head, sweaty locks of hair dangled across his brow. He would rather the Boss yell or shoot or *something*. Anything rather than condemn them with disappointment. Throughout Sly's life, when he did something wrong, it was a case of run or be beaten or arrested or some combination of those. Disappointment confused him. One thing was clear, though: his chances with the gang were fading fast.

"Boss?"

The Boss kept his head down but raised an open right palm. "Look, kid, don't talk. You're lucky I'm not fitting you with concrete galoshes right now. The last thing I want to hear is *you*."

"But, Boss, didn't you say you wanted to send a message?" The Boss didn't answer. "The way I figure it, every newspaper is flashing pictures of what we done. Your enemies are going to see what happens to them when they try to muscle in on you. *Everyone* is going to see that."

The Boss didn't move. Eightball turned toward Sly. "Shut up kid, the Bosss don't want to hear it."

"No, *you* shut up," the Boss said. He looked as though he was attempting to find a solution to world peace or what he was going to order at Cossetta's for dinner. He rubbed his chin and stared at his desk lamp until a smile squeezed between his chubby cheeks.

"This is better than letting them go. DeLuce will get the message and so will every family from Chicago to Minneapolis." The smile dropped away when the Boss eyeballed Sly. "This better work out, kid."

Sly understood that statement to mean that if the Boss took any heat, Sly had better run and hide or he'd end up in a ditch outside of town.

The Boss focused on Eightball. "I'll deal with you later. But for now, show the kid the ropes. Be back here first thing in the morning."

Sly tapped his toe and bit his fingernails.

"Welcome to the family."

Sly tried to act tough, but he couldn't hide the smile on his face. He shook the Boss's hand before moving closer to the door where Eightball stood.

"Bosss, I was the one who killed the first guy. It was my idea," Eightball said.

The Boss waved his meaty hand. "Shoo, fly, don't bother me."

Eightball slumped his shoulders and took one step back, being sure to throw a salty leer Sly's way.

"Thanks, Boss!" Sly said. The words rang through the room like the piano at a Harold Lloyd picture show.

Sly shoved his hands back in his pockets and turned to leave. The Boss stopped him with a question. "Have you got something else for me?" *One foot out the door. So close.*

Sly froze. His fingers took inventory of his pockets: two wallets, a flask, and a pocket watch in one, and the folded piece of paper wrapped around a loaded pistol in the other. He wasn't going to give up the paper.

"My men watched you pick Pancetti and the lookout clean. Show me what you got."

The trigger rubbed warm and smooth under Sly's fingertip as he thought carefully. He shuffled in place. Maybe they only saw him grab *something* and didn't get a good look at each item.

He pulled the wallets, flask, and gold watch from his left pocket and set them next to the short piles of cash. He kept his eyes on them and took two steps backward toward the door, using his sweaty hand to grip the pistol in his right pocket.

"Is that it?"

Sly nodded. "Yes, Boss."

"Everything?"

Sly's heart started kicking again. His tongue felt like sandpaper.

"Yes, Boss. That's it. I didn't have much time."

The Boss stood up. "Isn't there one more thing?"

Sly held his ground. He rubbed the trigger once again. He wasn't leaving without the paper. The blood in his veins coursed faster and ran hotter. He was hell-bent on deciphering that paper and the gold hidden in its creases. He'd take out the Boss, Eightball, and the man who took their coats if it meant keeping that piece of paper.

"Aw, hell, keep the gun. You did good after all, Sly," the Boss said.

"Thanks."

"I got showers in the backroom. I put 'em in so my men could clean up after a job. You two go and wash up. I'll have my assistant get a change of clothes for you. Leave those behind and I'll make sure they're taken care of." Sly hoped that involved burning Eightball's clothes.

Sly did as the Boss ordered, but made damn sure the paper was stuffed into the toe of his shoe, safe and sound.

The hot, soapy water felt like heaven against Sly's skin. He scrubbed and rinsed and repeated until no grime or blood swirled down the floor drain.

"See?" Eightball gloated as he used a horse brush to scrub his flaking, raw skin. "I told you he'd be fine."

Sly hadn't forgotten that Eightball tried to sell him out to the Boss. Though he made it into the gang, Sly knew if Eightball found out about the mysterious paper, Eightball would beat him to death and take it without a second thought.

After drying off, Sly hung his white towel next to the one Eightball had used, which had started out white but was now a yellowish-brown.

Sly dressed in the ragged, but clean, clothes the Boss had provided. He turned his back to Eightball before removing the paper from his shoe and tucking it in a pocket right next to his new pistol. He glanced at Eightball's knuckles and wondered if the new clothes had belonged to any of Eightball's seven beating victims. Sly put on a thick wool overcoat. The previous owner certainly didn't need it since the poor sap couldn't become warmer than ground temperature anyway.

Sly slicked his hair back, put on his wool cap, and started down the stairs with purpose. He felt the weight of the pistol tugging with each step. His life and his paper were still intact. Now he had errands to run.

7.

That Old Familiar Smile

SLY STEPPED INTO THE ENTRY and turned to look back upstairs. Eightball's heavy clomping shook the stairs on his way down. He slipped his arm into the sleeve of his new grey wool coat and grinned when he joined Sly. "Let's go celebrate at the Outhouse," Eightball said.

Sly smiled when he imagined Eightball's name carved into a headstone. "Can't. I gotta go."

Sly watched Eightball concentrate on buttoning his coat. The afternoon sun shining in the window illuminated the dust floating through the air.

"Where you going?" Eightball asked while modeling his new coat as if posing for the Sears, Roebuck and Co. catalog.

"I got shit to do."

"Like what?"

"Look, I got shit to do. What is this, the Spanish *Imposition?*"

"The what?"

Agony had yelled *Spanish Imposition* whenever Sly's mom sobbed for answers after Agony returned from a late night of drinking and carousing. Sly assumed it was the standard comeback for anyone who didn't want to answer any more questions.

"I gotta go."

When Sly flung the door open and stepped outside, icy wind punched his face. The robin's egg sky was speckled with popcorn clouds.

"Hey, wait up," Eightball said. He trotted out the door and down the sidewalk. "What time will you be done doing your shit?"

A ball of rusty barbed wire knotted tighter in Sly's gut. Eightball was far too eager to be friends now. Sly had to ditch him, and quick.

"Look, asshole. I don't appreciate what you did in there, okay?" Sly said.

"What? Tellin' the Boss it was all your idea? You kidding me? You made it in the gang and everything worked out great, right?"

"You got lucky, pal. Lucky the Boss knew you were full of shit. I saved the day and made the Boss see it was a good thing what we done. Now leave me be, or you'll find out just how fast your luck runs out."

"You threatening me?"

"Nope. Threats have a chance of not happening."

Eightball's glare burned the back of Sly's skull as he walked away.

Sly jammed his hand into his pocket and pushed the pistol aside to rub the warm paper. Images danced in his mind. Dark figures and shapes and wavy lines and a giant pile of gold—his gold. But he couldn't read the writing that told where the gold was. He needed someone to help him. And asking for help was something that curdled his stomach.

He needed the perfect place and person. The St. Paul Public Library sat next to the police headquarters and always had people and kids and cops walking past. Walking in there waving an old paper around and asking people to read it to him would draw too much attention, so Sly gave up on that idea. Then he remembered one of Dapper Dan's tobacco shops was located next to a bookstore that people rarely came in or out of. Unlike most businesses in St. Paul—even funeral parlors—the bookstore ran legit and had no speakeasy operating behind the walls.

Sly raised his collar and lowered his head. He turned left and quickened his pace, checking behind him often for any signs of trouble as he traveled the short distance to the store, one block down and three blocks over.

As Sly passed the limestone façade of the café, the red brick barbershop, and the concrete steps of the post office, the paper warmed his pocket. The same eerie whisper returned and caught his attention, telling him to look in front of him—*now*. A man walking on the busy sidewalk came toward Sly in the opposite direction. The man, wearing a long black overcoat and wide-brimmed fedora, made eye contact and politely smiled. Suddenly Sly's backbone felt as if it were starting to rot and his stomach churned. From a distance the man's eyes appeared to have no iris or pupils; they were as blank as milk. When the man got within a few feet, Sly swore tears of blood dripped down the man's smiling chalk-white face. Sly blinked and the man's eyes appeared perfectly normal. The man side-stepped and leaned away, looking quite annoyed. People bumped into Sly from behind when he stopped , to check over his shoulder and clear the cobwebs. The whisper went silent.

The closer he got to the bookstore, the more excited he became. The paper seemed to warm Sly all over—a strange, comforting warmth that welcomed him. The paper would have reminded him of a long lost friend, if he'd had one. He felt intoxicated, but without the anger or loss of control. This was how getting drunk with the blue bloods on Minnesota Thirteen must feel. His dreams were coming true.

The glass chilled Sly's cupped hands when he pressed them against the front window of the bookstore. Dirt caked the window, making it impossible to see inside. He had no choice but to enter the store. When he pushed the door open, a small brass bell announced his arrival.

As Sly walked through the door, he looked over his shoulder. A man with matted hair tucked under a mangy stocking cap ducked down the alley across the street.

I'm going to kill that son of a bitch.

8.

Untimely Death

"Chief! Chief!"

St. Paul Police Chief August Murnane pushed through the crowd using his forearms like a train's cow catcher. A roaring multitude of scoop-hungry reporters, gossip-seeking citizens, and outraged church folk covered the steps of St. Paul's city hall. Street vendors weaved through people and the smell of boiling hot dogs wafted over the crowd.

"Chief! Do you have any suspects in the Cedar Street killings that took place earlier today?"

Chief Murnane stopped halfway up the steps and addressed the locusts. The late afternoon sun punched him in the back of the eyeballs, but he didn't flinch.

"We are currently conducting an aggressive investigation." He walked toward the building as the crowd erupted again into a verbal smear of questions.

"Considering the brazen attack at Fifth and Cedar, are the streets of St. Paul safe or do the gangsters control them?"

The chief spun around and glared at the crowd. "These streets are safe." His hand sliced the air for emphasis.

"Isn't your entire office on the Boss's payroll and currently under federal investigation?"

Murnane grimaced and waved the questions from the air like he was dispersing gnats. "No more questions!" The boisterous interrogation continued until he entered city hall and shut the tall copper door behind him. Building security, two wide-eyed youngsters right out of the academy, locked the door to keep the crowd at bay. Murnane brushed himself off and eyeballed the reporters pressing against the glass and covering the steps of city hall thicker than maggots on a carcass. "Goddamned leeches," he murmured.

Murnane's shoes clicked against the marble floor. He gripped the polished brass handrail of the marble staircase, counting his steps. He came to rest at the unpolished wooden door of *Mayor Londell Hodgson*—the name emblazoned in gold leaf on the frosted window. Chief Murnane knocked.

The voice inside barked, "Come in!"

Murnane entered a cloud of cigarette smoke. He quickly removed his hat, which smelled strongly of Murray's Superior Pomade, his brand of choice. He began to pace, using emphatic hand gestures to keep cadence.

"Goddamn it, Londell. This shit has to stop. I don't care how much the Boss is paying. After I gave the Boss an earful, the feds called again, and they are none too happy. I've got a world of shit coming down on me."

Mayor Hodgson reclined in his leather armchair and folded his hands under a protruding chin. "That's a lot of shit for one guy."

"This shit isn't funny! They're telling me indictments are imminent for most of my force. I heard Hoover just got the use of wiretaps pushed through Congress. They can listen in on our phone conversations and then use them against us in court." He pointed at his chest. "I'm not going to prison. I'm not leaving my wife and kids alone."

Hodgson swung forward and thumped his elbows on the desk. "I'm not laughing, August. I only have three hundred twenty-five police officers for a city of over a quarter million people with more arriving every day. Then I have the worst criminals from every corner of this country flooding in here at a constant rate looking for us to protect them. What do you think happens to us when we turn our backs on them?"

Murnane considered the question carefully. He had benefitted from the O'Connor system. Under his watch, he and Hodgson had expanded the system and profited handsomely by offering asylum to felons. Murnane and Hodgson found themselves protecting mass murderers, rapists, violent bank robbers, and fugitives alike, all seeking sanctuary in St. Paul—but *receiving* protection came with a hefty price tag.

Whenever J. Edgar Hoover's FBI came to collect a captured criminal, Murnane's force would fix it so records got lost or witnesses came down with chronic bouts of amnesia (or disappeared). St. Paul cops freely provided false information to any straight-arrow Johnny Law the feds sent. Most politicians and police alike became entangled in the web of dirty money, which offered no way out except by federal prosecution, Tommy gun lead poisoning, or, as Dapper found out, exiting your car via the windshield.

Mayor Hodgson continued. "Be that as it may, the Boss broke a cardinal rule this time and we can't let it slide."

"I already told him how we're going to handle things on our end. He said Eightball and some new kid botched a snatch-and-grab. Have you talked to him?" Murnane asked.

"No. Not yet, but I will. But I *did* talk to DeLuce," Hodgson said in a low voice.

Murnane reveled in his own reputation as a man who chewed up fear and spit it onto a dirty sidewalk. He took pride in the fact that criminals feared his gun and his fists. But one mention of DeLuce and Murnane felt like the Devil had just laid flowers at his grave. "Don't tell me those were DeLuce's men."

"It gets better. One of his guys was carrying something on him that DeLuce wants back in the worst way."

The chief waved his hand. "Do what you want. I'm not risking my family's safety."

The average street grease never posed a threat to Murnane's wife and children. And the St. Paul crime syndicate would never upset the flow of dirty money by going after Murnane's family. But DeLuce was a different level of vicious. DeLuce had no jurisdiction, code of ethics, morals, or remorse. Murnane had covered too many of DeLuce's victims in white sheets.

"You're out when DeLuce says you're out. He pays us to keep eyes on the Boss's activities and that includes you too, don't forget that," Hodgson said.

"I don't owe that sick bastard a goddamned thing. The man is walking death." Murnane stopped pacing. "I heard he once interrogated a guy with a potato peeler. One slice at a time until the guy's forearm was down to the bone. What kind of a man thinks up something like that?"

"Do you think he'll try to *peel* you to death?" Hodgson chuckled.

"Maybe someone should take a potato peeler to your tongue so you shut up."

Hodgson repeatedly smashed his cigarette in the ash tray on his desk like it was a cockroach that wouldn't die. "Say what you want, but whatever this missing thing is, DeLuce said he won't stop until he gets it back."

"Must have been a lot of money—or? . . ." Murnane asked.

"He wouldn't tell me, but he's coming in on the three-forty train from Chicago. You can ask him yourself. He's pulling out all the stops. He's bringing the Butcher Boys in on this one, and he asked for *you* to help them."

Chief Murnane bowed his head and closed his eyes. He knew the Butcher Boys handiwork all too well. Orphans of Swedish immigrants, at a young age they rose to prominence on the streets of St. Paul. The twin brothers freelanced as killers for the highest bidder. A few months back Murnane arrived at a crime scene where the brothers had taken care of a snitch behind Mack's Dining Car on Seventh Street. The Butcher Boys had taken their time with the victim. When Murnane got to the scene he was told there weren't enough solids to take to the morgue. Police ended up washing the snitch down the sewers with a hose.

Murnane raised his head and stuck out his chest. "I'm taking my wife and kids and we're leaving town right now."

"No you're not. He wants you and that's that."

"I just told you I'm out. I don't give a shit what that maniac says."

Hodgson shrugged. "He asked for you specifically. What am I supposed to say? No matter how you slice it, you're helping DeLuce and the Butchers.

"And now, thanks to you, if I run he'll hunt me and my family down just for sport. Well fuck him if he thinks I'm scared of him." Murnane rubbed his fingertips into his temples and tried to loosen the knot tightening in his brain. "Goddamn you, Hodgson. Why did you agree to this?"

Hodgson set his forearms on the desk and opened his hands. "Take it easy, August. He's not going to carve you up or kill your family. All he wants is whatever the Boss's guys took. Get it back and he and his chopper squad leave town. Everybody's happy."

"A guy like DeLuce doesn't get happy, he gets even. Suppose we don't get his shit back from the Boss's guys, then what? You think he'll just head back to Chicago and say, '*Well, we gave it the old college try. No hard feelings*?'"

Murnane watched Hodgson's spindly shoulders bounce when he chuckled. "Don't turn him into some kind of boogey man, August."

"You've implicated me in something I can't get out of, you son of a bitch."

"Hey, watch who you're talking to, Chief. Know your place. I appointed you and you've profited pretty damn handsomely off the Boss as well as DeLuce—so consider this as DeLuce collecting on services yet to be rendered. Be careful, August. You're on thin ice."

"You think I'm afraid of you, you little sniveling pencil neck? Don't think for one second your title protects you from me snapping you like a twig if anything, and I mean anything, happens to my family. I seriously hope your will is up to date, because whether it's me or DeLuce, one of us will be the end of you."

"That sounded very much like threatening the life of a public official. I could have you fired, tried, and convicted before you could *snap* your fingers."

"Roll the dice, asshole. One or both of us is already dead, so save your empty threats for your boot-licking constituents. You know if you sell me down the river, we both go over the falls."

Hodgson leaned back and smiled. The leather crunched when his shoulders settled in, adding to Murnane's tension. "Now let's just calm down here." Hodgson put his palms up, facing Murnane. "Nothing is going to happen to your family, I swear. While you're helping DeLuce, I'll send my driver over to pick them up and take them somewhere safe. I'll even get a couple squads to escort them and stand guard until this all blows over. How's that?"

"Hand me the phone."

Hodgson slid the phone across the desk. "Who are you calling?"

Murnane picked up the receiver and checked his pocket watch. It was just after two in the afternoon.

"My wife. I'm telling her to grab the kids and get out of town right now." Murnane looked down at Hodgson. "I'm not helping him. I'll say it to his face."

A loud knock rattled the door. Murnane dropped the phone.

"Who is it?" Hodgson asked.

The door opened and a man wearing a long, black overcoat removed his wide-brimmed fedora and walked in. "Mayor Hodgson. Chief Murnane. Good afternoon, sirs."

DeLuce was early.

9.

A New Wrinkle

SLY HURRIED INSIDE THE BOOKSTORE and closed the door. The window blinds rattled and echoed through the large store and the bell jangled loudly. Sly looked through the blinds but didn't see Eightball. He shut the blinds. He held his breath and listened, but heard nothing. He flipped the *Open* sign to *Closed*.

Sly pulled his hat down, turned his collar up, and lowered his shoulders before shuffling one step closer to the counter. If there were people in there, he didn't want anyone to get a good look at him.

Hiding in plain sight meant staying small and never drawing attention. Sly had been doing it for years—every time Agony came home drunk looking for something to beat after a hard day at the railroad. Especially if Mom wasn't around to defend him, Sly tried to be invisible, but usually took a beating anyway.

"Hey," Sly called out. He pulled his hat up. "Anybody in here? Hello?" Still no answer. He lowered his collar and stiffened his backbone feeling confident enough that no customers roamed the store. He stepped back and locked the door.

The only sign of life was a fancy carved ivory pipe resting on the counter. Smoke rose to the upper level of the store. Books of every color and size lined the walls. The unfamiliar smell of musty leather and sweet pipe smoke made Sly uneasy. He guessed it equaled the discomfort Eightball felt around that bar of soap back at the Boss's. But

51

if Eightball survived the soap, Sly could survive the bookstore. And, if need be, Eightball.

A small desk bell sat on the counter next to a sign. Sly knew enough to ring the bell for service.

Ding.

Nothing.

Ding. Ding.

Still nothing.

Ding-ding-ding-ding-ding-ding-ding-ding-ding-ding-ding-ding!

"What is going on out here?"

An ancient man wearing a frown on his mush emerged from a backroom camouflaged by tall stacks of books.

"Take it easy. Take it easy, young man. Where's the fire?"

Sly never wanted to get that old. The man's sagging jowls wobbled when he talked. He wore small spectacles that hung on for dear life to the end of his long nose. The bags under his eyes pulled the bottom lids away from the eyeballs exposing bright pink flesh.

"Who else is in here?"

"Only myself. I'm the owner." His disapproving frown was replaced by a wrinkled smile full of stained dentures. "I'm Phel Borge. Been here forty years now. Ever since I emigrated from Switzerland." Borge spoke in an odd accent that made him difficult to understand.

"I don't care, old man. I need your help."

Borge raised one eyebrow. "With the economy the way it is I've had to let everyone else go. People aren't buying books like they used to, as you can see by the amount of books I have and the lack of customers." Borge put his pipe in his mouth and struck a stick match. Every motion seemed to tire him to the brittle bone. He puffed and wheezed as the packed tobacco flared orange and smoke surrounded Sly.

"Hey," Sly said, but not loud or firm enough to slow down Borge's pointless explanation. The man was dull as dishwater—and even less fun to talk to.

"Nowadays if people want books, they go to the library and get them for free. So I tend to specialize in books that you won't find in any library." The pipe clicked against Borge's dentures as he spoke. "Especially those on ancient cultures and civilizations. I find that subject matter so very fascinating. From the Kingdom of Aksum to the Yuezhi armies, I've studied them all."

"I need your help, fast."

"Oh, and me rambling on. Forgive me. The stairs to the second level are to your right."

"No. Not that kind of help."

"Okay then, how can I assist you, young man?"

Sly reached in his pocket and pulled the paper out and pressed it down on the counter. The filtered daylight coming through the dirty windows showed-off the paper's creases and wrinkles. The smeared, nightmarish images reminded Sly of when lightning flashes cast shadows of twisted oak braches on his bedroom walls as a child.

"Oh, you're looking to sell an item."

Sly snatched the paper back. "No, you old bastard, I don't want to sell it. I want you to tell me what it says."

"Reads."

"What?"

"Papers or books are *read*. They don't have the capacity to speak."

Sly reached across the counter, grabbed Borge by his collar, and jerked him forward. Borge folded his arms to his chest like a frightened turtle and his pipe dropped to the floor. His round, pink eyes grew even rounder and pinker when his glasses knocked off kilter.

"Tell me what this says, old man. Now." Sly's tensed knuckles rubbed tight against Borge's trembling chest. "Now get readin'."

When Sly released him, Borge straightened his bifocals and reached down to reposition the paper for a better look. Borge then readjusted his shirt, his red bow tie, and cleared his throat.

The look in Borge's eyes should have knocked Sly out faster than a pair of freshly polished brass knuckles. "How dare you manhandle me, you rogue! You unwashed miscreant! I've never experienced such a brazen lack of respect for one's elders in all my . . ."

Sly pulled his pistol.

Borge put up his hands and stepped backward. "Please."

Sly tapped the pistol barrel on the paper.

Borge looked over Sly's left shoulder toward the front door. Sly aimed the gun at the old man. "Don't worry, I locked it. No one's gonna bother us. And trust me, you got about five seconds before I turn your peepers into bullet holes. Now get readin'." Borge finally shut up long enough to gasp.

"What do we have here?" Borge adjusted his spectacles and his bushy, grey eyebrows rose. "This seems to be some type of drawing with writing as well. It's written in Hebrew. No. Aramaic, I believe."

"What does that mean? Can you read it or not?"

"I'm not very well versed in Aramaic I'm afraid. It's an ancient language from Syria and Israel. Well, many places really."

"Are they around here? Can I take a train there?"

Borge looked up at Sly. Drool glistened at the corners of Borge's mouth. Deep concern or concentration, Sly couldn't tell which, shown on Borge's face as though Sly's incredibly smart question had stumped him.

"They are on the other side of the world, young man." Borge looked down at the paper and continued. "There were so many Aramaic dialects it is impossible to place this particular writing's origins. Though I enjoy studying ancient languages, Aramaic is one language that gives a novice like me a devil of a time." Borge paused and leaned close to the mysterious paper.

"If this were indeed created by ancient Israelites, they were most likely employed by the Egyptians, working for them as artisans and engineers, as I like to hypothesize. And you see here, two smaller pyramids are still being built, which leads me to believe this is some type of construction plan, like a blueprint today. Or possibly a rendering of the event, like a photograph. This wavy line is most likely the Nile River."

"Tell me what it says."

Borge rubbed the thick, grey whiskers on his chin, which sounded like steel bristles dragging across burlap.

"This is very strange."

"What is? What's strange?"

"It's written on paper."

"So?"

"Based on what appears on this document, it should predate the invention of paper by at least two millennia."

"So?"

"The great pyramid of Giza was completed around twenty-five hundred B.C. This paper shows the other two smaller pyramids still under construction. They are believed to have been constructed shortly afterward. Paper is thought to have been invented in China around one-hundred A.D., over two thousand years later."

Sly blinked twice. Slow, heavy breaths from his gaping mouth filled the silence.

"If this were an accurate and timely account of the event, it should be written on a slab of stone or clay. Possibly, on a parchment, like calf- or lambskin or some other form of vellum."

Borge once again raised his eyebrows and lightly nodded at Sly. Sly blinked and swallowed and let his mouth hang open again.

"Paper didn't exist when this was written," Borge snipped.

"Can . . . can you read it or not?"

Borge removed his peeper cheaters, squeezed his eyes shut, and pinched the bridge of his nose.

"Where did you get it?"

"None of your business, old man. I just need to know what it says." Sly felt his skin start to heat up and the veins in his temples throb. "What about the gold. See here? That's gold, right?"

Borge shrugged. "Perhaps the Israelites could have been skimming artifacts and golden effigies during construction. This could have been passed between workers to show where to bring what they had stolen in order to hide it. Or it could show the route from the limestone quarry to the construction site. But as I said, being that it is on paper, it is either a replica or a fake."

"You never said that. What do you mean a fake?"

"As I clearly stated earlier, paper didn't exist in twenty-five hundred B.C. That's why it is either fake or a copy made much later."

"Stop saying it's fake! I want to know where this gold is."

Borge chuckled nervously. "I don't know. You have to read it, follow it."

"That's why I'm here, stupid. Tell me where to find that gold!"

"Find someone who can translate Aramaic and you should figure out the paper's origin and purpose. But don't you understand? I suspect someone is having a lark at your expense, young man."

"Who can read this shit? Who?" Sly wrapped the old man's shirt around his clenched fist. Sly then flashed his pistol in his other hand to make his message clear. Borge's glasses dropped onto the counter and slid along the polished oak.

Borge tried to lean back by pulling in his chin, but couldn't because Sly once again held his collar tight. "Rabbi Mendlebaum at the Chabad Shalom synagogue on Fifth Street or Father Patrick Murphy at the St. Paul Cathedral up on the hill! They're the only ones I know! I swear! Please let me go!"

Sly flung Borge backward, causing him to stumble and hit the wall of books behind the counter.

"You tell anyone I was here, I'll kill you."

Borge breathed hard. "I'm only guessing about the paper. You need a professor of archeology or ancient languages to study it. He could tell you everything. He would probably give you a lot of money for it. Go to the University of Minnesota Department of Archeology. They'll help you. Hurry." Borge pointed toward the door.

"Stop trying to trick me, old man. I show this to some know-it-all and the next thing I know he takes it away and shoves it in some museum, or worse, calls the cops. No way. The gold is *mine*." Sly tapped his sternum with his index finger.

"You are grossly misinterpreting my explanation. I understand it is not the answer you were expecting or want to hear, but that paper could be a multitude of things."

"Stop saying that! I've already killed today and I ain't afraid to do it again." Sly backed toward the door.

Borge raised his hands and stared down the barrel. "Something other than reason or common sense has a hold on you, young man."

Any words of reason fell on deaf ears because power and greed pumped through Sly, convincing him more than ever to find that gold no matter what the risk.

Sly stopped at the door and looked out through the blinds. Eightball leaned against the alley wall across the street, keeping his head down while smoking a cigarette.

Sly gripped the pistol so tight, he could feel his pulse. The pistol was the only thing in the world he could count on right now, the only friend he had.

Sly thought about how much attention a gun battle with Eightball would draw. And if he missed, Eightball would beat him to death and steal the paper. He turned back to Borge who trembled while picking up toppled books.

"You got a back way outta this place?"

"Through there." Borge pointed down a narrow corridor lined with more stacks of books. With the pistol clutched in his right hand, Sly turned and ran out the back door and down the alley toward the Chabad Shalom synagogue on Fifth Street.

◆

Eightball rattled the front door so hard the hinges might have loosened. He tried seeing through the window. Layers and layers of dirt and coal dust caked on the glass and blocked his view. He pounded on the door until an old man opened the blinds.

"What do you want?" The old man shouted through the window of the door.

"I'm looking for someone."

"Are you the police?"

"Hell nnn…" Eightball stopped and thought a moment. "Yes. Yes I am. Officer Hobbs at your service. That's Hobbs with two b's."

"Oh thank heaven." The old man wrestled the locks open and greeted Eightball. "Please officer Hobbs, do come in." Before Eightball could get both feet inside, the old man let loose with an emotional tale that Eightball paid no attention to. "A man was just here. He attacked me, officer. He had a gun. He had a gun pointed at me."

The large room looked empty of people as Eightball turned his head and looked in all directions while holding his pistol halfway out of his coat pocket. Every muscle in his body was tighter than a tow rope and the smell of pipe smoke made him crave another cigarette.

"Did he wear a checkered cap?" Eightball asked quietly while glancing into every dark corner.

"Yes he did indeed. He went out that way, officer." The old man pointed down the narrow corridor leading to the alley behind the bookstore.

"Ssson of a bitch!" Eightball sprinted out the back and into the alley. The alley was empty.

Eightball took deliberate steps, producing a slow thud as he came back inside. The old man stood behind the counter. Eightball rubbed his left thumb across the knuckles on his right hand and said, "You're gonna tell me everything you told him."

"Yes, please. Of course I will, officer." The old man stuttered a moment and adjusted his glasses. "In fact there is something I forgot to mention to the other man who just left. He pointed a gun at me you know. I've never had a gun pointed at me before. It's a harrowing experience." The old man looked at Eightball's empty hands. "You don't have a gun do you?"

"Yes. But I won't need it unless you make me mad. Start talkin'."

The old man fidgeted.

"You don't act like an officer of the law, Mr. Hobbs."

"I said talk."

"Um, yes. A little over a year ago, two archeologists from the University of Minnesota came in looking for books on Aramaic. That's the language written on the paper that other young man had with him."

"Paper? What paper?"

"They said they had found a document that showed the location of a fortune in Egyptian artifacts. They seemed very short tempered, much like your suspect."

"What about this paper?"

"They said once they could decipher the writing, they would know *everything*. I don't quite know what they meant, but I assume they meant where to find the artifacts. I'll bet the paper that young man has is the very same document. If you tracked down those two archeologists, they would be able to answer all of your questions. Does that help you out any, officer?"

Eightball slammed his gun on the counter. "I'm not a cop, stupid. And now you're going to tell me where he's going."

The old man raised his eyebrows and frowned. "There's no need for that. I'll tell you everything."

Eightball smiled. "I know you will, number eight."

10.

Heads I Win, Tails You Lose

SLY ARRIVED AT THE SYNAGOGUE to find a young, lanky man wearing a funny little black hat. The man carried a broom and a small bag of salt to clear ice and snow from the front stoop. The man kept his head down and twirled the broom like it was his partner in a waltz lesson.

"Hey you. Where's Rabid Mellonbomb?"

The man stopped midtwirl and focused on Sly. "You must mean Rabbi Mendlebaum. He's inside preparing for mincha." He used his free thumb to point Sly in the right direction.

Sly pushed the man aside. "Look out." After tromping past the sweeper, Sly heaved the weathered wooden door open. Blustery polar winds followed him inside until the door shut with a heavy, echoing slam.

Once the warmer air replaced the chill, Sly detected the smells of lemon soap and charred wood. A humming, empty silence filled the space and Sly strained to hear any sign of life. Polished wood prayer stations jutted out from the walls, and a wooden railing surrounded a raised, square platform in the middle of the room with an altar at the center.

Any type of church made Sly uneasy. Religion baffled him more than books. God proved a greater mystery than the Oxford dictionary. All things being equal, he felt more comfortable being surrounded by books he couldn't read than a God he'd never understood.

Sly looked for a warm body to interrogate.

A slight, bearded man wearing spectacles appeared from a door in the back of the room. His face was buried in a black book as he walked. A cloth was draped over the man's forearm and he wore the same little black cap as the waltzing sweeper at the front door. The man could read *and* believed in God, Sly hated him already.

"Hey," Sly said.

Startled, the man stopped and looked up from the book. "Oh, pardon me. I hadn't realized someone came in."

"Are you Mellonbomb?"

Rabbi Mendlebaum stepped back as if Sly might throw a punch. "I am Rabbi Mendlebaum. Who are you?"

"Doesn't matter who I am. I need you to look at something."

The rabbi held his ground as Sly approached. "I'm sorry, young man, but I am very busy today. I would recommend making an appointment. Please talk with my assistant, Tali Haven. I believe he's sweeping the front stoop. Good day."

Sly pulled the paper from his pocket and shoved it in front of Mendlebaum who tried to focus. Mendlebaum's mouth fell open and his eyes reacted as if the paper were his own obituary. Sly realized Mendlebaum had seen that paper before and hadn't enjoyed the experience. When Mendlebaum reached for the paper, Sly pulled it away.

"Hey. Don't grab at it."

"Let me see that." Color began to run from Mendlebaum's face. "Place it here on the railing."

Sly stepped to the platform, slapped the paper down on the railing, and spread it flat. Mendlebaum pushed his spectacles up the bridge of his nose and raised his grey caterpillar eyebrows before letting out a gasp that confirmed Sly's suspicion.

"Where did you get this?" Mendlebaum trembled.

"Never mind. What does it say?"

"I'll ask you once again before I call the police. Where did you get this?"

Sly revealed his gun. "You're gonna tell me what this says or you'll be eating a hot lead sandwich long before you reach a phone. Start talkin'."

Mendlebaum changed his tune real quick. His flushed and sweaty face squeezed into a frown. Sly was unable to tell if fear or anger or some combination of the two caused Mendlebaum to wobble a bit. But Mendlebaum never lost sight of the paper.

"That gun strikes far less fear into me than this document," Rabbi Mendlebaum said.

"What is it?"

Sly poked the gun into Rabbi Mendlebaum's ribs. Mendlebaum made his fear and discomfort clear by frowning and letting out a sigh.

"This is part of a museum exhibit I helped coordinate in conjunction with a team of archeologists from the University of Minnesota. This document along with several other artifacts, were stolen eight weeks ago from a customs warehouse in Chicago. You have no idea what you're dealing with here. It's best for everyone if you just give it to me now."

"Maybe you didn't hear me. Read it. Now." Sly wedged the barrel between two ribs and Mendlebaum made a sizzling sound through his gritted teeth.

"I was one of several scholars and scientists who studied this document for nearly two years. We hypothesize it's a copy of an original stone tablet from ancient Egypt dating around twenty-one hundred B.C. We dated this document around one-hundred B.C, which predates the accepted date for the invention of paper by several hundred years. We believe it shows the location to an as-of-yet undiscovered amassment of Egyptian artifacts that Hebrew workers pilfered while building the second and third great pyramids at Giza." Mendlebaum cleared his throat and his eyes darted over the floor.

Sly could see a lie brewing inside Mellonbomb—a monstrous lie the likes of which only Agony could easily pass off. A man with any shred of a conscience stood no chance of concealing the size of lie about to burst from Mellonbomb's yapper.

"However, we were unable to decipher a scale for the drawing, making it impossible to figure where exactly they hid their purloined bounty."

"But the guy at the bookstore said you knew what this shit meant. It looks the same as those scribbles on that book you got."

"The Siddur is written in Hebrew and this paper is written in Aramaic. They are different languages."

"He told me you could read it. Now read it."

"What good would it do you? The artifacts are somewhere in the Egyptian desert under thousands of years of sand. Without knowing the drawing's scale, it's hopeless. Even if you had a thousand men working for a thousand years you would probably never come close—*if* they exist at all." Mendlebaum was twitching and scratching his nose. Not the kind of understandable nervousness of having a gun held on him, but more like he had told a lie the size of an elephant then tried to hide it under a napkin.

"You know," Sly said, "my dad could lie his way out of the gallows if he had to. He was the king of all liars. He'd lie about drinkin', he'd lie about runnin' around on my mom, he'd even lie about liking my mom's cooking so he wouldn't get caught lyin' about something else. I got real good at spotting his lies. I listened and watched and got to know his signs—his little tells. Just like reading the face of the man across from you at the poker table. You're saying one thing, but everything about you is telling me something else. You remind me of him—and that ain't a good thing. I'm counting to three and you die." Sly ground the gun into Mendlebaum's rib cage. "One. Two. Th . . ."

"Okay!" Mendlebaum shut his eyes, turned his head, and raised his hands. His back leaned in hard against the railing. "There's more!"

"What else? Tell me, old man!"

"It's a warning. Only a man of God, as in a rabbi, priest, a man of the cloth who has dedicated his life to spreading God's word, can seek the pilfered artifacts without damning his soul for eternity. That is what is written on the paper. If you fall victim to its temptations any further with greed in your heart you will be *damned*." Tears washed across his cloudy pupils.

"Now I'm getting pissed. I'll ask you one more time before bullets start flyin'. Read it to me."

"I will not. You don't understand. There is a curse on it. We lost two men during our two-year study of the document. Their greed got the better of them and they decided to go after the artifacts. Both men died violent deaths before they ever got their bags packed. You see, you don't even need to find the treasure to invoke the curse, but simply attempt to pursue it. I never believed in such things before studying this document, and now I find myself refusing to damn your soul. That is something I could not live with." Tears used wrinkles as troughs to find their way down Mendlebaum's cheeks.

Sly clenched his teeth. As he raised the gun to Mendlebaum's head, the front door opened, startling Sly. His trigger finger tensed. The gun kicked in Sly's hand and let off a bright flash and a loud crack.

Blue smoke curled from the powder-burn hole between Mendlebaum's eyes. His face lost all expression and a line of blood dripped like hot candle wax down the bridge of his nose. The rabbi fell forward, sliding against Sly and smearing him with blood, before collapsing to the floor.

"Shit!" Sly kicked Rabbi Mendlebaum. "There has to be more, you son of a bitch!" He turned his attention to the stunned young man with wide eyes standing at the open front door.

Sly had to silence any loose ends before getting the hell out of there. With the paper firmly in his grasp, Sly ran past the young man and shot four times. He burst out the door, back onto St. Paul's frigid streets, and never looked back.

Sly kept one eye open, straining against the bright afternoon sun. Icy slush caused him to slip and careen off a snow pile. He regained his balance and fled down the sidewalk while stuffing the paper back in his pocket.

Sly had obtained just enough information to be dangerous, but still needed to complete the puzzle hidden within the paper, so he set a collision course for the St. Paul Cathedral and Father Patrick Murphy.

Eightball stepped out into the alley behind the bookstore. He scooped up dirty snow and used it to wash the old man's blood off his hands. He reached in his pocket and pulled out a nickel. He flipped it up and slapped it on the back of his hand, but didn't look at it. Heads he'd go to the Chabad Shalom synagogue on Fifth Street. Tails, he'd make for the St. Paul Cathedral. He removed his hand.

Tails.

11.

Hanging on by a Cord

CHIEF MURNANE WATCHED DELUCE enter the mayor's office with the same lust for suffering the black plague must have had when it entered England. DeLuce moved through the curling cigarette smoke as if the curtains had parted and the tragedy had begun. His left arm emerged from beneath the black wool coat draped over his shoulders to remove the wide-brimmed black fedora.

"Mayor Hodgson. Chief Murnane. Good afternoon, sirs."

The Butcher Boys followed close behind. The hulking Swedish twins came armed with a blue-eyed stare on loan from the Devil. They shut the door and stood silently behind DeLuce.

Murnane twisted a kink from his neck and straightened the coat of his blue uniform. He stood alongside Hodgson's desk. He quickly looked at the phone receiver swinging listless by its cord over the edge. That thin black cord represented his family's lifeline, and if he overplayed its importance in front of DeLuce, things could go from bad to dead in a hurry.

Hodgson stood and offered his hand to DeLuce.

"Mr. DeLuce, so nice to see you again. How are you?" The painful ticking of the wall clock had been replaced by Mayor Hodgson's disingenuous pleasantries. Murnane knew the sugar coating wouldn't work. One look from DeLuce's straight-razor glare prompted the mayor to lower his hand and sit back down.

66

"You know why I'm here."

Hodgson raised his dark eyebrows and nodded. "Um, yes. Well, sort of."

"Where are the guys who hit my men?"

"We don't know. But what I don't understand is why you would show up here at the mayor's office in broad daylight with hordes of reporters outside. Use your head," Murnane said.

DeLuce looked down at the swinging phone receiver. "Calling someone?"

DeLuce's voice chilled Murnane to the marrow. Murnane pulled the receiver up by the cord, holding it a moment longer than necessary before hanging up.

"No," Murnane said.

"Where are we going first?" DeLuce asked.

"I guess you should go see the Boss," Mayor Hodgson answered.

"I'm trying to set up a bootlegging operation right under that low-life gangster's nose and you want me to go have a face-to-face with the guy?" DeLuce rubbed his hand over his thick hair and put his fedora back on. "If we go to war, then so be it. But until then, I don't want him knowing the importance of what he has."

"What does he have? You mean money?"

"No, it's . . . something else."

"What then?"

DeLuce looked down at Hodgson seated behind the desk and gestured toward Murnane. "Tell him to stop asking questions."

"Fuck you. We have a right to know what the hell's going on here," Murnane said.

Mayor Hodgson gestured for Murnane to sit down. Murnane grabbed a chair and sat in the corner so he could face DeLuce and the Butcher Boys. If he had had the power, Murnane's glower would have burned a hole in DeLuce's arrogance—and his face.

DeLuce pulled out his gold pocket watch and flipped it open. "You have one hour."

Hodgson straightened his tie and gagged on the phlegm in his throat. "To do what? With all due respect, Mr. DeLuce, it would help us if we knew what we were looking for."

"Find the Boss's men. Let me worry about the rest."

A violent knock at the door rattled Murnane, causing a shock to course through him. He saw Hodgson jump.

"Chief! Chief!"

"Hit the bricks! I have no further comment!" Murnane yelled.

"It's me, Hilliard. We got a situation."

Murnane needed more trouble right now like a hole in the head. "What the hell could this be about?" Murnane asked no one in particular.

Hodgson crossed his arms. "For Christ's sake, August, get rid of him."

Chief Murnane walked past DeLuce and opened the door. Rookie officer Hilliard stood sweating and rosy-cheeked in the doorway next to a young, lanky man wearing a black kippah and a face soaked with tears and urgency. Murnane closed the door to block Hilliard's view of DeLuce and the Butcher Boys.

"This guy says someone murdered the rabbi over at the synagogue on Fifth Street about twenty minutes ago."

"Okay, so take him to the station and get a statement. What did you bring him here for? Can't you see I'm in a meeting?"

"Sorry, sir, but the whole precinct knows you're here. Reporters have been hounding us all day too."

"So what do you want from me?"

"This guy, Tali Haven, says he saw which way the killer went. It might have something to do with the Cedar Street hit earlier today. Based on the eyewitnesses I interviewed, it sounds like the same guy."

"What'd the guy look like?" Murnane asked the young man.

Startled, Tali composed himself and answered, "I got a good look at him. He took four shots at me on the way out but missed . . ." The kid smiled tentatively and reexamined himself for bullet holes. " . . . obviously."

"Okay, what did he look like, Tali?" Murnane asked again.

"He was thin and had on a grey overcoat and a checkered flat cap."

"You just described half the city," Murnane said.

"He was young. Early twenties, maybe."

"Anything else?"

"Yes. I don't know if it's important, but when he showed up he had a piece of paper in his hand. I saw him shove it back in his pocket when he ran away. I think it had something to do with why he killed Rabbi Mendlebaum."

DeLuce yanked the door open, grabbed the young man by the arm, and shook him. "Where was he heading? Which way? Speak up, kid! Which way?"

Tali recoiled and opened his eyes wide. "Toward downtown, I guess. I don't know. He ran down Fifth Street. Someone must have seen him. He's got blood all over him."

DeLuce pointed to Mayor Hodgson. "Talk to the Boss and see what he knows, but don't tell him I'm in town. Let him know if he's hiding that kid in his building somewhere, I'll burn it down to flush him out. Make sure he knows I mean business." He looked at Murnane. "I want all your men searching every speakeasy, blind pig, and alleyway in St. Paul. Flatfoots, patrol cars, horses, and even the motorcycles."

"Look, I run my men and I'll decide how we sweep the city for this guy, got it?"

DeLuce answered with a glare harder than coffin nails.

Murnane didn't acknowledge DeLuce's glare. Instead, he got on the phone to the station. DeLuce hovered over him as he made the call.

"Get every man out on the streets. I need a full sweep of every shithole and card game happening right now. Put out an APB. Suspect is a white male, in his early twenties with a grey overcoat and checkered flat cap. Last seen running south, away from the synagogue on Fifth Street. Suspect has victim's blood on the front of his jacket and should be considered armed and dangerous."

Murnane listened intently to the news from the officer on the other end of the line. "Uh huh. Okay. Good work, Sergeant." Murnane slammed the phone down and looked at DeLuce. "I know where he's going."

"Let's go. You drive," DeLuce said, pointing at Murnane as if commanding a dog.

Murnane picked up the phone again. "I'll catch up."

DeLuce waved Murnane to follow him. "Let's go. Hodgson, you stay here."

"I gotta make one quick phone call . . ." Murnane hoped DeLuce didn't catch the desperation in his voice. One of the Butcher Boys walked over and calmly removed the phone from Murnane's hand and hung it up.

DeLuce watched from the open office door. Murnane felt like he was being buried in an unmarked grave.

As he followed DeLuce out of the office, Murnane turned to meet Hodgson's eyes. Hodgson offered a slight nod. Murnane wanted to believe that his family would be safe, that the mayor would keep his word.

The Butcher Boys stationed themselves behind the mayor.

———————◆———————

Murnane let the sirens loose and the red light flared off surrounding alley walls. The siren rang out like a banshee's lament. The car slid through narrow back alleys, past a barrage of crates and burning barrels. With every bump, DeLuce swayed in the passenger seat while bracing himself against the glove box.

"Put the word out on the street that I want this kid. Put a price on his head so high his own mother will give him up. You listening, Murnane?"

"Yeah, I gotcha. I'm trying not to kill us before we get there."

Murnane heard the engine rumble and the siren wail, but the silence inside the vehicle was the harshest sound. Not knowing if his family was safe made Murnane's stomach tighten. "Almost there." He pressed the accelerator to the floor.

Murnane jammed the patrol car into second when he hit the incline of Cathedral Hill and felt the gears grind against his palm. The car bucked when the gears engaged.

The mammoth church doors swung open just as Murnane slid the car to a stop in front of the cathedral. Two altar boys sprang from the church and sprinted straight for the patrol car. The kids looked like Satan had just asked them to take his confession.

12.

Father Patrick Murphy

SLY RAN COVERED IN BLOOD down Fifth Street, through the frigid streets of St. Paul toward the cathedral on the hill. His lungs burned and his legs felt like overcooked spaghetti as he stumbled and slipped on the ice and snow, but continued driving forward no matter what. Gawkers pointed and gasped. Leaving a trail of witnesses didn't concern him. All that mattered was how many of the paper's mysteries Father Patrick Murphy could unlock.

Sly heaved the cathedral's thick wooden doors open and stood in the doorway letting his eyes adjust to stained glass colors and candlelight.

The doors shut behind Sly and the whistling winter air caused the candles to flicker. The scent of burning wax rekindled his aversion to churches. Two altar boys attempted to keep the candles from blowing out and then gave Sly a look filled with something quite the opposite of forgiveness. A few elderly women knelt, thumbing rosaries, and a man with a hymnal covering his face sat in a corner, cloaked in shadow.

Sly watched the boys slowly examine him. Their expressions grew more horrified as they studied the blood on Sly's coat. "May I help you?" one asked in a soft voice.

"Father Murphy. Where is he?" Both boys, their eyes wide, pointed to a hallway to Sly's left. His ragged shoes squeaked across the speckled marble floor as Sly ran down the hall.

"Murphy!"

Sly entered the first room he came to. Several brass candleholders and an oak podium occupied the darkness, but no priests.

"Murphy!"

Sly darted across the hall and looked in another room containing stacks of books and leftover seasonal decorations. Purple tapestries and mannequins dressed as Joseph and Mary knelt by a baby doll wrapped in a burlap sack. Sly recognized the Minnesota Thirteen oak barrel cut lengthwise and sanded down to look like a cradle. Prohibition's donation to the church. Even Joseph, Mary, and little baby Jesus got to drink with the blue bloods. Lucky bastards.

"Shit. Murphy!"

The deeper Sly infected the church's guts, the more suffocated he felt. He likened it to when he was a kid and watched a snake swallow a frog ass first—at the time, he thought it was keen, but now he understood how the frog felt.

Sly knew the altar boys were watching him, but as long as they weren't cops he paid them no mind.

"Hello?" A faint voice called from farther down the hall.

"Murphy? Where are you?"

"Here. I'm in here."

Sly darkened the entrance to a cramped office. The office smelled like the inside of a trunk found in a dusty attic. A small, bony man with thinning grey hair sat at a plain desk. He wore black trousers and a black shirt with the little white part of the collar priests wear to let you know they're priests. Even though the shades were drawn, shadows managed to crawl over the walls and floor.

The moment Sly laid eyes on the priest, Sly's backbone stiffened worse than a dead tree branch. His soul was being slowly dipped into an ice bath. Sly realized he could snap Father Murphy's frail neck without breaking a sweat, but something caused him to pause. Years of Agony's punches, cuts, and cigarette burns hammered through Sly in a flash—and the pain scared the hell out of him. Sly had walked into that church with a trainload of sins and a loaded pistol, and wondered if God might be a little raw about it.

But if this was a warning from God not to hurt the priest, Sly felt it was too little, too late. If God couldn't protect him from Agony, then no way was God going to scare him away from getting answers out of this little old man. God owed him one.

The priest sat at his desk sorting through piles of papers and addressed Sly without looking up.

"I'm Father Patrick Murphy. Please excuse the mess. My main office is in the rectory, but I haven't . . ." With a polite smile, he turned to pick up a book and caught sight of Sly. The smile slid off his face. He removed his reading glasses and looked Sly up and down. "My goodness, son, what happened to you? We need to get you to a doctor."

"No. I need you to look at something." Sly slipped the paper from his pocket and slammed it down on a small open spot between the stacks of paper. He shifted his weight from one foot to the other and back again.

"I think you need a doctor, young man."

"I don't need a doctor. Tell me what this paper says. Right now." Sly slapped the paper.

Father Murphy jumped when Sly hit the desk. He looked down at the paper and then up at Sly.

"Read." Sly pointed at the piece of paper.

Trembling, the frail priest put his reading glasses back on and turned to examine the paper. He slid a humming desk lamp closer, then backed away and squeezed his nose into the crook of his arm, like something rancid had slapped his face.

"Where did you get this?"

"None of your business."

The two boys peeked inside the doorway, catching Sly's attention. The two scrawny altar boys expressed four saucer-sized eyes. They startled Sly who drew his pistol and waved it across the doorway hoping to shoo them away. Father Murphy raised his hands and gasped and the boys yipped and disappeared. Cassocks swished and hard-soled shoes chirped against the marble floor, the sounds growing fainter with each stride.

"Please, young man, there's no need for violence."

"Read it! Now!"

"You don't understand. I've studied this document before." He closed his eyes and shook his head. "Please don't ask me to read it."

"Why not? Are you scared?"

"Yes. And you should be too."

Sly chortled. "Why is that, priest?"

"Get rid of it."

"That's what the other guy said. Why should I? What is it?" Sly asked.

The old priest looked as though he either didn't hear Sly or hadn't understood the questions. He sat up and leaned forward. "What other guy? Who have you already spoken to about this?"

"The Jew, Mellonbomb. He said it was cursed or some bullshit."

Father Murphy studied the flecks of blood on the back of Sly's hands and the stain on Sly's coat. Tears pooled on top of the bags under the priest's eyes. His fingers spread over his open mouth. "That's not your blood, is it?"

"Old Man Mellonbomb wouldn't answer my questions. And if you don't want to end up just like him, you better tell me what I want to know."

"Rabbi Mendlebaum is a dear friend of mine."

"*Was* a friend of yours."

Grief and fear curled Father Murphy's lower lip. "What have you done?"

"How do you know about this paper? Is it a treasure map? God-damn it, start talkin'!" Sly screeched.

When Father Murphy pulled a handkerchief from his pocket, Sly raised his gun. "Hey. No quick moves." Seeing the handkerchief, Sly eased off the trigger.

Father Murphy wiped his eyes, blew his nose, and drew a few sobbing breaths before speaking.

"We studied this document with a team of archeologists at the University of Minnesota. We hypothesized it may be a record of items collected by slaves of the Egyptians, or at least someone in their employ. However, we could not be certain of the document's accuracy or scale in portraying the artifacts or their location." He stiffened up before continuing. "Rabbi Mendlebaum would have told you that."

Sly reached across the desk and grabbed Father Murphy by the back of the neck and shoved his face in front of the paper. The old man's flesh felt like a stocking stuffed with pudding. Suddenly, Sly felt Agony grab him from behind. Agony's greasy, jagged fingernails squeezed Sly's neck so tightly, he felt warm blood oozing. Agony dug into Sly, like a vise lined with razor blades, and shook until stars appeared. When Sly released Father Murphy, Agony's grip released as well. Sly took a moment to look behind him. He and the priest were alone. He shook away the stars, rubbed out the pressure, and checked for blood.

Sly gnashed his teeth hard enough to make chalk dust.

"So, you're going to lie to me and you're not going to help me. Is that right?"

Sly pulled the hammer back with his thumb. The click was slow and purposeful. Father Murphy reacted to the sound of the cocking gun by slumping his shoulders and conceding a sigh. His eyes were the color of the winter sky outside—clear and blue—but were missing the sunlight. The priest wiped away tears with his handkerchief before straightening his glasses with trembling hands.

"At first we assumed the story written here was a metaphor—a story of the Israelites being enslaved, whether by the Egyptians or by their own greed. The paper teaches that they must follow one of two paths. One to the light or the other to destruction."

"What the hell are you talking about?"

Father Murphy ran a bony finger along the text, zig-zagging down the paper like the claw marks of a caged animal.

"The workers who built the pyramids speak of being cheated out of their rightful wages by the Egyptians. They continued to work only to amass more treasure by stealing from the Egyptians. When the pyramids neared completion, the builders placed a curse on anyone who dared to seek the treasure—anyone other than those involved in the original plot to steal from the Egyptians, that is. We think they did that for fear of the paper falling into Egyptian hands. The paper goes on to name the demon Mammon, known by men of the cloth as the demon responsible for greed, as the enforcer of the curse. Until this paper was discovered, the first time any scholar knew of Mammon being mentioned by name was in the Bible, which was written around two thousand years later. It seems as though Mammon took control of the thieving workers one by one and led to their destruction. Rabbi Mendlebaum warned you of the two archeologists in our group who decided to go after the artifacts, did he not?"

"Get to the treasure. What does it say about the treasure, god-damn it?"

"Please don't say *His* name in vain." Father Murphy looked up. "I've told you everything I know. That is all it says."

"There has to be more. It has to say where the gold is."

"Heed the warning written herein, young man. Your soul depends on it."

"Bullshit. You're just trying to trick me, just like Mellonbomb."

"You still don't understand." His voice was deep and calm and eerie.

"What? Understand what? Stop saying that!" Sly swatted a pile of papers sending them flying. They fluttered and rustled, coming to rest throughout the small office.

Father Murphy looked like a man forced to dig his own grave. "You didn't find this paper. It found you."

13.

Shoot-Out at the O.K. Cathedral

Sly felt the oily darkness slither across his skin. The dark in the small office became so thick it seemed to move like liquid throughout the space.

"You didn't find this paper, it found you." Father Murphy sounded like he was reciting a eulogy. Pools of warm lamp light glistened in the priest's eyes.

"What do you mean it found me?"

"This isn't the kind of thing someone misplaces. Malevolent forces brought this to you."

Blood, brains, and a thick skull-sludge oozed down a warehouse door in Sly's memory as he fought against believing the foolish old priest.

"I took it off a dead guy. He didn't hand it to me, I *took* it. You don't know what you're talkin' about!" Sly waved his hand attempting to shoo the omen away, but the father's eyes were cold and unnerving. The priest wasn't lying.

What Sly saw instead were drowning souls on the sinking train. He felt ice water ram down his throat and a thousand icy needles pinch his skin. Horror and panic gurgled up into his throat until he choked. A violent cough snapped him out of the vision. Father Murphy sat quietly in the dark, staring up at him. The priest held the one thing within his pale eyes Sly did not want to see: the truth.

"Try to scare me all you want, but I'm going after that gold."

Father Murphy ran a hand across his thinning hair, placed his palms together, and said, "I implore you, do not go down this path any further. You have no idea what you're dealing with."

"I know there's a big pile of gold on that paper and you seem to be doin' everything you can to keep it from me. But it ain't 'cause you're worried about my soul or none such thing." Sly narrowed his eyes, tilted his head, and smiled. He wagged his finger and said, "You know where the gold is."

"Dark entities want you to seek the gold because their only intention is to cause misery and torment. Mammon plays upon your greed. There is no reward at the end of this journey, my son, only suffering."

The Devil himself couldn't keep Sly from discovering the secrets the paper held. Agony had taught him well that causing pain is the easiest way to get what you want in life. Hell, the Devil had nothing over Agony when it came to making people suffer. Sly felt the gun in his right hand and began to consider his own ability to inflict misery on others. Agony would be proud.

"I don't believe in any of this. Paper can't do none of that stuff you're sayin'. It's just . . . paper." The knot in Sly's stomach kept him from laughing.

"You are a bad soul, my son. That paper sought you out. It seeks out the wicked and makes them pay for their sins—that is part of its purpose."

Sly picked up the paper with his left hand. "What a sack of shit. Besides, the Jew told me that a man of God can go after the treasure without getting cursed. Does it say that?"

Father Murphy bowed his head. "Yes."

"Then you're coming with me. You can believe in stupid curses all you want, I just want the gold." The paper felt like silk when he rubbed it between his fingertips—so *comfortable*.

"You are already cursed. The further you follow this path, the worse it will become. It frightens me to think about those two poor men from our research group who dared to go after the artifacts. They said they were seeking the artifacts in the name of science, but their greed consumed them. I'm telling you, your torment will escalate each day—I've seen it happen firsthand. We need to destroy that document before it's too late."

Sly held the paper tightly and twisted away. "You touch this and you'll regret it."

"Please. Let me help you."

"Oh, you're gonna help me all right. Let's get a move on."

Sly decided he needed two free hands to manhandle the priest, so he slid the pistol deep into his right pocket and shoved the paper into his left. He lifted the scrawny priest by the collar and hauled him to the office door. Sly peeked out the door to make sure the coast was clear. He had just taken the first step to becoming a very rich man. He was in control now and nothing stood in his way.

"Well, looky here!" Eightball's misshapen teeth ground out a sinful smile.

Sly recoiled and clutched the priest tightly. "How did you find me?"

"It wasn't hard. You're about as subtle as a train wreck."

"What do you want?"

"First, you can hand me over your gun. Real slow."

"Why would I do that? I ain't dumb."

"The main reason is because I had a nice talk with the old man at the bookstore after you left. Turns out he forgot to tell you somethin' real important on account of you sticking a gun in his face. He talked real careful to me. Told me a bunch."

"Bullshit."

Sly plunged his hand into his right pocket. Eightball flashed his pistol.

"No, no, no. Let's not get stupid. I heard what the priest said. I know a whole lot more about that paper than you do." Eightball extended his free hand. "So hand over the gun *and* the paper."

Sly slowly worked his hand over the gun in his pocket while keeping a close eye on Eightball's .38. Sly carefully slipped his finger over the trigger. "You shoot me, you'll never find that treasure. The Jew told me all sorts of stuff before I killed him—stuff you don't know. So you'll take the paper over my dead body."

"Pretty poor choice of words." Eightball cocked his gun. "Tell me what you know."

Father Murphy ducked and covered his head. Sly tried to pull his gun, but the hammer snagged on the lining of his coat pocket.

"This is the police! Stay where you are!" A voice bellowed from down the hall. Sly grabbed Father Murphy by the wrist.

When Eightball turned his head to look down the hall, Sly reared back and planted his foot square into Eightball's chest. Eightball grunted and flew backward, hitting the wall. He slid to the floor, coughing and holding his chest.

Sly got his pistol loose from his pocket and stepped into the hall, yanking Father Murphy with him. A large cop in a blue uniform and hat crouched at the end of the hall and held a very steady weapon.

"Officer, please help me. They have guns!" Father Murphy yelled out.

"Drop your weapons!" the policeman ordered and moved a step closer. The officer's silver badge and brass buttons shimmered. So did his gun.

Just over the cop's shoulder, Sly recognized something—a set of eyes set under a wide-rimmed black fedora. Sly froze. He recognized those eyes. They reminded him of when he was a kid and had gotten lost in the woods one night after Agony left him behind. Sly heard wolves yip as they followed him at the edge of the darkness, their eyes glowing in the full moon. He'd seen those eyes somewhere else, though. Very recently.

Sly's curiosity shattered when Eightball struggled to his feet and fired two quick shots at the police. The flashes boomed and slapped against Sly's ears causing a painful ringing. The officer and the other man ducked into a room off the hallway.

Sly pulled the priest closer. "Where's the back door to this place?" he asked, squeezing Father Murphy's wrist.

A bullet hit the door frame inches from Sly's face. Splinters pricked like sewing needles against his cheeks as he twisted away.

Father Murphy shut his eyes and covered one ear with his free hand. "Please stop shooting in my church!"

"Where's the back door?" Sly yelled.

The priest pointed in the opposite direction of the police. "That way."

Sly ran like hell down the hall, gripping Father Murphy's wrist tighter every time a gunshot rang out. He figured the next three shots he heard were fired by Eightball because the shots sounded like they were directed at the cops.

At the end of the hall Father Murphy waved to the right. "That way."

Sly looked behind to see Eightball running backward down the hall holding his gun in the air.

"Go left," the priest said. Sly tried to steady the stumbling priest as they ran. There was a small white door at the end of the hall. "Here." Sly skid to a halt.

Sly looked the door up and down and worked the knob, but it wouldn't open.

"Please hurry. I hear them coming." The father curled his hand to his mouth like a silent film star in distress. Sly stepped back and aimed, ready to shoot the door knob.

"Save the bullets," Eightball said. He kicked open the door, turned, and fired one more shot down the hall.

Sly had to shield his eyes from the late afternoon sun. Two quick shots from a larger-caliber gun hit the wall inches above Sly, creating a shower of plaster dust. Sly ran a few steps into the back parking lot before letting go of Father Murphy long enough to let loose two quick shots, keeping the cop and his creepy partner just inside the church.

"Why are they shooting at me? I haven't done anything! It's you they want!" Father Murphy ran away with his hands to his ears, looking exactly like a frightened priest caught in the middle of a gunfight. Sly caught Father Murphy by the wrist and Eightball ran up and hooked his arm around the priest's elbow.

Sly led the chain of men to a nearby cluster of bare saplings. He considered shooting Eightball and continuing with the priest on his own. But pictured what would happen to him if he missed. Plus Sly couldn't remember if Eightball had fired six shots or five. Bullets flying at him had a way of making a guy lose count. Also, two guns holding off their lead-slinging chaperones were better than one.

A path of dirty snow wound through a leafless woodland ending at a large group of makeshift hovels. Sly led the way, still holding Father Murphy tightly by the wrist. Eightball brought up the rear. The packed dwellings were built with driftwood logs, sheet metal, and anything else the residents had fished out of the Mississippi River. Wooden plank walkways, slick with ice, covered the mud between the shacks. The narrow passageways reeked of boiled cabbage. One thing Sly hated more than being shot at was boiled cabbage.

"Stop," Eightball said. He pulled Father Murphy into a nook along the path. Eightball popped open the cylinder of his revolver and shook the empty brass casings onto the frozen mud. He slid fresh bullets in with his thumb and snapped the cylinder shut with a flick of his wrist. "How many bullets you got?"

Sly opened his gun and counted two bullets. Even with all the running and shooting, Sly had tried to stay one step ahead. He wanted to make sure that after they escaped the cops, he would have enough ammo to finish off Eightball. Several bullets in his pocket tumbled loosely through his fingers. "A few extras. Maybe eight? Ten? How many you got?"

Eightball wiggled his gun in the air. "You're lookin' at it."

Advantage Sly.

"Please don't shoot. These are innocent people. Women. Children. Please."

"Shut up, Priest." Sly closed his gun and then looked behind them to check on the police.

A bullet punctured the sheet metal next to Sly's shoulder. He grasped Father Murphy's wrist tight and started running. Fear drove his feet hard and fast. Sly knew after looking into those eyes under the fedora, the men chasing them would not take them alive. This was a one-way trip, and his ticket looked just like a death certificate. Eightball brought up the rear and fired once more, but Sly couldn't see if Eightball made it count. Five bullets left.

Sly pushed over curious onlookers who came outside to investigate the shots. Father Murphy apologized to each person who fell in the mud or slammed into a wall. "So sorry. Excuse us. Oh my. So sorry about this." Women screamed and babies cried and dogs yipped. Bullets continued to ring out through the tight corridors.

The maze closed in on Sly. Sly felt like he was trying to escape being swallowed by a giant metal snake. He hoped he wasn't running in a circle because every turn looked the same. Father Murphy's sobbing breaths and slapping footsteps were the calling cards of an exhausted man. The cabbage smell was replaced by wet lumber and dog shit. Sly and Father Murphy continued to careen off walls as they jutted left, then right, then left twice more.

Sly skid to a halt. Fifteen feet ahead, a boy stared up at him. His solid black eyes resembled two empty wells. When the boy pouted, thick black smoke surged from his sockets. Sly tightened his grip on Father Murphy. "Ow. You're hurting my hand." The smoke thickened when the boy smiled.

"Why are we stopping?" Father Murphy asked while gasping.

Sly turned to the priest. "You see that?"

Father Murphy peered around Sly. "See what? The boy? Please don't hurt him."

When Sly looked again, the boy stood trembling, clutching a ragged, filthy teddy bear. No smoke. No smile.

Eightball crashed into Sly and Father Murphy. "Why'd you ss-stop? Move! They're right on our assses!"

Sly took off again with Father Murphy firmly in tow and Eightball a step behind. Disturbing visions forced their way into Sly's head. A dead mouse sprawled in a trap. Sly shook his head and focused on the sound of his feet pounding against the planks. A corpse with worms dangling from the eye sockets. *Goddamn it.* Maybe someone slipped him a mickey or he conked his noggin when he fell on the slippery sidewalk back on Fifth Street. He needed to run faster.

Sly was desperate to find a way out of this shanty nightmare. His legs started to feel like rubber bands. And if *his* legs felt tired, he wondered how Father Murphy's must feel.

Sly saw an opening. He burst from the shantytown and took a deep breath. Father Murphy stumbled and started to drag behind like a wagon full of bricks—not a good feeling when you're on the lam with the wolves closing in.

"There's the river!" Eightball yelled out as he ran past. Sly saw the limestone bluffs of the Mississippi River rising up against the horizon. The shore was less than one hundred yards ahead.

"Come on, Priest, you can make it."

Once Sly and Father Murphy reached the riverbank, Sly stopped. Eightball fired two more shots at the lousy coppers who had just emerged from the shacks. Eightball had three shots left, and counting.

Loud blasts from the cops were followed by tufts of snow and ice that popped-up around Sly, landing too close for comfort. The uniformed policeman slipped and fell. But the other man, dressed all in black, continued at a heated pace, his gun cracking and flashing.

Father Murphy cried, "I can go no farther. Please. I must rest." Father Murphy went limp as a ragdoll. Sly kept him from falling by gripping him with his free hand and pulling straight up. As much as Sly wanted to be rid of Eightball, he needed his help to get Father Murphy to safety. *Son of a bitch.*

"Eightball, get over here."

Eightball put one of Father Murphy's arms around his neck. Sly took the old man's other arm.

Train cars slammed and locked together a few hundred feet down the riverbank.

Sly looked over the limestone bluffs. "We gotta find a place to lay low for a while. I know some caves in the bluffs south of here where we can hide out." Sly stepped left, taking Father Murphy in the opposite direction of the rail yard.

"Bullshit, we're hopping a train and getting out of town." Eightball nodded toward the train yard. He stepped to his right, pulling Father Murphy's arm. Eightball stopped after only two steps. "And when I say *we're* hopping a train, I don't mean *you*, Sly." Eightball confirmed his statement with a waggle of his pistol and a crosscut-saw smile.

"I have the paper. All you have is the priest," Sly said with conviction.

Eightball steadied his gun at Sly. "How about I just take both and leave you here in a heap." It wasn't a question.

Eightball pushed Sly away and dragged Father Murphy toward the rail yard.

Sly's anger swelled, but pointed his gun away from Eightball in a sign of good faith. "What the hell are you doing? You won't get far without my help. Think it through," Sly said with less conviction.

"The priest comes with me. Between him and what the book man told me, you're as useless as a bent-dick dog. Good luck on your own."

Sly watched them walk away. "The Jew told me all sortsa stuff too. There's a whole lot you don't know. Without me, you got nuthin'."

Eightball stopped. Father Murphy calmly looked at Eightball's face. "That man," Father Murphy nodded toward Sly, "is partially right. You must work together to get through this. You both may know part of the truth, but only I know the *whole* truth. And if you get me to safety, I'll tell you everything I know. But we need to run because those men are approaching rapidly. Please!"

Sly flinched when a loud bang sounded and bullets whizzed by. The shots were so close he slapped his hands against his chest and checked for bloody holes, thinking Eightball had shot him. But Eightball was dragging Father Murphy toward the rail yard. Sly turned to see the cop running at him.

It was time to catch a train.

Sly lengthened his strides. He reached the tracks and jumped over and between rails, looking for a train heading out of town. A train up ahead let out a hefty moan and began to move. Each car tensed and lurched as the giant iron snake started to slink away.

"That one! Go for that one!" Sly pointed his pistol at the train. Eightball nodded, gave Father Murphy's arm a tug, and made for the train.

A bullet zipped and whistled by Sly's head. He ducked, but kept running right beside Eightball and the droopy priest.

"Please! I can't run this fast," Father Murphy said before his legs gave out again. He fell and dragged Eightball to the gravel. Sly ran around them and closed in on the train, which was gaining speed. A hail of gunfire told Sly the cop and wolf-eyes were closing fast. Rounds splintered the train car, shredded the railroad ties, and sparked off the rails. Sly heard Eightball fire his last three rounds. Eightball's bullets, and his luck, had just run out.

Looking behind him, Sly saw Eightball heave the father up and over his shoulder. Eightball quickly caught up to Sly despite toting the extra weight. Eightball pointed his empty gun backward toward the cop. *Wait. It's empty. Isn't it?* Sly tripped over a railroad tie.

Sly tasted blood and gravel when his face hit the frozen ground. He accidentally fired off a shot as rocks dug into his chest and legs. He rolled over and shook off the stars before shooting twice at the cop who was about fifty feet behind him. When the cop ducked away, Sly could see the man with the wolf eyes was much closer.

Sly pushed up against the sharp, cold rocks and his legs churned and spit gravel behind him. He put away his gun so he could grip the train with both hands—if he could catch it. Eightball reached an open cargo door. He flopped Father Murphy inside before lifting himself into the car. Eightball stretched out the door and yelled, "Come on!" Slippery railroad ties, and the snow and gravel between them, made Sly stumble and lose ground.

The silence behind Sly caught his attention. Sly turned to check on how close he was to taking a dirt nap. No one was chasing him. That is, no human.

A large black wolf was on Sly's heels. Snapping jaws clacked between growls. Sly's legs were driven by an overwhelming fear of being ripped to shreds, and then shot, just for good measure. Sly's heart thumped in his throat and his feet pummeled faster than if he were running on hot coals. He heard the wolf panting at his heels. Sly's mouth hung open in exhaustion as the snarls grew louder. Sly could see Eightball extend his arm, reaching, straining, only a few feet ahead.

Sly used the last drop of adrenaline in the tank and leapt to the cargo door. He grabbed Eightball's forearm and was pulled up and into the car. Sly rolled onto his side and took one last look out the door. No wolf—only the silhouette of a figure wearing a wide-brimmed fedora and a long overcoat, standing between the rails, the outline of a smoking gun dangling at his side.

Sly rolled onto his back and let his palms rest on his heaving rib cage. Wheezing sounds filled his ears and thick saliva coated his tongue. As the train hummed, Sly pulled his pistol out of his pocket and rested it on his chest.

Out of the corner of his eye, Sly saw Eightball rise up onto his elbow and pull his six-shooter. Sly sat up and did the same, feeling confident Eightball was out of bullets. Apparently, Eightball was worse at math than Sly.

Father Murphy stayed flat on his back and muttered, "Please put your guns away. No one is going to shoot anyone."

Eightball's eyes looked hard enough to crack granite. Sly wondered if sneaky Eightball had lied earlier about how many bullets he had left. A bullet in Sly's chest would make one hell of a lie detector. Eightball pointed his gun squarely at Sly and then slid Father Murphy up close and used him as a shield.

"Only if he puts his down first," Sly said.

"No way. You first."

Sly got to his knees, but couldn't get a clean shot at Eightball. Sly removed the paper from his pocket and held it out the open door. The paper flapped loudly in Sly's fist. The train rode along the high limestone bluffs of the Mississippi River and the river below was a *long* way down.

"You shoot me and the paper goes bye-bye. Plus, you're out of bullets, asshole. Give me the priest and I won't shoot."

"Bullshit. The priest stays with me. Give me the paper."

When Sly shook his head, Eightball pulled the trigger three times. Three clicks.

"Please stop."

"Stay out of this, Priest!" Eightball yelled.

"No more killing. I mean it. I will refuse to decipher the paper. Any treasure you'd find hidden within its writings will be lost forever. I told you I am the only person left who knows and understands its contents. Everyone else is dead. Like it or not, the three of us are in this until the very end. And you can threaten me all you like, but I am willing to sacrifice my life to save your souls."

The train clunked along the track. Wind swirled within the boxcar. Eightball lowered his gun. Sly did the same. Father Murphy's words started to sink in—especially *treasure*.

Sly furrowed his brow. "What do you mean we'll never find it?" The word *treasure* bounced around Sly's head. He rode in the back seat of a luxury breezer and waved at masses of people as ticker tape rained down from the heavens. Bluebloods chanted his name and all wanted to be his friend and invited him to their fancy outdoor parties he couldn't pronounce. That's the life the paper held for him. All he had to do was figure it all out—and Father Murphy was the key.

The bluebloods faded and Sly went back to speaking with the class of a plugged toilet. "Okay, old man, if you're saying we need you to find it, then you must know where it is, don't you?"

Father Murphy looked down and let out a heavy sigh. "Yes."

14.

Family Matters

CHIEF MURNANE PLACED HIS HANDS on his knees and took a minute to catch his breath. The warm gun rested against his right knee. The freezing air burned his lungs. He hadn't caught the bastards, which meant more time with DeLuce in tow. All that remained of the lumbering train was the choking cloud of black coal smoke that filled his nostrils. Murnane walked up behind DeLuce who stared down the tracks, his smoking gun dangling at his side.

"You were right on his heels. What happened?" Murnane said.

"Getting old?"

"Get the rail yard boss and find out where that train is headed," DeLuce replied.

Murnane heard steel rub against stiff leather as the pistol slid into the holster under DeLuce's jacket.

"Now!" DeLuce barked.

The expression Murnane flashed DeLuce was meant to translate as *Go fuck yourself*. He left DeLuce and searched between and around box cars until he came across a rail yard worker. The man wore a bushy beard and a red wool Stormy Kromer cap—both standard issue for rail men during the winter months.

"Hey, Mack. Where's that train there headed? The one going out along the bluff." Murnane pointed and the man squinted westward.

"Minneapolis, Officer. Just sent it."

"Thanks, appreciate it."

The man looked over Murnane's uniform and took an extra gander at his shimmering badge. "You Police Chief Murnane?"

"No." The last person Murnane wanted to talk to was anyone who wanted to talk to him, so he walked away. He hated people. Especially today.

Murnane's wife, Mary, continually teased him about his curmudgeonly disposition. She'd smile and rub his arm and accuse him of being a big teddy bear, but only she had the patience to see that side of him. She was the best thing to ever happen to a surly son of a bitch like him. He'd just kissed her goodbye that morning on his way out the door and he already missed her like hell.

He followed the cigarette smoke and his building disgust right back to DeLuce. "Minneapolis."

"Let's go."

Murnane trudged across the ice and snow toward the cathedral sensing DeLuce always kept within shadow distance. Even with the low winter sun casting elongated shadows, DeLuce was still too close for Murnane's comfort.

As he retraced their path through the shantytown, Murnane assured the folks who had gathered outside in response to the commotion that the suspects would be brought to justice. One woman shouted, "We read the papers! We know you're crooked!" The barrage of taunts continued with the crowd chanting "Inhumane Murnane" as he and DeLuce trekked over the dirty snow and into the woods. The only thing he hated more than people was a large crowd of people. *Goddamned leeches.*

By the time Murnane trudged up the hill behind the cathedral, dusk brushed deep purple across the sky.

"Let's warm up inside." DeLuce flipped open his gold pocket watch and studied it. "And I must use the phone, quickly," DeLuce said.

The only welcoming thing in that church was the warmth. DeLuce's presence made the *sanctity of the church* bitterly ironic.

Every minute spent in DeLuce's presence reminded Murnane of

the time he fell into the family's corn silo when he was nine. The corn sucked him down deeper, trapped his arms, and squeezed him tight. The more he struggled, the faster he sank. The corn had no remorse either.

Murnane watched DeLuce use the rectory phone. The first conversation was three words long. *Just checking in.* He looked at Murnane when he spoke and hung up quickly. Goosebumps riddled Murnane's flesh.

The second call was to the Butcher Boys back at the mayor's office instructing them to meet him at the Minneapolis rail yard near University Avenue.

Murnane watched DeLuce hang up the phone, letting his gaze linger a moment longer on the phone than he should have. DeLuce said, "Let's go," and subtly extended an open palm to let Murnane lead the way.

Murnane squeezed into the driver's seat and the thinner, but equally tall, DeLuce sat in the passenger seat. Sharing a confined space with DeLuce really made Murnane's skin crawl. What really tormented Murnane was that he didn't know for sure if his family was safe or not.

"Okay, Murnane. Start talking. Who were those guys?" DeLuce asked. The question hung in the air like a guillotine blade.

"The one fell down right in front of you. You didn't get a good look at him?"

A suffocating silence answered for DeLuce.

Murnane pushed in the starter pedal and released the hand brake. The car coughed out a cloud of thick, oily smoke before reluctantly starting in the cold. "Well, I know the asshole who got on the train first, the guy carrying the priest, was Eightball. He's part of the Boss's gang. Didn't recognize the other one, though. And from what that Jewish kid told us, he fits the description of the guy who killed Mendlebaum *and* hit your men." Murnane put the car in gear and wound down

Cathedral Hill, making his way to University Avenue. "I should check with the Boss. He'd give me the name."

Murnane knew the Boss would give up the kid with no fuss. The easiest way for the Boss to separate himself from a violent crime was to use a lackey as jail cover. The kid takes all the heat, the Boss walks away clean.

"Asking will tip my hand and waste time *we* don't have," DeLuce said.

As Murnane turned left onto University Avenue, gears churned out viable explanations in his head. But every explanation led to more confusing questions. *What were they chasing, if not money? And why was it so damn important to DeLuce?*

"There's one thing that makes absolutely no sense—why take the priest? I can't believe they would kidnap him. There are plenty more rich people in town who would be a lot easier to nab than a priest—and pay much higher ransom. All he did was slow them down. If they leave the priest behind, they get away easily. No, that was no kidnapping. They obviously need him for *something*." Murnane hoped thinking out loud might prod DeLuce into revealing an explanation.

"They must have tried getting the Jew first, but it went south," DeLuce answered. A pregnant pause caused Murnane to look over at DeLuce. DeLuce's eyes hooked into Murnane. "I know why they need the priest."

The Old Testament had a better sense of humor than DeLuce, so Murnane knew DeLuce wasn't joking. "What are we after, *really?*"

DeLuce took a slow, deep breath—the kind someone takes just before he sinks underwater for the last time. "Murnane, you have a family?"

The question made Murnane feel as though he had swallowed an angry porcupine. "Go fuck yourself."

"It's a simple yes-or-no question. What's the harm in answering?"

The wheels spun in Murnane's head harder than a hell-bound train. DeLuce never just made conversation. Every action, every word, was carefully calculated and had some morbid purpose. *How do I answer? Do I lie and tell him I have no family so I don't put them in danger?*

Or does he already know everything about me and my family and he's test-ing me to see if I'll lie? Murnane would rather choose which finger to cut off first, than answer the question honestly. *Goddamn it.*

"Yes," Murnane answered.

"How *is* Mary?"

"How do you know my wife's name?"

"It's my job to know."

The answer made the porcupine roll over. "And my kids?" Murnane asked.

"Jacob and Samantha."

"Are you trying to tell me something, DeLuce?" Murnane gripped the wheel so tight he hoped it would snap in two. He glowered at DeLuce.

"If we don't find what I'm looking for, well . . ."

"Well what?" Murnane clenched his teeth. "I don't take threats lightly, you son of a bitch. You go near them, you're dead."

The repeating light and dark patterns from the street lamps re-flecting off the wet brick avenue mesmerized Murnane as numbness covered him. The droning big six under the hood filled the silence. Desperation constricted his chest. "There's no need for this bullshit. We'll get whatever it is back. Just leave my family out of it."

"If you go near a phone, they die."

"Okay. Okay. If I help you, I want your word it ends there. Me and my family never hear from you or your men again, right?"

DeLuce stared out the window.

"Right?"

Adrenaline pumped like nitroglycerine through Murnane's veins, and the smile that crawled onto DeLuce's face ignited it. "*Fuck you,* DeLuce. Go find whatever it is yourself."

DeLuce continued smiling and looking through the window. "Do you live at 4926 Oakcrest Lane? The blue house with a white porch swing?"

"Don't." Murnane didn't squirm, despite the fact the Devil had him by the balls.

"My men live there too. Now whether or not everybody gets along is entirely up to you."

Murnane turned away and twisted his face so tightly it hurt. He fought like hell to hold back a sob. "You fucker. You touch them, you die."

"Not before they do."

The puttering car engine and the tires rolling over the wet streets were all Murnane heard for the next several blocks. Murnane's mind raced and raced and wished for some way out, any way out.

"Have you ever talked to God, Chief Murnane?"

DeLuce soaked every word in seething arrogance. Murnane pictured pressing his sidearm against DeLuce's head and blowing his brains through the window and out onto University Avenue. *Let them hose that shit into the sewers.*

"I am God to you right now. All you have to ask yourself is, *Do I want a peaceful God or a vengeful God.*"

Murnane wrenched his hands against the steering wheel, turning his knuckles white.

"And if I may offer some heavenly advice—start praying."

"Is whatever they have worth killing my family over?"

"Don't play altar boy with me, Murnane. You've been profiting off the gangs for years. Your deeds have racked up a hefty tab and now it's time to square it. You're a victim of circumstance—a circumstance you created. Playing both sides has a price."

"You have no right to hurt my family because of what I've done."

"It has nothing to do with rights. I'm in control and you'll do what I tell you."

DeLuce's fiery gaze burned the right side of Murnane's face. While thinking of all the ways he'd like to see DeLuce die, Murnane pictured jerking the wheel and plunging off the high bluffs and onto the jagged boulders below. Murnane would take himself out if it guaranteed DeLuce died by his side, but there was no guarantee his family would be safe afterward. Then again, a world without DeLuce would be a good world to leave behind. He inched the car closer to the guard rail.

"And if you get any ideas about killing me to save them, think again." DeLuce leaned in closer. "My men expect me to call at pre-determined times every few hours, but never the same time interval twice. So if a time passes and I don't call, there will be three little gutted pigs hanging upside down from your front porch." He pulled the gold watch from his vest pocket and flipped it open with his left hand. Murnane grew sicker as he watched DeLuce raise his eyebrows and look down his nose. "I would drive faster if I were you."

Murnane trembled. Vomit rose in his throat.

"I know how you feel, Murnane. Helpless. Alone. Like you let your family down. I understand that. I know what I would do if someone threatened *my* family. That man would beg for death."

"Then why are you doing this?"

"Because something very important has been taken from me, and there are no obstacles forged in Heaven or Hell that will stop me from getting it back. I feel I've been very clear on that point."

"Why is it so important, for Christ's sake?"

DeLuce turned and stared into the darkness once again. "I always thought the Devil was something the nuns at school made up to keep us in line. I never believed in God or the Devil before it found me."

When DeLuce spoke, Murnane heard a scared child sitting in the passenger seat.

"Before *what* found you?" Murnane asked.

"I know what they have, and who it belongs to—and he wants it back."

15.

No Rest for the Wicked

Sly took a moment to look over the snowy Mississippi river bluffs outside the open cargo door as the train clunked out of St. Paul. The cold wind swirled inside the boxcar and stirred up odors Sly easily recognized. Livestock had left behind damp straw and fresh manure that covered most of the boxcar floor. The train delivered beef cattle from the Minneapolis stockyards to the St. Paul slaughterhouse, and it was headed back to get another load of manure-filled passengers.

Sly puffed out his cheeks and blew straw out of the pistol barrel. "What are you holdin' back, old man? I want to know everything."

"Yeah, where's the loot?" Eightball asked.

Father Murphy sat up and rested his elbows on his knees. "Please let me catch my breath. Give me a moment, for I have never been shot at before. Oh my, I can't stop shaking." He held out his quaking right hand to illustrate his point. "I'm not used to all this running and shooting."

Sly got to his feet and put his hands on his hips the same way a child in a sandbox announces he is king. "You just said you know where the treasure is, now spill it."

Father Murphy's breathing slowed, becoming less forced. He tilted his head back and closed his eyes. "It's not a treasure map, at least not in the way you might think. The paper holds something far more valuable—and dangerous."

Eightball removed his knitted hat and scratched his matted hair. "What's worth more than gold?" he asked. Dandruff flakes drifted up and swirled in the wind.

"Priest, we will put a bullet between your eyes and throw you off this train if you don't start talkin'," Sly said.

"Can't you see that piece of paper is taking control of you both? It is pure evil and the only thing for you to do is be rid of it."

Sly bent at the waist. "I'm about to *be rid* of you—for good. Start talkin'."

"I'm frightened enough without you and your unwashed partner always threatening to kill me." Father Murphy's eyes moistened. "I can't even go home because those men who chased us will probably be there waiting. I don't know who to trust. Even the police were shooting at me." Father Murphy put his face in his hands. "What have you gotten me involved in?"

Eightball put his hat back on and glared at Sly. "Let him catch his breath. He ain't goin' nowhere. I'm gonna sssee where we're going." Eightball walked over to the door and hung his head out. After a few moments of wind-blown examination, Eightball slid the door shut. Straw settled to the floor.

"The lines switched as soon as we cleared the rail yard. Looks like we're bound for Minneapolis," Eightball said. Sly had already figured that out; the straw and cow shit were dead giveaways.

Sly knew the train routes as well as any conductor. Riding the rails was a way of life for many of those without means. Prohibition had lured plenty of poor folks to St. Paul, from near and far, looking for the golden meal ticket. Prohibition was a godsend for anyone with a little ambition and a lot of gutter-dwelling ideas on how to make a buck, and the trains hauled them in by the masses, including a young Sylvester Hobbs.

Sly looked down at Father Murphy who knelt on the dirty floor. Sly saw himself as a boy, kneeling in the snow, using his frozen fingers to load blasting caps because he didn't dare defy his father. Sly wanted to make damn sure *this* father was on the up and up. He needed answers and was in a position to take control. *He* could give the orders instead of taking them—and he liked it.

"I'm thinkin' you don't really know where the gold is, old man. You're just sayin' you do so we don't throw you off this train. But sometime sooner rather than later we're gonna get to the bottom of this paper. You hearin' me?" Sly asked while patting his pocket.

Father Murphy dropped his hands and looked up at Sly. "I am tired of your threats and I'm tired of you. I am cold and have no will to fight or argue anymore. I will tell you everything about the paper in good time. If that is not good enough for you, then by all means, please kill me and give me some peace."

Sly raised his gun high, ready to pistol whip the shit out of Father Murphy, but Eightball stopped Sly's hand.

"What are you doing?" Eightball growled.

"Nobody talks to me like that." Sly ripped his arm from Eightball's grip.

"We need him to find the treasure. Look at him. One hit could kill him. Use your head for something other than storing rocks."

"I make the rules here. I have the paper. You two assholes are just along for the ride." Close enough to touch eyeballs with Eightball, Sly grated his teeth and said, "You're only alive because Priest won't let me kill you. Remember that."

Eightball smiled. "You have to sleep sometime."

Father Murphy raised his hand. "If you want my help, I suggest you please calm down and focus on more immediate concerns."

"Oh yeah, like what? How I'm going to spend all my money?" Sly asked.

"Don't you feel we should address the far more pressing matter of the identity of those men and why they were trying to kill us? They certainly had no regard for your life *or* mine." Father Murphy touched his chest.

Sly slapped his coat pocket containing the paper. "This is my only concern." He pointed at Father Murphy. "You're a distant second. And you," he said, pointing at Eightball, "ain't even on the list."

Father Murphy rubbed his hands together, dropped his head, and muttered quietly to himself.

"Speak up, Priest. What are you sayin'?" Sly folded his arms.

"Those men weren't after you, or me. They wanted the paper."

Sly twinged like a pinched nerve in his neck had snapped. "What are you talkin' about? They was comin' to arrest us for what we did to those boys on the street." Sly spoke with the conviction of a king proclaiming a new tax. But his innards told him Father Murphy was right.

The priest continued, but faced the wall when he spoke. "It makes perfect sense. Why else would they shoot at us—even at me and the children we ran past? The paper must have hold of them as well." He turned to Sly. "You stole it and now they want it back."

Father Murphy's words rubbed Sly the wrong way.

"Oh, horsefeathers. I told you what they want—*us*." Sly pointed between himself and Eightball in a quick, repeating gesture.

"The dead man you took it from, who was he, exactly?"

Sly thumped his thumb against his chest. "I ask the questions around here."

Sly's comment spurred a hard look from Eightball. "You can eyeball me all you want, but remember, I'm the one with the bullets," Sly said.

Eightball stomped over to a pile of straw in the corner and sat down. Eightball's retreat tasted better than an extra dessert at the soup kitchen.

Father Murphy struggled to his feet and fought to stay balanced on the wobbling train. He walked a crooked line to the straw pile. The slight man bounced a little when he sat next to Eightball. Sly knew by looking into the two pairs of eyes studying him, the battle over who was in control was long from settled.

Father Murphy said, "I'll tell you this—that paper is the ultimate temptress. Remember First Corinthians, which tells us, *He has promised to limit our temptation to that which we can resist, and He always provides a way of escape.*"

Sly laughed and bowed, the pistol in his extended right hand. "Looks like we escaped just fine on our own, Priest, thank you very much. No help from no God or Bible or nuthin'. What does it say in your good book about them apples?"

"The point is, my purpose here is becoming clearer with every word you utter. I'm here to save you. Save you from that which you clearly do not see nor understand."

Sly smiled. "I understand perfectly good. I have the paper and you want to rip it up. That means it's definitely worth more than you're let-tin' on." Sly used his free hand to pull his checkered flat cap down just above his eyes.

"Please listen to me," Father Murphy said. "As wretched as you are, I cannot allow the paper to control you. I have to believe you can be saved. The book of James tells us, *But each person is tempted when he is lured and enticed by his own desire. Then desire—when it has conceived—gives birth to sin, and sin, when it is fully grown, brings forth death.*"

The more Father Murphy spoke about keeping Sly from danger and saving his soul, the more uneasy Sly became. Hearing Bible passages really made his skin itch. His skin itched like a son of a bitch.

Save my soul, my ass. Priest must have some trick up his sleeve. He's dealing from the bottom of the deck. The old man ain't on the level.

Sly smirked because no one was going to pull the wool over *his* eyes. "Okay, Priest, we'll do it your way. You're not gonna tell me about it, fine. I got you where I want you anyways." Sly held out his arm and wiggled the gun. "But if you try runnin', I'll bet my little friends here can catch you. So just tell me what you think we should do next and see if I agree." He placed his gun back in his pocket in a gesture of good faith. "Now what's our next move?"

Father Murphy replied, "The treasure is far, far away. A great distance."

"That's not a place. We need an address." Sly prepared to concentrate real hard to remember what Father Murphy was about to say.

Father Murphy settled into the straw, working his hands into it. "The desert doesn't have an address."

"Mellonbomb said it was nearby. Why are you lyin'?" Sly didn't move. He feared Father Murphy would call his bluff.

"My son, he would have said no such thing. What we seek is on the other side of the world."

Probably why Sly always lost at cards—he was a lousy bluffer.

Goddamn it.

Sly swaggered across the floor. He pulled his gun back out and used it to scratch his head as he paced. "Well, Priest, I don't care how far I gotta go, I'm gonna find out what's on this paper and there ain't a damn thing you or anyone can do about it. And then I'll be rich!" With all his false bravado, Sly couldn't shake the knot building in his stomach.

"Let's try to identify our pursuers, shall we?" Father Murphy said. "Who were those men? The one identified himself as a police officer. The other one wore a suit and tie. He must have been a detective. Oh, goodness. If these police officers are under the paper's control, we need to find honest policemen to turn to for help."

Sly laughed. "I don't go to the cops for help when I'm tryin' to outrun a murder rap. Plus, they're all on the take. We're on our own. Can't trust nobody from here on out."

Eightball turned to Father Murphy. "The cop was Murnane and the other guy was . . ."

Dapper Dan only got up the nerve to tell Sly about DeLuce after a few whisky shots had loosened Dapper's tongue. DeLuce's legend filled every shadowy corner of seedy alleys and blind pigs in St. Paul. Every hardened gangster whispered the evils of DeLuce, but never too loudly. Sly could add up the facts: They had knocked off DeLuce's men. Sly lifted from one of them a paper that led to a huge treasure. That was something DeLuce might want back. Even Sly could do that math, which added up to him being buried in a world of shit.

"DeLuce," Sly said like he had whispered a secret in the Devil's ear.

Eightball nodded.

Father Murphy raised his eyebrows. "Who is this DeLuce?"

"Man's meaner than a skilletful of rattlesnakes. In fact I heard a snake bit him once and the *snake* crawled off and died," Eightball said.

"And this evil man is chasing us, along with the policeman? If this DeLuce is as dangerous as you say, you should turn yourselves in before anyone else gets hurt. There must be honest police officers somewhere."

"You're not on the trolley. Between DeLuce and Murnane, there ain't nuthin' they can't cover up. Two thugs and a broken-down priest are less trouble than ants at a picnic to guys like them," Sly said.

"Okay, but have you stopped to think about where this train is heading? It would stand to reason those men will be waiting for us when we get to wherever that might be."

"Priest's right. We gotta hop off this train before it stops," Eightball said.

Sly noticed that Father Murphy watched the speed at which the trees sliced the rays of twilight beaming between the door cracks. Sweat dripped from Father Murphy's forehead.

"Can we wait until it slows down?" Father Murphy asked.

"Eightball, you help Priest off the train."

"Why me?"

Sly flashed his gun. "Because we all took a vote. You lost seven to one." Sly laughed at his own joke. "Seven on account a there bein' me with six bullets . . ."

"Yeah, yeah. I get it." Eightball turned to Father Murphy. "Priest, as soon as we slow down, we jump and run. If we land on solid ground, be sure to run *with* the train, never try to stop yourself. You could break your legs. Just hit the ground and don't stop running. And keep an eye out for anyone wearing a Stormy Kromer cap," Eightball said.

"I'm sorry, sir, I don't know what that is."

"It's a red cap you can see a ways off. All the railroad men wear 'em," Eightball said.

"Why would I look for them?"

Eightball smiled. "Because if you run into a guy wearing a Stormy Kromer, you're about to get a shotgun full of rock salt in your ass. They hate train hoppers."

Father Murphy pinched his thin face into a fearful ball. He rubbed his arms and blew into his hands.

"Why don't you get under this straw and stay warm?" Eightball asked Father Murphy. "You're no good to us sick—or dead."

Father Murphy seemed to fight back a smile and said, "Thank you." Eightball buried the old man under the straw. Eightball leered up at Sly and then buried himself up to his neck next to the priest.

"Well, aren't you just like two little peas in a pod," Sly said.

The pile heaved when Eightball said, "Go fuck yourself."

"You haven't experienced much love in your life, have you, my sons?" Father Murphy asked from beneath the straw.

"I've loved lotsa things," Sly said. "Mostly wads of cash and long-legged blondes."

"Yeah. And I'm John D. Rockefeller," Eightball said.

Sly stared at the closed cargo door and felt again hot wolf breath on the back of his legs. He knew Father Murphy had hit the nail on the head. Sly had stolen something belonging to a brutal man who would stop at nothing to get it back. Reaching in his pocket, Sly rubbed the soft paper between his fingertips. *If DeLuce wants this, he'll have to pry it outta my cold, dead hands.*

Visions of a king's wealth spun inside Sly's head. Gold and jewels stretched out before him as far as the eye could see. He pictured picking up a nugget big as an apple and biting into the soft gold. Tasted like karats, not apples. Sly smiled at his own cleverness. All his dreams were coming true. All he had to do was outrun the Devil.

16.

Twice as Much as Chicago

Sly had no idea how to outrun the Devil. Sooner or later it would come down to him and DeLuce, kill or be killed. He'd taken on plenty of challenges before, been thrown into the worst life had to offer and come out no worse for wear on the other side. But this was his first chance to prove himself as a leader, to take control of his own life and by doing so, get what he wanted. The train rolled over the gaps between where the rails butt up next to each other producing a rhythmic thump that kept cadence with Sly's throbbing head. The world was out of control and made him feel like he was tied to a canoe in a hurricane.

"What the hell are you doing?" Eightball asked. Only his head stuck out of the straw pile.

Sly tasted cold steel and realized he had placed the pistol in his mouth while thinking. He let the gun drop and swing from his index finger. "Wondering if you're worth the trouble to have stickin' around," Sly said calmly.

"I was kinda hopin' you'd pull the trigger," Eightball said. Steam rose from his mouth and hung near his face.

"Yeah, I bet you were. Nope, when I pull it, *you'll* be on the business end."

"How thick are you gentlemen?" Father Murphy asked, his voice muffled by the straw.

"Make some room in there for me. Priest, you get between us," Sly said, using the pistol to draw the picture.

Father Murphy popped up, brushed straw from his face, and frowned. "All you had to do was ask. My goodness."

Sly threw Eightball a look, and Eightball rifled it right back. The energy between them compared to two bulls and one cow in a small pen. Once Sly locked horns with Eightball, only one bull would be left standing, and Sly wanted to make damn sure it was him.

"Settle down, Priest."

"You're one crazy ssson of a bitch, and your time's coming. Mark my words," Eightball said.

Sly pocketed his pistol and immersed himself neck-high in the straw. It felt warm. Damp and itchy, but warm.

Sly welcomed the warmth when it finally took hold. The setting sun brought narrow beams of orange light into the cattle car that relaxed him into a dream-like state of unfamiliar comfort. He thought of his mom. No single thought in particular, more a jumbled bunch of pleasant memories mashed together. Sly rubbed a finger across the scar on his ear and stared into the setting sun.

Eightball broke the quiet. "Priest, where do we go next? Because if we're going around the world, we'll need some serious cake."

"Well, gentlemen, we need to go to Egypt."

"Egypt? Is that a real place?" Sly asked.

Father Murphy smiled. "If only you had been blessed with brains instead of ambition."

Sly wasn't sure how to take the comment, but figured it wasn't very good. He wasn't sure how sore to get about it.

"Egypt is a long ways away," Eightball said.

"You ain't got any idea where Egypt is," Sly accused, trying to prove he wasn't the only idiot in the straw pile.

"The hell I don't. I know it's a whole lot farther away than Chicago."

"Well, I knew that." Sly sneered and folded his arms under the straw.

"I also know it costs money to get to Chicago. So Egypt is gonna to be twice as much." Eightball said this as if he were a bank president watching ticker tape spit from a machine.

"You maroon. Egypt ain't even that far. I'd bet the farm on that."

"Please gentlemen, you're making my head ache. Oh my, what I wouldn't give for a Brahms violin concerto. A Walt Whitman poem. A game of chess by the fire. A warm coat."

"How much money you got?" Eightball asked Sly.

"The Boss took it all. How much you got?"

"I got nuthin'. The Boss took mine too. Priest, how much do you have?"

The straw bounced. "What little money I have is in my dresser drawer next to my bed." Father Murphy paused. "At home." He paused again. "At the rectory."

Eightball shook his head. "Goddamn it. If a trip around the world cost a dollar, we wouldn't make the state line."

"Please cease your blasphemy," Father Murphy said.

"We probably need at least a hundred dollars, but how we gonna get it?" Sly asked. "I'm sure there's a price on our heads so any job we pull off will get DeLuce or Murnane's attention. We need us some quick cash without them finding out. They've got eyes and ears everywhere."

"I know someone we can trust, maybe," Eightball said.

"Who? And what do you mean *maybe*?" Sly asked.

"Well, we gotta find him first."

"How?"

"Last I heard he was working as a bartender at a high-class speakeasy in Minneapolis called the Chap's Room. The place caters to a mixed crowd, whites and coloreds. He usually had a line on some job or another. Especially the kind we need right now—one that steers clear of the cops and the Mob."

"Hold on a minute. I don't like this idea," Sly said. His experience planning robberies with the Barker-Karpis gang was coming in handy. "I think we should take our chances with a bank, or the post office. Just wait for the payroll delivery and we can hit the post office fast and hard. That way at least Murnane and DeLuce won't have time to react before we hightail it outta town." He may not have the blue-blood smarts of Father Murphy with all his violins and playing checks by the fire—but Sly had smarts where it counted. Number one was how to stay behind, not in front of, a gun. Those smarts beat Walt Slimman, hands down.

"We hit the post office and we'll be all over the front page," Eightball said.

Sly leapt from the straw and began to pace.

Eightball said, "Say something goes wrong and we shoot someone? What if we shoot a flatfoot? We'll have every cop in the state on our ass. And they'll be happy to shoot us or take us right to Murnane. Too risky. We talk to Mudbone."

Sly stopped pacing. "*Who?*"

"Mudbone."

"What kinda name is that?" Sly asked.

"Maybe he's got a huge black dick," Eightball answered.

"Heathens," Father Murphy mumbled.

"Sounds like Shitbone to me. This is a bad idea." Sly knew no one could be trusted. This Mudbone guy would sell him to Murnane and DeLuce in a second. This situation was turning more rotten by the minute and Sly needed answers.

"Look, I decide what we do. If I'm going to go along with this, I got some questions." Sly searched for a question that a leader would ask. Something so impressive that Eightball would realize Sly was the new boss. "So how do you know this Mudbone guy?" He crossed his arms and stood straight and proud of his incredible question.

"I used to work with him at the Chaps Room and a couple other places. He was a bartender and I worked the doors. We also pulled a few side jobs together. Hijacked a couple small moonshine shipments and grifted here and there. Nuthin' big." Eightball laughed under his breath. "He's like you. One crazy son of a bitch."

Sly asked a straight question and got a straight answer. He hoped he looked stern when he kept his arms folded and nodded in response.

Sly felt something move under his collar, something like a spider's hairy legs. He performed part rain dance and part man-on-fire jig. He stopped to see two heads sticking out of straw, staring at him blankly.

"What the hell are you doing?" Eightball asked.

"Thought I had a spider on me."

"A what?"

Sly formed his hand into the shape of a spider and wiggled his fingers. "A spider. A big one. I don't like spiders, okay?"

Eightball giggled. "What's the big deal about a little spider?"

Father Murphy smiled for the first time.

"I hate 'em. Just never mind."

Eightball smiled and softly sang, "Itsy bitsy spider crawled up and *in your mouth*."

"Shut up."

The train brakes engaged and released to slow the train down, causing Sly to jerk forward and catch a wall for balance.

Eightball stood and brushed straw off his coat. He looked down at Father Murphy and said, "Okay, Priest, we're slowin' down. Just do what I told you and you'll be fine."

Father Murphy looked up at the ceiling and said, "I don't want to jump. I don't want to run. I don't want to do any of this." He raised his arms upward, tilted his head back, and closed his eyes for a few moments. Sly wondered what the hell he was doing. Father Murphy folded his hands and whispered. He put his hands down and looked up at Eightball.

Sly crossed his arms. "Tough hop. We'll be jumping soon, so get ready."

Father Murphy spit straw out of his mouth before he stood and brushed the rest off. When Eightball opened the side door and icy wind swirled inside the car, Father Murphy shivered.

Sly walked over to the doorway and used his left hand to brace himself against the opening. The city lights of Minneapolis glowed in the distance and landmarks became recognizable as the train slowed. Outside, bare trees cut in front of the warm, twinkling city lights. Minneapolis at night looked like some magical crystal palace from a faraway land.

Sly felt something bump his arm and saw Father Murphy sitting down and dangling his legs out the door.

Reaching down, he yanked up Father Murphy and yelled, "Hey!" Father Murphy slid up and back into the car. "What are you trying to do?" Sly asked.

Father Murphy looked like a lost puppy. "What do you mean?"

"What if we pass by a bridge or go into a tunnel? You dangle your legs out of a moving train, something is likely to come by and cut them right off. Use your head." Sly tapped his finger against his temple.

"I don't understand these rules. I just rested in a pile of malodorous, wet straw. It's freezing cold and I'm doing all I can to keep you from killing me and each other. Please understand this is all a lot to take in for someone unaccustomed to such a lifestyle. I'm trying to do my best, but jumping from a moving train is asking a bit too much, I'm afraid."

Eightball peeked out the door and smiled. "Well, Priest, the snow looks deep here so we might just have a real soft landing."

"Or you might land on a sharp rock under the snow. Good luck," Sly said.

"Can't you go a little easy on Priest?" Eightball asked.

"Just get ready to jump and try not to break any bones," Sly said.

Father Murphy whimpered. "If I am going to do this, I need help. Please?"

"What you need is a drink." Sly slapped his pockets and dug under his coat. Sly turned to Eightball. "You got anything? Boss took the flask I lifted off Pancetti."

"Yeah, but it's all I got."

Sly backhanded Eightball on the collarbone and motioned toward Father Murphy. "Give him some." Eightball looked sour, pulled the flask from his coat, and held it in front of the priest.

Father Murphy reached out as if being dared to touch a bee hive. He took the flask and tilted his head to one side as he examined it. "Please know that this is only to help build my courage and deal with the bitter cold, you understand." He hoisted the flask to eye level and recited, "*Do not neglect to do good and to share what you have, for such sacrifices are pleasing to Him.*" His Adam's apple bobbed with each swallow. He wiped his forearm across his mouth, screwed the cap on, and handed the flask back to Eightball. "Thank you, sir," he said.

"How do you feel?" Sly was unsure why he asked. Maybe he had an ember of care for the old man's well-being. Maybe he just wanted to watch a priest get drunk.

Father Murphy softly nodded and looked out into the night.

Sly's left arm gripped the train car for balance; his right hand latched onto Father Murphy's left wrist. Sly could tell Father Murphy would rather be swallowing thorn bushes. Eightball was holding the wall for balance with his right hand. Sly watched as Eightball grabbed Father Murphy's other wrist.

The train rumbled and the wind rushed in Sly's ears. "When's the last time you saw Mudbone?" Sly asked.

"About two years ago," Eightball yelled. He stuck his head out the door and looked up ahead. Sly assumed he was scouting a good place to land.

"Why did you stop working together?"

"We had a disssagreement, I guessss."

Eightball gripped Father Murphy tighter by the wrist and started pulling him away from Sly. When the priest started falling forward, he clung to Sly's arm like it was a life preserver in shark-infested waters. Sly crouched, ready to spring into the night and take Father Murphy with him.

"What happened?" Sly asked.

Eightball yelled, "I killed his brother! Jump!"

17.

The Chap's Room

SLY JUMPED and landed back-first, creating a cloud of icy sparkles. It was almost pretty. Despite the relatively soft landing, he let out a grunt when his ass hit the snow. Two lumps landed next to him, grunted, and made their own clouds, followed by gasping and coughing.

Sly lay still, looking up at the stars. The rail yard had several tower lights that not only did their best to drown out the stars, but also reminded Sly of a prison yard. Sly tilted his head and surveyed the surroundings through the thick purple dusk—until a fist came flying at him. Sly dodged sideways, but in a flash, Eightball had him pinned. Eightball drove his gnarled fist straight down, but it glanced off Sly's cheek and sank into the snow. Sly pulled his arms to his chest and pushed against Eightball. Sly heaved upward, rolling Eightball off and away from him. Sly pulled his right leg from the deep snow and stomped on Eightball's ribs. Eightball coughed and his eyes bulged before he rolled twice more, out of stomping range.

Sly pulled his pistol. "You son of a bitch!"

Eightball lay on his back and panted. "You don't have the balls."

Father Murphy let out a loud exhale that stopped Sly from squeezing the trigger. Sly backed up and pocketed his pistol, keeping an eye on Eightball.

Father Murphy was flat on his back and wheezing to the point of tears.

"What's wrong, Priest?" Sly asked.

Eightball got to his feet and high-stepped close to Father Murphy. "Got the wind knocked out of him is all," Eightball answered.

Father Murphy squeezed his eyes shut and made a sizzling sound through his gritted teeth.

"I think he broke his back. Now look what you done," Sly said.

"I didn't do nuthin'. You're the one who said he'd land on a rock."

"You're the one who made us get on the train!" Sly said.

"We were getting shot at, you palooka. And if he broke his back, it's only because you keep pulling a gun on him and asking about the paper. He wouldn't be here if it wasn't for you!"

Sly raised a crooked finger. "You dragged him out of the church, same as me!"

Sly turned his attention to what he thought was faint laughter. He looked down to see Father Murphy laughing into the darkness. Sly figured the old man hit his head so hard he couldn't get his mind right—or the booze was working its magic.

"Oh my goodness!" Father Murphy wiped away tears.

Sly reached for Father Murphy. Eightball helped pull the priest to his feet. His laughs trailed off into short huffs and smiles while he dug in his pocket and pulled out his glasses. "I haven't done anything like that since I was a child. Oh me, oh my, what fun!" He put on his glasses and finished brushing himself off.

"Did you break those peeper-cheaters of yours, Priest?" Sly asked.

"In all the chaos, I guess I forgot them in my pocket until now." Father Murphy held them up against the tower lights in the distance and examined them for cracks. "They look to be fine."

"You able to walk?" Sly asked. Father Murphy was the key to Sly's fortune. It was becoming painfully clear that Father Murphy's health was just as important as his own. No priest, no treasure. Sly had to take better care of the old-timer. And keep Eightball from killing either—or both—of them.

"If you gentlemen could stop fighting for more than one minute you could enjoy the little gifts life gives you." Father Murphy beamed like a child locked in an ice cream shop. "However, it warms my heart to see you have sincere concern for my well-being. I do believe there is hope for you after all." He cleared his throat into his cupped hand. "I don't suppose I could trouble you for one more nip? It is ever so cold and my old bones don't take to it very well."

Eightball rolled his eyes and dug out his near-empty flask and slapped it against Father Murphy's chest. The moonshine sloshed inside. "Here." Eightball looked at Sly. "See what you started?"

Father Murphy opened the flask like he would a Christmas present and swallowed heartily. "Ahhhh."

Sly tried to hide his satisfaction behind a smile when Eightball snatched the flask and turned it upside down over his open mouth only to have two small drops hit his tongue. He screwed the lid on and stuffed the container back in his coat. "Thanks a lot, Priest."

Father Murphy smiled and nodded. "No. Thank you, sir."

"Stop calling me that. You give me the creepy crawlies," Eightball said.

"I don't know what else to call you—either of you."

"And it's gonna stay that way," Sly answered. He turned toward the city. "Let's get movin'." Sly waved to Eightball. "You walk in front of me."

Like a gun-toting mother hen keeping track of her chicks, Sly looked back to check on Father Murphy. He remained up to his knees in snow and hadn't moved. Father Murphy was watching something in the distance. "Come on, Priest, fun's over."

"Why look. It's a gentleman wearing one of those hats you described." Sly saw Father Murphy smile and wave into the dusk. "Hellooo, sir!"

Sly peered around Father Murphy and almost shit himself when he spotted the railroad worker aiming a shotgun.

"Run!"

The shotgun blast flashed brighter than the surrounding tower lights. Luckily, the snow around Sly took the brunt of the shot. Eightball had followed orders, but Father Murphy didn't. Sly lunged back, yanked Father Murphy by the arm, and threw him over his shoulder. Deep snow tugged at Sly's legs making every step exhausting—but a shotgun proved to be a hell of a motivator. Sly's knees struggled to plow through the snow. The small priest suddenly felt like a full barrel of Minnesota Thirteen. Shotgun blasts stripped the bark off a tree next to Sly. He flinched but kept his balance as he hauled Father Murphy deeper into the trees. The shadows stopped the pursuit as quickly as it had started. Sly avoided tripping over Eightball, who was crouched among the pines.

Sly plopped Father Murphy on the ground. "Ow."

"Serves you right, Priest. What the hell were you thinkin'?" Sly asked.

"Why did we stop? Is that man still chasing us?" Father Murphy huffed.

"We're off railroad property. He's probably sipping from his flask by now." Sly had to rub it in.

"Goddamn it, Priest, I told you to let us know when you saw a railroad man," Eightball said.

"I did."

Despite the thick trees blocking the distant yard lights, Sly could see Eightball's face wrinkle as he mulled over the statement.

"There's a guy comin' at you with a shotgun and the first thing you notice is his goddamned Stormy Kromer? Jesus Christ, Priest, you are not cut out for this kinda life, that is for *damn* sure." Eightball spoke as though explaining to a child why he should look both ways before crossing the street.

"Priest, you're as sharp as a mashed potato," Sly said.

"Please cease your blasphemy. I apologize. I am not a seasoned travel companion, but I promise to do my best from now on."

"Good try. But we know you'll run to the cops first chance you get," Sly said.

Father Murphy grabbed Sly by the arm with a grip that would make a bear trap envious. "I swear to you . . ." His eyes pierced Sly and ricocheted from Sly to Eightball. " . . . I am here to save you both from a fate far worse than prison. From that duty I will not falter."

The look on Father Murphy's face kicked Sly square in the soul— and it hurt. Sly gently pulled his arm away when Father Murphy loosened his grip. "Then why'd you just call to the railroad man for help?"

"I wasn't waving for him to save me, I was being polite and friend-ly. Before you gentlemen came into my life, I was a kind and cheerful person."

Sly shook his head. "We'll be keepin' an eye on you just the same, so don't get any funny ideas. And keep your crazy Bible shit to your-self."

"Come on. We need to get him some clothes or get him inside. The cold just might kill him before you do," Eightball said and smiled a bit.

Father Murphy placed his right hand over his heart. He looked like a father walking his daughter down the aisle on her wedding day. "It's not only the spirits warming my spirits right now. But you are right, sir, I would welcome some warm clothes."

"Shit, the old man was silly enough when he was sober." Sly laughed. "And since when do you worry about anybody dyin'?"

"Since it would cost me a whole lotta money is when. Let's go."

Sly tapped his pocket, making sure Eightball watched him do it. "You lead the way. Slow and steady," Sly said.

Minneapolis twinkled in the distance. Sly kept Eightball far enough ahead so a sudden roundhouse punch wouldn't hit pay dirt. Sounds of crunching snow kept pace right behind Sly, so he knew Father Murphy was close. The more steps Sly put behind him, the brighter the city lights became.

"I hope to hell you know what you're doin'," Sly uttered into the darkness. "I still say this whole plan is a piece of shit. This Mudbone will probably kill you and then me and Priest." Sly listened for Father Murphy. Father Murphy hiccupped.

"I'm tellin' ya we could hit the post office payroll delivery and be outta town before the smoke cleared."

"Look, we're fresh outta options," Eightball said. "Mudbone's our best chance at getting some quick cake without attracting attention from the cops or the Mob."

Sly moved along, wishing every snapping twig were Eightball's neck. Despite the loud, satisfying cracks, Sly felt no better about the plan.

"What happened between you and Mr. Mudbone's brother?" Father Murphy asked.

"A couple years back I was supposed to fight him. The betting went through the roof because he was one tough black son of a bitch—everybody knows them coloreds can fight. The Boss fixed the fight so I'd win, but I was supposed to give Mudbone's brother a piece of the action for taking a dive. He double-crossed us and wouldn't throw it, so I beat him to death." Eightball looked back at Sly. "He was number five."

"Fighting, gambling, and murder—how egregious. For shame. Your lack of compunction is repulsive. Saving either of you will be a great challenge."

Eightball shrugged. "He got off light compared to what the Boss woulda done to him. Besides, he was an asshole."

Father Murphy passed Sly and caught up to Eightball. As Father Murphy trudged along, he bowed his head and mouthed a silent prayer while raising his palms toward Eightball.

Eightball turned and swatted the priest's hands. "Knock it off. I got enough on my mind without your shit."

Father Murphy recoiled and folded his hands to his chest. Eightball stopped walking. Sly saw Eightball's face soften—as much as a wrecked mug like Eightball's could soften—into an apology. Father Murphy put his hand on Eightball's shoulder. "It's okay, my son. You've had a time of it. What's troubling you?" Father Murphy asked.

"Well, to be honest, I don't know what Mudbone's gonna do when I show up on his doorstep. The guy is crazier than a shithouse rat. I don't know if he'll hug me or shoot me. Hell, he might do both. But we were friends for a long time and we been through a lot together. He's our best chance at some quick cash, so I hope it's worth the risk."

"You *hope*?" Sly stopped and crossed his arms. "You sell us on this plan of yours and now you think the crazy son of a bitch will kill us? I told you. I knew it all along. This is exactly why you should be listening to me. I say we hit the post office first thing in the morning."

"Mudbone will have jobs for us, trust me."

"Oh yeah, like what?" Sly asked.

"I don't know. Maybe we can ask him to loan us the money to get to Egypt. Hell, he'd be happy to take some treasure as payment when we get back."

"I'm fine with asking this asshole for a loan. But it's not coming out of my take. No way," Sly said.

Father Murphy turned to Sly. "My son, you must have faith. If this Mr. Mudbone can provide us with the means to travel to Egypt, then any plan is better than armed robbery. I will not hurt innocent people. The only way to break the curse is to seek redemption. And part of the redemption process is that you must first stop the wrong-doings in your life and aspire to something better."

"That's why I'm putting up with you—to be better by getting rich."

Something about the way Father Murphy offered to help get them to Egypt reminded Sly of Agony. Whether it was the tone, or the glint in Father Murphy's eyes, or his overall willingness, Sly couldn't put his finger on it. Sly almost laughed while straining to make any connection whatsoever between Agony and a little helpless priest who did nothing but find the good in every situation. But when Father Murphy talked about that Egypt place, it felt wrong—like a lie. Sly got the exact same bad feeling when Agony left the house well before noon to get him a cake for his seventh birthday. Sly waited on the front porch, on the front steps, on the tree swing, and finally looking out at the night through the front window. Sly awoke to a right cross. When he hit the floor, he had two loose teeth and no cake.

"Let's keep movin'," Sly said.

Sly followed three paces behind Eightball and Father Murphy. Eightball kept to the shadows and wove through back alleys and empty streets until he reached the Chap's Room.

Eightball stopped in front of a single unlit door positioned dead center along a red brick wall. A pipe pumped out steam at a constant hiss. The steam filled the alley and kept the heaps of garbage from freezing. It also helped spread the stench.

"This is it. Let me do the talkin'." Eightball kicked the door twice with the toe of his right shoe.

The door opened only two inches and a warm honey glow filled the crack.

Eightball leaned in. "I'm here to see Mudbone."

The door slammed.

Sly threw his hands up. "Well, that's just swell. You sure have a way with doormen."

The door opened again no more than three inches. "Who's askin'?"

"Tell him Eightball needs to see him."

Sly winced. Now Father Murphy knew Eightball's name.

The door started to shut again and Eightball yelled, "Tell him no hard feelings!"

The door slammed.

After a pause, Father Murphy asked, "Your name is *Eightball*? As in billiards?"

"You dumb shit, now he can give the cops your name," Sly said.

"I'm not leaving your sides. Your names are safe with me."

Eightball nodded at Sly. "Well if that's the case, he's Sly."

"You fucker." Sly wished knives could fly out of his eyes and into Eightball's laughing puss.

"Don't worry, he can't tell the cops shit. It's against church rules. I think," Eightball said.

Sly perked up. "What's that mean?"

"It means he can't tell them about any bad shit we done because it's like a . . ." Eightball looked down the dark alley for the right word.

"Confession?" Father Murphy replied.

Eightball smiled. "Yeah, that's it, a compression."

"You mean a *confession*, son."

Eightball's expression turned serious. "That's what I said."

Father Murphy straightened his shirt and his posture. "Very well. Since official introductions are in order, I'm Father Patrick Murphy."

"I don't care," Sly and Eightball answered at the same time.

"I'm still calling you Priest just the same," Sly said. Every move he made and word he chose tightened his control over the group. But control seemed to be slipping away by the second as he waited by the door.

The door opened again. Cold and shivering, Sly cautiously moved toward the warm light the instant it reappeared. An arm appeared around the door gripping a pistol.

"Gun!" Sly yelled.

Boom! Boom! Sly jumped on a pile of warm garbage.

Boom! Boom! Boom! Boom!

After the echoes faded, Sly uncovered his head. Eightball and Father Murphy were splayed on some splintered crates. The arm holding the smoking gun still stuck out from behind the door.

A voice inside called out, "Mudbone says *no hard feelings right back atcha.*"

"Is everyone okay?" Sly yelled.

"We're okay," Eightball answered from several feet away. "Mudbone was just kidding around. No problem. He won't shoot no more." Eightball sounded as convincing as the Grim Reaper selling life insurance.

Sly rolled onto his back and searched himself for bullet holes. He patted his chest before examining his hands for blood. Checking for bullet holes was happening far too often. Wilted lettuce and a blotchy tomato slice peeled away from his clothes when he jumped up. "Goddamn it!"

Sly ran over to help Father Murphy to his feet. "Priest, you okay?"

"None the worse for wear, I believe."

Eightball used the brick wall for leverage and lifted himself off the pile of crushed crates. "No problem at all. Mudbone's just being funny."

"I'd hate to see him mad," Sly said. Sly had nothing but hatred for the plan, the cold, Eightball, the rotten food stuck to his clothes, and oh yes, being shot at—especially that. Postal clerks wouldn't have shot at him.

The door slowly opened wide. The entry was empty, except for warm light, white walls, and a cobblestone floor.

Eightball approached the door.

"What the hell are you doing?" Sly asked. "You're going to get us all killed. Let's get the hell out of here." Sly's voice strained.

Father Murphy grabbed the crook of Eightball's arm to stop him.

"You sure about this?"

Eightball shrugged off the priest's hand. "Nope," he answered, and walked inside.

18.

Draw Blood and Erase the Past

CHIEF MURNANE DIDN'T PAY ATTENTION to anything beyond the headlights grazing the icy bricks that paved University Avenue. Noxious car exhaust fumes and his noxious travel companion made the bile in his intestines, and his soul, fester. Images of his family hanging upside down from his front porch with their entrails removed did not help. Every thought revolved around saving their lives—even if it meant sacrificing his.

The sweet, dry smoke from DeLuce's freshly lit cigar staled the interior.

"I know what they have and who it belongs to—and he wants it back," DeLuce said.

When DeLuce said the rightful owner *wanted it back*, Murnane heard frailty in DeLuce's voice. The way DeLuce said it sounded like a man staring at the gallows.

"I thought whatever we were looking for belonged to you. Whose is it then?" The time had come to stop the bullshit and grill DeLuce for answers. "I'll do whatever it takes to save my family. That makes me a dangerous man, DeLuce."

"Duly noted, now drive." DeLuce flicked cigar ash on the floor.

DeLuce was visibly rattled; his voice had weakened, his posture changed, his arrogance had dissolved into a puddle—only for a moment—but Murnane caught it. Whatever he and DeLuce were chasing down scared the hell out of the Devil himself.

The chess pieces were finally moving in Murnane's favor. He prodded DeLuce. "Something wrong?"

"Stop asking questions."

Murnane's streetwise mind was built for solving crime. He always thought one move ahead of the bad guys. His moral fiber, however, had suffered because he had used his superior sixth sense to line his pockets, which aided the criminals far more often than apprehended them. But he had a plan to find Eightball fast, and any idea that shortened his time with DeLuce was worth putting on the table.

"If they jumped in Minneapolis we could save some time and try to head them off. I think I know where they're going."

"All we know is they're heading toward Minneapolis. But we don't know if they got off there. We go to the rail yard and see if we can figure that out. Then we can plan our next move," DeLuce said.

"You're not thinking like a gangster. I've dealt with these slimy bastards for years now. It's easy to think one move ahead of them. All they care about is saving their own skins."

DeLuce straightened his fedora. "These goddamned gangsters have no ethics, no code of honor. They run around and shoot up everything like it's the Wild West. At least *we* have a code of honor."

"You mean *we* as in the Mob—not you and I."

Murnane glanced quickly, long enough to see DeLuce sneer. "Yes, we have a certain way of doing things. No one person is ever more important than the organization. With the gangsters it's every man for himself and fuck your partner." DeLuce cracked the window and flicked his cigar into the night.

"I say we track down Eightball's old crony Mudbone first. My gut says Eightball may try to meet up with him."

"And I'm telling you, our best bet is at the rail yard. So unless your gut wants a bullet in it, I suggest it stays quiet. In fact, I'd better not even hear it gurgle for a cheeseburger," DeLuce said.

Regret and remorse gurgled loudly when Murnane thought about the illicit deals he'd made throughout his career. He remembered the windfall of dirty money starting so simply. A rookie cop pocketing a five spot to look the other way while gangsters collected protection money from businesses on his beat.

The higher Murnane climbed within the department, the bigger and easier the money became. During his work as lieutenant, he took six thousand dollars on the sly to cover up a botched bank robbery. The following day he read in the St. Paul paper that a five-year-old girl was injured in the cross fire. Her blood stained the money he spent on Mary's anniversary present.

Every tarnished penny Murnane took over the years was meant to provide for his family's warmth, safety, and happiness. That same money now threatened their lives.

As he drove, Murnane vowed to create more memories playing catch with Jacob. He would do anything to ensure more time dressing up for tea parties with Samantha and her teddy bear Mr. Buttoneyes. To hold Mary in front of the fireplace just one more time.

None of his pocket-lining misdeeds could be undone now. The bitter taste in his mouth and the sweat on his palms came from the fact that the best chance of saving his family meant partnering with DeLuce.

"I deserve to know what we are after," Murnane said.

"I don't owe you a fucking thing. I'm the one with your family under my knife, remember that. You're lucky I don't dump you in a ditch right now."

"Either put a bullet in my head or answer my questions. I'm sick of your games."

DeLuce shifted in his seat. "All right, Murnane. I don't see the harm in telling you what I'm after. There's nothing you can do about it anyway."

Every muscle in Murnane's back stiffened as he drove.

"But be warned, when this is all over, you'll wish it *was* a game," DeLuce said.

Murnane smacked his palm against the steering wheel. "Fuck you and your riddles. Tell me."

"It's a document," DeLuce said.

"A document?"

"A document I was supposed to keep in my possession. And now it is no longer in my possession. I need to retrieve it before the rightful owner realizes I no longer have it."

Murnane heard DeLuce doing his best to keep the frightened child from reappearing.

"Oh, I get it—you got some dirt on a prominent politician. You were setting up the blackmail when our boys here threw in a monkey wrench. That makes sense. And this politician has enough clout to move heaven and earth to keep you from exposing his dirty laundry. Quite a web you're caught in, DeLuce. Good luck getting out of this one."

DeLuce's mouth turned up at the corners and his shoulders shook a little. "You have no idea who you're dealing with."

"First, there is no way I'm worried about some stuffed-shirt fat cat. And as for you, I've heard all about you. The way you torture people for fun. How you kill anyone who looks at you sideways. *Diavolo DeLuce*, that's what they call you on the streets. That doesn't mean a thing to me. I'm not scared of you, or your big, bad reputation. In fact, I think your reputation has bigger balls than you do."

"I'm not the one you should be afraid of." DeLuce spoke as if to himself.

"Hey, this guy's after you, not me. You're the asshole who dragged me into this mess." A horrific realization satiated Murnane. If some chopper squad gunned DeLuce down, DeLuce wouldn't be able to make the phone calls that were keeping Murnane's family alive. Murnane had to protect the one man he wanted to kill more than anything in the world. *Goddamn it.* A ticking clock thundered in Murnane's throbbing head. "How much longer before you have to call your men?"

"Twenty-two minutes," DeLuce said, without checking his watch.

Although the accelerator already touched the floor, Murnane pressed it until his ankle throbbed. The Minneapolis rail yard was just over the next hill.

Murnane slowed and turned onto a winding gravel road that he followed to a cul-de-sac. The headlights swept across a Minneapolis police car parked against a snow pile, a wood-sided pickup, and a black

Ford Model A. Murnane set the parking brake and forced himself to look at DeLuce. "Stay here."

Murnane got out through a thick cloud of car exhaust and walked across long wood planks covering soiled, hard-packed snow. He mulled over his excuse for being there as he tried to maintain his footing on the slick boards. A young officer was taking notes and questioning a stout, bearded man wearing a Stormy Kromer cap and holding a shotgun.

The officer stopped writing and gave Murnane the once-over. "What can I help you with? Are you lost?"

Murnane stepped lightly and said, "Well, I sure hope you can help me." He screwed on a smile deceptive enough to win an election. Murnane examined the railroad man's Stormy Kromer hat and thick beard and asked, "What's with the shotgun?"

"Who are you?" the officer asked.

"Officer Jacob Marley." The only name that sprang to mind came from reading Charles Dickens to Jacob and Samantha every Christmas. On second thought, he wished he had said Captain Nemo, but so what. No turning back.

The officer blinked. "That name does sound familiar. Anyway, what can I do for you, Officer Marley?"

"And what's your name?"

"Officer Sam Douse. What brings you to Minneapolis, Officer Marley?"

"Well, Douse, I'm trailing two murder suspects and tracked them here."

"Murder? You got a description?" Officer Douse raised his pad, ready to write.

"Well, I was hoping you fine gentlemen could help me out. What happened here?" Murnane turned to the bearded man.

Officer Douse started to answer. "Mr. Luf here . . ."

"Please call me Eric. Mr. Luf is way too formal for a man who works for a livin'." Eric used his fingerless gloves to stroke the shotgun like it was a purebred Persian cat.

"Eric here says three vagrants jumped off a train and ran into the woods. Nothing out of the ordinary—happens every day. But you know how it is, still gotta fill out a report, right?" The officer snorted a quick laugh. "Anyway, he got a couple shots off but doesn't think he hit 'em."

"What'd they look like?" Murnane asked.

"Wait. You said you were chasing two suspects. That is what you said. I wrote down *two*. Why are you interested in these three then?" Officer Douse asked. Douse was doing a fine job of being a tenacious cop and a pain in the ass.

Murnane turned to Eric. "What'd they look like?"

The ice chunks on Eric's hearty Scandinavian beard clicked when he spoke. "There was three of 'em." He held up two fingers and a nub. "I was working the up yard when I saw 'em jump off. Two were pretty tall, I guess, and the third was real small. I woulda thought he was a kid if it weren't for the grey hair and the fact he was dressed like a priest. The crazy bastard said hello to me when I pointed my gun at him. He mighta been drunk."

Murnane squared his shoulders to face Eric. "Which way'd they go?"

"Where do you think?" Eric pointed his shotgun toward the city lights.

Officer Douse licked the lead on his pencil and started to write. Every couple words or so, Douse would glance at Murnane's badge. Sneaky bastard was trying to get his badge number. Murnane turned his shoulders toward the city lights.

"That way, you say?" Murnane looked at the Minneapolis skyline through the skeletal trees.

"Do you think these could be your guys?" Officer Douse asked, still trying to catch a glimpse of Murnane's badge.

Murnane stepped backward. Slow at first, then picked up the pace. "Thanks Mr., um, Eric."

"Eric's my first name!" he yelled.

Officer Douse started to follow. "Hey, Officer Marley, if you believe they're still here in town, I need to know. We need to work together."

Murnane held up his hand and nodded as he stepped away. "Yes, absolutely. I'll meet you at the station to fill out some reports. See you there." Turning his back on Douse, Murnane waved toward downtown. He jogged back over the long planks, which shook under his weight.

Murnane jumped in the car, released the hand brake, and slammed into reverse. Douse followed Murnane to the cul-de-sac and approached the car, but when the headlights blinded Douse, he stopped. The car slid on the ice and spun. Murnane ground the gears until he found one and hit the gas.

"What happened?" DeLuce asked.

"They jumped the train and ran into the woods. I'll bet dollars to donuts they're going to see Mudbone."

Murnane checked the mirror to see if Officer Douse had followed him.

"Goddamn it!" Murnane slammed on the brakes. The car fishtailed until he let off the brake and hit the gas again. "How long have you two been here?"

The Butcher Boys loomed in the back seat.

"They got dropped off by the mayor's personal driver ten minutes ago," DeLuce said.

"You about scared the Christ out of me."

"So where are we going?" DeLuce calmly asked.

Murnane took a shallow breath and did a double-take in the rearview mirror at the two massive torsos blocking the back window.

"I told you we should have started with Mudbone," Murnane said. "Before Eightball worked for the Boss, he worked as a heavy at three speakeasies in Minneapolis. He and Mudbone were thick as thieves. I'll bet he's going to find Mudbone and hide out awhile. Maybe try to sell your document to the highest bidder."

"They won't sell it. If what you say is true, it's only a matter of time before this Mudbone finds out what they have and tries to steal it. And when he does, they'll kill him. We should keep an eye on the morgues for him."

DeLuce carried a certainty in his inflection that set Murnane's curiosity working overtime. "How do you know that? I doubt these fools can even read. Is that why they kidnapped the priest? So he could read it to them? They could have grabbed anyone on the street to read it to them, why did they target the priest? That part still makes no sense to me."

"Just find them."

Murnane quickly glanced in the rearview mirror.

"So you know where Mudbone lives?" DeLuce asked.

"No, the bastard never had a permanent address. And I can't waltz into police headquarters and start pulling files without answering a whole lotta questions. So I figured we'd head to the last speakeasy I remember him working at. If he's not there, someone should still know where to find him—if he's not dead or in St. Paul."

Murnane navigated the nighttime streets of Minneapolis. The streets took on a different personality at night. Shadows became a hiding place for danger that didn't exist in the daylight.

They arrived at the entrance to an alley cloaked in shadowy peril. The streetlights were too far away, and the buildings too tall to provide any light between the buildings. Three men, draped in tattered blankets, stood around a trash can seeming right at home in the cold darkness. Smoke and flames rose from the can. The men turned to look at the car when Murnane cut the lights.

"Here it is, the Broken Bone," Murnane said.

"Tubby Marcone owns this place. I'm going with you. That fat fuck owes me two big ones. Plus, if there's any information, I want to hear it firsthand."

"We can't be seen together." Murnane thumbed toward the back seat. "And I sure as hell can't be seen with *them*."

DeLuce nodded toward Murnane's uniform. "We need information and if you go in dressed like that, they're going to yell *raid* as soon as they set eyes on you."

Murnane frowned and examined the shiny buttons on his dark blue uniform. "Just stay here—all of you."

DeLuce pulled out his gold pocket watch and swung it like a sadistic hypnotist.

"Fine, but let me do the talking." Murnane turned and set his right arm over the seat and said, "You two stay put. Don't do anything to draw attention." The Butcher Boys looked at each other. "Better yet, don't do *anything*."

When Murnane and DeLuce exited the car, the three hoboes left the warmth of their fiery trash can. The vagrants kept their heads down as they moved closer to the car. Murnane kept a close eye on them.

"Hey, St. Paul, did you steal that car? Are you lost?"

Even from a few feet away, Murnane smelled the corn liquor on their breath. It was obvious they fought to stay upright. "Now's not a good time, fellas. Go sleep it off."

One of them stepped forward and pulled a knife. "We don't take kindly to St. Paul gangsters in our town. Toss your gun over there and give us your money, real slow."

"I'm a cop, you idiot."

"Yeah, right. I got a uniform too."

Chief Murnane had busted more than a few gangsters impersonating cops in his day, mostly after knocking off a bank or payroll transfer of some kind—or a blind pig that didn't garner the respect of fellow gangsters. Murnane figured these drunks were supposed to be guarding the Broken Bone from any such occurrence. He also knew these guys were serious enough to kill first and be too drunk to ask questions later.

"I want his badge!" one man said.

Murnane avoided lethal force at all cost, but these assholes were begging for it. "Guys, this is your last chance . . ."

Boom! The first man's right shoulder kicked back, and he dropped.

Boom! The second man's leg jerked before he fell face-first.

Boom! The third man bent at the waist and went down hard.

Murnane didn't duck until after the third shot. His ears rang, making his head ache. DeLuce held a smoking pistol in his outstretched arm. Murnane wiped his face and drew back his hand which was smeared with droplets of blood. The three men writhed and moaned on the alley floor, clutching their wounds.

"Goddamn it. Someone's probably calling the cops right now. You couldn't use a knife?"

"A knife? Do I seem like the kinda guy who brings a knife to a gun fight?"

"First thing you're going to do when we get in here is ask to use the phone, you got me?" Murnane poked DeLuce in the chest with enough force to push a man off balance. DeLuce didn't move. "How much time do we have?"

"Plenty."

"You make damn sure you get to a phone. If the cops show up, let me handle it. I don't want anything keeping you from making that call."

DeLuce examined his gun, studying the curling smoke. "Fuck the cops and fuck those assholes." He nodded toward the men rolling back and forth in the grimy slush, blood oozing between their fingers.

Murnane heard car doors open and shut. The Butcher Boys approached and stood alongside DeLuce. Using his gun as a pointer, DeLuce said, "Take care of this."

"Wait," Murnane said to the Boys. They ignored him. Murnane asked DeLuce, "What are they going to do?"

"Let's go inside. It's best not to watch," DeLuce answered.

"Get these guys outta here before the cops show up. Make it fast and keep it quiet," Murnane said.

The Boys followed Murnane's orders to a tee. They gathered wet garbage off the ground and crammed it into the wailing men's mouths until the men's eyes bulged. Gagging and choking sounds haunted the alley. The perilous shadows had lived up to their reputation once again.

Murnane melted snow in a handkerchief and used it to wipe the blood off his face. He did his best to ignore the sounds of slow death and multiple felonies unfolding only a few feet away. "Let's get this over with and get the hell out of here."

DeLuce looked at the Boys and said, "Take the car and park it one block down when you're done." He turned to Murnane. "Here," he said. DeLuce removed his long black overcoat and offered it to Murnane. "Put this on and button it up."

"I'm not wearing that." The thought of sharing anything with DeLuce repulsed him.

"You don't have a choice." DeLuce cocked his gun and pointed it down, but the message came through loud and clear.

"If you were going to shoot me, you would have done it by now. I have a gun too, asshole—don't forget that." Murnane yanked the coat away and swung it around, slipping his arms in the sleeves. The reek of cigar smoke punched Murnane in the nose.

"And lose the hat," DeLuce said.

Murnane tossed the hat in the car. He was close enough to hear the pop and rip a foot makes when snapped at the ankle and torn from a leg. One of the Boys opened the rear passenger door to retrieve a meat cleaver.

DeLuce swept his gun deftly, inviting Murnane to proceed to the steel door.

Murnane stopped before knocking and said, "For Christ's sake, don't kill anyone else. Let's find out everything we can and leave."

"I don't care who I kill. I'll do whatever it takes to get back that paper," DeLuce said. His stony face gave no delusions of empathy.

"Please."

DeLuce shrugged. "I'll do my best."

19.

The Apple of Her Sly

SLY BROUGHT UP THE REAR, keeping a cautious eye on Eightball and Father Murphy as they moved closer to the door. He held tight to the gun in his pocket while Eightball set one foot inside the door. Distracted by the warm and welcoming glow spilling from the doorway into the alley, Sly accidentally kicked a bottle, which clanked across the alley floor, scaring the shit out of him. Father Murphy turned in response to the ruckus and waved Sly closer. Sly neared the doorway and saw a hand the size of a baseball mitt reach out and grab Eightball by the throat.

Sly grabbed Father Murphy. "Let's go! Run!" Sly's retreat was cut off by a mountain of a Negro man who somehow had managed to sneak up from behind. His eyes were as dark as the shotgun barrel inches from Sly's face. Both the barrel and the mountain looked like they could inflict serious damage.

"Come join the party, ofay."

Swell.

Father Murphy raised his hands. "Please sir, don't shoot! I'm a priest. These men are with me."

The shotgun was quickly aimed at Father Murphy. The mountain squinted one eye and steadied the shotgun against his shoulder. "Then you best pull a miracle outta your ass."

"I don't find that amusing in the least, young man." Father Murphy's pinched face resembled a frustrated raisin.

Two quick jerks of the shotgun let Sly know that he'd better start moving toward the open door. "You go first," Sly said to Father Murphy who frowned. Father Murphy walked inside first with Sly right behind.

There was nothing comfortable about stepping through the door, other than the warmth. A thick hand grabbed the back of Sly's neck and pushed him against a brick wall. Being grabbed by the back of the neck was as enjoyable as being held at gunpoint. The right side of Sly's face was being ground into a cold brick wall by a meaty palm that felt like an overcooked steak. His lips puckered to the point of numbing. Sly would kick Eightball's ass for this little adventure—if Sly lived through it. And if Sly lived and Eightball didn't, even better.

Out of the corner of his eye Sly observed someone take Eightball's gun, two knives, and even the straight razor in his shoe.

Father Murphy whined when Eightball was relieved of his flask, "I was so hoping we could get that refilled."

Yet another man made quick work of frisking Father Murphy. He pressed Father Murphy against the brick, searching every pocket. "Indeed! Unhand me!"

The man with the meaty palm against Sly's face used his free hand to empty Sly's pockets. Bullets clicked together as the man took them from Sly and put them in his own pocket. He then took Sly's pistol and dropped it in the same pocket as the bullets. He pulled the paper from Sly's other pocket and held it up.

"What's this?"

Sly's heart pounded in his throat. Sweat dripped in his eyes. "A scrap of paper. It's nothing."

"Yeah. It looks like nuthin'." He balled it up and threw it at Sly's feet, all the while keeping Sly's face against the wall. Sly strained his eyes to keep the paper in his sight line.

Meaty Palm let go and turned Sly around to face forward. As Sly turned, he could see the other men turning Eightball and Father Murphy to face forward as well. Sly counted five large men under the dim electric light, three Negroes and two whites, armed with various blunt objects and one big shotgun.

"Which one a you is Eightball?" one man asked.

Happy to oblige, Sly looked over at Eightball. *Busted.*

The man stepped in front of Eightball and whispered, "Mudbone's got a message for you."

Eightball let out a painful grunt when the whisperer wound up and used Eightball's stomach for batting practice—Louisville Slugger–style. Eightball hunched over, but Meaty Palm and another man held Eightball's arms, not allowing him to drop to his knees.

"Please, sirs. You look like reasonable gentlemen. There is no need for this." Father Murphy raised a hand as if trying to stop them.

All eyes studied Eightball as he coughed hard and straightened himself. Sly used the opportunity to extend a foot and slide the paper closer, ever so slowly.

A black man wearing a tailored tuxedo sauntered in, preceded by a fog of cologne. All five large men turned and watched him enter. He stood a few inches shorter and was substantially slighter than his henchmen. Debonair as hell, the man posed in the middle of the room giving everyone a chance to admire him.

Sly had never seen a tailored tuxedo in person before—not even on a white person, except in pictures. This guy looked like he could run for president. A black president—that would be the day.

Eightball tilted his head back and raised his eyebrows. "Mudbone. How you been?"

"Shit, I figured you were dead—or in St. Paul." Mudbone's processed hair glistened against his round head. "I been waiting for this for a looong time."

Biting silence sank into both Sly and the room. Mudbone kept his glare locked on Eightball and stepped closer. Eightball flashed a smile as his eyes darted over Mudbone. Sly would never forget the look on Mudbone's face at that moment: as if Eightball was something Mudbone had just scraped off the bottom of his shoe.

Mudbone set his hands on his hips. "You mangy, low-down, dirty dog. You must carry your balls in a wheelbarrow, boy, showing your smelly ass 'round here." Mudbone's frown made his bottom lip curl up with every word he spoke.

"Mudbone, I swear I was going to split the money with you from your brother's fight. Honest Injun. I wouldn't double-cross you. He double-crossed *me*, remember?" The lump in Eightball's throat sounded painful when he swallowed. "The Boss didn't pay me right away. I had to pay some debts. There was a huge storm. My fuckin' dog died. You understand. Right?" Eightball spat out excuses faster than a Tommy gun spat out hot lead.

"You must be in some serious shit to show your raggedy mug around here." Mudbone flicked his wrist twice and the whisperer handed over Eightball's revolver. Mudbone opened the cylinder. "You come to see me carryin' an empty gun? You're dumber than you look." Mudbone tossed the pistol back to the whisperer. Meaty Palm handed Sly's gun to Mudbone. He opened the chamber and counted what few bullets Sly had remaining. Looks like you boys been in a scrape. Low on bullets *and* brains. Wonder what the reward for your mangy ass is? Whatever it is, I'm sure it's just the same alive . . . *or* dead."

Mudbone spun the chamber and snapped it closed. "Open your mouth," Mudbone said.

"What?"

"I said open your mouth, boy."

"What for?"

He pressed the gun against Eighball's forehead.

"Come on, Mudbone. We can talk about thissss. It was an accident."

"I thought you said you beat him to death on purpose," Father Murphy said.

"Shut up!" Eightball yelled.

Mudbone shoved the gun in Eightball's mouth. Convulsing coughs sent globs of snot seeping over the gun and Mudbone's hand.

Mudbone pouted angrily. "Now look what you done, you nasty bastard!"

"Please don't shoot him, Mr. Mudbone. You took his weapons. He is defenseless."

"He's 'bout as helpless as a pack a hungry wolves, old man. He'd beat you to death just as soon as look at you. Ask my brother. Or how 'bout I have Eightball ask him in person."

Sly pressed his lips together trying hard to will Mudbone into pulling the trigger. *Oh, please, please, please.*

Mudbone raised his left hand to shield himself from the splattering chunks of Eightball's face. "Back up fellas, this is gonna get messy."

Eightball jerked his head from side to side but couldn't escape the gun down his throat.

"Say hi to my brother for me."

Mudbone stiffened his raised elbow, squinted, and cocked the gun. Sly flinched.

Mudbone flashed a mouthful of wide grey teeth.

Then he laughed.

And then he removed the gun.

"I'm just foolin' with you, Eightball. Come on. You know that."

Eightball bent over, coughing and gagging. He bowed his head and gave a thumbs-up and nodded. He used his sleeve to wipe the drooping snot ropes away after he straightened up.

Mudbone slapped him on the shoulder. "So, how you been?" He handed Sly's gun back to Meaty Palm.

"I've been better, you crazy asshole," Eightball said, in a gravelly snort.

"And you, my favorite ofay!" Mudbone sounded like a leggy bombshell had just jumped out of his birthday cake.

"You mean you're not going to kill him?" Father Murphy asked.

"Not now. Maybe later." Mudbone examined Eightball's face. "Look at your face! It's bright red!"

"You're not upset about your brother?" Father Murphy asked. A henchman handed Father Murphy his glasses. The priest folded and tucked them into his shirt pocket.

"Hell no. He was an asshole. You sure ask alotta questions, little man. And why is the little white man dressed like a priest?"

Mudbone put his arm around Eightball and pulled him away from the wall. No gunshot wound to the head. No brains bashed against the brick wall with a Louisville Slugger. Eightball, like Sly's unlucky streak, remained alive and well.

"Actually, Mr. Mudbone, it's been quite an adventure. It started when ..."

"You didn't have to stick a gun in my mouth, you crazy son of a bitch," Eightball interrupted. He let his jagged teeth show when he threw his head back and laughed.

"Watching you shit your pants was a riot. I haven't had that much fun since we pulled that job on Exchange Street together."

"You stabbed me in the leg."

Mudbone hooted and slapped his knee. "But it was an accident, right?"

"I doubt it," Eightball said. "What do you have to drink around here?"

Father Murphy perked up at the inquiry.

"Come on, and bring your crazy friends." Mudbone waved for Sly and Father Murphy to follow.

Sly bent down, retrieved the balled up paper, and shoved it in his pocket. He rose and came face to face with Meaty Palm who silently watched Sly intently. His eyes, however, told Sly to get the fuck out of the room.

The hall widened just as Sly caught up to them. Father Murphy trailed the duo, attempting to explain how he was caught up with Sly and company to Mudbone who apparently couldn't have cared less. Sly followed them into the next room, which contained a small table and chairs and a large chrome ice box door against one wall. When Mudbone knocked, the chrome-plated handle slid aside and eyes looked out.

When the door opened, the smooth tones of ragtime music bounced around Sly. He noticed his foot tapping as he waited to get in. He followed them down a narrow hallway and past a doll-faced coat check girl who even brought a smile to Father Murphy's face.

The hallway opened into a grand room. Sly had never seen anything like it—any of it. Negroes and whites alike danced and spilled champagne and gin in equal quantities. Brightly colored suits and sequined cocktail dresses whirled through a haze of cigarette smoke.

Pounding piano and a brass quartet drove the rhythms that propelled a sea of people crowding the hardwood dance floor. A large ball made of small mirrors rotated above and reflected light in every direction. The room was alive.

"Come on, let's get some drinks." Mudbone led the way to the hand-carved hardwood bar inlaid with illuminated frosted glass panels.

Mudbone shouted over the music. "What'll you have? It's on the house!"

Sly had never ordered a proper drink before. He was drinking with the blue bloods now. He said, "I'll have what they're having," nodding toward the dance floor.

"Give me one dirty martini. Make that two. Don't worry, boys, this isn't your shitty bathtub gin. We get the straight stuff from Canada every other day. Real whisky, real gin, and real rum too. How 'bout you, pal?" He slapped Eightball on the back causing a couple more coughs to stumble out.

"Whisky."

"Give me some twelve-year Scotch! How about you, Father? You drink wine, right?"

Father Murphy tightened his face and surveyed the room. "Oh goodness, such a den of sin and decadence." He tilted his head and smiled at Mudbone. "I usually don't partake in such activities. However, the true sin would be not to accept your gracious hospitality. So I too will have Scotch. Only in the spirit of the moment, you understand."

Sly had to admire Father Murphy's caramel-colored hooch. *With ice. And a glass. Swanky.*

"When do I get my gun back?" Sly asked. Mudbone's paper-thin smile rubbed Sly the wrong way.

"When you leave, boy." Mudbone strained to keep that false smile on his face. He was hiding something behind it. Mudbone took a sip of his drink.

"What's your name?" Mudbone lightly elbowed Father Murphy.

"I'm Father Patrick Murphy." He raised his Scotch proudly.

Mudbone looked at Sly and asked, "What's your name, gunslinger?"

Eightball answered, "That's Sly. He's the reason we're all here. He's a mean cuss."

"Oh yeah? You must be one bad man if you got a priest runnin' from the law!" Mudbone's boisterous laugh almost caused him to spill his martini.

"Can we talk some business?" Eightball asked.

"Right now?" Mudbone asked.

"Right now."

Mudbone swung around and said, "Follow me."

Eightball glanced back at Sly and Father Murphy. "You two stay here, we'll be right back."

Sly watched Eightball and Mudbone disappear through a swinging door behind the bar. If those two scoundrels were going to meet in private, Sly wanted to listen in. As Sly turned to follow them, a platinum-haired waitress wedged herself between him and Father Murphy, using her elbows like crowbars.

"Lou, table fourteen is still waiting on those drinks! Come on, I ain't getting any younger!"

"Or smarter!" Lou replied.

She gave Lou a look that should have left scratch marks on his face. "You want I should rearrange your mush? Keep it up, Lou!"

Sly studied her bobbed hair before tapping her on the shoulder. "Hey, what's the big idea, buttin' in like that?"

She turned to look at Sly. Sly couldn't breathe. This woman could have made a charging tiger stop and purr.

If the music continued playing and the room still spun with alcohol-fueled merriment, Sly didn't notice. Only she mattered. She smelled like angels should smell. Her black satin gloves went all the way up to her dainty crowbar elbows and matched her ebony bustier. Her lips resembled wet cherries and her sultry eyes launched fireworks. He blinked and the music roared. The room burst with energy again.

She looked Sly up and down. "Move it, creep. I got mouths to feed, namely mine!"

She swung her tray and stomped back toward table fourteen. Sly watched the seam of her stockings—every inch, from ass to ankle—move toward the crowd. Despite his illiteracy, the poetry of her calves wasn't lost on him. After a few steps she slowed and looked over her bare shoulder. Sly's smile was as involuntary as panting. She returned the softest half-smile. His heart pounded so hard his teeth rattled.

"Well, Mr. Sly," Father Murphy said after a hiccup, "it seems you fancy that young lady." He used his empty glass to point at table fourteen. "This proves you have a heart. Otherwise she couldn't have stolen it."

Sly's only response was a slack-jawed gawk that followed the angel around the room.

"Mr. Sly?" Father Murphy leaned in. "Mr. Sly?" *Hiccup*. He tugged on Sly's sleeve. "Mr. Sly, are you feeling okay?"

"I think I'm in love."

20.

When Speakeasies Go Silent

MURNANE HESITATED before knocking on the frosty steel door. Small icicles hung off the door handle. DeLuce puffed hot breath into the night and slid his pistol under his suit jacket. Several feet away a cleaver hacked meat and thumped against bone, producing a sickening thud.

DeLuce said, "Knock."

Murnane rapped his knuckles against the cold metal. The door clunked open revealing nothing but an empty doorway.

"Please come in," a cheerful voice said.

Murnane entered in front of DeLuce and the door closed behind them. The stale stench of urine cut through the cramped barroom and made Murnane wrinkle his nose. A balding man wearing an eye patch busied himself behind the bar. He spit in a glass and wiped it down with the heavily stained apron loosely tied around his thin waist. Another man was slumped over the bar. A spilled drink pooled under his elbow and drool pooled under his cheek. Murnane assumed he was dead, which was fine since this wasn't Murnane's jurisdiction.

Murnane strolled around the room. Broken glass, cigarette butts, and what could only be blotches of dried blood covered the rotting wood floor. Dust and cobwebs coated every nook and cranny. Most chairs were broken and few tables still had their tops intact. A set of shattered false teeth lay under a stool.

DeLuce scanned the dank room as if it were an old friend suffering from a terminal disease. "What the fuck did Tubby do to this place?"

Besides the one-eyed bartender and the unconfirmed dead man, the only other person in the joint was the midget who must have been the cheerful voice who opened the door. The man stood maybe three feet tall and wore eighteenth-century carriage driver's clothes crowned by a ragged stove pipe hat. Murnane paused for a second and took in what he saw.

The midget tipped his hat and said, "Good evening, sirs."

"We're looking for a colored fella named Mudbone," Chief Murnane said.

The midget folded his arms and rubbed his whiskered chin, in a cartoonish look of concentration, but never answered. DeLuce stepped closer to the bar and addressed the one-eyed bartender.

"Hey, Deadeye, what happened to this place?" DeLuce asked.

"Sorry, friend, I don't understand your meaning." The bartender rubbed the glass harder.

"Does Tub-of-Shit Marcone still own this place?"

"Depends on who's askin'."

DeLuce shook his head. "This used to be a respectable joint. What happened?"

Murnane stepped forward, shoulder to shoulder with DeLuce, interrupting his nostalgic stroll down memory lane. "Marcone can wait. We need to find a darkie named Mudbone. Ever heard of him?"

Deadeye set the spit-shined glass on the bar. He grabbed an even dirtier glass, spit in it, and began to rub. He didn't smile but did wink his good eye. "What's that old saying? Oh, right—*penny for my thoughts?*"

DeLuce opened his suit coat and slipped his pistol out. Deadeye's eye narrowed when he saw it. DeLuce asked, "Do you know how much *lead's* in a penny? Because I know how much lead's about to go through your thoughts."

Murnane felt something odd at his crotch. He looked down to see the midget holding a pistol against the baby bank. The midget's other hand drove a pistol to DeLuce's crotch. By the time Murnane looked up, Deadeye had a shotgun pointed at their heads and the supposed dead man was picking both their pockets clean of weapons. The dead man opened Murnane's borrowed coat and stepped back. "He's dressed like a cop."

"So what." A voice boomed from the backroom as if speaking from the bottom of a well. A short, corpulent man waddled out. His hips rubbed against either side of the doorframe as he passed through. The floor moaned and stressed under his footsteps and Murnane felt the impact tremors from several feet away.

"What the fuck is this, Marcone?" DeLuce asked.

"I don't know how you got past my men out front, but this is not your lucky day, DeLuce. As you can see, we are no longer open to the public."

"Next time don't hire drunks to watch your front door," Chief Murnane said.

"I'll take that under advisement. However, you and *DeDouche* won't be around to worry about that," Marcone replied.

"Well, you look good, Marcone. Did you gain some weight?"

"Tie them up."

DeLuce laughed and held out his palm. "You still owe me two big ones from the Tunney fight. Pay up."

The dead man worked the rope into knots around Murnane's wrists and said, "They were asking about Mudbone." Murnane raised his hands and glanced down when the midget pressed the gun harder against Murnane's groin. DeLuce lowered his hand and looked down at his own crotch. The midget smiled.

"Mudbone? What do you want with Mudbone?" Marcone asked.

The bartender slid two chairs across the floor, one of them slamming into DeLuce's knees.

"The mayor wants to give him the key to the city and we need to let him know," DeLuce answered.

"Always with the wisecracks. You never change."

"I crack wise, and you crack sidewalks. C'mon, you lost two large on Dempsey, now pay up. It's been over a year now."

"You got a real fresh mouth for a man with such rotten luck."

"Just like Dempsey, I'm goin' down swingin'," DeLuce said.

"Look, I'm St. Paul Police Chief August Murnane. Let us go and I'll be sure to send some St. Paul hospitality you're way. Then we can forget all about this."

"Well, Chief, if you're hanging around this guy you're about as straight as a corkscrew, so give it a rest," Marcone replied.

"How much time do we have?" Murnane asked DeLuce.

"Four minutes."

"Please, Mr. Marcone, let us make one phone call, that's all I ask."

"You ask like I owe you a favor. Do I owe you a favor?"

"No. We just need to use the phone. It's a simple request."

"Relax, Chief. Tell you what I'll do." Marcone motioned to Dead-eye. "Go grab the phone off my desk and set it on the bar. The cord's plenty long."

Deadeye returned with the phone and set it on the bar.

"Thank you, Mr. Marcone. Just let DeLuce use the phone," Murnane said. He tried not to sound desperate, but asking for the phone was like tipping his hand to a table full of card sharks. And these sharks played for blood.

The dead man and the midget pulled Murnane and DeLuce down onto the chairs and tied them up with abrasive rope. The rope didn't burn Murnane as much as staring helplessly at the phone on the bar.

"Hey, how can he use the phone if his hands are tied? Will you work it for him? That's fine as long as he talks," Murnane said, feeling control slipping away.

DeLuce looked like a man feeding pigeons in the park on a warm summer day.

"This phone is obviously very important to you," Marcone said.

Murnane's eyes darted between Marcone and the phone.

Marcone smiled. "Tell you what, you sit there and get a good look at it while you die."

Murnane stiffened and thrashed. The rope burned and pinched into his wrists. The chair creaked and wobbled, but did not collapse. "You son of a bitch! I'll kill you!"

"No you won't," Marcone said, letting out a chortle.

DeLuce looked content, and it made Murnane's blood boil.

"What are you smiling about?" Marcone asked.

"I can't wait to watch you die, Marcone," DeLuce answered.

Marcone stopped smiling. "You're the one tied to a chair and I'm the one about to beat you into a pool of chowder. You must really be into some good hooch if you're seein' things differently."

Deadeye, the dead man, and the midget all closed in around Murnane and DeLuce.

Marcone stepped closer and crossed his arms. His eyes volleyed between Murnane and DeLuce. Chubby cheeks almost concealed a satisfied smile as if a whole deep fried turkey danced in front of him. "I want you to cut off their fingers one by one until they tell us why they're really here."

"I need that phone, asshole," Murnane said. Murnane twisted and rubbed his wrists raw against the coarse rope while sweat dripped into his eyes. The thrashing caused his hair to fall loose against his forehead. The phone mocked him from the bar.

"Start with Chief Telephone there. Cut his fingers real slow."

The dead man grabbed Murnane's left hand and gripped his index finger. Murnane's ears filled with his own huffing breathes as his fingers spread over the wood arm rest. Sweat rained from his forehead into his eyes and formed a rivulet down his nose. But when he caught the glint of his wedding band, he stopped fighting. Visions of Mary, Jacob, and Samantha ran through his thoughts, and he stared at the ring as if it were their smiling faces.

Deadeye raised a pair of pruners and squeezed them repeatedly. "These are steel anvil pruners. They'll cut straight through an oak branch three inches thick, like a hot knife through butter."

Murnane recognized those pruners. Mary used the same type to clip roses and trim branches off the apple tree in their back yard. *Now, there's one for the books*, Murnane thought. *Done in with Mary's pruners.*

Murnane squeezed his eyes shut and tears leaked out as he felt cold steel slide around his knuckle.

"Please, I need the phone," Murnane mumbled and looked over at DeLuce.

DeLuce looked straight forward and hummed "Let Me Call You Sweetheart."

Marcone frowned at DeLuce. "Keep humming, sweetheart. We're gonna wipe that smile right off your puss, because you're next."

DeLuce stopped humming. "No, you are."

Two blasts splattered Marcone's face across Chief Murnane. When Marcone dropped, Murnane's chair bounced a couple inches off the floor. The pruners clunked at Murnane's feet. Murnane turned to see the Butcher Boys behind the bar. Fresh from the back alley, their insane blue eyes beamed against their shimmering crimson masks. Their guns were poised squarely on Deadeye until DeLuce yelled, "Wait!"

Murnane let out his breath when they lowered their weapons.

"Untie me first," DeLuce said.

Before Murnane could blink, one Butcher had Deadeye clamped by the upper arm leaving the poor bastard with nowhere to run. The Butcher's other hand held the dead man tight, and Murnane saw the look on the dead man's face—he knew the jig was up. The other Butcher Boy made quick work of the knots and untied DeLuce.

"Oh God, me too," Murnane said. "Make the call. Make it now!" He tasted iron from Marcone's blood.

DeLuce rubbed his wrists and sauntered to the bar. He dialed the phone. The seconds tortured Murnane. DeLuce tapped his foot.

DeLuce turned his back on Murnane and spoke softly into the phone. "It's me. Just checking in. How is it?"

Murnane remained tied tight and watched DeLuce on the phone—talking to the men who held his family. It was the closest he'd been to his family since DeLuce intruded on his life. He wanted to tell Jacob and Samantha not to cry. That everything was fine and that Daddy would be home soon. He tried to ignore the taste of blood and the feeling of skull and hair on his tongue.

"We're good here," DeLuce said and glanced over his shoulder at Murnane.

"Tell them I love them. Please."

DeLuce hung up. "Untie him." The Butcher Boys sliced Murnane's ropes.

"How are they?"

"They'll be fine as long as you continue to play ball."

Murnane sighed and let his muscles relax. He twisted and rubbed each chafed wrist. Murnane spit and coughed trying to get the remaining debris off his tongue. "Damn you, DeLuce. Damn you to Hell."

"If you only knew . . ."

DeLuce examined Marcone's heaping corpse before he kicked it. "You fat fuck."

DeLuce picked his gun off the bar. "Take care of them," he said to the Butcher holding Marcone's men. DeLuce searched the room. "Wait. Where's the short one?"

The Boys pointed at Marcone. DeLuce moved in for a closer look. A top hat lay next to the body and a little hand stuck out between the fat folds. "Little fucker got off light," DeLuce said. He studied Deadeye and the dead man. "But *you* won't." He lifted the pruners from the floor and snapped them open and shut over and over. "You're going to tell me where Mudbone is—and you won't enjoy doing it."

DeLuce was about to do God knows what with those pruners. With every severed body part that splat to the floor, Murnane would be one step closer to freeing his family.

Get going, asshole.

21.

Fresh Love and a Rotting Corpse

SLY ADMIRED THE POETIC GAIT she used to float across the dance floor. The black seam of her stockings that disappeared under her skirt, leaving Sly to imagine where the lines ended. The swan-like grace she employed to balance a tray through flailing arms and kicking legs, managing not to spill a drop. The seductively sweet angel caused the words to pour right out of Sly's mouth again, "I think I'm in love."

Father Murphy tipped over his near-empty glass and the last sip of Scotch joined the ice chunks that slid across the bar top. He wiped his mouth and frowned at the whisky. "Did you say *love*, Mr. Sly?"

"Who is that girl?" Sly's eyes watered from lack of blinking.

"I never would have guessed you were capable of *love*."

"I'm capable of kicking you harder than an angry pack mule, if you don't shut up."

Father Murphy scooped the ice from the bar top and back into his glass and ordered a fresh drink by jangling the ice. The sound of ice against glass drew a seething glare from Lou, the bartender. "Well, you need to talk to her. The Bible tells us in Proverbs chapters eighteen and nineteen, *Three things are too wonderful for me; four I do not understand: the way of an eagle in the sky, the way of a serpent on a rock, the way of a ship on the high seas, and the way of a man with a virgin.*"

Sly snorted and slapped the back of his hand on Father Murphy's shoulder. "Trust me, Priest, she ain't no virgin. *Serpent*, maybe."

Father Murphy's face shriveled like someone had switched his Scotch for prune juice. He closed one eye and turned his attention to Sly. "Please forgive me, but I must say you look an awful fright. You should get cleaned up first. I think I saw a door that read, *Gentlemen.* I believe the washroom to be right over there." The ice jingled when Father Murphy used his glass to point Sly in the general direction.

Sly removed his hat and looked himself over. His greasy locks flopped down across his eyes and he brushed them back between his fingers before putting his hat back on. "Come with me," Sly said.

Lou set a fresh Scotch in front of Father Murphy and threw in a dirty look for good measure. Father Murphy looked as though wild horses would be unable to drag him from his refilled drink. "I think you are quite capable of washing yourself, Mr. Sly."

"I wasn't asking. Move." Sly yanked Father Murphy off his stool. As Sly towed Father Murphy toward the men's room, the priest kept turning back, apparently worried someone would swipe his whisky.

Sly swung the shiny black bathroom door open. Small black-and-white tiles covered the floor. He slowed down to admire the clean toilets inside each stall and two fancy sinks—*two*—near the door. The sinks had tall, polished brass spigots shaped like a swan's neck. A black man in a white tuxedo and black tie sat on a stool next to the sinks, handing out warm towels. He handed out candy mints and perfume too. Goddamned blue bloods knew how to live.

The giant wall mirror told the tale of Sly's adventurous day. Slumped and weary shoulders and splotches of caked mud across his weathered face were harsh reminders of what he'd been through so far—and also how much further he had to go. Straw stuck to his coat and Rabbi Mendlebaum's dried blood still speckled his clothing and hands. Father Murphy appeared out from behind Sly's left shoulder, more pleased than if he was about to go blueberry picking. "Let's make you presentable, Mr. Sly," he said.

Sly delved deeper into his reflection. He drew his shoulders back and stuck out his chest, just a little. His eyes were clear and bright and full of an agreeable energy he didn't recognize, but liked. He looked down at Father Murphy and realized the old priest wouldn't hurt him.

He was the first person Sly could remember meeting in a very long time who had absolutely no intentions of taking something from him. Not only did Father Murphy not want anything from Sly, but went out of his way to help.

All his life everyone Sly had ever crossed paths with or done business with—men and women—usually had something crooked up their sleeve. When the people he dealt with weren't on the level, it usually left Sly serving as jail cover, getting shot at, or taking a right hook from a jealous husband he never knew existed. But despite the hell Sly had put the little priest through, Father Murphy was more steadfast than ever about helping Sly. The more treacherous the situation became, the more backbone Father Murphy displayed. Priest showed honest interest in Sly's well-being, reminding Sly of the one other person on the planet who had cared: his mother. Sly had started to genuinely care for Father Murphy.

Father Murphy got right to work by grabbing a towel from the seated man and wetting it in the sink. "Wash your face with this."

The towel quickly became soiled as Sly rubbed and scrubbed his hands and face. Sly handed the towel back to Father Murphy, who pinched it between his thumb and index finger as if it were a small animal carcass. The seated man pointed to a wicker basket heaped with used towels.

Sly set his cap next to the sink, turned a spigot on warm, and held his head under the water. He ran his fingers through his thick hair, squeezing out the excess water. Grime, blood, and small pieces of straw twirled down the drain. Father Murphy handed him another towel and Sly ruffled his head dry. Wet hair fell across his eyes when he removed the towel. He almost smiled.

Father Murphy used Sly's cap to brush dirt from his coat. When he had circled twice, Father Murphy handed the cap to Sly.

Sly dusted off the cap by slapping it against his upper thigh, flopped it on his head, and tucked his drooping locks underneath.

"I think we are ready for your lady fair."

Sly posed before the full-length mirror. The mirror seemed far more agreeable this time. Father Murphy looked Sly over him from head to toe and nodded approval.

The seated man held out his hand when Sly passed by. Father Murphy shook it. "Nice to meet you. I'm Father Patrick Murphy." Father Murphy snatched the perfume bottle off the counter. "You will need some of this." He got three solid sprays in before Sly waved off the flowery stink.

"What the hell are you doing? I'm gonna smell like a daisy."

"Better than a pungent farm animal. Now let's go find her." Father Murphy grabbed Sly by the shoulders, spun him around, and nudged him out of the bathroom. Father Murphy gave Sly two solid slaps on the back. Sly appreciated the gesture without acknowledging it.

When Sly got back to the bar, he waved Lou over. Father Murphy rushed back to his unattended Scotch, examining it to make sure no one touched it while he was gone.

"What," Lou said, not in the form of a question.

"What's her name?" Sly asked. He looked around, but did not see her. "You know, the one who keeps stopping here."

"The little blonde? That's . . . Lilith. She *loves* when guys call her Lilith." Lou walked away.

Lilith, just as radiant as before, tromped back to the bar and set down an empty tray. She rested her elbows on the bar top. Sly walked up from behind her. Lilith had one hip protruding and one foot tapping the floor. When Sly leaned on the bar, Lilith turned and stepped back so she could look him over.

"Well, congratulations. Looks like you found the washroom." Lilith sniffed. "And smells like it too." She turned away and slapped the bar. "Lou, my customers are gonna die of thirst here! Stop beatin' your gums and make with the drinks!"

"They'll die of suffocation first, because your yackin's gonna suck all the air outta the room!" Lou replied.

"Hi, I'm Sly."

Lou set four fresh drinks on Lilith's tray.

"Sly? You look about as sly as a dead fox and only half as smart. Now move aside." Her elbow felt like a railroad spike when she prodded him on her way by. Lilith turned and said, "But if you're here when

I get back, I'll let you buy me a drink."

Father Murphy poked Sly in the ribs. "Mr. Sly, I think she is really warming to you."

"Stop calling me Mister. Just call me Sly, especially in front of her."

Father Murphy winked. "I certainly will, Mr. Sly." *Hiccup.*

Lilith came storming back to the bar. "Lou, water down table eleven's drinks, they're getting a little fresh for my taste, and they ain't tipping for shit. You gotta pay for the privilege of squeezin' my ass."

"Hi, again. I'm Sly."

"Yeah, you said that. Sharp as a cue ball, I see. So, what happened to you? You look like someone set you on fire and put you out with a brick."

Sly said the first thing that came to mind. "We know Mudbone."

"Well, that would explain the smell." Lilith smiled and flipped her wrist. "I mean before, when you smelled like a pig, not *now* that you smell like a pig rolling in flowers."

Sly scowled at Father Murphy, who was hunched over his Scotch and singing to himself.

"Is he okay?" Lilith asked.

"Oh, he's fine. Little stewed is all," Sly said.

Father Murphy slapped Sly on the back. "Hello, Mr. Sly. How is your lady fair?"

"Shut up, Priest."

Father Murphy raised his eyebrows and attempted to steady himself before pulling Lilith's hand closer to kiss it. She pulled it away. "Please forgive my uncouth behavior. The drink has gotten the better of me, I'm afraid, and I'm not quite myself," Father Murphy said.

Lilith set her hands on her hips and glared at Father Murphy like he had tipped her with an IOU. Ignoring the daggers flying from Lilith's glare, Father Murphy wielded a silly grin and raised his glass. "Please think on the book of Ephesians, chapter five, verse eighteen, which tells us, *And do not get drunk with wine, for that is debauchery, but be filled with the Spirit.*" He swallowed a gulp of Scotch. "I feel *the Spirit* filling me as we speak!" He set his glass on the bar and rubbed his belly.

Sly turned away from the embarrassment that was Father Murphy and turned his attention back to his gutter-mouthed angel. Lilith was as intriguing as a nest of baby rattle snakes—small, cute, and full of venom—and Sly knew what would happen if he touched the nest.

"Hi, Lilith," Sly said.

Lilith yelled over the bar, "Lou, you are the king of all assholes, you know that?" She turned back and poked Sly. "Don't call me that. I hate when guys call me that."

"But the bartender . . ."

"He's a jerk with a capital jerk. Name's Lily—nobody's called me Lilith since the nuns in school. And I wanted to punch them too." Lily raised her balled fist.

Sly felt like a world-class chump for letting Lou dupe him. Sly's reeling mind wrestled for a change of subject. "I gotta tell you, I think you're the bee's knees."

She curtsied and flashed eyes so amorous Cupid himself may have had a hand in their creation. "Well, thanks. I'm Lily Carlson outta Brainerd, Minnesota. Where'd you blow in from?"

"I'm from St. Paul," Sly said.

"You're from St. Paul? You and your friends must be in some serious trouble if you're running *from* St. Paul. What'd you do, kidnap the priest?" She nodded and giggled toward Father Murphy who had polished off his fourth Scotch and a second verse to whatever song he was mumbling.

Sly replied with an expression blank as a freshly washed chalk board.

"Holy shit, really?" She hid a little smile behind her cupped hand and then pointed. "You're a gangster, aren't you?" She put her fingertips over her puckered lips and moved in closer. "How many jobs have you done?"

"What kind? Robbery? Kidnapping? Bootlegging? Hijacking? I about done it all."

"Do you know the Barker-Karpis gang? Baby Face Nelson? John Dillinger?"

Sly was the king rooster about ready to crow at sunrise. He stuck his chest out and steadied himself into boasting position. "I know 'em all. Even worked with a couple of 'em. And don't call Baby Face, *Baby Face*, he hates it. Matter of fact, me and Alvin Karpis did a stretch together in Stillwater. His ma brought him biscuits every day. And he'd always give them to me."

"Aw. That was very nice of him."

"Nice? The woman can't cook for shit. They were hard as rocks and tasted worse. We used them as hockey pucks out in the yard. We carried a whole bucket of 'em around with us. Sometimes we'd throw them at the guards. Almost killed one once." Sly laughed and his heart fluttered when Lily giggled in return.

Lily slid in closer. "Well, my big, strong outlaw. What are we drinking?" Even the thick cigarette smoke from the room that swirled in the air between them couldn't hide her beauty.

He lifted his drink. "Two of these?"

"Two martinis? You sure drink high class for a skid rogue. But I like your style," she said before slapping the bar three times. Priest shot up from his Scotch and looked in all directions.

"Lou! Two martinis sometime today!"

Sly felt his cheeks warm while he tried to muster the balls to send a compliment Lily's way. "Well, Lily, you are a doll."

Lily's hand fell limp at the wrist and she batted her eyelashes. "Oh, dry up. You say that to all the girls." She poked him square in the left collarbone. Her finger felt like a hatpin, and her glare was as gentle as tractor tires. "And you better be the cat's pajamas if I'm spending all this time with you instead of hustlin' tables." She set one hand on her hip. "I don't want you to think I'm chippy, I'm just a woman who knows what she wants. And you look like the kinda guy I go for—tall, dark, and bad for my reputation."

Sly blushed and studied his shuffling feet for a moment before looking her in the eyes. Although it took a lot to shake him, her eyes left him defenseless and nervous to the bone. Her sultry ways rattled him like he'd just escaped a shootout by the skin of his teeth. Gunfights certainly rattled him as well, but his instinct was to run from a gunfight, not charge right into its arms.

She nodded.

Lou set two martinis in front of them and placed a Scotch in front of Father Murphy. Lou flopped a clean bar towel over his left shoulder and leaned closer to Sly. He used his chin to point at Father. "If he gets sloppy, he's outta here."

"Cool your heels, Lou, they're with me." Lily cold-shouldered Lou and fluttered her eyelashes again causing Sly's cheeks to turn a deeper shade of frost nip. "What's the priest's story?"

Sly's mind shot straight to the paper. He began to sweat and feared opening his mouth at the risk of exposing their plot. He feared telling Lily the truth because she'd think he was cracked, or worse, believe him and want to cut herself in on the treasure, or whatever the paper led to. He swirled his martini to buy some time. "We need him for something."

"Something like a hostage in case you get in a pinch with the cops?"

"Something like that."

"You are a bad man, Sly. My mother warned me about men like you." She raised her glass and they toasted. "Lucky for you I'm a bad listener."

The martini in Lily's hand soon flushed down her gullet. Sly liked a lady who could drink—at least one who drank enough to make some bad decisions.

Suddenly Sly felt a hand on his shoulder and Eightball said, "I need you and Priest in the backroom, now." *Son of a bitch.*

"I'm kinda busy here."

Eightball looked at Lily. "We'll be right back." Sly could tell Eightball meant business. "Now," Eightball said. Eightball scanned the bar and around the room. "Where's Priest?"

Sly spotted a small, grey-haired priest spinning across the dance floor holding a drink above his head singing,

"I'll tell me ma, when I go home,
The boys won't leave the girls alone.
They pulled my hair, they stole my comb,
And that's all right till I go home.

She is handsome, she is pretty,
She's the belle of Belfast City.

"Go get him!" Eightball yelled.

Sly bumped and nudged his way through the crowd, grabbed Father Murphy, and tugged him off the dance floor. Once Sly got the wobbly priest back to the bar, the two of them followed Eightball to a rear service door.

Sly yelled to Lily before entering the backroom, "Don't go anywhere! I'll be right back!" Sly pulled Father Murphy through a swinging door with a porthole window and entered the back storage area. A few waiters and waitresses, and one cigarette girl, sat and smoked, their feet propped up on crates.

Sly tapped Eightball on the shoulder as they walked. "What do you think of that waitress, Lily? She's a dish, ain't she?"

Eightball halted and grabbed Sly by the bicep. At the abrupt stop, Father Murphy teetered in Sly's grasp. "Look, now is not the time to get dizzy with a dame," Eightball said in a low growl. "First you won't stop thinking about the paper and now you're googly-eyed over some dish. Keep your noodle on the job at hand. Why are you askin' me for advice on women, anyway? Are you cracked?"

Frustrated, Sly cut in front of Eightball while still dragging Father Murphy along. He entered a small, dark backroom whose doorway was bordered by crates of wilting vegetables. Inside sat a small wooden table, three empty rickety chairs, and one Mudbone, eerily soaked in shadow.

Sly plopped Father Murphy down before taking a seat. Sly sat next to the old man, ready to prop him up when needed.

Sly thought Mudbone resembled a ghoul in the faded light coming from the lantern on the table. As if reading Sly's thoughts, Father Murphy said, "Are you a ghost, Mr. Mudbone?" The priest wiggled his fingers. "Ooooooooooooo."

"No, but you will be if you don't shut up," Eightball said. Father Murphy held back a giggle and folded his hands on the table.

"Okay, I got a line on a good payin' job. It's like this . . ." Mudbone began.

Father Murphy sprayed saliva across the table and pounded his fist twice in a fit of laughter. "Why don't you just join our merry band? There's plenty of adventure to go around." *Hiccup.*

Mudbone perked up and appeared dangerously interested in what Father Murphy had just said. "What's he talkin' about?" He looked at Eightball. "You told me you kidnapped the priest."

"We did. That's what he's talking about," Sly answered, trying to sound convincing.

"Oh, Mr. Mudbone, there is sooooo much more to the story than that. You wouldn't believe what we have."

"Don't listen to him," Sly said. "He's stewed to the eyeballs. You can't believe a thing he says." Sly gritted his teeth, grabbed Father Murphy's knee, and pulled in close to the priest's ear. "Shut your mouth or I'll shut it for you."

Father Murphy pouted like an antsy child during a Catholic funeral. "I merely jest, Mr. Mudbone," Father Murphy said, head swaying. "I would never condemn you to the hellish fate these two are doomed to suffer. I tell them to stop following the paper, but they won't pay attention. I tell them it's not a treasure map, but do they listen?" Father Murphy shrugged and pressed his lips together and let out a long breath, again spraying spittle across the table.

"What's he talking about? What paper? What treasure?"

"Nothing. He's talking about the newspapers," Sly was having a helluva time trying to think one step ahead of a half-conscious, Scotch-filled priest.

Father Murphy waved his arms. "Hot off the presses! The Devil gets your soul. Read all about it!"

Now Sly decided to listen—as if his entire existence depended on it. Even with Father Murphy's warnings soaked in booze, they carried weight. Raw and stifling, the omens ripped across Sly leaving him cold and alone. He swore he saw the lights dim and flicker when Father Murphy spoke. Sly moved his hand closer to the pocket containing the paper, but after seeing Mudbone watching him carefully, he stopped. The last thing Sly wanted was Mudbone for a shadow.

Father Murphy said, "The Devil is right behind us. He wears black and has a demon of wrath with him."

Sly squinted. "DeLuce?" he asked under his breath. Memories of the wolf returned and Sly felt his heart striking against the inside of his ribcage.

"What'd you say?" Eightball asked Sly.

"The Devil pretends to be one of us. He lies," Father Murphy whispered. The lantern cast light across Father Murphy's cheeks, but his eyes were swallowed by shadow.

"What's that crazy old coot talkin' 'bout?" Mudbone asked.

Priest bowed his head and whimpered, "I'm sorry I drank this evening. I've let down my guard when you need my vigilance to be at its most steadfast. I am heartily sorry. The book of Peter tells us, *be sober-minded; be watchful. Your adversary the Devil prowls around like a roaring lion, seeking someone to devour.*" Father Murphy sighed. "The Devil's coming, and he will devour you. Nobody listens until it's too late." His shoulders slumped and he fell silent. Sly held his breath and waited for Father Murphy to speak. The priest started to snore.

Mudbone focused on Father Murphy. Then he looked at Sly, then Eightball, then back at Father Murphy, as if every one of them held secrets. Mudbone shook his head.

"Like I was sayin' . . . I got a job for you ofays. Eightball told me about your problem with the cops and the Mob and the gangs." He counted them out on his fingers. "You boys really did yourselves in."

Sly scolded himself about getting dizzy over Lily instead of following Eightball and Mudbone, missing a golden opportunity to eavesdrop on their conversation. He was giving up control of his heart and his paper, and that would not stand. As usual, the whole god-damned world was plotting against him.

If the man who had graciously welcomed Sly to the Chap's Room by having Sly kiss a brick wall had already told Mudbone about the paper, it wouldn't take long for Mudbone to put two and two together. The job Mudbone set up could end up being a trap or an ambush.

"Why do you boys need this money anyways? I mean, if one of you comes to me looking for work, I usually don't ask questions. But I got you," he glanced at Eightball, "and gunslinger over here," he looked at Sly, "and some crazy old drunk priest. There is something more than a little strange going on here, Eightball."

Sly could hear the wheels spinning in Mudbone's mind. Mudbone was the smartest man in the room—the smartest *conscious* man in the room—and Sly hated him for it. Throughout the day, Sly felt like he was playing tiddlywinks while everyone around him played high-stakes poker. So he attempted to get Mudbone's mind off of anything concerning Father Murphy's sermon—a good ass-kicking would do just fine, but Sly was outnumbered and unarmed.

"We sure appreciate this, Mudbone," Sly said. He glanced at Father Murphy to see if he was still knocked out. He was.

"Don't sweat it, kid. But I got to ask you some questions first," Mudbone said.

"Sure," Sly replied.

"Are you okay with robbing people?"

Sly laughed. "We kidnapped a priest. There ain't too much we won't do. Robbing people ain't a problem, been doin' it for years. But if we run around robbin' folks, they'll call the cops." Sly said.

"You hear of Peacewood Cemetery?"

"Yes. Why?" Sly asked.

Mudbone rested his palms on the table and said, "I'll get you boys some shovels."

22.

Loosen Your Tongue

MURNANE REMOVED THE HANDKERCHIEF from his pocket and wiped blood off his tongue. The iron taste of blood, however, couldn't overcome the urine stench that filled the barroom. Or the sinking sensation in his chest of what could have been, having almost left his wife a widow and his children fatherless.

DeLuce tracked footprints in the thick dust coating the floor as he paced in front of Deadeye and the dead man. He watched DeLuce put his hand on the bartender's shoulder. One bloodshot eye responded to DeLuce's touch by wielding a sharp glare. "Where's Mudbone?" asked DeLuce.

Deadeye remained silent so Murnane decided to approach the other guy. Pale, sweaty, and shaking, the dead man was ready to talk, and Murnane knew it.

Murnane would use honey to catch this fly. "What's your name?"

"Francis, but people call me Santa."

"Santa? That's a funny name. I mean, you're skinny and have brown hair. You look as much like Santa Claus as I do," Murnane said. Murnane controlled the line of questioning by establishing a rapport with the person of interest—Cop School 101.

"It's a horse thing, sir."

"Oh, you're a heroine dealer. And your junkies call you Santa. That makes sense." Murnane wasn't sure if Santa's dripping sweat was

161

caused by being scared shitless, needing a fix, or both. Whatever the case, Santa would easily sweat out a confession of some kind, Murnane just hoped it would be something useful.

Murnane positioned himself in front of Deadeye and Santa. They glanced up from their seats, looking pretty damn uncertain what Murnane's next move was going to be. Santa's brown hair stuck to his forehead in loose, sweaty curls. A look of panic crossed his face and sent Santa singing. "We don't know! Mr. Marcone was the only one who knew where to find him. Honest!"

DeLuce waved the Butcher Boys closer. "Let's get to work, fellas." Blood soaked their faces, shoulders, chests, and arms. It tinted their blond hair pink.

The floor vibrated and glass shards cracked and crunched beneath each step the Boys took.

Santa's head pivoted side to side. "Look, we're telling you the truth. That's all we know."

DeLuce bent at the waist and set his hands on his knees. "I believe you. But when someone tries to kill me, I tend to take that shit personally."

"I'd tell him something quick, Santa." Murnane eyeballed DeLuce and quickly looked back at Santa. "Trust me, he is not one with whom to fuck."

Deadeye gritted his tobacco-stained teeth and snarled. "We ain't afraid of you. I lost this eye in the Great War. Do your worst." He lifted his chin in defiance.

"Any horrors you saw during battle are nothing compared to what *they're* going to do to you." DeLuce nodded at the Boys looming just feet away. DeLuce took his hands off his knees and straightened up, holding his gun at his side.

Murnane pulled DeLuce to the side. Maybe Murnane's mild coaxing of Santa wasn't going to work and he really didn't want any more bloodshed. "Hey, if they don't know anything, let's just get outta here and try the next place. I thought you needed that paper."

"You know as well as I do they know *something*. If you're getting uneasy about this, why don't you get on the phone to the mayor and see what he's found out on his end. And remember, dial that phone real carefully. I'd hate to have you dial the wrong number and inadvertently kill your family." DeLuce held his gun up and bent his wrist as if to say *tsk tsk tsk.*

Santa blurted out, "I heard he used to work a couple nights a week at the cemetery as the night watchman."

"Which one?" Murnane asked.

"Peacewood Cemetery over on Lyndale. I swear that's all I know."

DeLuce folded his arms and his gun stuck out from the crook of his left arm. "The cemetery, huh?" He unfolded his arms and pointed his gun between Santa's eyes. "I guess we'll meet you there."

"I *said* no killing," Murnane huffed.

DeLuce repositioned his gun at Murnane. "You got a problem?"

Murnane walked to the phone and dialed the mayor's office. He kept his questions and answers muffled and kept an eye on DeLuce.

"Looks like these two were telling the truth. Mudbone was askin' around on how to collect the bounty on our guys. We were right about one of them being Eightball and he says the other guy goes by 'Sly' and they still got the priest with them. Mudbone said we can nab Sly and Eightball down at Peacewood Cemetery at midnight tonight. The mayor thinks that would be the best way to go. That way we can control the scene and contain the situation. Oh, yeah, and Mudbone wants cash on delivery."

DeLuce chuckled like he was pulling the wings off a fly and watching it crawl around. "He rats out his friends and wants to get paid for it? If they don't kill him, I will. Lousy gangsters." He removed his fedora, slicked back his hair while still holding his gun, then put his hat back on.

"We're supposed to wait at the grave marked Lorraine Swenson, so let's go," Murnane said. He looked down at Deadeye and Santa and thought how close they came to meeting their maker at the hands of the Butcher Boys. Perhaps now the killing spree would end.

"Well, how big is this cemetery? I'm not searching in the cold dark for some gravestone that might not even exist."

"When we get there we look out for lantern lights. Then we follow the lanterns right to 'em. Use your head."

DeLuce stopped and savored Deadeye and Santa. Murnane recognized the way DeLuce looked at the bound men—the same way a cat peers through the bars of a canary's cage. A sick feeling simmered inside Murnane. DeLuce's thirst for blood was far from quenched, and these two assholes were about to fill DeLuce's big frosty mug of death.

"We got plenty of time before midnight. Let's have some fun," DeLuce said.

"C'mon, knock this shit off. Let's get out of here," Murnane said.

"These bastards just tried to cut off our fingers and then kill us. You're just gonna walk away?" DeLuce held up an open hand and spread his fingers and wiggled them before making a fist and spreading them again.

Murnane stepped closer to DeLuce. "I want to get the paper back so I can get my family back. All this bullshit is a waste of time. Let's. Go."

"Why don't you relax?" DeLuce strolled around the two sweaty men tied to chairs slowly. He grinned and nodded at Marcone face down at his feet, with a midget's hand sticking out from underneath. "I think the Bible teaches us *an eye for an eye*." DeLuce kicked the leg of Deadeye's chair. "Looks like you only got one eye left to give. Maybe you should stop pissing off the wrong people."

A silence filled the bar as if everyone waited for the gates of Hell to open. Murnane grabbed DeLuce by the elbow. "C'mon. The cops are probably right outside after your fireworks show in the alley."

DeLuce ripped his arm away. "If you don't have the stomach for this, go outside and wait. And when you're out there, take a good look at the bloodstains of the three assholes you had no problem with my boys ripping apart and stuffing into garbage cans."

"Why are we wasting time when we could be after the Boss's guys? These guys are tied to chairs. They can't hurt us." The river of blood that flowed from DeLuce's victims made Murnane feel further away from his family. He floated helpless in a canoe with no paddles against the raging current.

"You mean like we were a minute ago? You think these guys were just going to scare us? I know evil."

Murnane was growing desperately short of time and patience. He pinched the bridge of his nose between his thumb and index finger and squeezed his eyes shut to keep the knot in his head from getting any tighter.

"Look, I'm not sayin' they don't deserve to get worked over, but we have bigger fish to fry. We both need that paper and maybe we can catch Eightball and his gang on their way to the cemetery and save some time." Murnane offered reason in a last ditch effort to dam the river of blood threatening to flow freely again. But it seemed like he was attempting to divert the Mississippi River by using a popsicle stick. "Forget these small-time assholes."

"Yeah, listen to the cop. You got bigger fish to fry. We ain't worth the time," Santa said.

DeLuce pocketed his gun and nodded to the Butcher Boys, who grabbed Murnane and held him firm. DeLuce used the pruners to pry open Santa's mouth, jamming them deep inside. The sound of metal scraping against teeth caused Murnane to wince. Santa thrashed and gagged. Santa's feet kicked against the hardwood floor and Murnane felt the vibrations every time. DeLuce caught Santa's wagging tongue between the blades and squeezed. Blood poured and large bubbles popped from Santa's mouth. Gurgling wails filled the room. Murnane did not struggle against the Butcher Boys. All he could do was clench his fists and turn his head away.

When Murnane looked again, DeLuce had stepped back to admire his handiwork. He held the pruners chest high allowing the viscous red liquid to drip from the pruners to his hand, down his forearm, and finally to the floor.

"Oh, I'm sorry. Were you saying something?" DeLuce asked Santa. Deluce bent down and cupped his hand near his ear. Santa convulsed and spit up blood along with broken teeth. He wavered listless in his chair, fading quickly. Murnane stared at the severed tongue on the floor and knew DeLuce wouldn't have blinked an eye if it had belonged to Mary, Jacob, or Samantha.

Murnane dropped his arms to his sides when the Butcher Boys

let him go. He cast a sympathetic glance toward Santa whose head bobbed as he passed in and out of consciousness. Murnane felt sick about the junkie's plight and the fact that Santa's demise was part of a bigger world of pain and greed. A self-perpetuating machine of a world, whose only purpose is to feed on the blood and bones of its victims—the guilty and innocent alike. The machine was well lubricated as blood continued dribbling onto Santa's lap and flowed onto the dusty floor, pooling around his severed tongue. Murnane watched the puddle increase in diameter and realized he had helped build the machine.

Murnane dropped to a crouch when he heard the shot. The gunshot flashed and cracked, snapping Santa's head back and splattering the bar in red sludge and grey brain chunks.

DeLuce then aimed his gun at Deadeye.

The second shot sent Deadeye's one good eye staring off somewhere beyond the barroom walls and a thin line of blood trickling down the contour of his nose. His head fell limp and his mouth hung open.

Murnane stood and focused on the curling smoke rising from the small burn hole in the center of Deadeye's forehead. That was the moment Murnane knew the document was nothing more than an excuse. The reason DeLuce used to justify his blood lust.

"What the fuck did you do that for?" Murnane yelled.

"I think I've already explained myself quite well. Or weren't you listening?"

Murnane surveyed the carnage in a hazy fog, like coming out of a dream and not knowing where reality starts. Two drooping men tied to chairs, bullet holes between their eyes. At their feet lay a monster, a midget, and a severed tongue. Watching over the room were two giant, blood-soaked Swedes looking like a nightmare that would make the Devil wake up in a cold sweat. The bar front decorated with a fresh coat of blood and brain—a modern art masterpiece.

Murnane surveyed the room and couldn't help but wonder how long it would be before the machine devoured him. Or perhaps it already had. The thought socked him in the gut and made a cold, dark graveyard seem like something to look forward to.

23.

Grave Apples

THE CHAIR CRASHED BACKWARD when Sly lept up.

"You want us to rob graves? What the hell's wrong with you?"

Eightball's head jerked and his mouth and eyes flew wide open in response to the ruckus. Father Murphy snored. Every one of Sly's muscles stiffened as he confronted Mudbone.

There were lines even Sly wouldn't cross. After washing up in the Chap's Room bathroom, and Lily expressing her affections for him, Sly had started to feel, well, human. Only crows and coyotes lived off dead things.

Mudbone raised his hands. "Hey, you two said you need a job where the cops won't find you. This is the best I can do on short notice. Take it or leave it. It's duck soup, a clean sneak. Dead folks aren't gonna complain about gettin' robbed."

Sly waved his hands like an umpire calling a baseball player safe. "No way. That's as low as it gets—robbing dead people. What do you think we are?"

"I think you two is in trouble. And if you need money, you ain't got a choice."

Father Murphy raised his head. "The Devil is watching and waiting. He'll catch us all soon enough," he said in a sober voice reserved for funerals.

"Shut up, Priest. You been talkin' that same bullshit all day. Go

168

back to sleep." Father Murphy followed Sly's order.

Sly set his palms on the table. "Mudbone, you got to find us something different."

"Look, those folks get buried with all their jewelry. Lots of diamonds and lots of gold too."

When Mudbone mentioned gold, Sly had a choice to make, and the paper weighed heavily into his decision. On the one hand was Sly's desperate need for money to get to Egypt. On the other was the risk involved in following the plan of a man who had everything to gain from killing Sly and his companions and taking the paper for himself. But Sly wasn't sure how much, if anything, Mudbone knew about the paper Sly carried.

"What kinda gold we talkin' about?"

"Rings, watches, fillings, sometimes even full purses, like they tryin' to take it with them!" Mudbone slapped the table top.

Sly looked at Eightball. Eightball narrowed his eyes at Sly. "You picked Pancetti clean and *he* was dead. Now you're yellow about it?"

"Don't you call me yellow, you son of a bitch."

Mudbone nodded slowly. "Well it's good to see you ofays gettin' along."

"I get along with him," Sly thumbed the air in Eightball's general direction, "a damn sight better than I can see getting along with you," Sly said to wipe the smugness right off Mudbone's face.

A careful study of Mudbone's tuxedo and fancy bow tie tickled Sly's suspicious mind. Mudbone's glossy straightened hair and perfumed stink made Sly trust the muckety-muck even less. Sly had to ask himself why a man who had it made the way Mudbone obviously did, would moonlight as a grave robber.

"If you got this swanky gig here, why do you work at the cemetery too?" Sly asked.

The question caught Mudbone off guard. He fumbled with his bow tie while clearing his throat. "Well, you know, when a man has as many hens in the hen house as I do, them hens all need to be fed. But I can't feed 'em on chicken scratch. My little chicks need gold and diamonds all around. You understand."

Sly thought maybe Mudbone wasn't so smart after all if he gave gifts to chickens. Sly *ate* chickens and gathered their eggs as a kid, and sometimes he would even clean out their coop, but . . . *Oh, he meant dames.*

"Can we get enough to buy us a boat ticket anywhere we want to go? I mean in one haul?" Eightball asked.

"I buried a couple real rich folk last week. I would think you make plenty offa them," Mudbone said.

Sly did not like, in any way, shape, or form, the idea of creeping around a graveyard at night. Let alone digging up rotting corpses and robbing them.

Eightball leaned back in his creaking chair and folded his arms. "I'll do it."

"Fine," Sly said. "I'm in." Sly gave Mudbone the same look a man gives his cheating wife before he has proof. "And I want my goddamned gun back right now."

"Don't worry. Your guns are reloaded and waiting for you up front. But you seem a little hotheaded, gunslinger, so we'll wait till I'm sure you won't use 'em on me!" Mudbone's laugh felt like a drill bit inside Sly's ears.

"But we gotta wait until around midnight," Mudbone said.

"Bullshit. Why do we gotta wait until midnight? Let's get this over with," Sly said.

Mudbone's sweat shimmered in the dim lantern light. Sly saw him rub his knuckles while searching for excuses. "Um, because, the night guard ain't done till midnight is why."

Mudbone's excuses weren't making sense. And if something didn't make sense, it probably wasn't true. Sly had picked open a scab covering Mudbone's lies and decided to pour salt on the wound. "I thought *you* were the night watchman. What kinda shit are you trying to pull?" Sly asked.

Mudbone raised his hands and his sculpted eyebrows. "Nuthin'! Eightball, tell gunslinger here I'm on the up and up. C'mon you know me better than that. How many times we get into a scrape and I helped you out? More than you can count. I wouldn't do that to you. If you want to go now, we go now. No problem." Mudbone's movements became quick and short and his voice became high-pitched like he had attended the Agony School for Liars and graduated bottom of the class. "It's gonna take me awhile to button up things here and change outta this tuxedo though."

Sly searched Eightball's face for signs of disbelief, doubt, or suspicion toward Mudbone. He saw them all in heaping doses.

Eightball uncrossed his arms and rested them on the table. "Okay, Mudbone, it's your show."

The last thing Sly wanted to admit was that Mudbone was in control. Sly felt further from the truth of Mudbone's intentions than he did from Egypt, and he had no idea how to get to either of them.

"You sure about this?" Sly asked Eightball.

Eightball didn't answer. Sly looked down at the worn table top. *Goddamn it.*

Mudbone stood like a king in his castle. "Okay, boys, go get you some drinks while I change and then we'll get you your guns back, okay? I'll meet y'all by the coat check."

Sly was in no position to argue. A drink and a gun—that was the best he could hope for at the moment. Fingers crossed that Lily would change his luck back in the bar.

Eightball got up and pulled Father Murphy off his chair. Eightball shuffled while holding Father Murphy, whose head bounced with each step. Sly stopped by the bar and Eightball continued for the door.

"Where you goin'? Don't you want your drink?" Sly asked.

"I'd rather have my gun," Eightball replied. "I'll take Priest up to the front with me and wait for Mudbone there."

Sly saw his opportunity and took it to scout for Lily. When she approached, one corner of her mouth rose and her firework eyes sparkled and popped.

"I see you couldn't live without me. But then again I have that effect on men—usually bill collectors," she said.

"Mudbone got us a job, so I gotta go. Give me your address so I can see you again. Maybe I can drop by after I'm done tonight. Maybe."

The *maybe* was meant to be coy, but Sly realized it depended on what

Mudbone really had up his sleeve.

"Sure thing, outlaw."

When Lily grabbed a pencil and scribbled on her note pad, Sly winced. "Why don't you just tell it to me? I have a real good memory." She finished scribbling on her bar pad and ripped it out and handed it to him. "Here. It's only five blocks down. Look for the green-and-white striped awning. You can't miss it."

Sly pretended to read. "I know where that is." He folded her address neatly and put it in the same pocket as the paper. If Priest wasn't too drunk to see, he'd be able to read it for Sly later.

"I have a roommate. She's a singer at the Blue Bird down the street so if you come over, don't make a lotta noise."

All Sly and the men with him had done all day was make noise. He hoped if he made it to Lily's house, the noise wouldn't follow him. "Sure thing, doll. You're all aces."

"I thought gangsters didn't like aces, because they're bad luck or something."

Bad luck to Sly was just like having a hole in his shoe on a wintery day—a constant discomfort he could do nothing about until he stole a new pair of shoes. He had always avoided cards for that very reason. Well, cards, spiders, trains, shootouts, cops, the Mob, *women*. But hopefully his luck with women was about to turn around.

"I don't know. I don't play cards much. But I'll try to stop by tonight after work."

"All right, sweetie. Now don't leave me hanging out to dry, mama needs a little sugar in her bowl."

"Oh, I don't think I'll have time to stop at the store."

Her blushing cheeks cradled the sweetest smile. "Oh, you kidder. I love a man who plays hard to get." She shrugged and bent her knees slightly only to pop right back up with the cutest little bounce.

Sly stepped backward, unable to stop smiling. "Oh, I'll be there." He nodded and then disappeared through the crowd trying to think of a store that sold sugar that late at night.

Sly made his way to the front door where Eightball held Father Murphy up against the coat check counter. The priest's sweaty face was a couple shades of green. Sly reached into the coat check room and grabbed a stylish black tweed coat and rested it on Father Murphy's shoulders. A look somewhere between gratitude and seasickness washed over the priest's face.

Mudbone, now dressed in grimy canvas coveralls, gave Father Murphy's new coat the once-over, letting the thievery slide. He then approached the wall and tapped a square in the wood paneling. A small door opened to reveal a small safe. After unlocking the safe door, Mudbone pulled out Eightball's gun and handed it to him. Eightball pocketed all his knives and his straight razor as each was returned to him. Eightball grabbed his flask and shook it. The sloshing sound caused Father Murphy to pout and place his hand over his stomach.

Sly snatched his gun from Mudbone and opened it to check if it was loaded—six chambers, each containing a .38 caliber bullet, just as Mudbone promised. Sly kept his head low but his eyes raised and fixed on Eightball. Sly clicked the chamber shut and pocketed his pistol, but kept his hand wrapped around it.

Once outside Mudbone said, "I'll drive." Sly jumped in the passenger side of Mudbone's Lincoln Model L—damn swanky—and let Eightball suffer though riding in the backseat with Father Murphy. Sly put the odds at fifty-fifty that the priest would either yap the whole time or puke. Either way, Eightball would take the brunt of it.

The starter pedal squeaked when Mudbone pushed it in. The monstrous engine fought the cold and gasped and moaned for life before turning over.

Sly watched in silent contempt as they passed buildings and light posts along the icy nighttime streets. Mudbone pointed when the car passed a dark alley with an unattended burning barrel. "That's the Broken Bone. Used to work there. It used to be a real nice place, but nobody goes there since Marcone took it over and made it his office."

Sly turned and tapped Eightball on the knee and nodded toward a St. Paul police car parked on the street. DeLuce and Murnane must be hot on his trail and closing fast. Sly rubbed his neck, trying not to feel the rope burn as the noose tightened.

His thoughts bounced among DeLuce and Murnane shooting at

him, Lilith's tight bustier, and the paper tucked inside his pocket. The paper's velvet warmth felt soothing against his fingertips. The sensation of DeLuce and Murnane closing in on him faded and the comfort Father Murphy had provided throughout the day put Sly at ease better than a warm bed or his mother's embrace.

Comfort was replaced by a knot in Sly's stomach as the Lincoln neared Peacewood Cemetery. Every weathered headstone served as a reminder that death comes to us all. He especially didn't want to be reminded of that fact when he was at the beginning of a journey that would change his life forever—in a *good* way.

The paper warmed and his heart chilled. To hell with Father Murphy and his Bible bullshit—*the cursed paper found you*. Goose bumps covered Sly's arms and he shuddered to shake them off. He had to raise the money to get to Egypt and that was that. If it took robbing the dead to get to the treasure, then so be it.

The Lincoln slid to a halt outside the back entrance to the cemetery. The headlights shone across a thick, rusty chain and a heavy iron padlock on a wrought-iron gate with bent bars and rusted hinges. Mudbone left the car and removed a large key from his pocket. He wrenched his whole body in an effort to dislodge all the ice and rust fighting against him. The lock clunked open and the chain rattled against the bars as it slid away and formed a pile on the ground. Mudbone dragged the chain aside, got back in the car, passed through the gate, then leaped out again to close the gate behind them.

"He didn't lock the gate. That's a bad sign," Sly said to Eightball. When Mudbone got back in Sly asked, "Why didn't you lock the gate?"

"In case we gotta get away fast. You don't want to be trapped in here, do you?"

"Or maybe you're expecting company."

"Eightball knows I wouldn't sell you out. Right?" Mudbone turned to glance at Eightball in the back seat. Eightball sat in silence.

Father Murphy rested his head on the seatback. His hefty snores shook the windows.

Mudbone drove up the winding drive lined with towering elms, eroding tombstones, and granite angels.

"They buried Old Lady Swenson last week. It was a big shindig. All sorta people, so you know she had lotsa money." His headlights brushed across a large, polished grave marker and a small shack about twenty feet away between two gnarled oaks.

"What's that?" Sly asked.

"It's the shed where we keep all the tools for diggin' graves and keepin' up the place." Mudbone pulled out his pocket watch. "It's ten forty-five so let's get diggin'. I'll grab us some pickaxes and shovels out of the shed."

Father Murphy snored in the backseat.

"What do we do with him?" Eightball asked.

Sly saw the old priest curled up in the back seat wrapped in a warm coat looking like a hibernating animal. "Leave him. Best place for him," Sly said.

Mudbone walked to the shack, twisted the key in the rusty padlock, and swung open the door. Sly entered behind Eightball and Mudbone. Mudbone lit a gas lantern and blew out the stick match. He lifted two pickaxes off the wall and handed them to Sly and Eightball.

Sly examined the tool with wonderful thoughts of planting the sharp end deep into Eightball's dull head. Sly tightened his grip. Visions of blood pooling across Eightball's smelly, matted hair and dripping down his ugly, broken face warmed Sly better than hot chocolate ever could. Spittle foamed at the corners of Sly's mouth in anticipation.

Eightball faced Sly. Eightball's glassy eyes looked like he was probably plotting the exact same substitute for a nice hot chocolate.

"Let's dig," Sly said.

Mudbone picked up the lantern and a shovel and led Sly and Eightball from the shack. Sly and Eightball huddled around Mudbone, who lowered the lantern enough to illuminate Lorraine Swenson's name engraved on a freshly polished headstone. The grave was so fresh that the headstone still lay on its back next to Lorraine's plot. "Here she is. Let's get diggin'."

Sly thrust his pickaxe into the frozen ground, but made only a small dent. He made sure to face Eightball and stay out of his swinging range. Eightball's first swing tore out a small chunk of dirt.

"It's gonna be tough diggin' till we get below the frost line," Eightball said.

Sly raised the pickaxe over his head ready to thrust it deep into the hard, frozen ground. Mudbone yelled, "Wait!"

Sly let his pickaxe go limp and asked, "What is it?"

"There's something I should tell you. Watch out for grave apples. If you hit one of those, you're dead where you stand."

With his streak of bad luck, Sly's date with Lily might be postponed indefinitely. Peacewood Cemetery was making room for one more soul.

24.

The Last Place You Want

to Lie Down

SLY'S KNUCKLES TURNED WHITE as he gripped the pickaxe. The night air froze his ears and bit his cheeks and burned his lungs. The cemetery on a frozen winter's night felt worse than lying awake waiting for Agony to come home from a drinking binge. But his shitty feeling worsened when Mudbone warned them about hitting something he called a *grave apple*.

"What the hell is a grave apple?" Sly asked.

Mudbone smiled. "Nuthin' to worry 'bout. But thought I'd warn ya just the same. Sometimes rich folk bury all kinds of booby traps with the caskets to keep out ..." Mudbone's voice faded into a whisper as his round, glossy eyes scanned Sly and Eightball from head to toe.

"Grave robbers," Sly finished. "That's just swell. You're telling us this thing is booby-trapped?"

"Chances are she's not, but there's still a chance."

Sly pointed his pickaxe at Eightball, "Goddamn you. I shoulda killed you on the train when I had the chance. Now you got us diggin' up booby-trapped dead folks." Sly lowered the pickaxe and started pacing. "You're about as useless as chicken shit on a pump handle. I should be in a nuthouse for listening to you."

"Now hold on, chances are nuthin' will happen. And there's lotsa loot to be had, I'm tellin' ya," Mudbone said.

"So, what *is* a grave apple?" Eightball asked.

"It's like a big hollowed-out cannonball chock-full of gunpowder. They put a metal cover on top when they bury it so's the gunpowder don't get wet. When you hit it, it sparks underneath and triggers the gunpowder, and *boom!* You're lucky if half of you makes it outta the hole. The metal cover makes the whole thing kinda look like an apple, so's I call 'em *grave apples.* And the apple part is what breaks into pieces and slices you up real good."

Sly's mistrust for Mudbone showed plainly across his face. "And maybe you buried some here yourself hoping you'd have the opportunity to use 'em."

"Just keep your eyes and ears peeled and be quick on your feet. As soon as you hit something, jump outta the hole," Mudbone said.

Sly plunged his pickaxe into the ground. *Goddamn it.*

Sly worked in tandem with Eightball, tapping out the same rhythm railroad workers do when pounding spikes. Sly and Eightball hacked chunks of frozen ground and Mudbone scooped them out using a shovel. Below the frost line the digging became easier. They traded their axes for shovels and made faster progress.

After the hole swallowed Sly up to his waist, his back ached and his arms burned and wilted like rubber bands. His mind and muscles were too weary to concern himself with grave apples or anything else; he just wanted out of that hole and into Lily's nice warm bed. *Can't forget the chicken feed. No. Sugar. That's it.*

Ground was at eye level. Sly kept pitching dirt and rock and feeling every scoop in his arms and back. Mid-heave, he heard Eightball strike something solid and metallic.

A jolt of fear shot straight up Sly's ass, sending him half way out of the hole before Mudbone yelled, "Get out!"

Sly scrambled from the hole, clutching at rocks and grasping exposed roots. The explosion shot earth and rock twenty feet in the air. The blast pushed him up and outward. He bounced on his stomach, knocking the wind out of him. He rolled onto his side, curled into a ball, and covered his head as the dirt and rocks rained down. High-pitched ringing filled his ears.

Sly opened his eyes just as a falling shovel stabbed the loose dirt inches from his face. Sly sat up when the dirt and rocks stopped pelting him. He removed his flat cap and pounded it against a headstone. "Goddamn it!" He knelt and aimed his pistol and began to preach the merits of a world without Mudbone. "He tried to kill us! You saw it, plain as day. He tried to kill us."

Mudbone rolled onto his hands and knees, coughing. "I just dig the holes, I don't fill 'em back in. That's when they put in them grave apples. Have mercy!" He crawled a few feet and slammed into the next tombstone over.

"Put the gun away. He's had plenty of chances to kill usss. Plus, if he really wanted usss gone, he wouldn't a told us about them grave apples in the first place. Sssettle down," Eightball said. The statement made Sly aware of Eightball's whereabouts, only a few feet away. Unfortunately, Eightball had not taken a big bite of the grave apple—or vice versa.

Sly brushed the dirt from his coat and shook the earth from his hair. The moonlight did what it could to provide some light between the drifting clouds. The lantern lay on its side next to the hole having been knocked over by the explosion and did most of the work holding off the darkness. He inspected his gun by the lantern light. The gun looked able enough to put six wonderful holes in Mudbone.

Mudbone cowered against the headstone, keeping his hands raised. "I didn't think we'd hit any is all. Honest."

"What the hell was that? Is that what you were talking about?" asked Eightball.

"Yeah, just like I said." Sly scorned Mudbone, who picked dirt out of his ear using a few deep twists of his pinky finger. Mudbone then blew muddy snot into a lily-white handkerchief he pulled from under his coveralls. "And they usually don't go off at all," he said.

"Well this one did, you son of a bitch," Sly said through clenched teeth. "What other tricks you got up your sleeve?"

"Actually . . ." Mudbone said.

"Actually what?" Sly asked. He dropped his pistol to his side, but squeezed the grip like it was Mudbone's neck.

"I should probably mention about the spring guns too."

"Are you shitting us? 'Spring guns' and 'grave apples'? I smell a rat." The graveyard surrounding Sly was beginning to feel more like home by the minute. The broad side of his .38 served as an adequate head scratcher until he figured out what to do next.

"He was in the hole, Sly. He coulda blowed up too. I've known him a long time and he ain't no rat," Eightball said.

It was obvious to Sly that Eightball was a horrible judge of character. If the Devil had stolen Eightball's car, Eightball would have Jesus Christ arrested for the crime.

Mudbone raised his hands toward Sly. "Wait, don't you see? If it's booby trapped there must be something inside worth protectin'. We can't lose our heads now, we gotta keep diggin'!"

Sly got to his feet and paced—being sure to stomp while he did so. Following Mudbone was becoming more of a risky proposition by the shovelful. "Tell us about the spring guns."

"I got some stashed in the tool shed along with some grave apples I dug up that didn't go off. We find 'em sometimes when we gotta dig up a body to move it or for the cops to look at. Open the shed and see for yourself."

"Soon as I turn my back on you, you'll put a bullet in it. Start talking," Sly said.

Eightball watched from a few feet away, but as usual, said nothing. The stupid, helpless look on his face spoke loud and clear, though. Eightball didn't trust Mudbone either; he just didn't have the balls to say it out loud.

"It's a spring-loaded shotgun they rig in with the body just before burial. When you open the casket, a gun pops up and it pulls a trip wire attached to the trigger. They can get you anywhere from your balls to your head. Some of my guys have been hit by 'em, and I've had a couple close calls myself, believe you me. They're a lot more common than the grave apples because more folks can afford 'em. That's why I pry open the top," Mudbone stabbed at the air with his shovel to demonstrate, "and stand off to the side—safer that way."

"Thanks for the lesson. Now dig the rest of the shit outta that hole and open the casket," Sly said and rested his bent elbow on his pickaxe.

"Wait—me? Why me? This is you all's job, not mine!"

"That's before I almost got my balls blown off. Plus I can't hold a shovel when I got a gun in my hand." His thumb pulled the hammer back slowly. *Click.*

Eightball drew his pistol and held it on Mudbone. "Start diggin'," he said.

Sly was relieved that he and Eightball were together on this rather than he being the odd man out. Eightball set the lantern upright at the edge of the hole to finalize the majority's decision.

"Toss your iron over here, butt first," Eightball said.

After setting his hands on his hips and letting out a frustrated huff, Mudbone dug underneath his coveralls and tossed his gun at Eightball's feet.

Mudbone picked up his shovel and used it to hoist himself up, and shook his head. "Well, ain't this some shit."

"Take the lantern down with you. We don't need to draw attention." Sly handed the lantern to Mudbone with a whole lot of satisfaction.

Mudbone lowered himself into the hole and dirt started spurting out of it, one angry scoop at a time. He stopped every few scoops to peek out of the hole and look across the graveyard.

"What are you looking for?" Sly asked, trying to see why Mudbone kept checking their surroundings.

"Nuthin'. I ain't lookin' for nuthin'."

Mudbone stabbed the crumbling dirt and heaved. He hit wood and began clearing off the top of the casket. "What you boys really runnin' from? What's this all about?" he asked.

"Ask Sly, he's the one who's got it."

"Shut your mouth, Eightball."

"What's the big deal? He's down in a grave and we got guns on him, what's he gonna do?"

"Because it's none of his goddamned business, and I don't trust him. He's up to something, I know it," Sly said.

"We need money to get someplace far away," Eightball said to Mudbone.

"Like where? California?"

"A lot farther than that," Eightball said.

"Hey, enough," Sly said. He peered down into the hole. "Open it and toss the loot up here. And make it snappy."

Mudbone crawled over the casket and used his hand to sweep away the dirt. He took a moment to stare down at the lid and lick his lips.

"Stand back now, fellas. This gets damn ripe." Mudbone pulled out his handkerchief and placed it over his nose. "These dead folks swell up like a fat wood tick and sometimes they even explode. It's been a couple weeks, give or take, so she's about prime to pop." He picked up his shovel and stabbed it into the wood casket. A small geyser of liquids hissed and bubbled up and then quickly subsided. He leaned away from the casket and pried it open.

Every one of Sly's killings had one thing in common: he never stuck around to watch his victims become stiffs. Once the heart stopped pumping and blood stopped pooling, Sly was in the next county. He had never seen a decomposing body before. Sly didn't really want to see—but he couldn't look away.

As the casket lid creaked open, dirt and pebbles tumbled across the rich wood, and the stink hit Sly square in the nose like an axe handle. He spun away and fell to his knees onto the fresh dirt pile, covering his nose and with the crook of his arm. He tasted the corpse juice misting through the air and filling his mouth. He fought against three strained retches, using every ounce of energy not to spew the warm, thick vomit that was burning his throat. Sly heard Eightball gagging a few feet away.

Mudbone laughed and called out from inside the grave, "Yeah, you folks ain't used to that smell. I gotta admit, I usually stick mothballs up my nose before I open up a casket I suspect might be juicy, but you ofays were so hot to trot to get out here, I clean forgot 'em."

Mudbone puffed out his cheeks and exhaled. "See? We got lucky.

No spring guns. But lord, she is a rotten one."

Sly inched his head and shoulders out over the open grave for a better look-see.

"Grab the loot and let's go. Come on, I'm freezing!" Sly said.

Mudbone crouched and held the lantern just above the old lady's body. The lantern rocked back and forth, causing Lorraine, Mudbone, the open casket, and the dirt walls to swim in shadow.

Then the light shone across Lorraine's bluish-grey face. Thick yellow liquid bubbled from her eyes, nose, and mouth, and her skin was swelled as if stung by an entire beehive. Sly saw her eyes spring open. Her mouth formed into a scream before she vomited green bile that splashed across his face and into his mouth.

Sly fell backward, rubbed his face, spit, and coughed uncontrollably. When he opened his eyes, Eightball was looking down at him.

"What the hell are you doing?" Eightball asked.

Hitting the ground had shaken Sly out of the nightmare. He examined himself for green bile. But after wiping his face, his hands were clean. He searched the ground for oozing liquids, finding only muddy footprints in the snow.

"I musta tripped. Grab that shit and let's get outta here," Sly said. He stiffened his back and searched the graveyard for any signs of movement before crawling back over to check Mudbone's progress in the grave.

Mudbone moved in closer and nodded. "Well dip my balls in sweet cream and squat me in a barn full of kittens! Lookie what we got here. I told you. I told you we'd get something good."

Sly and Eightball crouched over the hole for a closer look. "What? What is it?"

Gold rings covered in sparkling diamonds shimmered in the lantern light. A large pearl necklace caught Sly's eye. That would fetch a pretty price from a fence he knew over on Wabasha Avenue. When Mudbone lifted the necklace, a trail of yellow slime came with it. Lorraine's skin had decayed to gelatin, which made tearing her fingers off and ripping the earrings through her earlobes effortless. He tossed the jewelry up to Eightball who caught it and flung as much slime off as he could before stuffing everything into his pockets.

Eightball raised his hand to his nose and gagged. He got down on the ground and rubbed dirt and snow all over his hands trying to rub the smell off.

Snow crunched beside Sly. Father Murphy had snuck up to the edge of the hole without being noticed. Sly jumped and Eightball reacted by spinning and drawing his gun.

"You want us to shoot you, Priest? What the hell are you thinkin'?" Sly asked.

Steam shot from Father Murphy's flared nostrils as he loomed, lit from below by the lantern in the grave.

The memory of Agony coming at Sly with a lit cigarette and bourbon on his breath couldn't match the fear Sly felt looking up at Father Murphy. The once cheerful little priest who couldn't stop smiling now looked like Death was climbing up his back. Father Murphy saw something—*something*.

"We got a book here too," Mudbone called out from below.

Father Murphy bowed his head toward Mudbone. "It's the Bible. Pick it up," he said. He spoke in the same grim manner a mother uses to warn her children not to play with dead animals.

The Bible rested between Old Lady Swenson's dress and the inside of the casket. As Mudbone lifted the Bible, Father Murphy said, "Read the marked passage."

"But how did you know? . . ." Mudbone said.

"Open it and read."

"What for?" Sly asked. Impatience was knocking, driving Sly to grab the jewels and get the hell out of there. But the change in Father Murphy was much more than a hangover. And whatever had brought the look of death to Father Murphy's face demanded Sly's full attention.

"Read it!" Father Murphy yelled.

Mudbone fumbled through the pages until he reached the marked passage. "It's the book of Mark, chapter six, verse nineteen," Mudbone said in a quaking voice. *"Do not lay up for yourselves treasures on earth, where moth and rust destroy and where thieves break in and steal; but lay up for yourselves treasures in Heaven, where neither moth nor rust destroys and where thieves do not break in and steal. For where your treasure is, there your heart will be also. The lamp of the body is the eye. If therefore your eye is good, your whole body will be full of light. But if your eye is bad, your whole body will be full of darkness. If therefore the light that is in you is darkness, how great is that darkness! No one can serve two masters; for either he will hate the one and love the other, or else he will be loyal to the one and despise the other. You cannot serve God and Mammon. "*

Mudbone stopped reading. His hands trembled as he closed the Bible.

"This is your final warning. Relinquish your quest for answers here and now. If you proceed, I will not be able to save you," Father Murphy said across the darkness to any and all graveyard inhabitants.

"What the hell is that all about? And what's a *mammon*? Has that old priest got a screw loose?" Mudbone asked. He set the Bible back in the coffin as if his fate depended on the tenderness of his touch.

"Never mind him, he's still drunk as a monkey," Sly said.

"The Devil is closer than you know. He wants the paper *and* your souls," Father Murphy said.

Sly noticed Father Murphy had not stopped staring into the darkness. "What the hell are you lookin' at?" Sly asked.

"There is a light coming toward us, and the Devil carries it."

25.

Anyone for Cornered Rat?

SLY SEARCHED THE DARKNESS for any sign of light. Storefronts, street-lights, headlights, all lit up the distance, but Sly could not see anyone closing in on them. The warmth of the Chap's Room had long worn off and the sweat on his brow was turning to ice. The corpse mist had combined into a rancid slime that clung deep inside his nose reminding Sly that this night would stay with him long after he left the grave-yard—*if* he left it.

The gun in Sly's hand offered him little comfort.

"Are you sure the light's coming at us, Priest?" Sly asked.

"Could be a street lamp shinin' off a headstone or a patch of ice," Mudbone said from down in the grave, sounding real interested in what was happening. "Can't be an auto, 'cause we woulda heard the engine by now."

Movement in the hole took Sly's attention away from the dark-ness. He watched Mudbone jump twice, attempting to see out of the hole. Mudbone's round head popped above ground for good after the third jump when he climbed up and sat on the edge of the open coffin lid.

"Priest is right," Eightball said. "Someone's comin'. Put the light out."

Mudbone handed the lantern to Sly, who doused it. Now Sly could see the approaching light. A single lantern moved slowly and stayed low to the ground, swaying from side to side.

Mudbone grabbed some roots and pulled himself up onto the ground, shimmying along on his belly before getting to his feet.

Sly squinted into the dark. "Can you see who it is? How many of 'em are there?" Sly asked Father Murphy, who did nothing to acknowledge Sly's questions. Sly didn't need an answer. He already knew the light drawing closer belonged to DeLuce and Murnane.

The moon emerged from behind thick clouds again, its light bouncing off the snow and showing off the bare, twisted branches overhead. Sly tried to use the light of the full moon to see the people approaching, but couldn't make out his pursuers.

Sly could, however, clearly smell Eightball right next to him. The shower Eightball had taken at the Boss's office earlier in the day had fallen victim to Eightball's natural odors.

Eightball and Father Murphy flanked Sly and joined him in searching the graveyard.

"Too dark to tell how far off they are. I say we pack up our shit and get the hell out of here," Sly said—feeling very much like the man in charge.

Sly heard some movement behind him. "Hey, fellas . . ." Mudbone said. Sly began to turn and noticed Eightball turning fast. A shovel cracked off Eightball's sternum, knocking him to the ground. His gun hit the packed snow and pin-wheeled on its side and skittered away, stopping close to a nearby oak.

Sly twisted around and raised his gun, but Mudbone moved quicker, swatting his shovel against Sly's wrist. Sly yelped and watched his pistol tumble into the open grave.

Mudbone swung the lethal garden tool at Sly's head, close enough that Sly felt the breeze the spade created. Sly used his forearm to partially block the thrusting shovel. The glancing blow stung and landed with enough force to drive Sly backward, causing him to trip on the dirt mound and fall. Mudbone closed in, clearly intending to send Sylvester Hobbs straight to Hell earlier than scheduled.

Click. Click. The sound of a misfiring gun drew Sly's attention. Eightball aimed his pistol squarely at Mudbone and pulled the trigger.

Click. Click. No cracks, no flashes, no bullets. No molten lead to wipe the grin off Mudbone's face. Eightball looked angry and confused as he examined his pistol by pale moonlight.

Mudbone dropped his shovel and picked up the gun Eightball had relieved him of earlier. Mudbone laughed and stepped closer to Sly. "I had my boys file down your firing pins while you were in the bar. Your guns are as useless as you are. My gun's the only one that works, just like it should be."

When Sly realized Mudbone was taking aim at him, Sly tried to stagger to his feet. The loose dirt kept Sly from gaining a foothold and he flopped flat on his ass. Now Mudbone had ample opportunity to punch Sly's ticket to Kingdom Come.

Father Murphy lunged out of the darkness, hitting Mudbone harder than an angry linebacker. Father Murphy drove his shoulder into Mudbone, knocking a possibly deadly shot off target and knocking Mudbone to the ground. Mudbone's hand smacked against a rock and his gun skid out of reach.

Fists made of bone and fury balled up at Father Murphy's sides as he panted over Mudbone. The priest's body quaked, his chest raised and lowered, and steam fumed from his flared nostrils. *Crazy bastard thinks he's Tunney!*

Mudbone chose the weapon nearest to him. He swung the shovel across his body, aiming for Father Murphy. A whooshing sound cut the night air followed by the clanking of metal against frozen ground.

Dirt and ice peppered Sly's mouth as his teeth ground and crunched against sand and pebbles, enraging him further. Mudbone got to his feet the same time Sly did.

"I knew you were a rat," Sly said. Sly planted his feet. "Oh, I've been waitin' for this, asshole. Come and get it." Sly waved Mudbone closer, ready to dance. Mudbone wielded his tool-turned-weapon and balanced his stance. Sly circled Mudbone intending to use every weapon at his disposal, including dirty fingernails, to gouge the life out of the rat-faced son of a bitch.

Mudbone drew back the shovel and charged. From Sly's right, Eightball jumped in and drove his heel into Mudbone's knee. A loud pop and a pain-filled groan dropped Mudbone to one knee. Mudbone let go of the shovel. He stared at the ground and appeared to try to figure out just where his plan had gone wrong. Mudbone strained to his feet and looked his predicament right in the eyes.

Confidence drained from Mudbone as he saw Sly, Eightball, and Father Murphy circling him. Mudbone's first move was to punch Father Murphy, knocking him flat. Father Murphy whimpered and rubbed an open palm against his ailing chin. Mudbone seemed to gain a little confidence. Sly planned to squish that growing confidence, like he would a spider.

Sly understood Mudbone's strategy to take out the weakest threat. While Father Murphy was busy listening to *chin music*, Mudbone could choose his next target from only two remaining opponents and plan his next move.

Two weapons lay on the ground near Mudbone: the shovel and Mudbone's gun. The pistol was a few feet farther away from Mudbone, so Sly figured Mudbone would go for the shovel instead. Sly charged in that direction. Mudbone clutched the handle first, leaving Sly grasping at air. Mudbone walloped Sly across the jaw, landing one well-placed backhander.

A shovel slapped a hell of a lot harder than any dame Sly had ever insulted. The world spun as if someone had thrown him inside a Minnesota Thirteen barrel and kicked it down a hill. Sparkling stars filled his vision and the left side of his face burned and swollen. He rolled and moaned and checked for blood. Sly saw Father Murphy still on the ground. Sly wasn't as bad off as the old priest, but was still too dizzy to stand, so Sly could only watch.

Mudbone faced the only man left who could stop the rampage: Eightball.

"Why are you doing this?" Eightball asked, sounding wounded.

"Why you think, you dumb fucker?"

"Because of your brother? You told me we were square on that. You said you hated him."

"I did. He was an asshole. But so are you." Each man slid two steps to his right. Eightball took a step forward.

"You stay back," Mudbone said. The shovel sliced the air. "I ain't gonna let you get close enough to hit me."

"Then why? I thought we were partners," Eightball said.

"For the money of course. You know how much those ofays want for your ugly ass? More than I make in a year! Which got me thinkin' you boys must have somethin' real important. So I figured I'd just take it and run. I had you dig a hole, shoot you, and leave you for the cops to find. But not before takin' whatever it is you all so secretive about."

Sly rattled the stars and cobwebs from his head. The bash to his noggin knocked something into place and Sly was able to put two and two together. *Mudbone had turned them in.*

"You called DeLuce," Sly said in a wheezing moan.

Mudbone laughed. "You dumb sons a bitches still don't know how much trouble you in, do ya? The word on you two is that anyone who wants to cash in has to call the mayor of St. Paul hisself. You boys made some damn powerful, not to mention good-payin', enemies!"

Sly thought about the St. Paul squad car they passed on the way to the cemetery. The car belonged to Murnane all right. DeLuce had to be with him too. Everything fit perfectly.

"You double-crosssssing ssson of a bitch!" Eightball blurted.

"You just figurin' this all out now? You're dumb, boy—real dumb."

Eightball cocked his fist and charged at the same time Mudbone swung. The shovel clanked off Eightball's stocking cap, knocking him over.

As Sly fought to crawl onto his hands and knees, Mudbone kicked Sly in the ribs hard enough to cave in a lesser man's chest. Sly was on his back again. Mudbone planted his feet and positioned himself over Sly, ready to drive the shovel's edge straight through Sly's neck. Sly almost prayed, but having Death stare him in the face made it hard to think of the words.

The deep, meaty sound of tearing flesh and cracking bone were followed by a liquid gasp.

Mudbone's shoulders jerked back and his eyes bulged. His hands remained in the air as the shovel dropped away. A gurgling sound made Sly think Mudbone was choking on his own blood. When Sly looked closer he saw the point of a bloody pickaxe protruding through Mudbone's sternum. *Couldn't happen to a nicer guy.*

Mudbone's knees thumped against the frozen earth. He fell onto his side, his bloodshot eyes staring into the afterlife.

Sly took his eyes off Mudbone and saw Eightball let go of the pickaxe handle. Eightball panted and let his exhausted arms dangle.

Eightball shuffled over and helped Father Murphy to his feet while Sly lifted himself off the ground. Sly felt every bruised muscle, cut, aching bone, and now, his swollen face, warning him to stay alert at all costs—the paper depended on it. Valuable time had been wasted during the skirmish, allowing Murnane and DeLuce to close in. The lantern light was growing brighter.

"We gotta get outta here," Sly said. He took a few relieved breaths and brushed the muddy snow off his clothes.

Eightball rubbed the lump on his head.

"That blow should have knocked you out cold," Sly said.

Eightball patted his hair. "Ain't no shovel gonna get through this mangy mess."

"He'd been planning this ever since we showed up at the Chap's Room. The rat-shit son of a bitch," Sly said. The brawl had kicked the shit out of Sly, body and soul. But as the light closed in, the time for *I told you so's* would have to wait.

Sly searched his pockets in a frenzy. When the soft paper rubbed against his knuckles, he clutched it tight for reassurance. The paper made him feel safe until he realized his useless gun was still down in the grave. The only working pistol was in the snow—and up for grabs.

Sly scanned the snow for Mudbone's gun. When Eightball crossed Sly's field of vision it looked pretty damn apparent Eightball was doing the same thing. The search stopped abruptly when Sly found the gun.

Father Murphy cupped the gun in his hands as if he held a wounded baby bird.

Sly stepped slowly and carefully, afraid of what the crazy old priest would do if Sly made any sudden moves. Sly approached him as if trying to catch a butterfly with his bare hands.

"C'mon, Priest. Hand it over," Sly said in his most pleasant voice.

"No, over here. You don't want that nasty gun, Priest," Eightball said as he approached from the opposite side, his outstretched hand begging for the gun—every step landing so softly they wouldn't crack eggshells.

Father Murphy started to cry. Tight wrinkles formed across his forehead and mouth as his eyes welled. His gaze rebounded from Eightball to Sly and back again. Father Patrick Murphy looked absolutely helpless, despite the fact he held all the power in his palms.

"Time's runnin' out, Father Murphy. Hand me the gun and I'll protect you from the bad guys," Sly said, nice and gentle.

"Don't listen to him, Priest. He's been ordering you around all day. I'm the one who's been taking care of you. Give *me* the gun," Eightball said.

Sly took a slow, gentle step. Eightball did the same. Father Murphy pulled his elbows in tight, shrinking into himself. When Sly got about two feet from the priest, Sly lunged. So did Eightball.

Father Murphy shrieked and flung the pistol over his head into the night air just as Sly and Eightball crashed into him.

Sly tried to see where the gun had gone, but couldn't get a fix on it. The gun, like his control over Eightball, was lost.

"Well, you sure fucked us, Priest," Sly said.

"Please, Mr. Sly, we have to run now," Father Murphy said, followed by a sniffle. "They are here and they want the paper. You can't let them get it. Should we hide in there?" Father Murphy asked as he pointed at the tool shed.

The surrounding shadows harbored men who were willing to get bloody. Men who carried guns and knew how to use them. Men who knew more ways to hide dead bodies than Sly knew how to create them.

The tiny shed was built from nothing more than wood planks held together by a lightweight timber frame. Sly's desperation was running hard and time was running out. "Guess you're right, Priest. Let's make our stand in the shed."

"Are you crazy? That's the first place they'll look," Eightball said.

"Look, we'll never make it to one of those mausoleums. Plus, they don't know the tool shed's full of grave apples and spring guns. They won't expect that," Sly said.

"I thought Mudbone said they didn't work," Eightball said.

"He said the grave apples were duds they dug up, but the spring guns might still work."

"What if there ain't no shells?"

"You got a better idea? Murnane probably called in every department from every nearby county. They most likely got us surrounded. If we run for it, they got us for sure. Shed's our only chance. We can buy some time and maybe see how many guys we're up against."

Eightball looked sour, but nodded.

Sly guided Father Murphy by the elbow and followed Eightball toward the shed a few yards away. Once Eightball and Father Murphy were inside, Sly shut the rickety door and locked the slide-bolt.

Lily's bed never seemed so far away.

Sly could see, through a crack in the wall, a pinpoint of light weaving between the winding group of eroding tombstones that followed the slopes of the cemetery. The light swayed and threw shadows across naked tree branches that resembled arms ready to snatch unsuspecting passersby.

Labored breaths and a squeaking lantern handle announced Murnane and DeLuce's arrival.

The lantern DeLuce carried was the only light Sly had to see by because the clouds had swallowed the full moon. He watched Murnane and DeLuce study the tombstones at their feet, stopping to read the names and examine the disturbed ground. The men drew close to where Mudbone's double-crossing carcass had fallen. The shiny brass buttons on Murnane's uniform glinted in the soft light when he knelt next to the body.

"This must be Mudbone. I told you they would kill him," DeLuce said.

Murnane took a closer look. "Yep, that's him all right."

"They couldn't have gotten far. The blood's still steaming." DeLuce reached down and touched something on Mudbone's face. "Eye's still warm and moist."

Sly blinked quickly to keep from feeling like a finger pushed against his eye.

Murnane bent down and rifled through Mudbone's pockets. Murnane stopped and pulled out something small and flat and held it up to the light.

"What is it?" DeLuce asked.

"A matchbook from someplace called the Chap's Room—probably where he worked. Could be a solid clue."

Murnane studied the snow. "Looks like there was a hell of a struggle. Bring the light over here more and I'll see if I can tell which way they ran off," Murnane said.

"Why don't you have a flashlight?" DeLuce asked.

"You want to run back to St. Paul and get it, asshole? You didn't really give me any time to gather supplies, remember?"

DeLuce did not reply.

Murnane examined the ground and the story it told. Sly knew Murnane's well-deserved reputation as a hardened cop. Word throughout the blind pigs was Murnane could track a bird through a blizzard. Sly's bad luck had just turned to *no* luck.

"Look," DeLuce said. Sly felt his luck draining away when DeLuce pointed at Sly's gun in the grave. "Go get it."

"They can't have more than a minute head start, let's go after them," Murnane said and started walking toward the shed.

"Get the gun." DeLuce pointed into the grave. His tone could have carved an epitaph into granite.

Sly watched Murnane climb down to retrieve the pistol. As Murnane climbed out, DeLuce extended his hand to pull him up, but Murnane smacked it out of the air. DeLuce chuckled. Apparently Murnane and DeLuce got along just as well as Sly and Eightball. Murnane pocketed the useless pistol.

"Keep an eye on those guys. I'm gonna look for guns," Sly whispered to Eightball. Sly peered out the crack once more before feeling through the darkness and finding a dusty sheet. Ever so slowly, Sly pulled it aside and exposed a pile of sawed-off shotguns. He ran his hands over several of them, able to make out only the guns' outlines in the dark. Some were attached to springs, some remained attached to wood planks. He pulled a couple out and after carefully cracking them open, stuck his fingers down the cold, empty barrels to find they were not loaded. Sly paused to see if DeLuce and Murnane reacted to the noise.

Father Murphy tapped Sly on the arm. Sly couldn't make out Father Murphy's face, but could sure as hell smell the Scotch on his breath. "I'm so very scared. Please don't start shooting again," Father Murphy whispered.

The full moon broke free of the clouds and beamed in through the wall cracks. Sly chose three shotguns free from planks or springs. Then, like a hungry, blind mouse, he searched the workbench for shells. Inside a dusty cupboard, he touched a box of shells, which he held close to his face. He rolled the shells between his fingers to verify they matched his twenty-gauge shotgun. He stashed a handful of shells in his pocket, away from the paper.

Sly had three fully loaded shotguns ready to do what they were built for. He passed a gun and the remaining shells to Eightball.

Sly kept his face pressed against the crack, breathing in the faint scent of engine oil, as his left eye focused on the men outside.

"Get ready," Sly said.

Father Murphy crouched and rolled into a ball in the corner. Sly heard a faint moan that only dogs and angels were supposed to hear.

Sly leaned against one side of the door and Eightball against the other. Eightball lifted his shotgun, aiming it at the door. Sly grabbed a shotgun and aimed it as well. He leaned the third against the wall next to him. It slipped, creating a thud. Sly squeezed his eyes shut, gritted his teeth, and tapped the shotgun barrel three times against his forehead.

When Sly peered through the crack once again, he noticed Murnane catch DeLuce's attention before pointing at the shed. DeLuce nodded and cocked his gun. *Click.*

Sly whispered, "They know we're in here. When they kick the door in, start blastin'."

"This is the part I really hate," Father Murphy rubbed his hands together and mumbled a prayer.

Sly's fears were confirmed when he saw DeLuce jump behind a nearby tree. He had heard the thud. Sly no longer felt like a blind mouse. Now he was a cornered rat.

"Okay, we know you're in there." Murnane's baritone voice rang out through the darkness. "Come on out and hand over the priest and we promise to go easy on ya!"

"Go eat a shit pie, copper! Come in and get him!" Sly answered.

"Please, no, Mr. Sly. Don't threaten him. He'll kill us," Father Murphy said.

"Listen to the priest, Eightball. You know if we come in there, you're coming out in a pine box! Don't be a fool!" Murnane said.

Eightball stiffened and looked at Sly. "I didn't tell you to eat a shit pie!" Eightball yelled. "But go eat a shit pie!"

"Well then, I'm talkin' to Sly. Use your head, kid. You got a lot to live for."

How'd he know my name? Damn, Murnane is good.

"This is DeLuce. You know what we want. Hand it over!"

Even the wind seemed to stand still out of respect when DeLuce spoke.

"Right! As soon as we hand it over, you're going to kill us. I didn't just fall off the turnip truck, you greasy wop son of a bitch!" Sly figured taunting a hardened cop and a ruthless killer was a solid plan.

"We won't! Just toss it out the door and run like hell. You have my word," DeLuce said.

"Your word ain't worth shit! Come and get it!" Sly said.

"We have twenty officers here and you are completely surrounded," Murnane said. "You have no way out, kid. Give it up. You still have a chance to live through this."

"Please don't let them have the paper! I'm begging you. You have no idea what horrific fate awaits you if you hand over that paper, Mr. Sly."

Sly let go of his shotgun and rubbed the paper in his pocket. Soft, supple, warm—like Lily's skin, no doubt.

"Why don't you two back way off, and we'll send the priest out with the paper. How'd that be?" Sly shouted, snatching up his shotgun again.

"Bullshit, you're all coming with me!" Murnane yelled.

"Okay, send the priest out with my paper! You have to the count of three!" DeLuce said.

Sly whispered, "We let Priest out first and once they come out from behind the trees we blast 'em good and proper."

"Please no, Mr. Sly. That's a terrible idea. I don't want to get shot."

"Hold on! You boys all come out with your hands up and nobody has to get hurt," Murnane said.

"One!" DeLuce yelled.

"I gotta ssside with Priest on thisss one. This is a pretty shitty idea," Eightball said.

"Priest, when the shooting starts, cover your head and run like hell to the back of the shed." Sly asked Eightball, "You loaded?"

Eightball snapped his shotgun open and double-checked the fresh shells.

"Two!"

Sly reached down and used his free hand to grip Father Murphy by the arm. "On your feet, Priest. Let's go."

"Please don't make me do this. Please don't make me do this. *Please* don't make me do this."

Eightball reached over and slid the bolt-lock open. Sly nodded. Eightball nodded.

"Three!"

26.

Last Rites of a

Scotch-Filled Priest

SLY HEARD PISTOLS BEING COCKED. The wood plank wall felt icy against his ear. He was trying to think of the next move, trying to think of *anything*. Swirling clouds of hot breath shone across what little light the moon provided through the wall cracks.

The world was spiraling out of control, making Sly feel like a turtle on its back on a busy street—his head spinning from too many near misses.

"Okay! Okay!" Sly yelled. The four ramshackle walls closed in.

"The priest better have that paper raised high in the air!" DeLuce said.

Sly didn't know whether to love or hate the paper. It made him wonder if he was following the paper or the paper was leading him. Something within the scribbling and pictures lurked, waited, and he hoped it was answers. The paper had brought nothing but worse luck than even he was used to. It filled him with doubt. Like the paper was *lying* to him. Perhaps leading him to a treasure that didn't exist. He felt trapped. All those feelings were wrestling with greed, delicious greed. He wanted to burn the paper and at the same time would kill to protect it.

"Okay, he's comin' out," Sly yelled. Father Murphy's eyes met Sly's. Sly did his best to offer comfort using only a glance, but he was fresh out of bullshit. Father Murphy would be the first to die, then Sly, then, hopefully, Eightball would get his too. Sly's gaze couldn't hide the truth. The old priest started crying again as Sly pushed open the door.

Father Murphy kept his hands folded in front of him and sobbed as he shuffled toward the door. Sly looked through a crack between the shed's wall boards and watched DeLuce close in, using a nearby woodpile for cover.

"Please don't shoot me!" Father Murphy cried.

Father Murphy raised his hands above his head and stepped carefully outside the doorway before stopping. Sly heard the frigid wind howling through the tree branches over his own kick-drum heartbeat.

DeLuce stayed behind the woodpile and waved Murnane in. Murnane used a large oak for cover.

"Show us the paper, priest," DeLuce shouted and peeked over the woodpile.

Sly tucked the spare shotgun under his left arm and held the other in his right hand. He held up three boney fingers and began counting down.

"Priest, do you have the paper? Yes or no? Step closer where I can see your face!" DeLuce said.

"We go on three." Sly curled his first finger. *One.*

"What?" Eightball asked, alarmed.

Sly checked on Father Murphy. The priest's fear screamed from head to toe: his head was down, his hands were up, he shuffled but didn't move, and his whimpers would make anyone's heart melt—except DeLuce.

"Where's the paper?" DeLuce asked.

Second finger. *Two.*

Father Murphy lowered his hands and looked back at the empty doorway. Sly studied Father Murphy standing alone in the cold facing armed men and crying his eyes out. Sly's fear eroded into an unfamiliar emotion—*pity.*

"Show us the fucking paper or I will send you all to Hell!" DeLuce screamed.

Sly curled his last finger.

Three.

Sly leapt out the door and shoved Father Murphy toward the outside corner of the shack.

Sly let both barrels loose on the woodpile. The second barrel ripped a hole in the woodpile because it dared to protect the Devil. Before Father Murphy had hit the ground, Sly had dropped the first gun and used the spare from under his arm. He unloaded and let the oak have it. Sly's arm took the brunt of the shotgun's thunder that punished the tree for protecting Murnane. Splinters and buckshot gouging into tree bark shattered the night, taking everyone by surprise—especially Sly.

"Move, Priest, move!" Sly yelled. Father Murphy lay frozen, staring up at Sly. "Hightail it behind the shed and keep goin'." Father Murphy scrambled to his feet.

Eightball blasted the woodpile. DeLuce ducked and Eightball turned on the tree screening Murnane. "Son of a bitch!" Murnane yelled.

Over his shoulder, Sly watched Father Murphy scamper around the corner and out of sight. Bullets whizzed and whistled by as Sly reloaded.

Protecting Father Murphy felt good, it felt *right*. Sly even seemed to aim better after helping Father Murphy. Sly had regained his balls.

Murnane shot twice more before Sly heard *click*.

"Shit!" Murnane yelled.

As Sly reloaded, Eightball kept DeLuce pinned behind the woodpile to Sly's right.

Several clicks came from near the tree.

Click.

A pause.

Click-click-click-click.

Sly realized Murnane was trying to fire Sly's broken gun.

"Goddamn it!" Murnane yelled, loud enough to wake the dead. The sabotaged pistol bounced off the woodpile.

Eightball shot at the woodpile and DeLuce popped up every

other shot and returned fire as Sly slide-stepped backward to the side of the tool shed.

Sly stopped just around the corner, snapped open the break-action shotgun, and reloaded using the final two shells from his pocket. He slapped the gun shut, emptied both barrels at Murnane, and ran like hell.

He heard Eightball blast two shots. Sly twisted as he ran and spotted Eightball hotfooting it across the snow on Sly's heels.

"Priest!" Sly ran and called out. "Priest?" By the light of the full moon, Sly was able to follow a fresh set of footprints in the snow leading to a small iron gate and one scared priest—both looking old and rusty.

Father Murphy lay behind a tree and covered his head. "Please stop shooting!"

Sly secured the empty shotgun under his armpit and bent down before touching Father Murphy on the shoulder. Father Murphy yelped and cringed when he looked up at Sly looming over him.

Sly clamped onto Father Murphy's right arm and Eightball grasped his left. Sly reared back and kicked the gate, which let out a moan when it swung open.

Five blocks and three alleyways later, Sly, Eightball, and Father Murphy slid to a halt under a lone streetlamp, put their hands on their knees, and fought for breath. Poor Father Murphy's pink cheeks puffed and sucked air with enough force to fix a flat tire. Three sets of slushy footprints would be easy to follow, but they were away from danger for a moment.

"You son of a bitch. I told you Mudbone was no good." Sly stiffened into striking position, as did Eightball, like two rattlesnakes hunting the same mouse. *Now was the time for I told you so's.*

"Look, don't start with me. And get out from under the light. What are you, stupid?"

"This was all your idea! You brought us here! You trusted him!" Sly said.

Eightball clenched his fists at his sides. "I never trusted him, but it was all I could think of. If you haven't noticed, we got nowhere else to go. I thought he could help us. I sure as hell didn't hear you come up with any ideas."

"I said we should rob the post office, remember?"

"Well . . ." Eightball said.

"Well, you were wrong." Pointing out Eightball's faults exhilarated Sly as much as helping Father Murphy. If only Eightball would get lost, or better yet, die, Sly and Father Murphy could continue as a two-man team.

"Look, they gotta be right behind us. Let's go." Eightball walked away down the street.

Sly held an empty shotgun and was out of shells. His unlucky streak had to wheedle him one more time—no gun, no shells, no luck. When Eightball opened a nearby trashcan and tossed his shotgun inside, Sly figured they were in the same boat.

"Then I'd say we're pretty fucked," Sly said in his closing argument. It felt pretty damn good to recite a closing argument rather than be run over by one.

"Why don't you tell me what you know about the paper? I mean, in case we get separated," Sly said, calling after Eightball. *Or you get yourself killed.* The fact Eightball never slowed down lathered Sly something fierce.

As Eightball walked away, he said, "Oh, the old man at the bookstore told me plenty, believe you me."

Sly shrugged and called after him. "So what are we supposed to do? Is Jack the Ripper a friend of yours too?" Sly considered hopping over to Lily's place, but vital information concerning his paper was strolling down the street so he had to follow Eightball instead.

"This is madness. Absolute madness. I cannot do this anymore. Men are dying all around me and the Devil smells our souls."

"Take it easy. You can't smell a *soul*, Priest."

"The Devil can sniff out souls like bees and dogs smell fear. Like the righteous smell filth. Mark my words, he'll find us no matter where we go, or how far we run."

Sly faced Father Murphy and poked a stern finger into the priest's collarbone. "Shut up. I've had enough of your bullshit. There ain't no

God, there ain't no Devil, and there's none such coming to get us. So pull yourself together. As soon as we find someplace to sit tight, you're going to tell me what that paper means. What it *really* means. And no more boogie man bullshit. You got me?"

Father Murphy slouched and pouted. Sly felt like he had just kicked a puppy. He set a hand on Father Murphy's shoulder. "Don't crack up now, Priest. You're doin' real good." Sly almost smiled, but paused. "But after getting so drunk, and all this runnin', you're gonna feel like shit in the morning."

Father Murphy lifted his head and glistening trails of tears shimmered against his reddened cheeks. "Why is this happening to me? Is there any good in this world? You care about nothing but yourselves." Father Murphy kicked at the ice chunks along the street. "Every day I see innocence ground up into meaty bits small enough for the Devil to eat. You have shown me a side of humanity I only read about in the newspaper from the comforts of the church rectory. That's as close as I ever got to the violence. That's as close as I ever *wanted* to get. Even the people who came to confession never spoke of grave-robbing and murder." Father Murphy used his sleeve to wipe away his tears. "That man back there you call DeLuce is twisted and comes from a very evil place."

"DeLuce is from Chicago," Sly said.

"He represents all the wickedness from which I try to shield the innocent souls I am obligated to protect."

Sly turned to see that Eightball was a good half-block away. The pools of light and shadow Eightball passed under grew smaller as did Eightball. "Come on, Priest, let's go. We're gonna lose Eightball." Sly figured Eightball wouldn't leave him and Father Murphy behind since . . .

A sudden overwhelming fear made Sly plunge his hand into his pocket. The soft paper greeted and reassured him. *The jewels in his pocket are nothing compared to the treasure. Eightball won't go too far.*

"No. I must tell you something," said Father Murphy. "I didn't get a look at that DeLuce, but I could *feel* his evil."

Teardrops glistened across the crosshatched wrinkles on Father

Murphy's cheeks. He sniffled twice through his chafed, red nose while glancing behind him toward the graveyard, like he'd just left his own funeral.

"DeLuce knows we have the paper. I'm afraid I've only made things worse."

"What do you mean? How did you make things worse?"

"I haven't been completely forthright with you about our predestined destination."

"Huh?"

"Egypt. I'm afraid I've misled you. That's not where we need to be."

27.

Sink the Eightball

"WHAT DO YOU MEAN? We're not going to Egypt?"

Sly wasn't sure he had heard Father Murphy right. The night grew colder and darker. Sly didn't understand how that was possible either. His feet and hands were numb. His face burned and felt drier than cracked leather. He could only imagine how frail, little Father Murphy was managing to survive.

The priest looked like he'd been through a hay thresher—twice. His coat, permanently borrowed from the Chap's Room, was covered in dirt, which matched his gloomy face. The bags under his eyes could carry water. Sly figured the old priest would probably say anything about the potential treasure if it got him out of the cold. Sly couldn't believe anything coming out of Father Murphy's mouth, unless it was half-digested Scotch.

"I know we've run you through the ringer today, old man." Sly put a hand on Father Murphy's shoulder. "We'll get you a hot meal and a warm bed and set you right."

Father Murphy staggered to the closest streetlight, setting one hand over his stomach and the other against the post. "You killed Mr. Mudbone." He turned a shade of pale green Sly had never seen before. "Oh dear, I just want to go home. I don't feel so well."

Father Murphy braced himself against the light pole and let loose a bucket of Scotch and warm stomach acid that splattered on the icy street and dissolved into the snow. Sly wondered how one little man could hold that much in his stomach. Guttural howls and retches echoed down the vacant street as steam rose from the puddle. The retching must have scared something in the alley because a trash can fell over followed by the sound of empty bottles rolling along the alley floor. Father Murphy spit twice and cut loose any remaining strings of spit clinging to his quivering bottom lip.

Sly noticed Eightball was way down the block now. Too far to even hit with a rock—and Sly had a pretty good arm. When Sly wanted Eightball to leave, he wouldn't go. Now Eightball was leaving and Sly needed him to stay. Eightball was as screwy as, well, a woman. *Sugar. Don't forget the sugar.*

"C'mon, Priest. We gotta get goin'." Sly patted Father Murphy on the back and took him by the arm and gently, but quickly, led him down the street. Men who craved another chance to watch the life drain from Sly one bullet hole at a time were hot on his heels.

"Hey, wait up," Sly said when he and Father Murphy caught up to Eightball, hoping to slow him down, but it didn't work. Sly considered grabbing a rock. "Where we goin'?"

"I know a flophouse just up here where we can lay low tonight," Eightball said.

Sly followed in Eightball's tracks through the drifting snow. Sly gripped Father Murphy's clammy hand. Somehow, the old man hadn't dropped dead right there in the alleyway. Sly kept Father Murphy moving in and out of the narrow back streets, using the shadows for cover. Eightball stopped at a small door, tucked into a tall brick wall.

Eightball opened the door. Father Murphy looked the building up and down. "Is this safe?"

"It's a room for the night. Or would you rather sleep outside?" Sly pulled Father Murphy close.

The door opened to a narrow staircase that led up. Under the dim light, Sly noticed the heavily pocked tongue and groove wainscoting that ran along the walls. Sly stayed right behind Father Murphy as they climbed the stairs, which ended at a small lobby containing a counter. A portly man wearing glasses and reading a newspaper sat behind the counter. In front of him rested a service bell and a short stack of newspapers.

Sly watched Eightball approach the clerk. Sly could only see the back of Eightball's head. *Please don't smile. You'll scare the shit out of him.* The clerk looked up from his paper and flinched like he'd seen a large, hairy spider on Eightball's face. Sly smiled when he pictured the clerk smashing Eightball's face with the heel of his shoe.

"We need a room for the night."

The desk clerk bowed his head and looked over his glasses. "How many rooms?" His eyes bounced from Eightball to Sly to Father Murphy before returning to Eightball. Sly propped up Father Murphy who seemed to have the bones of a scarecrow.

The clerk reached for an array of tarnished brass keys hanging on a peg board behind him.

"Just one."

The clerk stopped for a moment, then grabbed a single key. He stiffened and examined Sly, Eightball, and Father Murphy again.

"What's with him?" He pointed his chin at Father Murphy.

Sly hitched up Father Murphy like a pair of sagging trousers. "He's got a stomach bug. Real bad. We're taking care of him," Sly answered.

"What's he got, the bottle flu?" The clerk snorted at his wisecrack and set the key on the counter. "If he gets sick, you clowns are cleaning it up, you got me?"

"Yes, sir," Eightball said.

"Yes, sir," Sly said.

"And you'll be charged for an extra linen service," the clerk said. "That'll be two dollars."

Eightball turned away from the clerk. He reached in his pocket and pulled out a diamond ring—with most of Lorraine's finger still attached. He kept the thawing finger low and close to his crotch, out of the clerk's view. Eightball twisted and pulled, attempting to separate the ring from the rotting flesh and bone. "Ssso sssorry. Looking for my wallet."

Eightball stuffed the bone and slime back in his pocket. He pulled out the pearl necklace instead, covered in frozen yellow tendrils. He gave the necklace, and his hand, a quick wipe on his pant leg, turned back around, and set the jewelry on the counter.

"What's the big idea? Do I look like a fence?"

Eightball set his elbow on the counter. He raised his wrist and pointed down at the necklace. "These are *real* pearls. I bet the wife would love something like this. Am I right?"

The clerk pouted, causing his mouth to sink into a deep frown that looked like frustration-meets-curiosity. Armed with the silver tongue of a salesman, the persistence of a toothache, and the stink of a sweltering outhouse, Eightball pitched the clerk.

"These here pearls come all the way from Egypt."

"Egypt is a desert and pearls come from the ocean. Mostly the Atlantic."

Eightball snapped his head back like the clerk had just used a glove to slap his face and challenge him to a duel. "What are you, an oyster doctor? These are good pearls, real good quality. If you were so smart, you'd know that."

The clerk gave Eightball a salty look and took a closer look at the necklace. Lines of doubt and mistrust formed across the clerk's forehead. Sly figured the clerk was about to call the cops. After what seemed like ages of eyebrow furling and chin rubbing, the clerk caved. He picked up the pearls.

"What's that smell?" the clerk asked.

"None of us have had a shower in quite a while. We must smell a bit *ripe*," Eightball answered.

"I want you out before eight a.m., got me? And if I hear one peep, I'm calling the cops." The clerk slid the key across the counter. "Take room two. Down the hall and to the left. One bathroom per floor and that's at the end of the hall on your right. If the shower don't work it means the pipes froze up again, so too bad."

Eightball swiped the key. He grabbed a newspaper off the counter too. "Can I have this?" The clerk shooed him away and continued to examine the wife's new gift.

Sly reached behind Father Murphy, propped him up by his armpit, and followed Eightball to room number two. Over his shoulder Sly watched the clerk start to pick off bits of hardened yellow flesh. The clerk held the necklace up to his nose and sniffed. His face contorted into something bitter and disgusted before tossing the necklace down the counter and batting the air.

When Eightball pushed open the door to room two, paint flakes fluttered to the hallway floor. The place looked a damn sight better than the graveyard, but barely more welcoming than the tool shed they had just blasted their way out of. The room contained a stained mattress on a rusty metal frame, a pillow as thick as a deck of cards, a spindly nightstand, and the stale smell of desperation. The view outside the lone window was dark, cold, and as desolate as the view inside. But the joint was heated. The overworked radiator clunked and rattled and popped as hot water coursed through it.

"Let's get Priest some food. Poor bastard's starving," Sly said.

"There's a bakery two doors down. Check the garbage cans 'round back. They're always throwing away yesterday's bread. Sometime's there's cake." Eightball acted like the bakery threw away birthday cakes with his name written in frosting.

"Priest, get on the bed while I run out for some food." Sly dragged Father Murphy from the door to the side of the bed.

"Hey, hey, hey. What the hell are you doin'?" Eightball stepped closer to the stained mattress.

"What does it look like I'm doing?"

"I'll take the bed," Eightball said.

"Bullshit." Sly let go of Father Murphy, who dropped to the hardwood floor letting out a thud and a grunt. "We should draw straws."

"No need." The bedsprings squeaked when Eightball sat on the bed, bounced a little, and rubbed his knuckles.

Sly took the pillow, all the while giving Eightball the stink-eye, just daring him to say something. Sly sprawled Father Murphy on the floor in front of the door—to use him as a stop in case anyone tried to kick his way in—and set the pillow under Father Murphy's head.

Eightball unfolded the newspaper and started spreading it on the floor around the bed.

"What are you doing?" Sly asked.

Eightball paused and sneered at Sly. "I put newspaper around my bed so no one can sneak up on me when I'm sleepin'."

Sly thought that was pretty clever, but huffed as if it was the dumbest idea he had ever heard of. Sly lay down on the floor, used his rolled up coat for a pillow, and positioned himself so he could keep an eye on the old man.

"I thought you were going to get Priest some food," Eightball said.

"Don't order me around. He's sleepin' anyway," Sly responded.

Just as Sly settled in, he heard Father Murphy mumble. The old priest sat up, leaned against the door, and put his face in his hands.

"What's wrong, Priest? Can't sleep? You're safe," Sly said.

"I can't take this anymore. I feel terrified and alone. This has been, most assuredly, the worst day of my life. Please forgive me for wanting to be safe at home in my own bed."

"Look, all of us would rather be someplace else right now. Why don't you get some shut-eye and we'll get the full skinny on the paper first thing in the morning."

Father Murphy let his head wobble. He wiped his nose on his sleeve, producing a slurping sound. He examined the snot smeared across his arm. "Oh dear. I fear your lack of manners is rubbing off on me."

"Stop cryin'. You ain't done nuthin' wrong," Sly said in a voice he might use to comfort a scared child, if he ever cared enough to do so. "You're doing great."

Eightball lay on his side, propped up on his elbow, which sank into the mattress. "Yeah, you're doin' great. There's nuthin' to worry about, just like Sly said."

Father Murphy's sniffles broke the silence. "Nothing to worry about . . ." *Sniffle.* "Perhaps a story would take us out of this room and let us forget our troubles, even for a few minutes."

"You should be sleepin', Priest. Get some shut-eye, we got a big day tomorrow," Sly said.

"I know, why don't you tell us how you got your name, Mr. Eightball? I'll bet it's very interesting."

Sly quickly changed his tune and sat up. "Yeah, I gotta hear this."

Eightball focused on picking lint off the mattress. He rolled a little ball between his thumb and middle finger and flicked it away, one after the other.

"Aw, it's no big deal."

"Please, Mr. Eightball. I'd really like to hear the story behind such a unique name."

Eightball searched the watermarked walls like the past was hard to find.

"I was maybe five years old, I guess. Me and my old man used to go from town to town hustlin' pool. He'd clean out gin joint drunks and take me along for the ride. He told me my mom died when I was born, but I think either she ran off or he killed her."

Eightball's stare traveled back through time and Sly could see, by the way Eightball's eyebrows squeezed together and his voice cracked, it wasn't an easy trip to make.

"Anyway, one night I remember he took on this really drunk guy named Artus. Artus couldn't hardly stand up and my old man beat him pretty good. Artus musta been embarrassed because every time he lost he'd challenge my old man again, and kept right on losing. Before he knew it, he was into my old man for at least three large. So Artus says to my dad, 'One last game at double or nuthin'. My dad agreed and played real serious. I could see he was concentratin' on every shot. And Artus played him tough, the whole way through."

Eightball sighed before plunging back into the grueling memory. "Artus had one solid and the eight ball left to sink. He kisses the first ball, but it hits the eight and both balls stop right on the lip of the pocket. It was right then that I leaned forward on my stool to get a better look and fell to the floor. Apparently, when I hit the floor, the eight ball fell in—just before the other ball. The whole barroom seen it and no matter how much Artus screamed about a rigged game, he owed my old man six large."

Eightball's face hardened like he was fighting off the images left behind from a bad dream.

"Then my dad told Artus that if he took me off his hands, my old man'd call it square. My dad handed me over right then and there and walked out. Never saw him again." Eightball studied the cracks in the plaster wall as if he were trying to find his father somewhere beyond.

"Don't even remember what he looks like. My old man never told Artus my name. So then Artus named me Eightball because of how he lost the game. I'm sure my old man called me somethin', but I've been called Eightball for so long I can't remember my real name. I spent the next ten years hustlin' and working cons with Artus until he died in a knife fight in some bar up in Forest Lake."

Eightball turned to Father Murphy. "So now you know." Eightball laced his fingers across his chest.

Sly realized he and Eightball were more alike than he ever considered. Both their fathers weren't worth a shit. While Sly had spent his childhood wanting Agony to leave him alone, Eightball wanted to spend more time with his dad—maybe just enough to ask him why he left. *How do you hold on to someone who wants to leave and how do you get rid of someone who doesn't want to go?* Sly and Eightball were two sides of the same coin.

Father Murphy sniffed and said, "After decades of confessions, that may be the saddest story I've ever heard."

"Oh hell, it wasn't all bad. I know what I did wrong that made him want to leave," Eightball said.

"You weren't at fault, Mr. Eightball. You were just a child." Father Murphy consoled Eightball as he might any lost member of his flock.

"Sure it was my fault."

"How could you possibly justify what he did to you? What did you do wrong?" Father Murphy asked.

"I was born."

Father Murphy bowed his head and closed his eyes. "Let us pray."

Sly watched Father Murphy reach, using blind faith to find Sly's hand. Sly jerked away in blind frustration from the priest's cold palm. Father Murphy opened his eyes. "A silent prayer, perhaps, would be best."

"Take it easy, Priest," Eightball said.

"I don't know what else to do. You killed Mr. Mudbone and I will not let anyone else die because of me leading you astray. Maybe the treasure is the only answer. Maybe the treasure is the only thing that will make it all stop."

Eightball sat straight up. Sly listened and felt a shock of anticipation shoot through him. "What do you mean?" Sly asked. "You were sayin' somethin' about not needing to go to Egypt. Are you saying there *is* a treasure?"

"I have kept the full truth from you both. I'm afraid I've been leading you astray in order to stall for time. I needed time to figure out how to save you." He rubbed the top of his head and winced, like the confession had stung him.

Sly was more confused than ever. *Leading me astray? How?. . .* "What do you mean?" Sly asked.

"The truth is the treasure *does* exist. Not only does it exist, but it's already been found. I accompanied the team of archeologists to the Sahara Desert and we excavated it and cataloged it and . . ."

"You found it? All we need to do is haul it back, right?" Sly reached behind his head and found the paper in his coat pocket. He massaged the paper and it instantly sent warm tingles through his body.

Father Murphy narrowed his eyes into a penetrating stare. "We dug it up. And we brought it back—along with the curse, mind you."

"Back? Back where? Where is it?"

"It's in St. Paul."

The desk clerk heard the street door slam, followed by methodical footsteps approaching from the stairs. Tremor rings broke the surface of his steaming cup of joe. He lowered his newspaper to see two monstrous, pink-haired, blue-eyed men standing across the counter, staring at him.

28.

Devil Got Your Tongue?

EVEN THROUGH HIS thick wool uniform, Murnane felt the coarse oak bark against his back. The rough sensation compounded his already surly attitude. Sly and Eightball had escaped with the priest in tow. Again.

At the edge of the lantern's light, weathered tombstones sulked in the shadows, looking as though they were creeping up on Murnane. Gun smoke filled his nostrils despite the blustery, swirling winds.

Stars glimmered throughout the crisp night sky like sequin-laden ribbons tied across the heavens. Murnane remembered singing "Twinkle Twinkle Little Star" to Samantha at bedtime—her favorite song. And Jacob's as well, until Jacob decided he was too big for little baby songs. Murnane wished he could smile at the memory.

Murnane pushed against the oak for support and struggled to his feet. Woodchips tumbled from his coat.

"How the fuck could you let them get away?" DeLuce lay on his back waving his gun toward the moon.

"Me?" Murnane asked. "You're the one flat on your ass."

"Why didn't you shoot them?" DeLuce asked. He pushed himself up quickly as if doing calisthenics.

Murnane reloaded his empty pistol and looked at the useless gun lying in the snow. "Some asshole filed off the firing pin on that gun."

Murnane surveyed the graveyard, looking in the general direc-

214

tion of where he had parked. He saw nothing but distant street lamps through the oaks.

"You let 'em get away, Murnane. I'm starting to think you're doing this shit on purpose." DeLuce picked off bits of loose debris from his collar and fedora.

"Well, if your goon squad was here, we would have caught them. But you made 'em stay back in the car, remember?"

"After you jumped out of the car and ran in here in a big damn hurry, I calmly stayed back and told one of them to stake out the west gate, and the other the east gate. If these assholes ran out, the Boys will let us know. Now let's get away from this goddamned smell."

"I want to know why Sly and Eightball are so damned determined to keep that document. What's on it, exactly?"

DeLuce examined his coat and brushed off the remaining splinters.

"There's a tear in my coat," DeLuce said.

"It was fine when I gave it back to you in the car on the way over here."

While walking past Murnane, DeLuce brushed against the chief's arm, enough to move his shoulders. "Let's get back to the car," DeLuce said.

Murnane picked up the lantern. "I mean it. Start talkin'."

DeLuce stopped and turned. "Look, just help me get it back and I'll leave you and your family alone."

Murnane heard an honest vulnerability in DeLuce's offer, but didn't fall for it. "Yeah, but every time I get shot at, I'm reminded that your word ain't worth shit. At this rate I'm not going to live long enough to see them again anyway and then there's nothing stopping you from killing them. Tell me. And no bullshit."

DeLuce walked away, fading a few steps into the night. Murnane stayed put, leering at DeLuce's back.

"Somethin's got you scared. And as much as I would like to think it's me, I doubt that's the reason. And whatever scares you, interests me. What's on that paper?"

DeLuce laughed. "I'm not afraid. You'd know if I was."

"I know when a man's afraid and pretending not to be. What's on that paper that would scare the mighty Devil DeLuce himself?"

DeLuce stopped, his back to Murnane. The faint light barely touched DeLuce's form across the darkness. "I need that paper more than you know." DeLuce trudged ahead, leaving his statement to further chill the night air.

Murnane followed the same path through the snow they had created on the way in. The snow crunched and twigs snapped underfoot as Murnane caught up to DeLuce. Murnane took the lead. The lantern swung at Murnane's side except when he raised it every so often to get his bearings.

"What's the matter, DeLuce? Devil got your tongue?"

Murnane stopped and pivoted to face DeLuce. The wind tousled the bottom of DeLuce's coat. His feet were firmly planted shoulder-width apart. DeLuce's head was down, but his eyes looked straight through Murnane.

"That paper belongs to someone you don't ever want to meet."

Murnane had found DeLuce's Achilles heel.

"Why not? Who is he?" Murnane asked.

"Someone you don't want to cross."

"By cross you mean, make mad, or cross paths with?"

"Either."

"You stole it from Capone?"

"You think I'm afraid of Capone? Not a chance."

A list of well-known politicians and Mob bosses rattled through Murnane's mind like an open file cabinet caught in a propeller. "Tell me."

DeLuce raised his chin and balled his hands into fists. "I should just shoot you and dump you here."

Murnane knew when a suspect was about to crack under questioning, and DeLuce was cracking like an overcooked egg. Whoever this guy was, he had burrowed under DeLuce's skin and created a burning rash.

"You can stop with the empty threats. You need me." Murnane felt the seconds tick by. *Let the egg boil.*

DeLuce remained planted, but his slumped shoulders and low-hanging head reminded Murnane of a scolded child. "It was a few months back. We got a tip about a shipment coming into Chicago customs from overseas—Egypt or someplace—with a bunch of arche-ological artifacts the likes of which you've never seen. I took two guys and we checked it out. We slipped the night guard a few bucks and had the place to ourselves. Every one of those crates was empty, except for one. The last crate had one piece of paper in it. I thought it was the manifest, until I took a closer look."

"And? What was on it?"

"A bunch of shit I couldn't understand. That's not important."

"That's the whole reason we're out here chasing these assholes. How is that not important?"

"If you shut your mouth and listen, I'll tell you." DeLuce puffed out his cheeks and exhaled hard. "It wasn't what was on the paper, it was who came looking for it."

Murnane let DeLuce spill the beans at his own pace. When a person of interest decides to talk, let him talk. DeLuce looked as if he could smell the roses someone had set on his coffin.

"Later that night I'm alone in my office looking at the paper under my desk light. All of a sudden there's this guy standing across the desk from me. The guy came out of *nowhere*. The building was locked up tight so I have no idea how this guy got in without me hearin' him. He says it's his paper, and I tell him I don't know what he's talkin' about. And to go fuck himself. I pull my gun and all he does is smile."

The wind chose that moment to moan across the graveyard, on cue.

"What'd he look like?" Murnane asked.

"That's the thing. My office was dark except for my desk lamp. Every time I tried to get a good look at him, it was like the shadows followed him and covered up his face. But the weird thing is I could see his eyes—I'll never forget 'em."

DeLuce squinted and frowned, drifting through the memory of the night in question.

"So I pull the trigger and my gun jams. I pull the slide back, eject the bullet, and there was no jam, so's I reload and pull the trigger again but nuthin' happens. This whole time the son of a bitch is just standin' there, fuckin' smilin' at me." DeLuce blinked twice, trying to decipher the sequence of events.

"So I'm fuckin' with my gun," DeLuce said as he mimed the jammed pistol, "and swearin' up and down I don't have his paper . . . as it's crammed down by my crotch under the desk. He says I can keep the paper under one condition." DeLuce dropped his arms to his sides.

When DeLuce looked at Murnane, Murnane raised his eyebrows and nodded, prodding DeLuce to continue.

"So I ask him, 'Oh yeah, what's that?' And that's when he stopped smiling. My office got *real* cold. It was August and humid as hell, but I swear you coulda stored meat in there. He says all I needed to do was *keep it safe.*"

"The paper?"

"Yeah, the paper. So I decide to take him by surprise and flip my desk lamp and shine it in his face. But as soon as I did, the bulb popped and my office went black. By the time I found my lighter, he was gone. It's a good thing too because I was two seconds from getting up and stomping a mud hole in his ass. Crazy thing is, I checked my office door and it was still locked. The outside door too."

"That doesn't tell me why these guys want the paper so badly." Murnane said. Across DeLuce's face was a visceral, tangible fear Murnane empathized with. DeLuce envisioned something only he could see.

"I started having these nightmares. The guy would start out smilin' at me, then I'd be runnin' for my life from wolves with fire coming outta their eyes, and all sorts of crazy shit. Every night—same fuckin' dream. I couldn't sleep for months. So I figured if I got rid of the paper, I might get some sleep. I gave the paper to Pancetti to take to St. Paul. When it was stolen this morning, the guy shows up again and says I broke our deal. . . ." DeLuce swallowed hard. He looked at Murnane and then at the ground and said, "I broke our deal."

Murnane chortled. "I can't believe I'm listening to this."

"I need that paper."

"You are so full of shit. You know, there's an old saying. Fool me once, shame on you. Fool me twice, and I'm a fucking idiot."

"What time did the Boss's guys hit my men this morning?" De-Luce asked.

Murnane was surprised by the random question. "About noon. Why?"

"Didn't you wonder how I got to the mayor's office so fast?"

"Trains move fast. Doesn't take long—Chicago to St. Paul."

"The guy showed up at seven thirty this morning. Before the paper was stolen. Told me I needed to hightail it to St. Paul."

"The guy is obviously working with the Boss and his gang. He's yankin' your chain, DeLuce."

"This guy works alone."

"Why would you say that? How can you be so sure? It's definitely someone with some money and power. You're letting yourself get played like a fine-tuned fiddle."

"This guy works alone." DeLuce carried such conviction in his voice, it frightened Murnane.

"C'mon. He's not going to get you this riled up without a whole gang of people backing him. This was an orchestrated setup. You probably have a rat inside your organization feeding these jokers information. Oldest story in the book."

"He didn't threaten to kill me. What he has in store for me is worse than death. I saw it in his face. I heard it in his voice. I *felt* it every time I tried to sleep."

"What are you saying?"

"I'm talking about the Devil, God, Heaven, Hell—all that shit."

The distinct feeling of being duped left Murnane with a heel's hangover—an angry heel. "You think this is funny? You threaten to kill my family and then give me this bullshit? You're one sick son of a bitch, you know that? Next phone we come across, you're calling and letting my family go."

Murnane stormed away. After only three steps, DeLuce caught up and squeezed Murnane's arm, stopping him. DeLuce was scared. Scared.

"I know it sounds *pazzesco*, and I guess I don't care if you believe me or not. But I need that paper back, end of story," DeLuce said.

"And it's one helluva crazy story." Murnane ripped his arm away. "I can guarantee you it won't end with 'he lived happily ever after.'"

Murnane trudged in the car's general direction. DeLuce caught up and walked beside him, shoulder to shoulder.

"Do you know what St. Paul is, Chief? It's one giant meat grinder that feeds on innocence. You cram honest people with good intentions in one end, and when you turn the crank, guys like us come out the other end." DeLuce let his observations of St. Paul sink in. "The guy who came for the paper is the one turning the handle."

Something sickening congealed in Murnane's veins. He fought to understand how his view of the world could so closely parallel De-Luce's view of St. Paul. Murnane had never shared his thoughts with anyone. The coincidence was uncanny. Disgusting.

Murnane was fully cognizant of his role in creating and maintaining the twisted greed machine that had consumed St. Paul. He remembered happily floating on rapids of flowing dirty money, all too eager to go over the falls and crash into the voracious meat grinder below. Once he cleared the rapids, life was clear-sailing. Only later did Murnane realize the deep churning current below the surface had drowned the honest man he used to be.

"*Greed* turns the handle, DeLuce. Men *line up* to jump in that meat grinder, they don't need to be forced."

"Nobody gets away from St. Paul, and nobody gets away from *him*."

"Enough with the Devil bullshit. That's just your guilt fucking with you, DeLuce. I know guilt all too well, thanks to you, but I'm not afraid to face the consequences. And more important, make things right. Guilt is the chink in your armor, the crack in your tough-guy façade. You don't know how to handle it like a normal person—a person with a *conscience*. Or, maybe this is all an act and you are just that fucking crazy."

"You'll know what I mean when he finds us. And he will."

"Knock it off, DeLuce. We aren't little kids around a campfire.

You know what I think? I think you got to the docks and found empty crates because someone jumped your claim on all those pricey artifacts. But maybe in their hurry to get away, some idiot accidently drops an important document. The kind of document that can sink folks with power and money. Those people will do whatever it takes to keep afloat." Murnane saw the streetlights becoming brighter up ahead. "You send the paper to St. Paul for safe-keeping, but these two palookas steal it and now are buying time until they cook up a solid blackmail plan. Makes sense."

The main gate released a groan when Murnane pulled it shut after he and DeLuce passed through.

"Forget what I said. Just find the paper."

Murnane spotted the car down the block. "But why would they need Mudbone? Why were they digging up graves? And what's with the priest?"

"What's that you say?" DeLuce asked, cracking half a smile. "Pieces not quite fitting together the way they should?"

"I know I'm on the right trail. What do you take me for?"

"I take you for a cop. You can't get any dumber than that."

"Fuck you, DeLuce."

As he approached the car, Murnane noticed the Butcher Boys had not returned.

"Maybe your boys got a tail on our suspects," Murnane said. He felt equal parts relief and curiosity. "We'll swing by the east and west gates and see if they are still out there."

As Murnane reached for the door handle, one of the Boys stepped from the shadows only feet from Murnane, causing him to jump. "What the? . . . Where did you come from?"

The lone Titan pointed westward, down the empty street.

"He says they went that way. Let's go," DeLuce said.

I didn't hear him say anything. The car started after a few harsh coughs. Murnane flipped on the lights and headed west, slowly. DeLuce rode shotgun and the Butcher pointed from the back seat.

"What's with him? Well, *them*. Why don't they talk? Are they mute?" Murnane asked.

"I never inquired," DeLuce said.

"How'd he get cleaned up? They looked like hell back at the Broken Bone."

The Butcher had washed his face and changed into a white tailored shirt and tan trousers held up by dark brown suspenders. He looked like he could have just left a job at the bank and was heading home to his family—other than the blood-dyed hair.

"They always have an extra set of clean clothes with them. What they lack in conversation, they make up for in cunning," DeLuce said.

"And brutality," Murnane added.

Pointing out each turn, the Ghost of Christmas Yet to Come guided Murnane down avenues and through alleyways. He pulled over when the Butcher Boy squeezed his shoulder. Murnane now understood how a rabbit felt when an eagle swooped in.

Murnane set the parking brake. He followed DeLuce and the giant to a doorway tucked into a brick wall. The small doorway led to a narrow staircase. Murnane held the door and let DeLuce, and his pet, lead the way. At the top of the stairs sat a counter and on top of the counter was a stack of newspapers. Behind the counter sat a portly clerk wearing an expression one would get when two giant Swedes stare at you without saying a word.

"Thank goodness you're here, Officer. I was just about to call you guys." The clerk thumbed in the Boys' direction. "Tell them to beat it."

The Butchers had led Murnane and DeLuce to their quarry. Murnane was within feet of the paper and saving his family. The last thing he needed was the clerk to panic and call the Minneapolis cops.

"These men are special agents," Murnane said. He motioned toward DeLuce. "And him too."

DeLuce smirked.

"Well, why didn't they tell me they were cops? They show up together about twenty minutes ago, then one leaves and comes back with you guys while the other one just stands there. They didn't say anything, the creepy bastards. What kind of an outfit are you running here? And why is their hair pink?"

"They have explicit instructions not to divulge information concerning our ongoing investigation."

"Well, not saying anything is just plain rude." The clerk folded his arms. "What is this all about, anyway?"

"We are tracking two murder suspects who are holding a priest hostage."

"Room two." The clerk pointed and stepped back from the counter. "Will there be shooting?"

Murnane saw the clerk focus on DeLuce's sidearm sticking out from under his coat. "Can you go somewhere in the back, perhaps? That would be best. Please stay down and be quiet."

The clerk slunk through a door behind the counter, closing it behind him. As Murnane examined the layout down the hall toward room number two, he heard the clerk's door lock and a chair slide across the floor before being propped up under the door handle.

Murnane took lead. DeLuce crept close behind. The Boys remained by the desk.

Each step was slow and methodical. The floorboards creaked and moaned. Murnane winced at every sound that bounced through the hallway. The chief stopped at the paint-chipped door displaying a worn and tarnished number two—screwed in place with one round head and one flat head screw. Murnane heard muffled voices inside. Someone was in the room.

Murnane rested his right shoulder against the door frame. DeLuce mirrored Murnane on the other side of the door. DeLuce slid the hammer back on his pistol and slowly loaded a round before pressing his gun against the door. Murnane popped open the chamber of his revolver, making sure it was loaded.

His heart punched hard inside his chest. Sweat condensed on his upper lip. Murnane needed these bastards—alive or dead.

29.

When Priests Fly

"You mean the treasure's been in St. Paul this whole time? While we're runnin' around getting shot at?" Sly asked. Sly leapt to his feet, clenched his fist, and punched the wall. Plaster cracked and fell, exposing bare lath beneath.

Father Murphy covered his head as if Sly's next punch would crack *his* plaster. "You *kidnapped* me—at gunpoint I might add. We then jumped on a moving train while being shot at. I haven't taken a breath since." Father Murphy appeared to hold back tears when he fixed his gaze on the hole Sly had punched in the plaster. "Everything I've done is because I'm trying to protect you, don't you see?"

Father Murphy sat cross-legged in front of the door and looked up at Sly like a lost puppy. Sly cooled his boiling blood down to a simmer and took pity on the old man.

"But the treasure is in St. Paul, right?" Eightball asked.

"Yes, but let me explain. It holds something more malevolent than you can imagine."

Now we have to worry about elephants? Sly felt more confident than ever because he knew there were no elephants in St. Paul.

"We're going to St. Paul," Sly proclaimed. He commanded attention and took charge. And he put on his coat. The paper comforted Sly when he stroked it inside his pocket, like a child stroking his safety blanket.

Father Murphy shifted on the floor in quick, nervous bursts. "Please, please, listen to me."

Something outside the door made Sly twist his head, allowing his ear to confirm fear. He raised an index finger to his lips. "Shhhhhh." Sly pointed toward the hallway.

Eightball jabbed his elbow down against the worn bedsprings, causing them to creak loudly in protest.

Sly extended his right hand behind him, attempting to hush a restless Eightball and a whimpering priest because one peep might be the end of them.

Eightball eased off the mattress and stepped lightly on the newspaper spread around the bed. He backed up toe to heel, toe to heel, slow and precise, toward the back of the small room, toward the second-story window. Sly latched onto Father Murphy's wrist and pulled him off the floor. Sly backed away from the door with steps so light they wouldn't crack an egg. He remembered, all too clearly, his useless pistol tumbling into an open grave.

A drawn-out creak on the hardwood floor in the hall announced someone's arrival just as clear as a bookstore owner's jangling bell. *Shit.*

Sly inched farther from the door and nearer the small window on the opposite wall, afraid of what was coming next. He watched Father Murphy bring his knuckles up to his mouth and squeeze his eyes closed. The priest barely opened one eye then quickly closed it again.

Inside the room, the paint-chipped radiator made the only sound when it knocked and pinged as scalding water pumped through its innards. From outside the door, Sly heard a hair-raising *click.*

Sly let go of Father Murphy and reached for the spindly nightstand, using the nightstand to smash the window and the quiet.

Gun shots louder than Dapper Dan's swan song tore through the door before Sly heard someone attempting to kick open the solid oak door. Three more bullets came through the door split seconds apart. Sly ripped the mattress off the bed. Eightball helped him curl it up and shove it through the window. It flopped into the night and Sly checked where it landed to get a distance measurement before grabbing Priest. Despite the forceful kicks, the door held.

Father Murphy gasped as though Sly was shoving a pistol up the old man's nose. "What are you doing?"

"Out we go, Priest." Sly squeezed Father Murphy by the back of the neck and hurled him out the window like a sack of potatoes. He shrieked much louder than the nightstand had. The priest hit the mattress and bounced once before landing safely in a snowdrift.

Sly turned to see the door swing open and slam into the wall.

The gunshots were followed by the man wearing a black fedora. Sly recognized the hat and the wicked, fiery eyes as belonging to De-Luce. DeLuce's entire face became engulfed in flame, causing it to melt. That was enough to send Sly out the window.

Sly jumped and smacked against the mattress, feeling the metal coils dig into his back. He bounced into the snow next to Father Murphy, who was trying to stand. Landing back-first in the snow drove the air from Sly's chest.

Sly lay in the snow between a pile of crates and a broken fence, trying to catch his breath. Light filtered through windows as curious onlookers opened their curtains to see what all of the ruckus was about.

Eightball fell from the sky, bounced off the mattress, and landed ass first in the parking lot a few feet away. Sly yelled, "Let's go!"

Trudging through knee-deep snow, Sly reached Father Murphy and tugged him to his feet. Gunshots blistered the ice around Sly. Sly looked up at the broken window to see Murnane and DeLuce looking back at him, guns firing. Sly pushed Father Murphy forward. The bullets stopped, but the clicks continued. A man yelled, "Goddamn it!" Sly had dragged Father Murphy no more than ten steps when he heard the telltale sounds of a fresh clip.

Sly gripped Father Murphy's coat tightly at the shoulder and shoved him around the side of the building as six more rounds rang out through the night. The gawkers scurried away from their windows.

Father Murphy's coat was on the verge of ripping when Sly pulled him around to the sidewalk out front. When Sly turned the corner he smacked face first against the barrel chest of a monster-sized man. Sly fell and cracked his head on the icy sidewalk. When he stopped sliding backward, Sly took a moment to shake out the cobwebs.

Sly noticed the monster standing over him appeared to have pink hair. *I must be screwy.* Sly glanced over to see the same giant pick up Father Murphy by the head. *There's two of 'em. Jesus, I must be* double *screwy.*

The monster looming over Sly smiled and slipped on brass knuckles the size of a ship anchor. Smiley cocked his arm back. Sly crawled backward, trying to keep from being crushed under a fist that could pound mountains into sand.

Smiley halted, turning to look at his monster twin. Sly stopped crawling. The twin dropped Father Murphy and gazed off in the distance. Blood trickled from the twin's mouth as he dropped to his knees. Smiley lunged, attempting to catch his collapsing brother. Once the monster fell, Eightball let go of the knife handle sticking out of the monster's back.

Father Murphy sat on the sidewalk and rubbed his head. Sly managed to spring from the sidewalk and, at a dead run, scooped up the priest. Eightball joined Sly, helping to carry Father Murphy away at a full sprint.

Hard leather soles slapped on the wet pavement no more than a few steps behind. *Why aren't they shooting? Must be out of bullets. Finally a lucky break. Keep running.* Every pounding step blurred Sly's vision and jarred his teeth. His burning leg muscles fought to keep pace. Father Murphy felt like a load of bricks.

Sly made a hard left and pulled Father Murphy and Eightball down the first alley they came to. They ran through it and came out the other side and Sly pulled around a corner. Sly stopped and looked back, pretty sure he saw a blur wearing a fedora soar past.

Sly helped Father Murphy over to a stack of nearby pallets to rest. Sly rested against the cold brick building and fought for air.

"Do you still got the paper?" Eightball asked.

The question took Sly by surprise, but he was far too tired to wonder why Eightball was so worried about the paper. Inside his pocket, he recognized the warmth and comfort of his best friend. Sly swallowed and left his mouth hanging open and nodded. "Why wouldn't I?"

"Double-check," Eightball said.

"I got it." Sly let his neck muscles slacken.

"Well, make sure, goddamn it," Eightball said.

Sly pulled out the paper, shaking it in front of Eightball. "See! Now stop asking about it!"

Eightball's fist delivered the blow better than a sledgehammer. To add insult to injury, Eightball snatched the paper from Sly's hand before Sly had time to fall backward. All he could see were flaring, painful bursts of stars, and his jawbone felt like part of his ear. Yet another large garbage pile had broken his fall. Sly was able to get one last look at Eightball running around the corner, paper in hand. *No luck. Goddamn it.*

Sly pushed himself off the garbage and gripped Father Murphy by the arm. Father Murphy's head snapped up in surprise. Sly took one running step trying to pull the exhausted priest along for the chase. Father Murphy fell off the pallets and onto the alley floor. The pursuit was over before it had started.

Father Murphy lay on the ground, looking lost in every way a man can. Sly leered at him and then studied the big, empty alley where Eightball used to be.

"Fuck!" Sly kicked the wall next to him. "Fuck, fuck, fuck!"

Father Murphy uncovered his ears and stared down the dark alley. "Don't worry, Mr. Sly. The treasure is locked up tight, and I know where the key is. We'll see Mr. Eightball again soon enough."

———————◆———————

Eightball felt his heart in his throat and the warm paper in his hand. He had run only two blocks when he spotted a taxi idling on the corner. He sprinted over and jumped in the back. The driver slammed his newspaper down and yelled, "What's the big idea scaring me like that? Hit the bricks, I'm off duty."

Eightball pressed his straight razor to the driver's throat. "Consider this overtime. Drive." The newspaper floated onto the passenger seat. The clutch moaned and the cab bucked into gear before peeling down the street.

"Make a right here."

The headlights hit DeLuce and Murnane spilling out of the alley, right in front of the cab.

"Keep goin' or I'll give you a St. Paul smile from ear to ear. Get me?"

Eightball jerked when the driver hit the gas. He felt the driver's Adam's apple move against the razor's edge when the driver swallowed hard. Eightball looked out the back window and grinned wide at Murnane and DeLuce. The two louses stood there looking like they got stood up on prom night.

"Go East on Hennepin Avenue."

Eightball turned and watched Murnane and DeLuce disappear around the corner. Once his pursuers were out of sight, Eightball focused forward, his eyes narrowing in the rearview mirror.

"Take me to St. Paul."

30.

Sugar in Her Bowl

SLY COULDN'T REMEMBER a colder moment or a colder night. His paper—along with Eightball—were gone. A ruthless Mob boss and a relentless cop were running him down and would love nothing more than to identify the remains of one Sylvester Hobbs. He felt cold to the bone, dirty, hungry, tired, and goddamned horny. And all he had to pin his hopes on was one scared little priest. The treasure seemed harder to get to than Lily's sweet honey pot. *Shit! Sugar.*

"What should we do?" Father Murphy asked. "We have no money for a cab and I certainly don't think I will survive another train ride."

Sly pulled Lily's address from his pocket and unfolded it. "Here, tell me where this is." A less-than-romantic sensation was building in his trousers.

Father Murphy took Lily's address, removed his spectacles from his shirt pocket, and examined the writing.

Sly had forgotten all about Father Murphy's glasses. Somehow they had survived without bending or breaking. Then Sly remembered Father Murphy stuffing them in his pocket once the idiots were done frisking him at the Chap's Room.

"What is this place?" Father Murphy asked. He brought the address close to his face. "You certainly have exquisite penmanship."

"Just get us there."

"I believe it to be a few blocks that way." Father Murphy nodded west.

Now that the paper Sly had been coveting was out of his reach, different feelings simmered inside Sly and his desire to see Lily swelled. That feeling was very familiar, and hopefully curable.

Sly and Father Murphy walked side by side. Father Murphy squinted at Lily's address every half-block or so. Sly kept Father Murphy very close as they moved along the icy, sandy sidewalks, keeping to the shadows. Every small movement around them drew Sly's complete attention. Steam rose from the sewers and puffed like a dime store cigar. Every plume turned into a frightful ghost before blowing away in the frigid winds. Sly rubbed his eyes and kept the idea of specters to himself.

"Mr. Sly? How can you live like this?"

"What's that mean?"

"We should have, by all reasonable accounts, been dead no less than four times today. Is that the life you envisioned for yourself as a child? Looking over your shoulder and dodging death around every corner?"

"Never really thought about it."

Father Murphy slowed his pace. "You should reexamine your choices, Mr. Sly. Reasonable people don't live like this. Reasonable people get married and raise children and go to church on Sunday."

"Regular folks settle for what life gives 'em. I take what I want, and I don't let no woman or job run my life. The working man's a sucker. I watched my old man work his whole life just so he could lose his shitty job and drink himself into an early grave. But not before he beat the shit outta me and Mom every chance he got. I'm not going to be stupid and work just so's I can give money to the church. No way."

"So giving money to the church is stupid?"

"*Going* to church is stupid. You tell folks that if they don't behave, they'll go to Hell. You scare them into giving you money. What a scam."

"That's not really our message."

Sly could tell by Father Murphy's silence that the old man had no response to Sly's insightful views of the church.

"Are you not afraid of Hell?" Father Murphy asked.

Sly examined the concerned look on Father Murphy's wrinkled, frost-nipped face. "No."

"Why not?"

"Because it don't exist."

"Well, Mr. Sly, I happen to know it does."

"Why are we talking about this? Maybe you should rest your jaw awhile—it's probably tired."

"I've devoted my heart and soul to loving and caring for my fellow man, no matter how vile they may be." Father Murphy raised his eyebrows and peered over his glasses to study Sly. "But you, dear boy, have proven to be the greatest test of my faith in mankind."

"Thanks. I guess." The wheels turned in Sly's head. He thought about the comment a bit more and realized it was not a compliment after all. Anger simmered to the surface. "And look where all your Bible learnin' and Hell-fearin' got you. Today you seen how people *really* live. What do you think? Where's your God now? I don't see him tryin' to help you out none too much." Sly raised his chin and stepped just a little higher.

"He never gives us more than we can handle. He believes in you, as do I. I see a light in you, Mr. Sly."

"Well then, you're *blind*. I'm just fine the way I am, so bite your tongue next time you feel like preachin'." Sly quickened his pace just enough to signal an end to the conversation. Father Murphy caught up to Sly quickly. Apparently, Father Murphy wasn't ready to give up.

"I'm just worried about you, Mr. Sly."

"I've kept myself above ground this long, haven't I? And now I'm about to be rich." Sly smiled and rubbed his hands together.

"Mr. Sly, about that . . . We have a problem."

Sly stopped. He heard a loose shutter, caught by the wind, slamming against a wall. "What now?"

Father Murphy stopped and faced Sly. "It's that man, DeLuce. He's not a normal man."

"Ach!" Sly waved his hand trying to shoo the crazy talk from the air. It was easier to label the priest as an old, drunk, crazy, tired fool than admit to himself that Father Murphy just might be telling the truth.

"Don't believe anything DeLuce says. That man is pure evil. He wants you to think he's just a man, but he is not."

"Enough, Priest!" Enough! It's not like the goddamned Devil is chasing us."

"As a matter of fact, He is."

"Bite your tongue and chew on that for a while." Sly really wanted the conversation to end so he walked away and shut his mouth. Guilt, and the effort it was taking Father Murphy to keep up, slowed Sly's pace. "Look, get us to the treasure and I'll make sure the church gets a nice fat donation. How'd that be? Huh? Will that shut you up?"

"That paper is a magnet for evil. How do you think DeLuce keeps finding us?"

"He's just a guy. You have no idea what you're talking about."

"I have faith in a higher power, Mr. Sly. My faith gives me a strong intuition when evil is near. The more powerful the evil, the stronger the sensation. The officer accompanying DeLuce—I think you said his name was Murnane. I don't get that feeling about him. He must be a good man."

"Ha! Are you kidding me? Murnane is as crooked as a trout stream. If DeLuce *was* the Devil, Murnane would be holding his pitchfork for him while he took a piss. And by pitchfork, I mean tally wacker."

"Despite your crassness, I see good in *you*."

Priest's statement floated through layer after layer in Sly's mind. Sly didn't believe there was good inside himself, so he found it unlikely someone else could see any. Sly turned away from Father Murphy and smiled.

"We'll get to where we're going and hole up for the night. We'll get you warmed up and hopefully get something to eat. You sure Eightball won't find the treasure?" Sly asked.

"Without the key, he has no chance. Even if he figures out where in St. Paul it is."

"You better be right, Priest. I'll whip you good and proper if you're still lyin' to me." Sly felt his threats holding less and less venom.

"I assure you, Mr. Sly, he needs us. But please take heed. Mr. Eightball may not be our biggest concern when we arrive in St. Paul. DeLuce may already be waiting for us when we get there," Father Murphy said.

Sly spotted a green-and-white striped awning. "There it is, just like she said."

"She? She who?" Father Murphy asked.

Sly stopped under the awning. Father Murphy held the address up and checked it against the numbers on the building. "This is it," he said.

"Let's go," Sly said, and held the door open for Father Murphy.

The window in the door rattled when it slammed behind Sly. Their weary footsteps creaked against the worn wooden stairs. Father Murphy stopped in front of Lily's apartment door and Sly knocked quietly. Sly wondered what time it was. *Probably around two in the morning.*

From behind the door, a lady's voice yelled, "Who is it?"

"It's me. Sly." Sly winked at Father Murphy who frowned in disapproval and shook his head. "Your outlaw. Sorry to bother you this hour."

"No bother. Just got home from work. I'll be there quicker than a bunny whisker!"

Sly turned to Father Murphy. "Get behind me."

"What?" Father Murphy asked.

"Get behind me. If she sees you out here, she might not let us in."

"I don't think the young lady would send us out into the cold. Reflect on the story of Mary and Joseph . . ."

Sly presented a tight fist. "Shut up and get behind me or I'll slug you—so help me God."

Father Murphy looked three shades past aggravated, but he slid behind Sly. Sounds of doors closing and furniture sliding across hardwood floors made Sly wonder what exactly she was up to in there.

Lily flung open the door. She wore a red silk robe over a black lace negligee that left little to Sly's reeling imagination. Tied loosely at the waist, it seemed the only thing holding that robe closed was Lily's will.

The hallway light played upon her supple skin, offset by the darkened apartment behind her. He really wanted to turn this moll into his doll—his drumming heart confirmed it. *What a dish.*

She smiled and opened her arms for a hug—until Father Murphy popped out from behind Sly. Lily's face went from happy to shocked. She clasped her robe tight across her breasts and shrieked. Father Murphy gasped and slapped his hands over his eyes.

When she tried to slam the door, Sly stuck his foot out and yelped when it struck against his instep. The door bounced open and Sly hobbled into the darkened apartment. He could barely make out a couch and a coffee table. A cat streaked across the living room, its claws clicking against the hardwood floor, following Lily into her well-lit bedroom.

Sly couldn't help but notice how much her ass looked like two perfect scoops of ice cream. The only thing keeping him from solving the mystery of where the seams of her stockings ended was a loosely tied red silk robe.

"What the hell is the priest doing here? Get rid of him," Lily yelled from inside her room.

Sly raised his eyebrows and removed his flat cap and shifted his weight from one foot to the other.

"How was I supposed to know you'd answer the door wearing next to nothing?"

"That was meant for you to see, not the whole world! What kind of a girl do you think I am?"

"I can't just send him out in the cold, doll face."

"The hell you can't!"

"Oh, come on, sugar-pie, don't be a flat tire. He don't mean no harm. He's a *priest*." *Oh, shit. I forgot the sugar for her bowl.* "Are you mad about the *sugar?*"

"What?" Lily peeked out the doorway, grimaced, then retreated like Sly had stuck a dead fish under her nose. "I've done some pretty seedy things in my life, but being half-naked in front of a priest takes the cake. I've never been so embarrassed in all my life."

"Don't you think you're overreacting? I mean it's not like he hasn't seen stuff like that before."

"He's doesn't run a burlesque bar, you idiot! He's a priest!"

Sly's comment drew a queer glance from Father Murphy as well.

"Now get out, the both of you. Go, before I call the cops."

"Sweetheart, we got nowhere to go. The job went south and we lost our partner. The cops and the Mob are already after us and we need your help. Please."

Silence beamed from Lily's bedroom. The cat peeked out before Lily reappeared, the red silk tied tightly around her. She set her fists on her hips.

Sly lowered his head and tried to loosen the ties with his smile. "Please?"

Considering the look on Lily's face, Sly knew he would need to be a safecracker to remove that robe. She crossed her arms, stomped twice, and pouted. "Oh, I sure know how to pick 'em. When the sun comes up I want you gone. And don't ever come back, *or else.*" She wagged her finger like it held the power to cast evil spells. "You're real lucky my roommate's not coming home tonight. *Real* lucky. She woulda called the cops for sure." Sly's eyes had adjusted enough to see Lily pointing at the worn, brown couch with stuffing sticking out of various rips in the fabric. "You two should be very cozy right there."

Sly shuffled over to the couch and sat down. Father Murphy sat next to him. In the shaft of light coming from the bedroom, Sly saw dust and cat hair float up.

Sly peered at Lily's silhouette. "This will do just fine. I knew I was right about you. You're the bee's knees."

"Hmpff." Lily crossed her arms again and withdrew back into her bedroom. After the cat followed her inside, Lily slammed the door.

"Well, I guess it's just you and me, Priest."

"Indeed."

"Go ahead, Priest, take the couch. I'll take the floor." Sly wanted to follow Lily and try to explain his way into her room, and then into other things, but set a blanket on top of Father Murphy instead.

The streetlight cast shadows throughout the second-floor apartment. A tear trickled down Father Murphy's cheek and his lip quivered. Sly rolled his eyes. "What now?"

"Mr. Sly, what is happening to you? You just gave up your spot on the couch and subjected yourself to the cold, hard floor. Also, you could have easily barged in with threats of violence and forced that woman to take us in, but you didn't. I am so happy to see this new side of you."

"I don't have a gun, or I would have barged right in."

Father Murphy smiled and shook his head. "No. I know you wouldn't have hurt her."

"Shut up and go to sleep."

Priest fell asleep the second his head hit the couch. His snoring rattled the windows and Sly's nerves.

Sly lay on his back on the cold, hard floor, his fingers intertwined behind his head, and studied the long shadows creeping across the ceiling.

He couldn't stop glancing at the warm glow under Lily's bedroom door. The light called to him and he had to answer.

31.

Bitter Medicine

MURNANE LOOKED THROUGH THE WINDOW of the passing cab. Eightball held something sharp and shiny to the cab driver's throat. *Only Eightball. No Sly. No priest. Damn.*

Watching Eightball slip away yet again left Murnane feeling like a heel who had just been stood up on prom night. Murnane had had more than his fill of being made the fool and wanted those sons of bitches locked up till the Rapture.

Brooding silence enveloped the walk back to the flophouse. Murnane couldn't understand how those inept greaseballs kept getting away. And judging from DeLuce's tense demeanor and loud, clomping steps, he assumed DeLuce contemplated the same thing.

When Murnane returned to the flophouse, curious gawkers were milling about like sedated cattle let loose from their pens, too dumb to run away. Luckily, they kept their distance. Murnane studied the fresh tracks in the snow, which diagrammed one hell of a struggle. A bloodstain on the sidewalk marked where Murnane remembered Eightball had sliced open one of the Butchers. Only the bloodstain remained.

DeLuce circled the blood stain on the sidewalk. "Look, I don't care how many questions you have to answer once we get there, but we are going to Minneapolis police headquarters to wait for that cab driver to show up. He'll be able to tell us where he dropped Eightball off," DeLuce said.

Murnane also wondered how the Butchers kept sliding in and out of his evening—especially now that one of them was seriously injured. However, the Butcher Boys' whereabouts were of little consequence versus the whereabouts of Sly and Eightball.

"How the fuck do they keep getting away while hauling an old priest around with them. It's like they have a guardian angel," DeLuce said. "Son of a bitch!" He kicked a nearby lamp post and hobbled away in pain.

Murnane would do exactly as DeLuce had suggested—not because DeLuce said so, but because DeLuce's suggestion was the next logical step in the investigation and had the greatest probability of yielding a solid clue. Murnane was prepared to be asked a shitload of questions from the Minneapolis cops. A St. Paul squad car parked outside Minneapolis police headquarters in the middle of the night would draw some attention.

Murnane had his own questions. Something about that matchbook he lifted off Mudbone kept gnawing at him. He pulled out the matchbook, rubbed his thumb over it, and read silently. *The Chap's Room.*

"How long until you have to make the next phone call?" Murnane asked.

"Hours. Let's get to the station." DeLuce stepped off the curb and made his way to the patrol car.

"I think we should check out the Chap's Room."

DeLuce stopped, keeping his back to Murnane. "The cab driver is a sure bet. I'll admit I fucked around a little bit back at the Broken Bone, but now it's time to get down to business. The clock's ticking for both of us. I say we get to the station and wait for the cab driver."

There was more worry in DeLuce's voice than before. His frustration was the lit fuse on a powder keg and dangerously close to detonation. Murnane was ready to watch the fireworks.

"This place is only a few blocks away. Let's check it out," Murnane said.

Murnane followed DeLuce to the car.

The ride over to the Chap's Room was quiet, the way Murnane

liked it. Murnane parked near the speakeasy entrance.

"Give me your coat again," Murnane said.

"What are we playing, musical *coats*?" They exited the car and De-Luce removed his coat and handed it to Murnane for the second time.

Murnane tugged on the lapels before quickly bending over and double-checking his hair in the passenger side rearview mirror.

DeLuce searched the steaming alley. His apprehension could be seen from Wisconsin. He scowled and raised one eyebrow. "You better be right about this."

Murnane nodded. "The entrance is down the alley by that steam pipe."

"If you're wrong, your family's going to pay." DeLuce started down the alley. "Hold up a minute," Murnane said.

DeLuce stopped. "What is it?"

Murnane removed DeLuce's coat and tossed it on the squad's hood. He unbuttoned his uniform jacket and folded it as he would an American flag presented to a fallen officer's widow. Mary flashed through his mind. He pushed the image aside and set the uniform in the patrol car, and closed the car door. He put DeLuce's coat back on and said, "Okay."

DeLuce chuckled. "*Now* you listen to me."

After what happened in the Broken Bone concerning his uniform, Murnane wasn't taking any more chances. It seemed to be a beacon for bloodshed.

Thawing garbage met Murnane at the alley's entrance and the smell poked up his nose like a sharp stick. He checked the rotting piles of discarded food, broken bottles, and smashed crates, half-expecting to spot protruding limbs as he walked past.

Murnane knocked on the inconspicuous Chap's Room door. Steam hissed and clouded his view. Despite the chill of the night and his partner, the warmth was welcome.

"Don't tell them Mudbone's dead. Act like we have business with him."

DeLuce didn't respond. The fuse was burning.

The door opened about two inches, shining a slice of warm light into the darkness. No demands for a password, no questions, no voices heard. Murnane slipped his hand over his pistol resting snuggly in the holster under his coat.

"We have business," DeLuce said.

The door opened a bit wider allowing more light to escape. "We need to see Mudbone," Murnane said.

"Who's askin'?" The authoritative voice sounded like it belonged to an authoritative man who most likely held an authoritative gun.

"Open the fucking door, asshole." DeLuce pounded the butt of his fist against the metal door, sending the sounds reverberating through the alley.

Murnane held up his hand, urging DeLuce to stop. DeLuce sneered, but settled himself and answered, "DeLuce outta Chicago and his . . . associate." Being called DeLuce's associate made Murnane feel worse than if he had swallowed a coffee can full of rusty nails.

"I heard a you," the authority responded.

"We have business with Mudbone," Murnane said.

"What kinda *business*?"

"The kind that will make you all a lotta money. Now open the fuckin' door, it's freezing out here," DeLuce said.

When the door swung open, a deluge of warm air swept over Murnane. He kept his head on a swivel and stepped inside.

A callused vise of a hand welcomed Murnane by grabbing the back of his neck and shoving him against the wall. Coarse brick dug into his cheek. The door slammed. A shotgun barrel pressed up under Murnane's nostrils. The smell of gunpowder and gun oil rose from the barrel. His nose hairs itched, but he didn't dare move to scratch.

Despite having the side of his face kissing the brick wall, Murnane had a clear view of DeLuce, who was no better off. A shotgun was aimed at the back of his skull.

These guys weren't going to shoot, not inside the speakeasy. But that knowledge didn't mean Murnane could lose his composure or make a move to disarm his welcoming party.

Unable to see who owned the hands patting him down from behind, Murnane felt his gun slide from its holster. Next they grabbed his shoulder and spun him around so his back was to the wall.

The eyes staring through Murnane were tortured, deep, and as menacing as the sawed-off double-barrel under his nose. The ebony man looked like someone who would pull the trigger and then kick the corpse for making a mess. "What you want with Mudbone?"

One man lowered his axe handle and turned DeLuce away from the wall to get a good look at him. "Shit. This guy really is DeLuce," he said.

Another man slapped a Louisville slugger against his palm. "How do you know that?"

"I seen lotsa his wanted posters. Yeah, that's him all right. Leave them alone."

The thugs appeared to back off of DeLuce as a sign of respect mixed with a healthy dose of fear. When the shotgun slowly withdrew, Murnane rubbed his nose and counted four other men holding axe handles, pipes, and baseball bats.

"You treat all your guests like this? You must make a killing on tips," DeLuce said while straightening his necktie.

"Sorry, Mr. DeLuce, but Mudbone say anyone who come askin' for him gotta be treated rough on account of he don't trust *nobody*."

"What's your name?" Murnane asked.

"They call me Bumble Zee."

"That's one hell of a name," Murnane said.

"My last name starts with Z, and when I punch a chump, my right hook stings awful bad."

Murnane watched DeLuce eyeball each man. If DeLuce's eyes had been gun barrels, every man would have been dead before he hit the ground.

"We need to see Mudbone." DeLuce said. Emotionless.

"He ain't here," Bumble Zee answered.

"Do you know where he went?"

"Peacewood Cemetery. Said he'd be back in a few hours."

"Well, I really don't feel like going back out into the cold. Is it okay if we go in and have a drink while we wait?" Murnane asked.

"Go ahead inside. Tell Lou the bartender you're here to see Mudbone. He'll take care of you."

DeLuce followed two of Mudbone's men from the room. Murnane brought up the rear. He wanted to keep as many people in front of him as possible. The men led him and DeLuce to an empty room containing a giant aluminum freezer door against one wall. After Mudbone's men opened the freezer door, Murnane followed the group down a long narrow hallway. When Murnane entered the main room, he stopped cold.

The sheer size and audacity of this establishment impressed the hell out of Murnane—and made him feel helpless. In spite of Prohibition's watchful eye, the Chap's Room operated as though the Purity Squad had never existed. The crowded dance floor, vibrant music, and booze-fueled laughter served as a painful reminder of Murnane's choice to take kickbacks and payoffs. His remorse grew, thanks to every clinking glass and gleeful squeal.

As Murnane stepped up to the bar, Lou was wiping up a melting ice chuck with a clean white linen towel. *The one-eyed bartender back at the Broken Bone could have taken a lesson or two on cleanliness from this place.* Lou stood about two inches shorter than Murnane, but looked real sturdy. The crude tattoos on Lou's forearms were done in prison, not the armed services. Lou was the type to have held his own in many a prison yard tussle. Knotted knuckles and a bent nose meant he had boxed—possibly semipro, or for back-alley money, or both. Lou did his best to shout over the raucous music.

"What can I do for you gentlemen?"

"We're here to see Mudbone. They said you'd take care of us while we wait." Murnane attempted to look pleasant by grinning like an asshole, as if everything Lou said was compelling.

Lou flashed a half-cocked grin. "Sounds good to me. What'll you have?" Lou flipped the towel over his left shoulder. His right hand was scarred by powder burns. So he knew his way around a firearm—a definite sign Lou moonlighted as an enforcer.

DeLuce sat on a stool and set his forearm on the bar. Murnane saw him swivel to get a better view of the clientele, letting his eyes linger on the ladies. "Gin is fine," he said, never taking his eyes off the dance floor.

"Whatever you got is fine," Murnane said.

As Lou poured the drinks, Murnane asked, "So did Mudbone leave with anybody?"

"The only people who ask those kinda questions are cops." Lou used the towel on his shoulder to dry his hands. "You know we make a great pulled pork sandwich. Do you like roasted *pig?*"

"We just heard a couple of our friends were with him earlier. We need to talk to them too," Murnane said.

Lou set the bottle next to the two glasses on the bar. "My memory ain't so good lately—used to be a boxer—took a lotta shots to the head. There's medicine I can take, but I can't quite afford it. You understand."

DeLuce understood the sound of a bribe as well as any cop in St. Paul. He spun around to face Lou. Murnane closed in on DeLuce in case they had to make a quick getaway.

"I'd love to help you out, pal, but I left my wallet at my boss's office," Murnane said. Murnane turned and spoke directly into DeLuce's ear. "Some asshole made me leave it behind because he was in such a big damn hurry."

When DeLuce reached below the bar, Murnane put even odds on DeLuce pulling out a gun or a wallet. DeLuce's black leather wallet appeared and he slid out a ten spot.

Murnane snatched the money from DeLuce and slapped it on the bar. Lou swiped it up. "Three of 'em. Real shit rats, these guys. One was even dressed like a priest. I've heard of gangsters dressing up like cops to blend in during a robbery, but a priest is just wrong. Then the priest went and got himself hard boiled."

"Did they talk to anyone but Mudbone when they were in here?" Murnane asked.

"Goddamn that medicine can be expensive."

DeLuce attempted to jump across the bar, but Murnane grabbed his forearm and held him down. DeLuce slapped a second ten on the bar and crossed his arms. The bank was closed.

"Matter of fact, one of them got sweet on the waitress, Lilith."

"Where is Lilith?"

"She got off about an hour ago. She never consorts with the cus-tomers, but she really had it bad for this guy. Batting her eyelashes, swinging her hips like they were greased. She liked him, all right. The guy smelled like a barnyard too. But that didn't stop her from getting all googly-eyed and giving him her address."

"Do you think *I* could get Lilith's address—just to find out where the guy is, you understand. You'd be doing us a huge favor. Especially after we paid for you to get your mind right and all."

"Sure thing. Any pal of Mudbone's is a good egg in my book." The sarcasm in Lou's voice could have poisoned every person in the joint. Lou grabbed the pencil from behind his ear and licked the lead before scribbling on a notepad. Murnane didn't know why Lou was selling out Mudbone, nor did he care. Any clue that got him one step closer to saving his family was all that mattered.

Lou handed Lilith's address to Murnane who studied it before sliding it into his coat pocket.

"Lilith Carlson. Many thanks, Lou." Murnane slid off his stool and knocked twice on the bar top.

Apparently, spending twenty bucks left DeLuce sour and unwill-ing to bid Lou a cordial good-bye. Murnane waited for DeLuce to leave and followed right behind.

"Hey," Lou said. DeLuce and Murnane stopped and turned. "Thanks for the memories!"

DeLuce pointed at Lou and said, "Go fuck yourself!" Murnane turned and pushed into DeLuce's shoulder, urging him closer to the front door.

When Murnane and DeLuce arrived back at the entryway, the merry little welcoming party sat on stools and smoked liked clogged pot-bellied stoves. Axe Handle rose and approached a wall safe. He worked the combo and handed DeLuce and Murnane their guns. When Murnane retrieved his gun, he examined it to verify no joker had filed off the firing pin while they were talking to Lou. Still intact.

The outside door clunked behind Murnane. Murnane pulled De-Luce's coat tighter.

"What did I just pay twenty bucks for?" DeLuce asked.

"He just told us where to find those shit rats. Let's go."

DeLuce threw his hands in the air. "All they care about is the paper. They sure as hell aren't out chasing dames."

"It's a solid lead," Murnane said.

"Solid as cat shit. Let's get to the station and wait for the cab driver. And give me back my damn coat. I don't want you ripping it any worse than it already is."

Murnane removed the long, black coat and tossed it at DeLuce. "The address is three blocks away. Get in."

"That cab driver is sitting at cop shop headquarters telling everyone who will listen where he dropped off Eightball. That is where we need to be," DeLuce said, stuffing his arms into his overcoat and reexamining the tear in the sleeve. He then opened the passenger door, plunked his ass down, and slammed the door.

Murnane got behind the wheel and reveled in the heat from De-Luce's sparking fuse. Murnane pushed in the starter pedal and the clutch, but didn't put the car in gear. He could hear DeLuce's teeth grinding.

"You're willing to put your family's lives on the line for a *hunch*?"

"We came out with a lead and we're going to follow it." Murnane jammed the car into gear and pulled away from the curb. He pulled up in front of a door under a green-and-white striped awning. He parked and double-checked the address. "This is it," he said.

"Have fun," DeLuce said.

Murnane walked up the stairs, trying to step lightly and not make noise, remembering the reverberations his heavy feet caused at the flophouse. The thought of using Lilith's phone while DeLuce languished out in the car crossed his mind. He got to Lilith's door and pulled his pistol. He felt warm breath on the back of his neck. Two mountainous men loomed; one had a blood-soaked bandage wrapped around his neck.

32.

Kiss or Kill

SLY LAY ON THE COLD, hard floor unable to sleep. One reason was Father Murphy snoring louder than a locomotive crashing through the Lake Nebagamon ice. The other was the welcoming light calling to him from under Lily's bedroom door.

The wind outside whipped against the second-floor apartment window and howled through the back alley. Newspaper pages and ice crystals fell victim to the harsh updrafts. Sly related to the feeling of being caught up in a whirlwind. He had fought hard throughout the day to be the leader, but couldn't shake the feeling of being *led*. And he knew that when the wind finally stopped, the paper would have nowhere to go but down.

The alley lamp provided the same soft light as the full moon, just enough to cast shadows across the dark apartment.

Sly wanted nothing more than to barge in on Lily and take charge, like a real man would. To have his way with her, because that's what she wanted him to do—*right?*

Sly never considered himself an expert on dames, dolls, or molls. For all his bravado, women scared the shit out of him. Lily was the first girl in a long time to take an honest interest in him without intending to stab him, rob him, or press charges. Sly continued to study the light, letting his mind drift into his muddy past.

A long, heavy sequence of embarrassing events trailed out like a rusty chain tied to a sinking boat anchor.

He remembered kissing Tammy Lynn Johnson behind the church when he was six. Neither understood what kissing really meant, but Tammy explained that she watched her parents kiss and all Sly and Tammy had to do was put their lips together. Since Sly never saw his parents do such things, he did just as Tammy instructed.

Kissing felt awkward, but exciting—until Father Vaughan came around the back of the church and caught them. Vaughan could run fast for an old man and proceeded to chase Sly with a broom. Vaughan could also hit with the best of them, getting in a couple good whacks before Sly outran him. At school the next day, Tammy claimed that Sly had attacked her. No girl would go near him for years to follow.

Next he remembered playing kiss or kill with a group of cute girls when he was thirteen. The girls screeched and fought like feral cats to avoid his grasp. Sly wasn't sure if they hated him because of his smell, the dirt on his face, or Tammy Lynn's nasty rumor. When he finally caught a girl, she immediately cried and punched at the air, screeching *Kill! Kill! Kill!* It was the first time he ever pushed a girl in anger, but not the last. When she got up and ran away, she seemed pleased at having escaped without a kiss.

Then the shameful tale of Emma Norton rekindled. Emma reminded Sly of a coyote—because of her matted hair and how she'd eat things she found on the ground. Also in the way she always walked alone, almost prowling.

Emma was about as cute as an old potato sack, and every bit as dirty, but Sly knew his choices were limited. Emma had the one quality Sly needed in a girl—low standards. Her nickname in school was *pincushion*. Sly found a kindred spirit in Emma; they were both outcasts.

The first time he attempted to kiss Emma, she asked, "What are you, six? Kiss like a man." When Emma closed her eyes and opened her mouth and cocked her head to one side, Sly did the same. When their mouths collided, Sly swore he chipped a tooth.

One day he picked brown-eyed Susans for Emma. He went to her farm, but no one was at the house. He heard noises in the barn and walked in on her and skinny Lloyd Martin rolling naked in the hay.

She looked at Sly and smiled, but kept right on riding Lloyd, using her knees to keep from being bucked off, like Lloyd was some untamed horse. Sly envisioned plunging a hatchet into their skulls but chose to drop the flowers and walk home instead, vowing to kill every coyote he ever came across from that day forward.

Now he stared at the line of light daring him to knock on Lily's door. But the past was a leg iron shackling him in place. Lily was only a few feet away. Courage surged as his feelings for her ignited.

He used the couch for leverage, being careful not to disturb Father Murphy, and stood. He crept to Lily's door like a thief willing to steal her heart, if she'd let him in. He rested his shaking fingers on the door handle and turned it at a snail's pace trying to keep it from squeaking.

"Who's there?" Lily barked. Sly had been bitten by less hostile guard dogs.

Sly bowed his head and released the handle like it had turned white hot. "It's me."

"Go away. I'm not talking to you."

Sly opened the door and peeked his head in. A pillow bounced off his face.

"Get out."

"I just want to talk to you. Give me one minute." He slipped inside the room and gently closed the door behind him.

Lily sat up in bed and crossed her arms and looked at him like he was something her cat had thrown up.

"What do you want? I hope you don't think you're getting in this bed."

He stopped creeping toward her bed and raised his palms. "No, not at all. I would never think that."

"Well, are you going to stand there like a sap all night, or are you going to spill it? A lady needs her beauty sleep."

He studied the way her bobbed hair curled over her ears and just touched her soft neckline. His weight shifted from his left leg to his right and back again.

"I want to say I think you're really swell and that I am sorry for bringing Priest here, but we had no choice. We were sitting in our flophouse room and the cops busted in and there was a big shoot-out and we jumped out the window and ran and then got shot at some more. I didn't think I'd get outta there alive, honest."

"You got shot at?" A favorable combination of worry and sympathy softened her voice and her eyes. She inched closer. "What else happened? Did you kill anyone?"

"I think we got one of the big ones. Giant blond guy with a twin brother."

"Oh, you poor thing." She patted the chenille bedspread next to her. "Come sit next to me." Sly slide-stepped to the bed and sat down next to Lily. He realized being shot at was far less nerve-racking than talking to a beautiful dame.

"Tell me all about it—my big, bad gangster," Lily whispered, touching Sly on the knee.

Sly felt his knees lock together. He really appreciated her concern. This was by far the best he'd felt all night. Hell, maybe in *years*. "I think that's about it," he said.

She used her fingertips to caress the top of his thigh. "Well, be glad you got away no worse for wear," Lily said.

Nothing could ruin this moment. "Other than Eightball stole my paper . . ." *Goddamn it.*

"Paper? He stole your newspaper? I have today's edition right over there." She pointed to her dresser cluttered with open jars of radium-glowing cold creams, perfume bottles, piles of unwashed clothes, and one folded newspaper.

"No." Sly fought the urge to tell her the truth. Every fiber of his being told him to lie, but when his eyes met hers, the truth flew out of him faster than Priest through a second-story flophouse window.

"Priest is here to tell us about a piece of really old paper I found. He knows what it means and we need him to tell us where it leads to. And it belongs to the mobster chasing us and he's got a tough cop helping him track us."

Lily folded her hands in her lap and lifted her shoulders. "It leads someplace? Like a treasure map?" She swung her gams over the bedside and moved well within kissing distance to Sly. When he looked at her stockings, tingles appeared in long-dormant places on his body.

Don't say yes. Don't say yes. Don't say yes.

"Yes." Sly's frustrated brain tied in knots while he watched the cat sit at the end of the bed and lick itself with one rear paw straight up in the air. "At least that's what Priest said just before the cops came bustin' in on us. But we never got the whole story."

"Do you want me to talk to him? Ask him where the treasure is, maybe? He might be more inclined to talk to a woman." She batted her butterfly eyelashes.

"He's a priest. He ain't gonna go for any of that flimflam."

She let her shoulders drop. "Guess you're right. So what are you gonna do?"

"He says he knows where the treasure is, so in the morning we're heading back to St. Paul."

"The treasure is in St. Paul?"

"That's what he says."

"Where in St. Paul? It's a big city." She ran her candy-apple-red fingernails gently across his knee. "You can tell me, sweetie. I want to help you."

If some palooka had been asking questions about the treasure, Sly would have been suspicious. But a beautiful dame like Lily wouldn't double-cross him over some loot. No way. "I don't know. He fell asleep before he could say anything more. I figured I'd let him sleep. He's had a helluva day. Plus, he's not going nowhere." The last thing Sly wanted to do was talk his way out of Lily's bedroom.

Lily cocked her head. "What makes you so sure?"

"He's been going on and on about some curse. About how the Devil is chasing us and he's gonna take our souls and all kinds of crazy shit. Priest says he won't leave our sides until we're safe, whatever that means." Sly attempted to use a frail laugh to dismiss Father Murphy's predictions. The laugh didn't work.

"Well, I'll go with you boys to St. Paul in the morning."

"I don't think that's such a good idea. We've been getting shot at all day. I don't want to put you in danger."

Lily set her hands on her hips. "Well, that's a fine kettle of fish! I can handle myself, thank you very much."

Sly turned a concerned ear. Lily must have seen the concentration on Sly's face. "What is it?"

"You hear that?" he asked.

"Hear what?" she asked.

"Exactly."

The silence from the living room caused more fear in Sly than the sound of a gunshot. Something wasn't right.

Father Murphy let out a yell much too big for such a little man. Sly leapt and noticed Lily at his side when she clasped his arm and cowered behind him. Sly swung the door open. Father Murphy was standing next to the couch.

"The treasure. The treasure. The treasure," Father Murphy said.

Sly moved in close enough to shake the old man firmly, trying to wake him. "What is it, Priest? What are you saying?"

"The basement. The basement. The dark basement."

"What basement? Where?" Lily asked, her grip cutting off the blood supply to Sly's arm.

"The museum. In the basement." Father Murphy's head swayed from side to side. His eyes remained closed.

"He must mean the History Museum. He was tellin' me and Eightball about him and a bunch of scientists at the St. Paul History Museum. How they were studying the paper. It must be there—in the basement," Sly said. So much joy shot through him, his toes curled. He grasped Lily's upper arms. His smile was reflected in hers. Father Murphy lay back down on the couch and started sawing logs again.

Shit. That's where Eightball took my paper. Sly let go of Lily.

Lily tapped Sly on the arm and directed him to look to his right. Sly noticed several shadows cutting across the hall light leaking under the door. Too many for one set of legs. Sly could take three guesses as to who was in the hallway, and the first two wouldn't even count.

Sly reached down and covered Father Murphy's mouth to keep him from making noise. Father Murphy opened his eyes in a panic and struggled like a drowning man, gasping and kicking.

Sly raised his finger to his lips, signaling to Father Murphy to be silent, then escorted Father Murphy quickly and quietly to the front door. Lily grabbed a candlestick and held it over her head.

Someone knocked at the door and Death knocked on Sly's nerves.

Lily backed away from the door and asked, "Who is it?"

"Open up. It's the police."

Murnane.

33.

Back to Satan Paul

Sly recognized Police Chief Murnane's gruff voice all too well. Sly didn't understand how Murnane had found them again, but obviously the chief's tracking abilities far exceeded any rumors Sly had heard. Murnane had the nose of a bloodhound, the cunning of a fox, and the ferocity of a wolf—traits Sly feared and admired.

Sly used his hand to cover Father Murphy's mouth and nodded for Lily to answer the door. Father Murphy struggled under Sly's grip. "Be quiet. Murnane's at the door." The smell of a litter box in need of a cleaning added to Sly's choking tension.

Sly watched Lily's every move through the shadowy apartment, his eyes so wide they began to hurt.

Lily slid the door chain into place and opened the door until the chain went taut. The hallway light sliced across Lily's face and into the dark apartment, and finally cast across the floor. She rubbed her eyes.

"Yes?" She clutched her silk robe at the neck. "Who are you? What do you want?"

"I'm Police Chief Murnane. I need to ask you a few questions. May I come in ma'am?" Murnane asked.

"What time is it? Can't it wait until morning? I'm really tired."

"Sorry ma'am, it can't. Is your name Lilith?"

"Hopefully not. What's this about?"

"Did a man visit you at the Chap's Room earlier tonight?"

"Lots of men visit me at the Chap's Room *every* night. I'm a waitress. But I'll bet you already knew that."

"There are two men working together. One goes by the name of Sly, the other Eightball. They have a hostage—a small man dressed like a priest. It was one of these men we believe showed a particular interest in you."

"I don't know what hooch you got into, but you should save these stories for your wife. You could even send them into *True Detective* and get 'em published."

"Are you saying you haven't seen these men?"

"Like I said, I see men every night."

"Lou told me one of them took a special interest in you."

"First of all, Lou is a lying son of a bitch who gossips more than an entire sewing circle. Second, I come home every night with my ass covered in bruises from hooch-jockeys pinching it thinking they're taking a *special interest* in me. If that's all you got, I would really like to get back to bed. Have a good night."

As Lily started to close the door, Father Murphy fidgeted, knocking a lamp off the table. The lamp landed softly on some dirty clothes on the floor. Priest gasped between Sly's fingers. Lily paused before closing the door.

"What was that?" Murnane asked.

"Oh. Just my cat. She gets into everything and loves to come and see who's at the door."

Sly slid next to the wall making sure his hand remained firmly across Father Murphy's mouth. Lily looked at Father Murphy and said, "Bad kitty." Sly watched her turn and smile at Murnane.

"Have a good night, Officer. Hope you find your bad guys."

Sly could see the top of Murnane's head cross the threshold, his eyes surely searching the darkness behind Lily. "Oh, I will. Goodnight."

Lily shut the door, cool as a cucumber. After looking through the peephole, she fell gently against the door, letting out a sigh. She set her right hand over her chest. "My God, is my heart pounding," she whispered.

Sly released Father Murphy, who looked angry as a wet hen while catching his breath. Lily checked the peephole once more, then under the door. The shadows were gone.

"We gotta get outta here—now," Sly said. He felt Murnane and DeLuce taking turns choking him as he spoke.

"Why? I just got rid of him."

"He's coming right back with a lotta guns, trust me."

"Oh, applesauce. He is not." She ran her fingernails up and down his bicep. "Please don't leave. It'll be worth your while."

"I'm afraid Mr. Sly is right. These men won't stop. I can feel De-Luce very close now."

"DeLuce?" Lily asked. "As in the DeLuce crime family outta Chicago?"

"The very same, I'm afraid," Father Murphy answered. "Now may be a good time for a prayer." Father Murphy closed his eyes, folded his hands, and mumbled in the dark.

"Knock it off, Priest," Sly said. He shrugged and turned toward Lily.

"We gotta leave and the front door's no good," Sly said.

"Take the fire escape."

Sly realized this was the beginning of their good-bye. He pulled Lily close by placing his hand against the small of her arched back. He wrapped his other arm around her waist. She squeaked in the most adorable way, somewhere between surprise and giggle.

Her soft lips tasted like warm honey when they brushed against his. She touched his face and moved her tongue in ways Sly wasn't used to—but loved. It was a real kiss. A *first* kiss.

"Amen," Father Murphy said.

After floating back to earth, Sly noticed the stupid grin on Father Murphy's face.

Sly released Lily. She flew out of his embrace and into her room. Sly moved over to the window and opened it, questioning in his head Lily's hasty retreat. Lily reappeared less than a minute later wearing a powder-blue overcoat and carrying socks, shoes, and a knit hat.

"What are you doing?" Sly asked, one leg already out the open window.

"I'm coming with you."

"No you're not."

"I'm not going to be here if DeLuce is coming."

Knock. Knock. Knock.

Muscles clenched in Sly's body and fear clenched in his mind. His attention flashed to Lily, then to Father Murphy, then at the door itself—expecting the door to smash open and guns to blast away.

Murnane spoke through the door. "Sorry to come right back, but I need to ask you one more thing."

Sly ducked out the window and tripped onto the fire escape. He lay on his back, the rusted iron grate digging into his shoulder blades. Father Murphy poked his head out the window. Sly maneuvered and reached over to help Father Murphy climb out.

"Hold on a second, Officer. I'm not decent!" Lily pulled the window down half way. She wrenched and pulled, but the window would not close.

"Go. I'll stall him as long as I can and I'll meet you at the History Museum," she said.

The finality in her eyes shimmered, thanks to fresh tears that tore Sly apart inside. Sly tried his damndest not to look at her as if it were the last time, hoping she really would meet him at the museum. But he didn't like his odds.

"See you in St. Paul, doll face," Sly said. The words crumbled like dried ash in a blustery night wind. Lily wrestled the window shut then disappeared from view.

Sly worked his way down the rusted and wobbling fire escape, looking up frequently to see how Father Murphy was managing. The escape rattled and separated a few inches from the building every time Sly shifted his weight. The rickety ladder slid out of place, then banged against the building, causing Father Murphy to let out several *whoas* accompanied by nervous chuckles.

Sly hung momentarily from the bottom rung before dropping to the ground. Father Murphy clung to the ladder no more than six feet off the ground.

"Goddamn it, Priest. Let go!"

Father Murphy looked over his right shoulder, then his left, then his right again. He latched on to the ladder like it was being lowered into a pond full of crocodiles.

"Just let go and fall backward. I'll catch you. Trust me." Sly meant it. "It's a lot shorter drop than from the flophouse window."

"I had no choice in that matter, if you recall."

"C'mon. Do you want to get shot? On three." Sly raised his arms. "One. Two."

Father Murphy tumbled through the air for the second time. This time Sly caught him like he was a dame jumping from a burning building. He set Father Murphy on his feet and slapped him on the back. "See. No big deal."

"Sometimes I think breaking my neck might be a nice relief from you and this whole experience. If there weren't so much at stake I would seriously consider that option."

Sly had to agree. Escaping through windows was becoming far too routine, but beat being shot at.

"You okay?" Sly asked.

Sly examined Father Murphy. It would take a lot of Scotch to wipe the weariness from the old man's eyes. The exhaustion cut straight to Father Murphy's bones; he had aged a few decades in only a few hours. The poor man had experienced more danger and peril in a few short hours than most people endure in a lifetime.

Sly wiped the rust from his hands.

"We need a taxi," Sly said.

"How will we pay?"

"I got it covered. Follow me."

The night's events taught Sly enough not to barge into the street. He snuck along the brick wall and stopped to peek around the corner. Sly spotted a St. Paul squad car parked only yards away. And a man wearing a fedora in the passenger seat. *DeLuce.*

Sly stopped and grabbed Father Murphy's sleeve. "Hold on. De-Luce's sitting in a squad car right around the corner."

"But look." Father Murphy tapped Sly on the arm. "A taxi."

The taxi was idling across the street. There was no way of getting in that vehicle without DeLuce seeing them.

Father Murphy tugged on Sly's sleeve. "What should we? . . ."

Sly yanked the priest by the wrist and ran for the taxi. He turned to see DeLuce shoulder the car door open. The bullets began to fly. Sparks and gravel pinged off the boulevard at Sly's feet. Father Murphy kept his head low and covered.

Sly dove in the back seat of the cab and pulled Father Murphy in on top of him. Sly yelled, "Drive!"

DeLuce fired again, hitting the rear of the cab.

"Son of a bitch!" the driver yelled before he cowered and jumped from the car.

A bullet shattered the rear window, sounding like a crate full of bottles had fallen from the sky. Sly covered his face. The pointed shards bounced off the back of his hands.

He wriggled out from under Father Murphy and into the front seat. He jammed the taxi in gear and popped the clutch. The car sputtered and jumped but kept gaining speed.

Sly hurled the taxi through the icy streets. He kept his eyes even with the top of the steering wheel and tried like hell not to smash into anything. After a few blocks, a quiet settled in, like the one between a lightning strike and a thunder clap. Sly relaxed a bit and sat taller in the driver's seat.

The distinctive sound of broken glass tumbling off Father Murphy came from the back seat. In the rearview mirror, Sly watched Father Murphy sit up and remove the larger shards from his coat.

"This all needs to end, Mr. Sly. I can't do this anymore. The sooner we get to St. Paul the better," Father Murphy said while Sly listened to him shuffling glass off his head, neck, and clothes. A pause set in. The kind Sly didn't want to acknowledge because he knew Father Murphy was thinking the same bad thought. Sly allowed the quiet to fester a bit, not wanting to pollute the taxi with more bad luck.

"What do you think will happen to her?" Father Murphy asked.

The question cut into Sly, deep and slow. "She'll be okay." He gripped the wheel a little tighter. "She'll be okay." As if saying it twice would make it so.

"We should go back and help her. They're going to hurt her—or worse." Sly looked in the mirror. Father Murphy folded his arms. The condemning eyes reflected in the mirror were every bit as sharp as the glass shards at Sly's feet. Oily exhaust combined with Father Murphy's rotten stare and filled the taxi's interior, making Sly sicker than he had felt all day. He hit the gas and let the fumes rushing in through the missing rear window make him queasier. Guilt was a bitch.

"Let's just get to the museum in St. Paul."

"I only said we need to get to St. Paul. How did you know we need to go to the museum?" Father Murphy asked.

"Not only do you snore like a buzz saw, you talk in your sleep."

Sly kept his foot to the floor along University Avenue. His eHxcitement grew as he closed in on the treasure—*his* treasure. Bitter cold wind flowed in, punishing him all the way back to St. Paul.

Sly slid to a stop in front of the museum and jumped out.

"Aren't you going to turn off the car?" Father Murphy asked.

"No. We might need to make a quick getaway."

Sly ran up the steps, leaving Father Murphy on his own. Sly rattled the locked brass door. He gritted his teeth and turned toward the cab. "Goddamn it, Priest! It's locked!"

Father Murphy closed the passenger door, waved from the sidewalk, and shouted, "Of course it's locked. What time do you think they open? Not for several hours yet."

Sly gazed at the horizon, painted a deep orange. *Christ, I'm going to live to see the sunrise.*

"We need to go around back. I know where they hide the spare . . ."

Eightball jumped from the shadows and interrupted Father Murphy. The priest thrashed his elbows side to side, but Eightball held him tight, holding a razor to the old man's throat.

"What's the point of that? There's no reason to kill Priest."

"I got it all now, Sly. The paper, Priest, everything, and there's nothing you can do about it."

"Then why kill him?" Sly stepped closer to Eightball, but not too close.

"I'm not going to slit his throat." Eightball removed the razor from Father Murphy's neck. "I'm gonna slit yours," Eightball said, using the razor as a pointer.

"I'm telling you, Mr. Eightball, if you kill him you will never see a penny of that treasure."

"Bullshit. What do I need him for? He's got nuthin'."

"We need Mr. Sly to access the artifacts. You see, he is the key. He has been all along."

"What do you mean?" Sly asked. He stepped onto the sidewalk, still well out of Eightball's reach.

"I'll explain once we are inside. Please, let's go. DeLuce won't be far behind," Father Murphy said.

Eightball released Father Murphy and took a step back. "You better not be jerkin' me around and makin' me look like a maroon."

Sly formed his hand into the shape of a gun, wishing the gun were real, and poked the air in Eightball's direction. "Once I get the treasure, you're dead, asshole."

Eightball folded the razor and put it back in his pocket. "All right, Priest, I'll play it your way. There ain't nuthin' anyone can do to stop me anyhow."

"How did you know where to find us?" Father Murphy asked Eightball.

"I listen good and have a great memory. Now get movin'." Eightball prodded Father Murphy.

"Do you still have my paper?" Sly asked.

"No. I have *my* paper."

Father Murphy used his right hand to push Eightball away from Sly. "Just know that what I am about to show you has no bearing on my ultimate goal to destroy the paper for the good of us all. Now please, let's get inside."

Sly let Father Murphy lead and stayed a few steps behind Eightball in case a razor came swinging at Sly's face. Father Murphy walked around the back of the museum to a small stairwell that sank below street level. A few steps closer to Hell, Sly thought. At the bottom stood a worn wooden door with a small jelly-jar light wrapped in chicken wire just above it.

"They showed me this entrance when I was working here all hours of the day and night." Father Murphy used his fingertips to pull out a loose brick. He retrieved a key and slid the brick back in place.

Father Murphy led the way and Eightball jumped in right behind him. Sly followed them in.

The darkness was thick and Sly feared razors slicing at him. Father Murphy said, "This way." Sly followed the sound of the priest's voice and the clicking of his heels.

Sly began to salivate in anticipation of seeing the loot. He smiled and clapped his hands. "After all the shit we've been through today, we're finally gonna get the treasure!" Sly's imagination overflowed with liquid-gold waterfalls, jewel-covered crowns too big for his head, and endless piles of cash money, far as the eye could see.

The old priest stopped at a cramped, dimly lit room. Crates were stacked along the walls. Thick clumps of dust covered the floor and cobwebs hung from the ceiling corners. Not even the cobwebs could curb Sly's excitement.

"Before we go any farther I need to explain something. We have come to the crossroads of your personal battles between good and evil. You can either save or condemn your souls by the choices you make here and now."

"Are the goods in these crates?" Sly asked, imagining this was how Christmas mornings *should* have felt.

"Listen. Or you will be sorry."

"Yeah, yeah, yeah, the curse and all that hooey. That's why we got you, remember? Where's the loot?" Sly asked.

"Be careful, Mr. Sly. The time has come to pay the bill for your actions—throughout today and your life—and it is a hefty sum."

Father Murphy spoke as though he had just found the remains of a missing loved one.

Sly shut up and listened.

"You see, the ancient Hebrews who pilfered the artifacts you are about to see did not do it alone. They had help."

Sly and Eightball responded in unison, "So?"

"The workers couldn't get the treasure out of the work camps without the Egyptians catching them. And after decades of pain and torture and unanswered prayers, the slaves turned to someone who *would* answer their pleas."

"That's all real great, Priest, but let's make with the goods." Sly felt like he might burst if he didn't see something golden in the next minute.

"They turned to someone who ultimately betrayed them. Someone who made their torture at the hands of the Egyptians seem like child's play," Father Murphy said. His voice conveyed a mixture of condemnation, foreboding, and hopelessness. Sly began to feel like insects were attempting to chew their way out of his stomach. "He promised them all the riches they could imagine and wanted only one thing in return. In exchange for helping them steal from the Egyptians, he took possession of their souls. He eternally damned them and bound their souls to the very paper Mr. Eightball holds. Their tortured souls are trapped inside, condemning anyone the paper chooses to seduce. It serves as the beginning of Purgatory for those of ill-conduct and wretched spirit. The paper's only purpose is to use one's own greed against him, thus trapping him, much like a spider and a fly. You haven't been following a map—you've fallen victim to a contract with the Devil."

34.

When Lilies Break

MURNANE STOOD BEFORE his person of interest, who sat on the couch with her arms crossed. Wearing a powder-blue overcoat, she was dressed like she had somewhere important to be at almost four o'clock in the morning.

DeLuce entered the apartment, followed closely by the Butcher Boys. DeLuce slammed the door, causing the cat to hiss from somewhere in the dark. The Boys planted themselves across the doorway, blocking it completely. If DeLuce let things get out of hand with Lily, Murnane figured the Butchers would keep him from interfering.

DeLuce elbowed Murnane aside and stood in front of Lily. The Butcher Boys flanked DeLuce, staying one step behind him.

"Tell me where they're heading, you bitch."

"I don't know what you're talkin' about."

"How stupid do I look?" DeLuce asked.

"Compared to what?"

DeLuce dug his fingertips into her supple cheeks, making her lips pucker.

"Oh, you're a real tough guy aren't you? Knockin' dames around makes you feel like a man, doesn't it." Her words became distorted through her squeezed face. "Who are those two creeps? They do your heavy lifting? Not quite man enough to get your own hands dirty?" The dame tried to act like she had nerves of steel, but her voice held the ferocity of a wet butterfly. She was scared, and Murnane knew she had a right to be.

Using his free hand, DeLuce removed his black fedora, exposing his slicked-back hair. Murnane smelled the combination of sweat and pomade—the scent almost overpowered the litter box. DeLuce set his hat on the couch.

"Do you know who I am?" DeLuce asked.

"Yeah. A guy who needs some mouthwash." Lily tried to lean back, but DeLuce's hand was clasped tight across her cheeks.

"You got a real fresh mouth for someone so close to death."

Lily's tears glinted in the dim light.

"You see, I can smell fear in people. I smell fear like regular Joes can smell a rotten skunk. I've built my empire on my ability to sniff it out and exploit it." DeLuce leaned in and sniffed her neckline. "The fear in you, my dear, is stronger than road kill on a hot day. Oh, your mouth puts up a fight, but your eyes tell a different story. I've never smelled anything so beautiful. Now . . . tell me where they went."

She turned away, shut her eyes, and contorted her face into a restrained sob. Her mascara dripped onto DeLuce's hairy knuckles.

Murnane knew when interrogating a person of interest that eventually she would wear down. Sooner or later the person being questioned realized she had one of two choices—talk or suffer. Murnane had seen more than enough suffering today.

Murnane held up his hand. "Enough."

DeLuce squeezed tighter, squeezing small, painful squeaks from Lily.

"*Enough*," Murnane said. DeLuce stepped back and folded his arms. Murnane had given DeLuce enough leeway earlier that night with the thugs in the alley outside the Broken Bone, and then again with Marcone and his men. He wasn't going to let DeLuce's nature out of its cage again.

"Look, Lilith."

"Only cops and clergy call me Lilith."

"Oh. What should I call you then?"

"Lilith."

Murnane held back a smile. He liked Lilith, finding her fresh mouth aggravatingly charming.

"They've already killed three people we know of. We don't want anyone else to get hurt." Murnane tried to sound convincing—a type of comforting authority he'd perfected through the years.

Lilith narrowed her eyes at the Butcher Boys. Arms folded, they continued to block the apartment door. They didn't blink. "Yeah, what are those two here to do? Teach me the Charleston?"

"Take it easy. No one's going to hurt you. Tell us where they went and we leave—it's that simple," Murnane said.

Murnane's person of interest smirked and looked at the floor.

"Looks like you have a pretty good thing going here. Nice apartment, good paying job . . . I can make life real difficult for you. I could have you out on the street by this time tomorrow. No job. No swanky apartment. No prospects. Is that what you want?"

"Cut the pussy-footing around, Murnane. Let's break her legs." DeLuce reared back, ready to strike the back of his hand across Lilith's cheek. Murnane stopped him by using a flat hand against DeLuce's chest.

"I said, wait."

DeLuce dropped his mitt to his side.

"Trust me, Lilith, a nice long stint in the cooler will make you see that piece of street-grease you're trying to protect isn't so attractive. Court systems these days are so backlogged, hell, it might be six months before we could get you in front of a judge. That should be enough time for Prince Charming to turn back into a frog. This is obstruction of justice, aiding and abetting a criminal, sweetheart," Murnane said.

Lilith swallowed a gulp of tears and anger before bending to Murnane's interrogation, showing defeat in her narrowed eyes and clenched jaw. *That's it—checkmate.* She used her index finger to motion for Murnane to come closer. She whispered, "St. Paul."

Murnane straightened up and looked down on Lilith. She set her face in her hands. Her shoulders bobbed in cadence with her silent sobs. *Another interrogation ends in tears.* This one, however, was by no means satisfying to him.

"What'd she say?" DeLuce asked.

"She says they're going to St. Paul."

"Where in St. Paul? It's a big fucking city." DeLuce situated his fedora on his head.

"Where in St. Paul, Lilith?"

She lifted her face from her hands. "The History Museum. They're going to the History Museum."

Murnane said, "Let's go," while stepping closer to the door.

DeLuce pulled out his pistol. He jammed it into Lilith's cheek. The muzzle tugged at her upper lip, inflicting a sneer across her face.

Murnane used a swift uppercut to knock DeLuce's forearm away from the girl's face. The gun flashed bright as lightning and just as violent, punching a hole in the plaster ceiling.

He saw a cut on Lilith's cheek start to bleed. He saw her scream. All he heard, though, was a high-pitched whine tearing at his eardrums.

Murnane grabbed DeLuce's wrist as if it were a rattlesnake in a baby's crib. "Leave her alone," Murnane said before shoving DeLuce toward the door. DeLuce spun and pressed the gun to Murnane's forehead. This time, Murnane heard Lilith scream. And out of the corner of his eye, Murnane saw Lilith faint.

"Now that I know where to find them, what do I need you for?" DeLuce asked.

"Pull the trigger," Murnane answered.

The gun burned against Murnane's skin, but he didn't pull away.

DeLuce squeezed his lips together. His dark twitching eyes appeared bottomless as they dared Murnane to make a move.

The drips of sweat between Murnane's shoulder blades felt like crawling snails leaving cold, itchy slime trails, heightening the tension as DeLuce's gun barrel looked him in the eye.

DeLuce white-knuckled the pistol and started to tremble. He clenched his jaw and inhaled. Murnane felt the forceful exhale against his face. DeLuce's breath smelled like car exhaust. He dropped the gun to his side.

DeLuce opened the apartment door and walked into the hallway, the Butcher Boys on his heels. "You drive," he said.

Murnane drove, savoring the silence as he neared the glowing St. Paul skyline. DeLuce hadn't said a word since the stare down ended at Lilith's apartment. The tension in the patrol car pulled tight against his thoughts.

"Why do you have to kill everyone you come across?" Murnane asked.

Passing streetlights, and the shadows between them, cast repeating light and dark bands across DeLuce's blank expression. "Because killing is the quickest way to get what I want."

"She was no threat to us. Why would need to kill her? You're just that evil? What the fuck did life ever do to you to make you this way?" Murnane had assumed God created DeLuce while nursing a hangover.

DeLuce lit a cigarette under his cupped hand and blew out the match. His cheeks went gaunt as he sucked in and the ember glowed. Murnane heard the dry tobacco crackling as it burned. DeLuce cracked the window and flicked the match into the cold night. Murnane checked the rearview mirror. The two masses in the back seat rendered the mirror useless.

The only thing colder than the wind rushing in was DeLuce's demeanor. The remainder of the ride back to St. Paul was as pleasant as being at a friend's funeral.

Murnane brought the patrol car to a sliding halt in front of the museum, parking it behind an idling taxi. DeLuce forced the car door open and ran up the museum steps. Murnane calmly exited the vehicle and stayed on the sidewalk. DeLuce rattled the front door, then cupped his hands against the glass.

"Let's check around back," DeLuce said, running down the steps.

Murnane followed fresh tracks in the snow leading to stairs behind the museum. The door at the bottom of the stairs was unlocked. He held the door open for DeLuce and the Butcher Boys, who dutifully obliged.

Once inside, Murnane sped past the other men and took the lead. He held his gun up and at the ready and treaded lightly through the narrow, dark hallways. Murnane spotted a light up ahead and paused. He turned to listen, noticing the ringing in his ears had disappeared. "I hear voices," he whispered.

DeLuce flicked his cigarette into the darkness, the ash exploding like a silent firecracker. Murnane heard DeLuce exhale, then smelled the smoke.

"Time to get back what's mine," DeLuce said.

35.

Cursed

MURNANE FOLLOWED THE SOUND of voices. The light up ahead grew brighter at a sluggish pace, step by methodical step. The surrounding darkness stank like a wet dog and had the consistency of thick oil. Someone's breath warmed the back of Murnane's neck. The fact Murnane couldn't see his hand in front of his face was the most charming aspect of this place.

Murnane heard someone laugh and say, "You're so full of shit, Priest. There ain't one thing that's happened to us that can't be explained."

Murnane witnessed three men huddled under a single bulb, its heated filament barely making a dent in the surrounding darkness. The two taller men had their backs to Murnane, mostly blocking the third, much smaller man, from view. *Father Murphy. Thank Christ he's all right.*

One man put his hand on Father Murphy's shoulder. "You had your fun, now tell us where the goods are. Don't worry, the Devil ain't gonna come poppin' out at us. I promise." The man speaking wore a checkered flat cap. He removed his hand from Father Murphy's shoulder before shifting his weight from one foot to the other and back again. He looked down for a moment at the footprints he had created on the dusty floor.

Murnane figured the young man wearing the cap must be Sly because Murnane recognized Eightball's mangy ass standing closest

270

to Father Murphy.

"C'mon Priest, enough with the Bible hooey. Let's see the loot!" Eightball said.

"That is what I have been *trying to tell you*. If you move or disturb the artifacts in any way while harboring greed inside you, your soul is doomed to the contract for eternity. That's why DeLuce wants that piece of paper back so badly. With that paper DeLuce gains ultimate power over his adversaries."

"You're saying DeLuce is the Devil?" Sly asked.

Murnane listened with a vested interest, but figured they were giving a brutish thug like DeLuce way too much credit. The Devil would conduct himself in a much more calm and collected manner. The Devil would sneak up on you, earn your trust by convincing you what a nice guy he was—*nothing like DeLuce*. Murnane squeezed his pistol tighter, feeling its clammy grip in his hand.

Sly grabbed Father Murphy by the lapels. "You better make with the treasure right now."

Murnane raised an open palm for DeLuce and the Butchers to hang back for the moment. He stepped from the shadows, gun held at eye level. Sly and Eightball flinched. Father Murphy immediately covered his head and dove behind some stacked crates.

"Hands up. Where I can see them."

Sly and Eightball put their hands up.

Murnane strutted in front of them to get a good look at his captured prey. "Eightball, how've you been? And you must be Sly." Murnane made sure his face expressed his tattered tolerance for bullshit. "With what you've put me through today, I should shoot you on principle." Murnane addressed the void outside the halo surrounding the light. "Come on out, Father."

Father Murphy did not respond.

When DeLuce stepped from the shadows, Sly and Eightball looked as though they were about to be fitted for nooses. DeLuce's face hardly reflected light. The shadows seemed to follow him as he slowly circled the men huddled under the humming bulb. DeLuce prowled in his long, black overcoat, and black fedora, his eyes soulless as a dead fish. Each deliberate step of his hard-soled shoes ground sand and grit into the floor.

DeLuce circled behind Sly and Eightball. He pulled his gun from its holster and held the pistol behind Sly's back. The kid looked like an ant on the sidewalk with a boot heel coming down from above. De-Luce's eyes scraped up and down Sly and Eightball several times, deep enough to leave scars. Murnane knew DeLuce took great pleasure in basting the young men in their own sweat.

Next, DeLuce rummaged through Eightball's pockets, pulled out a knife and dropped it to the floor. The second knife he tossed into the dark. The third was a shiv, which DeLuce quickly glanced at before tossing it, too, into the dark. "Give me the one in your shoe."

"What makes you think I have a razor in my shoe?" Eightball asked.

"I never asked for a razor, dumbass. Now give it to me."

Eightball pulled the straight razor from his shoe and slapped it in DeLuce's outstretched palm.

DeLuce continued rifling. He paused, then he pulled out the pa-per. He holstered his gun and caressed the paper like he would a lover's skin.

"Is that it? Are we good?" Murnane asked.

DeLuce smiled. "We're good. We're very, very good." He ran his fingers along the paper and his eyes widened as he stroked the docu-ment. Sweat glistened on his brow. He licked his lips.

"You got your paper, now get on the phone to your guys and call them off my family." Murnane twisted Sly's arm behind his back and raised his pistol toward Eightball. "Okay, you two are under arrest. Up against the wall."

"Kill them," DeLuce said. He folded the paper tenderly and placed it in his pocket..

"What?"

"Kill them. Now."

"They're unarmed and under arrest. I'm takin' them in."

"They know too much. Witnesses are bad for business."

The turmoil churning inside Murnane tasted bitter. It tumbled like broken glass and rusty nails. His eyes darted from DeLuce to Eightball to Sly and back again. "I'm not going to kill them."

DeLuce pulled his gun and took aim at Sly's head. "Then I'll do it."

"Wait!" Father Murphy cried out from the dark.

"It's okay, Father. Nobody's gonna shoot anybody. Come on out— it's safe. We got the bad guys," Murnane said. He pushed Sly against the wall. Eightball followed suit on his own accord. Murnane holstered his pistol and reached for the handcuffs in his back pocket.

"Please don't kill us," Father Murphy said, his voice frail and uncertain.

"Come out, Father. No one's going to hurt you," DeLuce said. He smiled like the Grim Reaper admiring a packed church engulfed in flames.

"I need your word no harm will come to these men or myself," he said from behind the crates.

"I told you, Father, we won't hurt *you*," DeLuce said.

"Please don't kill them. They can be saved."

DeLuce laughed. "Saved from what, Father? I have the paper. I'm in control, now. Just like you said."

Murnane held the cuffs in his hand, but didn't put them on Sly. At the risk of having the bastards turn on him, Murnane wanted Sly and Eightball to have a fighting chance against DeLuce and the Butchers if all hell broke loose. *No good deed goes unpunished.*

"I know why you want the paper. I know who you *really* are, Mr. DeLuce." Father Murphy had lowered his voice by an octave.

Movement caught Murnane's attention. Sly and Eightball were shimmying away from the wall. Murnane raised a hand, signaling them to stop. DeLuce still held a gun.

"Look, Father, I'm sure these two told you all sorts of things about me. I promise I will not hurt you. Now come on out or I'm coming back there to get you," DeLuce said.

After DeLuce threatened the feeble priest, Murnane realized the legend of DeLuce far exceeded the truth. DeLuce was just another insecure man who used fear to control those around him. Take away his two monstrous playmates and his gun, and DeLuce was as threatening as a rolled-up newspaper.

"I know you're lying, Mr. DeLuce. That's what the Devil does."

DeLuce's laugh bounced off the thick stone walls and hardwood floors, sounding like a murder of crows.

"You're goddamned right I'm the Devil. I wipe out everyone who crosses me, like a plague. I make their families suffer, worse than a . . . a pestilence. So yes, I am the Devil and you'd better fucking fear me, old man." DeLuce held his hands out at his sides, like a stage actor ready to take a bow.

With Hell fire in his eyes, DeLuce flew toward Murnane and jammed a gun in his face. Murnane's pistol rested snug in its holster. It may as well have been on the moon.

DeLuce moved the gun just enough to make direct eye contact with Murnane. "You let me walk outta here with the paper and the loot and I'll let you live," DeLuce said, then nodded in Sly and Eightball's direction. "These two are dead where they stand already, but you and the priest still have a chance to walk outta here just like I promised."

"I knew it! I knew you were the Devil!" Father Murphy cried.

"Shut up, old man. Now get out here before I lose my temper and blast you too. The last thing you want is the Devil's wrath."

"Don't do this. Take whatever you want and go. There doesn't have to be any more killing. Just call your men off my family."

"There's plenty of time. Don't worry. And let me take this time to thank you, Chief Murnane, for helping me track these assholes down. You still don't understand how important this paper is, do you?" De-Luce looked so damned satisfied, pleased. Firmly in control. "That man in my office said as long as I kept the paper safe, I had the power to control the fate of anyone I chose. So when those two fuckers stole it, I had to get it back before he realized it was missing. If I hadn't gotten it back, my fate could have been controlled by these two idiots. No way was I going to let that happen. Don't worry there, big chief, I'm taking the treasure too. I deserve to be paid for my time in this shithole town of yours. I swear I'd rather be dead than spend one more day in St. Paul." Sweat gathered on DeLuce's upper lip.

"Now get out here, Father, or I'll shoot them all, so help me God."

Father Murphy whimpered from the darkness. "Okay, you've won, DeLuce. I'm coming out."

The diminutive grey-haired priest walked out from behind the crates. He held his quaking hands in the air. He was depleted to the bone, caked in mud and sweat. Shadows cast across him when he emerged, as if the light feared touching him. He walked behind Sly and Eightball and stepped out from between them. The shadows lifted.

When DeLuce laid eyes on Father Murphy's pale face, DeLuce stopped smiling.

"No," DeLuce whispered. His bottom lip curled and he lowered his gun. Murnane watched every ounce of DeLuce's sadistic vitality being drained, leaving behind a pathetic shell.

The filament glowed white hot and vibrated a high-pitched hum when Father Murphy looked up at DeLuce. "I have a feeling you will not live to see one more day in St. Paul, Mr. DeLuce. I wish we could have met again under more fortuitous circumstances. How *un*fortunate—for you."

The floor shook when DeLuce dropped to his knees. Fish hooks could not have pulled his eyes open any wider. Murnane had never seen a more complete look of hopeless desperation poison a man's face.

"It can't be. It's not possible." DeLuce sounded like a lost child.

Father Murphy pointed a crooked finger toward DeLuce, who cowered as though it were a loaded gun. The Butcher Boys emerged from the hall and stood on either side of Father Murphy.

"Please. Please, no. I've been trying to get it back for you. It's not my fault. They stole it. I have it now!" DeLuce extracted the paper from his pocket and waved it in front of Father Murphy.

A man seemingly incapable of emotion knelt sobbing at the old man's feet for reasons Murnane couldn't comprehend. Tears dripped between DeLuce's fingers and across the grip of the gun he had pressed against his face.

"Be that as it may, the parameters of our deal were well defined and left no room for alteration, deliberate or otherwise, I'm afraid," Father Murphy said. "My boys here have been keeping an eye on you,

Mr. DeLuce, while I kept an eye on my paper. I like to hedge my bets."

Father Murphy hovered over DeLuce like DeLuce was a bully he had just beaten to a pulp in a school yard brawl. DeLuce's arms fell to his side. His wrists went limp and the tip of the gun smacked against the floor.

"What's going on here?" Murnane asked. "What's this all about? Father, are you okay?" Though he enjoyed watching DeLuce cry like a little girl nursing a skinned knee, something about the scene wasn't on the level. Murnane suspected something far worse than DeLuce was in control.

"It is time for Mr. DeLuce to fulfill his contractual obligations, I'm afraid."

"You two know each other?" Murnane asked.

"Oh, Mr. DeLuce and I go way back. The last time I saw him was in his office a couple months ago. Isn't that right, Mr. DeLuce?" Father Murphy smiled down at DeLuce, who nodded and continued sobbing. "I know him so well that I can describe that sick feeling in his stomach as hope eroding away."

DeLuce raised the gun and used the side of it to rub his temple. "Please, God, let me go."

"You know that's not my name. I never took you for much of a fool, but if you think *He* hears *you* cry out in the dark, Mr. DeLuce, I gave you far too much credit. When all you have left is darkness, I'm the one who answers your prayers."

36.

The Agony of Defeat

SOMETHING ABOUT FATHER MURPHY seemed odd, almost *cruel*. Hell if Sly knew what it was, but his mind worked a double shift trying to figure it out.

"Why are you talking like that?" Sly asked Father Murphy.

The room grew colder and the air held the taste of curdled milk. Sly's gut hurt worse than if someone had pumped it full of gasoline, castor oil, and barbed wire—and thrown a lit match down his throat. All day his heart had been pounding harder than a stampede of horses, and his back had become covered in horseshoe prints. His bones ached.

Murnane still held the cuffs in his hand and pointed at Sly and Eightball. "You two are coming with me." Murnane sure was jittery. For a man who should know what to do in every situation, his movements made him look like a kid entering his first day of kindergarten.

"Father, I need you to ride with me to the station and make a statement. Let's go." Father Murphy didn't move. "Look, I don't know what kinda shit you're pulling here, Father, but the joke's over," Murnane said.

Father Murphy's laugh sounded like someone attacking a chalkboard with a rake. "Such a sense of duty." Father Murphy poked at the air in DeLuce's direction. "You could have learned something from Mr. Murnane. Despite straying many times, the selfless acts he made for his family saved him from me. But the route you chose led right here,

277

Mr. DeLuce, didn't it? I want that to be perfectly clear—you chose this path. And that is why I chose you."

DeLuce's face dripped with sweat and tears. He looked up at Murnane and whispered, "Run."

Metal scraping against teeth made a strange hollow clicking sound from inside DeLuce's mouth when he inserted the gun. A bright flash lit up the room as the bullet sent the back of DeLuce's head into the blackness. The gun smacked against the wood floor when DeLuce's body fell, facing toward Hell.

Sly jumped.

Father Murphy turned to Sly. "You see, Mr. Hobbs? I've told you all along you should fear the curse."

"Why did he do that?" Sly examined what was left of DeLuce. Terror coated his mouth, blocking his screams. His feet were solid blocks of ice; he couldn't make them move. Sly didn't know which was worse—being unable to run or having nowhere to go.

"Mr. Deluce assumed it was his only way out, his only chance to escape the curse. A self-inflicted gunshot will not keep him from fulfilling our contract, however. As long as we have a binding contract, Mr. Hobbs, there is no way to escape me. Ever."

"What is that supposed to mean? Escape what? *The curse*? Are you crackin' up?" Sly asked. He made a weak attempt to mask his deepening fear with shallow anger.

The Butcher Boys never took their eyes off Sly. He didn't enjoy the feeling of footsteps across his grave.

Father Murphy was no longer the fraidy-cat Sly had come to know and trust and care for. The Father Murphy he knew couldn't strike fear into a housefly. But there stood Priest showing off a vicious arrogance that confused Sly—and scared the hell out of him.

Sly panted. His chest heaved. The surrounding darkness held something more than an absence of light, rippling like a stone breaking the surface of a calm pool of water. Callused hands suddenly tightened around his windpipe. The hands wanted Sly dead. Then they let go. Sly gasped and looked around. The Butcher Boys were gone.

If someone or something was trying to scare him off the treasure, they had another thing coming. Sly stood too close to the treasure to turn back now.

"Who are you?" Murnane asked. He pocketed the cuffs, drew his pistol, and aimed carefully at Father Murphy.

"You know who I am, *Mister* Murnane."

"You're an old man who's obviously had a helluva day. I'll get the boys at the station to clean this up and we can get you some food, water, and some blankets." Sly heard uneasiness building in Murnane's voice that Sly very much related to.

Father Murphy nodded toward DeLuce's bloody corpse. "It's your love for Mary, Jacob, and Samantha that kept you beyond my reach."

Murnane's expression looked as though he had driven into oncoming traffic. "You couldn't possibly . . . How did? . . ." he asked, looking toward Sly and Eightball.

If Murnane was counting on Sly for a reasonable explanation, the chief would have better luck deputizing him. Sly shook his head slowly, eyes wide open.

The crease between Murnane's thick brows deepened. Sly could see him searching. That's how cops operate; they always gotta have answers for everything.

Murnane wiped sweat off his upper lip. "I've never met you before. How could you know that? You're just a priest."

When Murnane uttered, *You're just a priest*, Sly knew Murnane had the same questions he did. Murnane, too, recognized that Father Murphy was unrecognizable. There was no answer.

"I am whatever you believe."

Sly watched Murnane's eyes focus. Father Murphy was being scrutinized more thoroughly than bloody fingerprints at a murder scene.

"I should have possessed you too, Chief Murnane. But when you vowed to give up your life for your family, you slipped through my fingers." Father Murphy smirked and wagged his finger. "No matter how much I stack the odds in my favor, I don't always win."

"I need to go home." Murnane lowered his gun. It swung listless at his side for a moment until he relaxed his fingers, letting the weapon drop to the floor.

Sly noticed how close Murnane's gun was to his own feet.

"Now you're beginning to understand, Mr. Murnane. You've built a career on knowing how to tell when someone lies. So tell me. Am I a liar?" Father Murphy cocked his head. Sly's uneasiness increased in heaps when Father Murphy finished up by slipping on a con man's smile.

"I . . ." Murnane wavered in place and appeared to be choking down a bird's nest when he swallowed.

"I've brought much stronger men than you to their knees, Mr. Murnane. I helped Nero light the Great Fire of Rome. I turned a tumultuous village boy named Temujin into the most formidable ruler the world has ever known, simply by showing how best to place a vanquished foe's head on a pike. I dined with Vlad the Impaler, advising him on which cut of human flesh tasted best with Bordeaux. All of them bowed before me."

Sly figured those must be names of other cops.

He glanced again at Murnane's gun on the floor. Sly looked at Eightball, who was bird-dogging DeLuce's gun.

The weight of Father Murphy's leer broke Sly's concentration on the guns and forced him to pay attention to the old man. Father Murphy's eyes were so cold and unfamiliar they dared Sly to dive for Murnane's gun and at the same time told him what would happen if he tried.

Murnane looked as lost as Sly felt. Murnane wiped his tears away and stopped wavering. The chief gnarled his fists at his sides and looked Father Murphy in the eyes.

"You have your family back—for now."

Murnane walked back into the shadows of the entrance before Father Murphy stopped him by saying, "Remember, I'm always watching."

Murnane's right hand appeared out of the blackness. His middle finger stuck out of a balled up fist hard as dried rawhide. The hallway door slammed behind him. And he was gone.

Father Murphy turned back to Sly and Eightball. "And then there were two." He clasped his hands together as if to pray and said, "You two, I'm happy to say, are mine—*all* mine."

Sly heard the dirt being shoveled onto his casket.

"I'll make you a deal, Mr. Hobbs. If you kill Eightball right now, I'll set you free."

"Free from what? What the hell is going on here?" Eightball asked.

"Exactly. *Hell* is going on here," Father Murphy replied.

"So, Murnane is coming back with more cops? No wonder I feel queer about this whole thing. You led us right into a trap!" Sly yelled.

Sly knew there were no cops coming—no one was coming. Life experience served as a barrier between what he knew to be real and what he feared was reality.

"Quit acting crazy, Priest, and tell me where the fucking treasure is!" Sly picked up Murnane's gun and aimed. Father Murphy didn't duck, cower, flinch, or blink.

"You have a murderous rage inside you, Sylvester Hobbs. I love watching you work."

"Stop with the hijinks, Priest," Eightball said. Sly heard the hollowness in Eightball's voice.

"Shoot Eightball and claim the treasure for yourself."

Sly lowered the gun slightly. "Why would I shoot Eightball? What's wrong with you, Priest?"

Father Murphy laced his fingers at his waist. "Don't be a fool, Mr. Hobbs. This is what you've wanted all along, is it not?"

"Stop actin' like a horse's ass and tell me where the treasure is!" Sly rocked from one foot to the other, the gun locked between Father Murphy's eyes. Sly saw his breath as the air chilled. Goosebumps raised the hair on his body, caused more by his fear of Father Murphy than the bitter cold.

Eightball picked up DeLuce's gun. Sly turned and took aim at Eightball.

"What are you doing?" Eightball asked. He sounded like Sly had stuck a knife in his back.

"Drop the gun, asshole," Sly answered.

"I'm not going to shoot you." Eightball nodded toward Father Murphy. "Let's make him tell us where the treasure is."

Confusion, fear, and greed all sounded to Sly like great reasons to turn the gun back on Father Murphy. "Look, goddamn it, no more games, Priest. I want to see the treasure!"

Father Murphy extended his hand. "The treasure is right through that door behind you." Father Murphy spoke with a tenderness reserved for sleeping children.

Sly looked quickly over his left shoulder to see a closed door he hadn't noticed before. He walked toward the door, keeping his gun trained on Father Murphy. Sly reached for the handle, but withdrew his hand for fear the handle might bite him. When nothing happened, Sly gripped the handle tight, tugging and rattling the locked door. He was trapped. First, by the locked door, second, the impending darkness, and worse, Father Murphy's smile.

"Shoot the fucking thing!" Eightball yelled.

Sly closed one eye and pulled the trigger. *Click.* He pulled it again. *Click.* Sly kicked the door with all he had, but fell backward. The door fended off his kick with no effort, leaving him with a throbbing ankle.

Sly picked himself off the dusty floor, panting. "You try."

Eightball pointed and shot. *Click.*

"Open it!" Sly yelled at Father Murphy.

"How does it feel to be so close to that which you most covet and not be able to possess it?"

"What is this, a Bible lesson? You've worn out your welcome, Priest," Sly said. Kindness lingered within Sly like the last drunk to leave the bar after closing. But eventually, that drunk has got to go. "Eightball, beat the shit out of him."

Eightball pocketed DeLuce's gun, rubbed his knuckles, and nodded at Father Murphy.

"It's been good to know ya," Sly said as Eightball closed in.

"Is it really *me* you want out of the way?" Father Murphy asked Eightball.

Eightball slowed.

"If you eliminate Sly, the treasure will be yours—*all* yours."

Eightball stopped.

"Don't even think about it," Sly said.

Eightball turned toward Sly. Strings of drool sagged from Eightball's snaggy teeth and swollen gums. He continued rubbing his left thumb across his right knuckles and closed in on Sly.

"Hey. Stop. I mean it—stop!"

Sly aimed for the dead center of Eightball's forehead, but Eightball was close enough to slap the gun aside. A right cross glanced off Sly's temple but didn't fully connect. Another blow followed from the left, hitting the back of Sly's head and causing a quick burst of stars in his eyes. Sly swung his gun and hit Eightball square in the jaw. Eightball fell back against the stacked crates. Eightball shook out the cobwebs and charged.

"Wait!" Sly yelled before Eightball thrust his shoulder and nailed Sly in the breadbasket. Sly tumbled into the crates next to where DeLuce lay, hugging Eightball tight. It was the best way to prevent Eightball from delivering a knockout punch. Splinters and dust filled the air. They burned Sly's eyes and coated his throat.

Eightball kneed Sly in the balls. Sly let out a moan and held his breath as the pain shot up into his stomach, forcing him onto his side. Eightball stood and kicked Sly in the kidneys. Sly flattened out. Eightball pounced, using his knees to pin Sly's shoulders to the floor.

Father Murphy stepped closer and said, "Finish him."

When Eightball cocked his fist back, Sly knew Eightball was hellbent on ending their partnership.

Sly felt the useless gun in his hand and raised it in desperation.

Sly pulled the trigger.

The pounding flash walloped Sly's wrist, shooting pain up his arm. A single dribble of blood trickled down the bridge of Eightball's crooked nose and his empty eyes focused on nothing. Eightball's body listed forward, pinning Sly underneath. Sly pushed and pulled on limbs until he was able to wriggle out from under Eightball's body.

Sly examined the smoke curling from the gun barrel. Once on his feet, Sly turned to Father Murphy and set a tense finger on the cold trigger. Sylvester Hobbs had every intention of sending Father Murphy straight to Hell.

"Open the door."

"Well done, Mr. Hobbs."

"I said open the fucking door! You gotta know where the key is."

"Indeed I do."

"Then where is it?"

"It's inside you, Mr. Hobbs. It has been this whole time."

"Stop talking in riddles. Just 'cause I ain't so smart don't mean I can't plant one between your eyes, you double-crossing son of a bitch."

"You don't need me in order to acquire the treasure you seek. All the answers are right here in front of you." Father Murphy's straight teeth beamed against the dim light.

Submerged below broken ice, Sly could see the water's surface growing distant. Agony's cigarettes glowed orange and hot under the surface of Sly's crawling skin. The pliers ripped his ear open, but when he checked for blood, there was none. Baby spiders erupted across his face and wriggled inside his mouth. He mourned at his mother's grave a thousand times over, and his hands were scalded worse than when he pulled his toy soldier from the wood stove. All Sly could see from his past and present, and the future was a heavy grey cloud. The fear of dying alone in the dark was his only companion—other than Father Murphy armed with a wretched smile.

Sly pulled the trigger.

Click. Sly flinched, but Father Murphy did not. Sly pulled it again. *Click.*

"Son of a bitch!" He pulled the trigger in rapid succession. No flashes, no bullets, no recoil, no dead Father Murphy.

Father Murphy looked on, his hands folded in front of him. "Perhaps you got the bullets wet, Mr. Hobbs. Or there could be *spiders* on the firing pin. These things happen."

"Open the door!" Sly yelled in equal parts frustration and defeat. He stepped forward, doing his best to suppress his growing fear by contemplating pistol-whipping the truth out of the old man.

"I hope you realize what you're asking. If I open that door, there is no turning back."

"I don't care. I want it—it's mine!" Spittle shot from Sly's mouth and heat raced up his neck.

"I'll give you everything you have coming to you. Everything you could imagine and so much more."

The door behind Sly unlatched and creaked open about two inches. The dark crack beckoned, waiting to devour him. Hollow whispers filled his ears convincing him to open the door. Begging. Commanding. He figured the sounds were a draft from the open door. Sly studied the crack.

"There it is, Mr. Hobbs. Through that door are the answers to all your questions."

Vomit burned its way up Sly's throat. When he swallowed, it burned on the return trip as well. Every limb tingled and trembled and urine pressed against his bladder to the point of bursting. He made no move toward the door. He had never felt more alone.

Father Murphy bent down and pulled the contract from DeLuce's fingers. He rolled it up and used it to point at Eightball's body.

"I take special pride in watching you work—especially what you and your father did. When you helped sink that train, it was one of my proudest moments. How did it make you feel to watch those people drown? How did you feel when your father, Agony, I think you call him, smiled and held your hand? That was the moment you caught my attention, and I've been watching you ever since."

"How do you know about that? Did Eightball tell you?" *Did Eightball even know?*

"Your father and I are old business associates."

"You knew my dad?"

"The paper came into your father's possession before you were born, when he stole it from his boss, Mr. Avery. Agony coveted it, loved it, well, *agonized* over it. Avery always suspected your father had stolen the paper, and insufferable loathing finally drove Avery to fire your father. Thanks to the paper, Agony was quickly consumed by wrath, which I preyed upon. I showed up one day and made your father a deal he couldn't refuse."

"What do you mean? What deal?"

"I helped him plot to kill Avery. I didn't tell him directly, I just instilled the vengeance necessary for him to take matters into his own hands. That way, I got Avery's soul and your father had no escape, thus forfeiting his soul upon death. When I came to collect the debt Agony owed me, he begged and cried and bargained. The usual. But then he did something curious. He offered to make a trade—your soul for his."

"My soul? Wait, I helped him kill Avery. I don't remember seein' you there, old man." Sly had finally proven, most satisfactorily, that Father Murphy was full of shit.

"Oh, I was there. When the train sank, I thanked you from under the water. It was a beautiful day to drown, as I remember."

Sly pictured the man with the missing eyes sinking into the depths of Lake Nebagamon. Streams of blood had poured from his hollow eye sockets. He remembered the man mouthing the words *thank you.*

Sly pictured a death certificate signed in his own blood.

"I proceeded to tell your father that I already owned his soul, but would gladly take your soul in trade for a more lenient sentence for him in eternity. In the end, I got your soul while your father suffers through the worst Hell has to offer—and that is truly saying something."

"No. You're *Priest*. We kidnapped you! You're afraid of everything. We took care of you this whole time. You'd be dead if it wasn't for me."

"Correction, you'd be alive if it weren't for me, but I digress. I merely went along with you because I love a ringside seat."

"You're a weak, old fool."

"If that's how you feel, then you have nothing to fear, correct? There's the door, simply walk through it."

"Is this a setup? Are Murnane and the cops on the other side waiting for me?"

Father Murphy laughed. "As much as I love our little chats, my patience is wearing thin. I need you to walk through that door."

"That room doesn't look big enough to hold all the treasure."

"Oh, you'd be surprised. But you need to stop making excuses and walk through the fucking door." Father Murphy's voice reminded Sly of a dull axe grinding against a sharpening stone.

"No."

Sly aimed again and fired. The gun blew up in his hand. The pain loosened his grip on the gun and he dropped it. Sly let out a feeble yelp. The truth of who Father Murphy really was poked sharp sticks into his body. A hopelessness deeper than an abandoned well trapped Sly, squeezing every part of him—inside and out.

"That's it, Mr. Hobbs. Now you understand."

"Please, no," Sly murmured.

Sly wept hard enough to purge a lifetime of misdeeds. His chest heaved, full of mournful sobs reserved only for men who have abandoned hope. He knelt before the Devil and cradled his throbbing hand inside his good one while warm blood flowed down his forearm.

Father Murphy bent at the waist. "I'm a little disappointed you didn't see this coming. Didn't you find it odd that this whole time I, one of *His* supposed servants, never called Him by name? One of the little nuances of my banishment, you see." Father Murphy shook the paper in front of Sly's face, close enough he could smell its musty stink.

"Even now, after all hope has abandoned you, is your little mind still working out an escape plan? I love your *can do* attitude. But this makes you mine."

"Why are you doing this?"

"I've done nothing. You have put yourself here. I merely opened doors you were all too willing to walk through. And now you are in a place where even He can't save you."

"You mean God?"

"Yes, you idiot. Because when he fucks up and creates vile, repugnant beings like you, I sweep you under the rug of existence so his devout followers don't lose faith. That deal has been in place before time began. He gets the blind admiration he loves so much and I get souls to play with as I please. Who knew His greatest sin was vanity?"

Sly bowed his head and continued to sob. Bottomless.

"Oh, Mr. Hobbs, stop. You are acting like quite the fool. Are you ashamed of what you've done? Of who you are?" Father Murphy slapped the rolled contract across his open palm.

Sly nodded.

"Do you wish to beg for forgiveness? To be set free from your contractual obligation?"

Sly's head snapped up. He thought on his mother's smile. How she would hold his hand during long walks on warm spring days through the woods. He thought about Lily and how his heart beat just a little faster every time she smiled. And he thought about Father Murphy. The Father Murphy he came to care about, the one person who treated Sly with respect. All those wonderful things seemed like a lifetime ago. All those things had happened to someone else.

"Yes, God, please. I'm sorry. I'm so sorry for everything I've done."

Father Murphy narrowed his eyes and tilted his head as if a disturbing sound scratched against his eardrums.

"That sounded dangerously close to repenting."

Father Murphy grabbed Sly's chin between the knuckle on his index finger and his thumbnail and lifted Sly's wet face. A sharp fingernail pinched Sly's skin.

"Are you *worried?*"

"Yes."

Father Murphy laughed and nudged Sly's chin. He examined Sly the same way a boy cherishes a spider after he pulls off its legs.

"Now you repent?" Father Murphy placed his hands against his lower back and began to pace.

"Shine a light on a cornered cockroach and it will seek out the shadows. Do you know why? Because that is where it was born. All the times we've been through this, this is the first time you've ever tried to repent. Why now? Tell me what makes you sorry this time."

Sly stopped crying and looked into Father Murphy's empty eyes.

Father Murphy stomped his foot. "Tell me why you are sorry!"

"I feel . . ."

"You feel what?"

"I feel . . . I can be a better person."

"You don't know the path to salvation. You're only repenting because fear permeates every fiber of your crestfallen being. The light is as unfamiliar to you as a father's compassion. The darkness is your home, little cockroach."

"You're wrong. There is good in the world and I've seen it. You showed it to me." Sly looked at the floor.

"Good? *Good?* I am the knot in your stomach that warns you of the misdeeds you are about to inflict on your fellow men. I occupy your most iniquitous thoughts by day and the shadow under your bed by night. I have the power to fill your mouth with your dead mother's feces if it pleases me to do so. I have always been with you and always will be. If I have shown you anything it is that your propensity for greed and violence knows no bounds."

Sly wiped his nose. "Why did you say *all the times we've been through this?*"

Father Murphy bent down and set his hands on his knees. "The truth of who I am is nothing compared to what I am about to tell you."

The following moments drew out like his fate was being skewered by a long, serrated knife over an open flame. He feared the impending seconds, and what words the Devil would fill them with, more than he feared the Devil himself. Sly knew Father Murphy's next words would be carved into his headstone.

"You shouldn't fear who I am nearly as much as where you are."

37.

Dark Doorways

Sly cowered and used his bloodied sleeve to wipe tears from his face. The basement air left his skin clammy and covered in goose bumps, which throbbed like a thousand bee stings.

"What are you talking about? You told me who you are. I believe you. Please just let me go. I really am sorry—for everything I've done."

Father Murphy remained bent over Sly. "We've been through this all before, Mr. Hobbs, many times."

The surrounding blackness curled and moved to the rhythm of Father Murphy's words. Sly couldn't tell if the tears in his eyes caused him to see things or the dark had come to life.

"Please let me go."

The room suddenly smelled like an open sewer on a hot day. Sly buried his nose in the crook of his arm. Inside his nostrils, maggots wriggled and scurried against his nose hairs. He blew his nose and checked his hand for bugs, but saw nothing.

Father Murphy tapped the contract on Sly's head to accentuate each word. "You're. Not. Listening. Mr. Hobbs. This concerns you."

"You said you'd let me go."

"First, I said no such thing. Second, even if I had, why would you believe me now that you know who I am? Even if I was to let you go, you have nowhere to run. Don't be so pathetic. Take some responsibility for your actions. Only scoundrels repent at the last possible moment."

Sly snatched the contract out of Father Murphy's grasp and jumped up. He stepped out of Father Murphy's reach and held the paper up by two corners, threatening to tear it. The light above them throbbed and brightened every time Father Murphy took a deep breath.

Father Murphy stiffened and his smug face fell away. "What are you doing?"

"One more step and I rip this fucker to shreds." Sly trembled and every muscle tensed. He finally understood what caused the uneasiness he'd always felt around Father Murphy. Sly hadn't been unnerved by Father Murphy's unwavering belief in God, but by the Devil's desire to torture Sly at every turn. Sly was here because the Devil wanted him to be. It was that simple. The Devil had led him here.

Father Murphy held up his hands, palms forward. "Please. Just wait," he said in a soothing voice.

"Okay, asshole, now who's in control? It's going to be like this. I'm leaving and you're not going to follow me, got it?"

Father Murphy raised his hands higher. "Please don't destroy it. You're free to go." Father Murphy gestured with a flattened palm toward the crack in the open door behind Sly.

"Nice try, asshole. I'm walking out the *front* door."

"Okay, okay." Father Murphy stepped aside and let Sly pass. Sly held the paper between them as he shuffled closer to the hallway door.

"Wait, before you leave, there is something you should know."

Sly shook his head and clenched the paper tighter. "No more tricks. I'm leaving and there ain't a thing you can do about it."

"And I'm trying to tell you there is. Don't you want to know the truth about the treasure?"

"The truth? Ha! You just got done tellin' me you can't be trusted."

Father Murphy looked like he was holding back a giggle. "I did and I'm sorry." His bottom lip pouted. "Please lower the contract and, after you listen to what I have to say, you are free. I swear—you are free forever. You've outsmarted me. You win."

Sly stopped shuffling. His eyes darted from DeLuce's corpse to Eightball's body and back to Father Murphy.

"You got one minute."

"Fair enough, Mr. Hobbs. Thank you." Father Murphy bowed.

"Well, start talking!" Sly held up the contract.

"Okay!" Father Murphy arched his shoulders, planted his feet, and put his hands on his hips.

"Do you know where you are?" Father Murphy asked.

"What?"

"Do you know where you are, Mr. Hobbs?"

"Yeah, I'm in the museum. I can find my way home just fine, if that's what you're asking."

"What if I said you *are* home."

"What's that supposed to mean?"

"In fact, you've been home for centuries."

"This is bullshit. I'm leaving. You had your chance."

Sly took one step closer to the hallway door.

"Have you ever asked yourself what Hell *really* is? When we discussed its existence earlier, you didn't believe in it. I'll bet you're singing a different tune now."

Sly felt his life burning away like a crackling fuse growing shorter by the second.

"What do you mean?"

"Hell isn't a place, Mr. Hobbs, it's an event. A never-ending looping event of my creation."

"What? That doesn't make sense. You just keep making up stories, hopin' I'm dull enough to believe 'em."

"I'm telling you there is no treasure and there never was."

"You're a liar! You got me thinking you're the Devil because I ain't so smart and you figured I'd believe you. If you were the Devil you could take this paper away from me and there ain't no way I could stop you. You almost fooled me." A fiery pain, the likes of which Sly had never experienced, flared and scalded him from the inside. He doubled over, screaming. His chest squeezed the air from his lungs. The truth of Sly's existence rolled over him like a slow-moving tractor. Sly fought against the pain of the truth using what little he had left in the gas tank. He looked the Devil straight in the eye.

"I know where the treasure is now. I'll come back for it later. I'll get a gang together and take it. I don't care how many cops you have guarding it. And I have the map too!"

"How many times must I tell you? It's not a map, it's a contract."

Sly clutched the paper in his bloodied hand and shook it in front of Father Murphy's gloating face. Blood dripped and blotched across the floor. "This! Whatever *this* is! I have it and you want it."

"No, I don't."

Sly laughed. "Yeah, right. You would kill for this."

Father Murphy shook his head. "It's not real, Mr. Hobbs."

"Look, I'm holding it right here, stupid. Are you blind?"

Father Murphy pointed at the paper. "And I'm telling you that it is not real. None of this is." He raised his hands at his sides, pivoted at the hips, and scanned the nothingness surrounding them.

"I'm done with you."

"The only thing that *is* real here is your soul, and I already own that. Your soul is bound to me in flesh and blood, but never paper. Flesh is the currency with which I obtain my souls. I seal the fates of my clients by counting corpses and measuring the anguish they inflict on the innocent. I have owned you for a very long time, Mr. Hobbs. Ever since you prayed to get into the Boss's gang so many centuries ago. After Dapper Dan was killed, you felt lost, alone. You had no direction and were desperate not to have to carve out a living back on the streets. I was the one who got you into the Boss's gang. There were no contracts to sign, no papers to destroy, only your thirst for power and money. You greedily accepted my terms and I got your soul. However, I could not take possession of it until after your death. So I arranged that as well, I'm afraid."

"I rip this up and I'm free, so you don't own shit!"

"Go ahead. Rip away."

Sly grabbed the paper, or map, or contract. He no longer cared what it was, he just wanted it gone. He wanted out of that basement. He wanted to be out from underneath Father Murphy's shadow. His hands slid off the paper; he couldn't get a grip on it. The tighter he grasped, the worse the blood on his hands smeared over the paper.

Father Murphy stood by and showed off his perfectly straight teeth.

"This is your reality, Mr. Hobbs. Every facet of your existence is controlled by me—and always will be."

Sly slapped the paper against the brick wall and rested his forehead against his forearm as he wailed and moaned. Between breaths, he asked, "Why did you act like ripping the paper would save me?"

"Providing false hope is exhilarating—one final rush before the end."

Sly ran to the hallway door. He yanked the handle over and over and it rattled and clunked. The door did not budge. He screamed and grunted until blood covered the handle and pooled on the floor. He shrieked and pounded and kicked, draining everything he had.

"Help! Let me out! Someone please open the door. Help me!"

Sly shut his eyes, set his forehead against the door, and wept. The door felt cold against the sweat on his forehead. He turned and slid down until he sat on the floor. As the truth of his reality soaked in, tears poured out of him as quickly as his doubt. He repeatedly knocked the back of his head against the door. He looked up to see Father Murphy gazing down at him as if Sly were the first crocus of spring after a brutal winter.

"You do this every time, Mr. Hobbs. There's nowhere to run. You've completed your loop again. It's time to send you back to the alley."

"The alley?"

"The one in which you and Eightball are hiding, ready to take down Pancetti and his bodyguard."

"How do you know about that?"

"I was there. I just told you I arranged your death. Remember? The truth is, when you walked out from behind those crates with your hands in the air, the man spun and fired, nailing you between the eyes. You were dead before you hit the ground."

"I'm here right now, see?" Sly slapped an open palm against his chest. "I'm alive and that proves you're a liar!"

Father Murphy watched Sly like he was freshly carved prime rib.

"Oh, how I savor your pain. Your mournful laments are symphonic perfection. The salt in your tears is delicious."

"Stop talking like that!"

"Witnessing your soul dissolve before my eyes makes this whole journey worth the effort. You are one fine piece of sin, Mr. Hobbs. I truly cherish that moment when you give in and accept your fate. But for the first time, you felt genuine empathy for Father Murphy. That fact intrigues me—and made this particular fall from grace so much more rewarding than the others. You usually just grovel like everyone else. From now on I must make sure you have a change of heart every time. It is simply wonderful to behold the utter look of devastation on your face."

Sly jumped to his feet and ran across the room to the doorway. He flung open the door. A hideous abyss stared back. A curtain of hopelessness stretched across the doorway. With one final look over his shoulder at Father Murphy, Sly wept, "It's only a room. I'm not afraid of you!"

Sly stepped over the threshold. Memories of past lives flooded and rushed through him. Countless visions of gunfights and bloodshed pummeled his body and soul. He had never known such agony. He wavered and used the door frame to steady himself. As he took another step, he remembered walking through this door many, many times.

The door slammed shut behind him. He heard Father Murphy say, "Welcome back to Hell, Sylvester Hobbs."

38.

And So It Begins

SLY FELT HIS STOMACH TWIST and kick and checked the pistol in his pocket for reassurance. He didn't remember swallowing an angry wolverine, but that's how he felt. Pancetti unlocked the door and went inside, shutting the door behind him.

"Walk up like a bum looking for change. Distract him long enough so I can move in behind him. And let's keep this quiet. Don't shoot unless you have to."

"Are you crazy? He's got a machine gun," Sly said.

"I'll take him out before he can get off a shot. Don't worry about it. Now go."

"Don't worry about it?"

Eightball gritted what teeth he had left. "Pipe down." Sly felt a pistol barrel press against his rib cage. "I swear I will plug you right here and do this myself, the hard way. Now move."

Sly palmed the pistol in his pocket and considered slinging hot lead at Eightball, but the thought of getting cut down by a Tommy gun seconds later kept his anger in check.

The same chill Sly had felt in the Outhouse the day before crawled under his skin again. He stepped from behind the crates and approached the gunman. Sly took two steps before the lookout spun and the barrel emerged from beneath his coat.

Sly's world squeezed into a tunnel of vision focused on the tip of the gun. Lightning struck from the Tommy. The movie of his life flashed like the start and end of a picture show—showing nothing in between. Sly closed his eyes and waited for the burning bullets to rip through his flesh. Nothing. Sly opened his eyes. The man was still holding the Tommy on him. But no holes. No blood. No smell of burnt skin from the entrance wounds. No sensation of falling to the sidewalk. Sly raised his hands slowly as his heart tried to kick its way out of his chest.

Coming Soon from
Three Waters Publishing

Moonshine, Madness, and Murder, Christy Marie Kent.

In Quacker Holler, Tennessee, in the foothills of the Smoky Mountains, the monks make moonshine to support the school and one seventy-five-year-old nun writes and self-publishes redneck vampire nun erotica.

Until someone kills her.

When a recently fired reporter fears she is losing her sanity because of the voices in her head trying to persuade her to kill herself, she focuses instead on discovering the nun's killer. She fears she is slipping further into madness, however, when a new voice—that of the dead nun—urges her to fulfill an unconventional final wish.

Carrying out the nun's request might lead her to the killer—but it will also lead the killer to herself.

Visit us online at:

http://threewaterspublishing.com

Save 10% on Every Order

Subscribe to our email list at http://threewaterspublishing.com, and we'll give you a coupon code to save 10% on every order—*and* we'll update you on new releases, events, and meet-the-author opportunities.

About D. B. Moon

Born and raised in St. Paul, Minnesota, D. B. Moon was brought up to appreciate meat raffles and pull tabs, same as any fine St. Paulite worth his salt.

Fishing and reading take up a large amount of Moon's free time, mostly because both can be enjoyed with a cold Grain Belt. His favorite literary genres include hard-boiled, mystery, horror, and comedy—anything with dynamic, engaging characters and a twisted plot. An intelligent woman who can turn a form-fitting cocktail dress into a weapon doesn't hurt either.

He lives on a Minnesota lake and tries not to answer his door if at all possible. However, rumor has it he will let you buy him a Sailor Jerry & Coke if and when you find him in some local dive. Look for him in places where the bar top is oversaturated with stale beer and sad stories.

Coming Soon from D. B. Moon

Kiss-Proof World

Learn More about Mr. Moon at

http://dbmoon.com